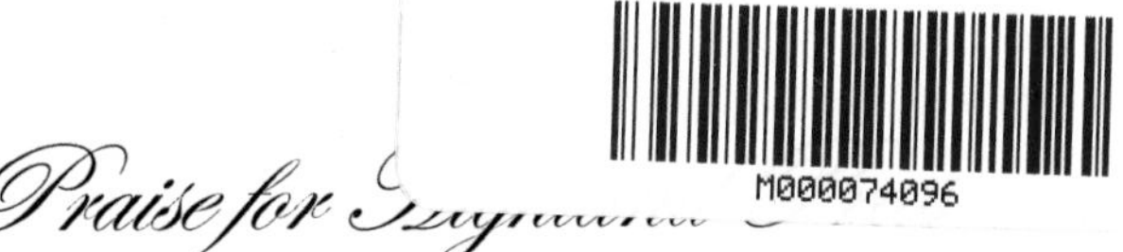

Praise for ... *Books!*

BLUE MOON MAGIC is an enchanting collection of short stories. Each author wrote with the same theme in mind but each story has its own uniqueness. You should have no problem finding a tale to suit your mood. *BLUE MOON MAGIC* offers historicals, contemporaries, time travel, paranormal, and futuristic narratives to tempt your heart.

Legend says that if you wish with all your heart upon the rare blue moon, your wishes were sure to come true. Each of the heroines discovers this magical fact. True love is out there if you just believe in it. In some of the stories, love happens in the most unusual ways. Angels may help, ancient spells may be broken, anything can happen. Even vampires will find their perfect mate with the power of the blue moon. Not every heroine believes they are wishing for love, some are just looking for answers to their problems or nagging questions. Fate seems to think the solution is finding the one who makes their heart sing.

BLUE MOON MAGIC is a perfect read for late at night or even during your commute to work. The short yet sweet stories are a wonderful way to spend a few minutes. If you do not have the time to finish a full-length novel, but hate stopping in the middle of a loving tale, I highly recommend grabbing this book.

Kim Swiderski
Writers Unlimited Reviewer

~~~
~~~

Legend has it that a blue moon is enchanted. What happens when fifteen talented authors utilize this theme to create enthralling stories of love?

BLUE MOON ENCHANTMENT is a wonderful, themed anthology filled with phenomenal stories by fifteen extraordinarily talented authors. Readers will find a wide variety of time periods and styles showcased in this superb anthology. *BLUE MOON ENCHANTMENT* is sure to offer a little bit of something for everyone!

Reviewed by Debbie
CK²S Kwips and Kritiques

~~~

NO LAW AGAINST LOVE - If you have ever found yourself rolling your eyes at some of the more stupid laws, then you are going to adore this novel. Over twenty-five stories fill up this anthology, each one dealing with at least one stupid or outdated law. Let me give you an example: In Florida, USA, there is a law that states "If an elephant is left tied to a parking meter, the parking fee has to be paid just as it would for a vehicle." In Great Britain, "A license is required to keep a lunatic." Yes, you read those correctly. No matter how many times you go back and reread them, the words will remain the same. Those two laws are still legal. Most of the crazy laws in these wonderful stories are still legal. The tales vary in time and place. Some take place in the present, in the past, in the USA, in England, may contain magic... in other words, there is something for everyone! You simply cannot go wrong. Best yet, all profits from the sales of this novel go to breast cancer prevention.

A stellar anthology that had me laughing, sighing in pleasure, believing in magic, and left me begging for more! Will there be a second anthology someday? I sure
~~~

hope so! This is one novel that will go directly to my 'Keeper' shelf, to be read over and over again. Very highly recommended!

Reviewed by Detra Fitch
Huntress Reviews

~~~

HIGHLAND WISHES - This reviewer found that this book was a wonderful story set in a time when tension was high between England and Scotland. Burroughs writes a well-crafted story, with multidimensional characters and exquisite backdrops of Scotland. The storyline is a fast-paced tale with much detail to specific areas of history. The reader can feel this author's love for Scotland and its many wonderful heroes.

The characters connect immediately and don't stop until the end. At the end of the book, the reader wonders what happens next. The interplay between characters was smoothly done and helped the story along. It was a very smoothly told story. This reviewer was easily captivated by the story and was enthralled by it until the end. The reader will laugh and cry as you read this wonderful story. The reader feels all the pain, torment and disillusionment felt by both main characters, but also the joy and love they felt. Ms. Burroughs has crafted a well-researched story that gives a glimpse into Scotland during a time when there was upheaval and war for independence. This reviewer is anxiously awaiting her next novel in this series and commends her for a wonderful job done.

Dawn Roberto
Love Romances
www.loveromances.com
~~~

Holiday in The Heart

Highland Press
High Springs, Florida 32655

Holiday in the Heart

For information, please contact Highland Press, PO Box 2292, High Springs, FL 32655.

All characters in this book have no existence outside the imagination of the author and have no relation whatsoever to anyone bearing the same name or names, save actual historical figures. They are not even distantly inspired by any individual known or unknown to the author, and all incidents are pure invention.

ISBN: 0-9787139-1-5
PUBLISHED BY HIGHLAND PRESS
A Wee Dram Book

To those who love the magic and beauty of Christmas, Chanukah and the entire Holiday Season.

Happy Holidays!

ACKNOWLEDGEMENTS

Grateful thanks are due to the many staff editors who helped with this book:

Kristi Ahlers
Cheryl Alldredge
Victoria Bromley
Patty Howell
Deborah MacGillivray
Marilyn Rondeau
Diane Davis White

And a very special thanks to Monika Wolmarans

~ LLB

Table of Contents

Christmas Wonderland

by Leanne Burroughs

1944

Samantha Noelle looked over the swarm of people—mainly mothers and children—and shook her head. The store was a madhouse!

How would she ever survive this next month? If she didn't need the money so badly, she never would have let Monique talk her into replacing her after she'd broken her leg. But Santa's helper couldn't be seen walking around with a cast on her leg, could she? At least that's the argument Monique had used.

So here she was—the day after Thanksgiving—dressed in an elf costume!

Samantha rolled her eyes. If one more teenage boy came by and made a wisecrack, she'd belt him. And there would go her job—and the money she needed.

As if that wasn't bad enough, the store manager had laughed when he'd seen her in the elf costume. His manners left the man far lacking. Such a shame, too, because he was drop-dead gorgeous with black hair and the clearest blue-grey eyes she'd ever seen. Eyes that seemed to look into your soul.

If she was lucky, she wouldn't have to deal with him very often.

The line of children wrapping through the toy department seemed endless. With most men in the war in Europe, few fathers were present. Management certainly had been smart to put Santa where little ones could beg and plead for toys they passed while in line. Everyone knew families would try their hardest to make Christmas special for the children, feeling they had to compensate for daddies not being home on Christmas morning.

Some little ones were whiny, but most looked excited and awestruck. The guy the store hired was good. White hair and a real beard. And his size was just about right—tall, with broad shoulders. No pillow necessary. What really caught a person's attention were his eyes. They twinkled when he spoke, giving the impression he really cared. Not just for the children, but their parents, too. His rapier wit had everyone laughing. He was exactly what Santa Claus should be—if he were real. And the children actually thought they were seeing the real Santa Claus.

Samantha sat with *Santa* in the employee cafeteria and wiped her fingers on a napkin after finishing her hamburger.

She watched him eat his cheeseburger and fries with relish. "So, Joe, what made you decide to brave being Santa?"

"Daughter insisted I'd be perfect for it. Told her she was crazy, but she thought I should try it now I'm retired. And with the war going on and so many men away, I figured it was the least I could do to put a smile on children's faces. It's bad enough most of them will have to spend the holiday fatherless." His rueful smile told her he wasn't pleased about that.

"You're perfect at it. And the children love you. You're...nice."

Joe laughed. "That's not something many people tell me. Usually they tell me I'm mean, rotten, and smell bad."

Samantha furrowed her brow. "Really?"

He wiped his mouth with a napkin and leaned back in his chair. "All right, I confess. That's what I usually tell them. So, Miss Elf, what made you decide to walk around in a green outfit?"

She smiled. "My friend was supposed to work here, but she fell and broke her leg while I was visiting my cousin, Allison, in Chicago. She knew I needed extra money, so when I came home she talked me into taking her place."

"Need it for Christmas presents?" A smile lit his eyes, then quickly faded. "Even if you do save some money, with all the rationing going on now, you might not be able to find whatever you want. It's even hard to find Christmas ornaments this year since silver's at such a premium."

"My friend's been working overseas as a fashion consultant for the past year and I've been staying at her house. She used to go overseas to view the Spring and Fall collections and bring them back for her company, but last year she stayed. With the war still going on, her employer's worried she might be injured by a bomb falling on London. So they're insisting she return home. She loves living in London and tried to find another job, but even Harrods had to turn her away now that it's focusing on the war effort."

Joe arched a brow. "So it's true? I'd heard their sales have lagged with people having little money. One of the newsreels at the theatre announced Harrods had switched to producing uniforms, parachutes and parts for Lancaster bombers. Even claimed sections of the store had been taken over by the Royal Navy."

Samantha nodded. "So, she's resigned to coming home and I have to find someplace else to live. Which is why I need extra money for a deposit."

"You're going to pay for an apartment on an elf's salary? I hope you don't want anything larger than a closet."

Samantha sipped her Coca-Cola, set the glass back down. "Oh, I have a job during the daytime, too. Since I set my own hours there, I shouldn't have any conflict that would keep me from being here on time so *Mr. Grumpy* doesn't have an excuse to yell at me for being late."

Joe laughed out loud. "By Mr. Grumpy I assume you mean Mr. Giovanni?"

"Yeah. I've never seen anyone so grumpy." *Or so handsome.*

"You really like that stuff?" He nodded toward her glass of soda.

"Coca-Cola? I love it. And I think it's awesome the company pledged to provide Coke to every U.S. soldier fighting overseas."

"That's the spin they give on it anyway."

Samantha laughed. "So now the truth comes out, *Santa*. You're really a grump."

"Guilty as charged."

They threw their trash away and headed out. Busy talking to Joe, Samantha didn't pay attention as she opened the door—and ran right into Gregory Giovanni. His hands shot out to brace her from falling.

Heat flooded her face. She was sure her complexion could compete with Joe's Santa suit. "Oh, I'm sorry. I wasn't paying attention—"

"Clearly," he interrupted, dropping his hands as if touching her burned them. "I do hope you pay more attention to the children visiting our Christmas Wonderland than you pay to your surroundings." He moved around her and headed toward the grill.

"Inconsiderate oaf!" Samantha grumbled.

Although he obviously tried, Joe couldn't conceal the gleam in his eyes. "You did practically knock the boss off his feet." As she shot him a glare, he continued, "You could do worse, you know. Most women consider him 'a good catch.'"

Samantha huffed. "As if I'd pay someone like him any attention."

Liar! You couldn't take your eyes off him during orientation. Hard not to look at someone that takes your breath away.

"From what I heard, the man gives a lot to the community. When you signed your employment paperwork you should have seen Nickel's Department Store is promoting a War Bond drive. I've heard Giovanni pledged to match everything his employees donate." He raised a brow as he watched her closely. "That's a mighty generous man, if you ask me."

With the onslaught of little boys and girls waiting to see Santa, Samantha had little time to think about *Mr. Gregory Giovanni.*

She'd run straight into him. The beautiful little elf that probably thought him the biggest Scrooge around. She should. He'd been nothing but unpleasant, if not rude to her from the moment he first saw her.

He had to. Had his daughter to think about. She was so fragile. In so much pain. He needed to spend every minute away from work with her. Not mooning over some beautiful, lithe girl that took his breath away.

When her friend had broken her leg and suggested Miss Noelle be allowed to take her place, he'd almost said no. Her resumé seemed too good. Too perfect. Then she'd walked into the interview room.

His brain had ceased functioning. All blood traveled south and left him without a sane thought. All he could think about was the young woman standing before him. Light brown hair cascaded halfway down her back. And her eyes. Eyes the color of brandy. She'd smiled, and the smile had reached her eyes. Surely they'd seen clear into his soul. Seen his loneliness.

He'd hired her on the spot. First time in his life he'd made such a reckless decision.

Surprisingly, he didn't regret it. He'd watched her today. Not that she'd seen him. He imagined she wouldn't have liked it if she'd known. He doubted she knew he owned Nickel's as well as the entire shopping center. Most people assumed he was merely the manager. He liked it that way. He wanted people to judge him for himself, not for his family's money. Ever since Amanda walked out on him, he'd made it a point not to let people know his family connections—still primarily in Chicago. Only a few people locally knew his background.

He'd been pleased with her performance throughout the day. Keeping children and their parents happy hopefully meant they'd shop in his store and other stores in the center—pleasing his store managers. And happy managers meant healthy profits. Not that he needed more money—his family's extensive business interests kept him more than comfortable—but he enjoyed what he did.

But she'd gone far beyond his expectations of an *elf*. She'd acted like she cared—not just automatically directing each child to Santa's lap. She actually talked to them. Paid attention to what they said, often kneeling on one knee to look into their eyes. Make them feel important.

Greg wondered what it would be like to have those eyes peer into his for any length of time. Talk to him like she had the children. Care about what he felt.

Stop it! She's not a date—she's an employee. Nothing more, nothing less.

Not since he'd met his wife had a woman affected him like this. He'd thought their love would last forever. Had wanted it to. Clearly Amanda hadn't felt the same. After their daughter had been born she'd told him she was leaving. She'd met someone else. Someone who could advance her career. She'd left and never looked back. Divorce papers had arrived in less than a week. He'd felt gut punched when she told him she'd never loved him. Had only wanted his money.

For the first time in years, Greg found himself wanting to open up to someone again. Be near someone other than his tiny daughter. He'd shut out everything—everyone— after Amanda left.

He'd seen Miss Noelle every day for the past week while she'd been in training. Greg shook his head. Whoever heard of week-long training to be an elf? He'd devised the class for employees from all the stores who rented space from his shopping mall merely as a means to see her. The woman with the Christmasy name. The woman with the haunting brown eyes. Eyes that called to him. Made him want more.

He was a fool.

Samantha didn't think her legs would hold up much longer. Hundreds of children had come with their parents to the store today. And every one of them wanted to see Santa.

She couldn't imagine how Joe had held up so well and still had a smile on his face as the last child of the day climbed up on his lap and recited her long list of everything she hoped to get for Christmas. She'd heard him trying to talk the little ones' lists down to only one or two items, knowing with the war on there'd be little extra money for Christmas presents. He'd told her earlier that he didn't want them to be disappointed.

With the store closed for the night, they walked briskly back to the employee lounge to get their coats.

She tried to open her locker, but the door stuck. *Just my luck*. Jiggling the handle again, she couldn't get it to budge. "Stupid door."

Drawing back her foot, she let loose and kicked the door. "Ow, ow, ow! That hurt." Holding her painful foot off the ground, she hopped around on the other foot.

"I don't imagine the door is very appreciative either," a voice said behind her.

Samantha groaned. She recognized that voice. Had listened to it every day for a week in the ridiculous elf sessions he'd made her take. As if she couldn't have figured out she needed to smile and talk sweetly to the children.

Bracing her shoulders, she turned to face—*him*. "It's been a long day and I want to go home. I work at an old age home during the day and have to be there early tomorrow. "

A smile pursed his lips as he moved to her locker, lifted the handle and easily opened the door. He chided, "Haven't you ever heard the old saying, 'you can catch more flies with honey?' Clearly the same applies to temperamental lockers."

He turned and walked to the far side of the room, spoke with someone else.

Why was he always walking around the store? Why didn't he just stay upstairs in his office? Samantha had the overwhelming urge to kick him in his oh-so-fine backside just like she had the door.

Greg parked his car in the garage and opened the door to his kitchen. "I'm home! Where is everyone?"

His housekeeper, Mrs. Watson, came around the corner from the living room. "We're right here. Missy wanted to play a game of *Snakes and Ladders*, so we've been down on the floor." She turned to smile at the small girl trailing slowly behind her. "Have to admit she's a good player. Beat me three games in a row."

Greg picked his daughter up and twirled her around. "You did? It's a good thing I wasn't here. You would have trounced me." He smiled when her eyes lit with joy.

"It was easy, Daddy. Mrs. Watson isn't a very good player. She kept moving the wrong way."

Setting her back on the floor, Greg riffled her long black hair, so like his own. Then again, Missy was the spitting image of him. He was glad. Didn't know what he would have done if she'd looked like her mother. Or should he say the woman who gave birth to her? She'd certainly been no *mother*.

He wished there was someone in his life that could spend time with Missy. His housekeeper was wonderful, but Missy needed someone besides himself to do things with. Someone younger than Mrs. Watson. To spend time away from home and the doctors' offices.

Some day his daughter would be free from the pain she was in now from when she'd broken her leg. He didn't doubt it—much. *No, I can't think like that. Melissa's leg will heal. It won't always hurt when she walks. She'll grow up and be a beautiful young woman. Help people who are less fortunate than she is. Maybe help elderly people.*

Where had that thought come from? Oh, he knew exactly why he'd thought it. Knew the woman he'd thought about all the way home.

He'd read on her application that she worked with the elderly. He thought that a strange vocation for a woman so young, so vibrant. He couldn't picture someone her age wanting to spend time with old people. Most without families wound up living in public institutions, ineligible for Old Age Assistance. That someone as beautiful as his *elf* wanted to be with them fascinated him. *She fascinated him.*

Stop it! She's just an employee.

As he walked Mrs. Watson to the door to tell her good-night, Greg acknowledged it was a lie. He wanted Samantha Noelle to be a whole lot more.

Every day for the next week Greg watched the clock waiting for his little elf to arrive at work. His elf? What was he thinking?

And every day she arrived on time, put on that ridiculous elf costume and went out to interact with the children. And with Santa.

The two clearly had bonded with each other. Become fast friends. For the first time in his life, Greg felt jealous. How he'd love to have her feel that way about him.

He'd watched the elderly man—Santa—as he worked with other employees throughout the day. They were pleasant, but his face came alive when Samantha arrived. Although he seemed like a nice man all the time, she brought out the best in him.

Greg imagined she could bring out the best in anyone.

He'd actually checked her references today—something he should have done before she'd started. They'd all been glowing.

Miss Noelle seemed perfect. But everyone had a flaw. He'd learned that quickly enough with Amanda. He'd thought his wife perfect. In a way, she had been—perfectly groomed, perfect manners, perfect face and body.

And shallow.

Miss Samantha Noelle was probably no better. Part of him believed it to be true. The other part wanted him to be wrong. He wanted her to be different. *Needed* her to be different. He knew from her application that she had no close family. She'd listed only one cousin in Chicago.

Could it be Miss Noelle was as lonely as he?

The following evening Greg entered the crowded cafeteria. He got his grilled cheese sandwich and started to take his food back to his office, but stopped when he spotted Samantha sitting alone.

Mustering his courage, he approached her table and set his tray down. "Hope you don't mind if I join you. Room's pretty crowded today."

He pulled a chair out and sat before she could tell him no.

She quickly wiped her lips with her napkin. Started to edge her chair back. "I was almost through anyway. You can have the table. I might run down to Grant's to see if they have any knitting supplies in their yarn department. I promised one of the elderly ladies I'd pick some up for her."

"Stay where you are, Miss Noelle," he ordered. "You weren't finished eating. If you find me that offensive, I'll leave." Greg stood, picked up his sandwich and drink and turned to the door.

A hand on his arm stopped him before he reached it.

"Mr. Giovanni, please don't leave. I'm sorry. I was rude. It's just that you make me feel..."

"Uncomfortable?" he finished for her. At her nod, he added, "I tend to do that with most people. Guess it goes with my position."

She continued to watch him, but said nothing. Her hand remained on his arm. The sensation of warmth seeped through his shirtsleeve, permeated his body, shot straight to his groin. Melted some of the ice around his heart.

"Please stay, Mr. Giovanni. Eat your sandwich before it grows cold."

Greg glanced down at his plate. He'd forgotten all about the grilled cheese. Cared less about it. He wasn't hungry for food. He wanted something much more elementary—companionship. Someone to spend time with, to talk with. He wanted it to be with Miss Noelle.

Placing his hand at the small of her back, he ushered her toward the table. After seating her, he drew out his own chair again and sat.

They sat in uncomfortable silence for several minutes until Greg could stand it no more. "Tell me about yourself, Miss Noelle. Why did you take this job?"

She looked surprised. "You already know why. Monique broke her leg."

"Yes, but that doesn't explain why you took over for her. We had dozens of applicants for the position. I could have filled it with one of them."

Those brandy colored eyes met his. "I've wondered about that. Why did you hire me when other people had applied before me?"

Damn! He'd walked right into that.

"Just seemed the thing to do since your friend recommended you so highly." *And because I wanted to drag you home and make love to you. See your long hair spread over my pillow, see your naked body writhing under mine.*

No, it wouldn't do to tell her that last part.

"Hmmm." Her eyes told him she didn't believe that.

"But you didn't answer my question. Why did you take this job?"

She smiled. "That's easy. I need the money."

"Your application said you already have a job. Something about elderly people."

Samantha chuckled. "I do. But I need a deposit for an apartment. I've been staying at a friend's house for the past year, but she's being transferred home because of the war. I have less than a month to find a place of my own." She sighed and took a deep breath. "I thought it would be easy, but I've been looking for the past week and haven't found anything I can afford."

He quirked a brow. "Haven't saved any money from your other job? Too busy partying and spending it on clothes?"

She looked insulted.

"I don't party, Mr. Giovanni, although I do attend USO dances now and again. And although I like to look nice, no, I don't waste my money on clothes. I can barely afford the material to make them, let alone buy them ready-made. With the war on, stores like this are only for the wealthy." She threw her napkin onto her plate. "Now if you'll excuse me, I have to get back to work."

"You still have twenty minutes before you have to leave, Miss Noelle." Her look told him he'd surprised her. "I saw you walking down the stairs from the toy department on your way to the cafeteria. Unlike someone else I know, I pay attention to my surroundings."

"Oh, I—" She looked flustered. He hadn't meant to upset her, just tease her about walking into him.

"I didn't mean to offend you, Samantha. I apologize. It's just that I'm used to women that—"

"Let you down?"

He said nothing.

"She must have hurt you badly for you to be so bitter. You're too young to have built such a wall around yourself."

A small gasp escaped her lips. "I'm so sorry. I didn't mean to say that. That was rude of me. Please forgive me."

He waved her remarks aside.

"Young? I'm hardly a child, Samantha. I'm thirty-five."

"Ah, almost ready for a walker." She smiled and placed her hand over his on the table. Her touch was light. Her warmth sent heat through his reserves, filling the emptiness within him.

"Yet you're hurting like a child. It shows in your eyes."

Greg shifted in his chair. He didn't want to talk about himself. Didn't want to think about his ex-wife.

"Again, please forgive me for intruding on your privacy."

"You must not make much at your day job if you need to take another job."

Samantha shook her head. "Changing the subject, I see. That's fine. You don't have to talk about it with me." She stopped and pursed her lips, clearly thinking. "Why don't I have any money? With the war going on, few people have money. However, I use what little I have to help senior citizens. I told you before that I help at old age homes. I do simple things for them to let them feel independent. I often run errands. I promised a few ladies I'd pick up some trinkets and some knitting materials for them. They can't get out to shop, but they wanted to buy a few simple Christmas presents." She ran her tongue over her lips before continuing. "They have very little money, less than most of us. The majority of what they have—including their ration coupons—goes to pay for them to stay in the nursing home. And those in public facilities have even less. So I buy them little things. They don't know it, of course.

They'd never let me do it if they did. I just let them think the homes cover their expenses."

Greg frowned. "You use your own money?"

She nodded.

"Why?"

"My grandfather lived with us when I was a child. We did everything together. He was my best friend. But he'd had a rough life. My grandmother died from cancer and he never recovered from that. They'd thought she was pregnant with her second child; instead she had a tumor. He became an alcoholic, and that took a toll on his body. When we could no longer keep him at home, I visited him every week. Watched him decline—physically and mentally. Watched the people who lived in the home do with very little. I vowed then to make a difference. To try and help people forced into that predicament."

As she'd done for him earlier, he reached out and covered her hand with his.

Who was this woman who wanted to make a difference in the world? Was she real? Or was this all an act? Maybe she'd found out who he really was and hoped to get his money.

Slowly moving her hand from beneath his, Samantha moved her chair back and rose. "And now, if you'll excuse me, I really must get back to work." She picked up her tray and turned to leave. Glancing over her shoulder, she impishly called back, "Wouldn't want my boss to think I was taking a longer dinner break than allowed."

No, she didn't know who he was. He was sure of it.

Greg walked slowly to his office the next afternoon, holding his young daughter's hand within his own. He'd taken Missy to the specialist that morning. How dare the doctor suggest his daughter could walk if she wanted to? Evidently the man was a moron! Didn't he realize how much it hurt her to take more than a few steps? Didn't he care?

Well Greg did, and no one would hurt his daughter! It was bad enough her mother had walked out on her. He'd never let anyone hurt her again.

Before heading home for the day, he had some things he needed to address in the office. Missy would be fine in the adjoining room while he worked. She stayed there often when his housekeeper was unavailable. She had strict orders never to leave the room. He'd stocked it with toys and books for her in the past so she could stay there after her numerous appointments.

Finding the room empty thirty minutes later, he panicked. Melissa had never left the room before. She knew not to. *Merciful Mary, has someone kidnapped her?*

Frantic with worry, Greg dashed out of his office, ran through Nickel's, then ran down the sidewalk in front of the shopping center looking for her. He looked in every store, every restaurant. No Missy.

Almost ready to head to his office to contact the police, Greg hurried back into Nickel's to recheck every department. Strains of Bing Crosby's *White Christmas* played throughout the store. Greg could have cared less about a white Christmas. All he wanted was to find Missy. Heading upstairs to the Christmas Wonderland display, he barely spared a glance for Santa and the beautiful elf. Except the elf wasn't there. Parents and children were lined up waiting to see Santa, but there was no elf to direct them.

His eyes scanned the area. What did it matter that she wasn't there? He was worried about his daughter. Yet an inner sense made him slow down and search the nearby surroundings.

Children were seated on the floor, watching cartoons in the children's play area he'd set up to keep them occupied while their parents shopped. His breath caught when he saw the green elf costume surrounded by children. Her head was bent low, talking to a beautiful little girl. A girl with black hair. His daughter.

Greg thought his knees would buckle. She was safe. His daughter was safe. Forcing himself to walk slowly to the play area, he stood behind them.

"Miss Noelle, Melissa, is everything all right?"

Samantha's head jerked up, her eyes seeking his. "You know her?"

"Yes, she's my—"

"Daddy!" Melissa scrambled up off the floor. She dragged her right leg as she moved toward him.

Greg lifted her into his arms. His eyes searched her to assure himself she was fine, then turned to Samantha.

"How did—"

Eyes bright with excitement, again Melissa interrupted. "Daddy, did you see? Santa's over there." She pointed back to the Christmas Wonderland area. "I heard your *sec-tary* talking about him, so I had to come see. I haven't been able to see him yet, 'cause my leg hurt too bad when I stood in line. And his elf helped me over here to sit when I started crying."

A wide smile crossed Missy's face as she looked at Samantha. "She's so nice, Daddy. Her name's Sam, and she's been talking to me for such a long time. Can you marry her, Daddy? Santa won't mind if she stays with us instead of with him."

Greg was sure his eyes were as wide as Samantha's at his daughter's exclamation. Where had she come up with an idea like that?

"M-Missy, I'm afraid Miss Noelle has to stay here with Santa. He...he..." Greg couldn't think of a thing to say.

Samantha came to his rescue. "I have to stay here, Missy. What if another little girl needs help and I'm not here to take care of her?"

Pouting, Missy's lower lip pouched out. "I don't care. I saw you first."

Samantha laughed. "Sweetheart, Santa needs me. I have to stay here until he leaves."

"Do you have to go home with him?"

"No, I go to my own house at night and he goes home to Mrs. Claus."

Missy brightened. "Good, then you can have supper with me and Daddy. He's making *pas-ghetti* tonight. Usually Mrs. Watson gets the noodles at the general store, but my grandma made these for us. Sometimes when I'm over at her house she lets me help."

Greg groaned and interrupted her monologue. "Melissa, I'm sure Miss Noelle has far more important things to do tonight than have dinner with us."

Missy shook her head, her black hair swinging from side to side. "No she doesn't, Daddy. She told me earlier she doesn't have nuffin' to do tonight. Didn't you, Sam?"

Looking guilty, Samantha nodded. "Well, yes, but—"

"Puh-leeeeeeze!"

Greg wished a hole would open up and he could drop into it. How could he politely get out of this? This young woman wouldn't want to spend dinner with him and his daughter. She'd barely wanted to share a table with him yesterday. Besides, she probably had a boyfriend waiting to take her out when she left work.

"Miss Noelle, I'm sure you have other plans, but if you don't..."

The smile that lit her face warmed his heart. "Actually, I was going to make myself a sandwich and read a good book." She blushed when she added, "Romances are my favorite."

"See, Daddy. I told you." His daughter looked triumphant.

Why did the thought she didn't have a date so please him?

Missy held Samantha's hand as she proudly showed her the Christmas tree. "Isn't it beeeeeautiful, Sam? Daddy and I put it up last week. And I helped decorate. Didn't I do a good job?" She looked up to wait for Sam's answer. At the nod, she added, "But I couldn't reach up high. Daddy had to put the angel on top. And he gave me a job 'cause I'm a big girl. He says I have to help him water it every day." She pulled Sam closer. "Look at the ornaments we got this year, Sam. One for me and one for Daddy. Mine's red and his is blue. Look really, really close. You can see right through them. And look at the top. Daddy said they had to use paper 'cause of the war. They can't get silver something or other. Daddy said they're red, white and blue because we're *pate-tic.*"

Greg laughed and swung his daughter up into his arms. "Patriotic, sweetheart. We're patriotic."

"We should have got a white one, too, Daddy. That could be Sam's."

Sam laughed in embarrassment. "It's sweet of you to think of me, but I have my own tree." She pointed toward the elegant tree. "But I have to admit I love those lights that bubble. I haven't seen any like that before."

As soon as Greg set her down, Missy pulled on Sam's hand again. "Sit on the floor with me, Sam. You can play with my Tinker Toys."

"Are you sure you don't want me to help with anything?" Sam called while Greg prepared dinner. She sat cross-legged on the floor helping Missy build a bridge with her Tinker Toys.

"I'm fine. I'm used to cooking. It's just me and Missy, so unless my mother feels sorry for us and brings food over, I cook every night."

This was a side of Greg Giovanni she imagined few people saw. She doubted most even knew he had a daughter.

Now that she'd seen a chink in his armor, she could see she'd been wrong in her first impressions of him. He might be someone she wouldn't mind getting to know better after all.

But did she dare? He was her boss—even if the job was just temporary. Somehow she couldn't imagine the manager of Nickel's Department Store wanting to date one of its elves!

"It's done!" Missy shouted as she put the last piece of the Tinker Toy into place, stood and walked back to her bedroom. Sam watched her. She took five steps, then dragged her leg. She'd dragged it when leaving the store after seeing Santa Claus, too. Sam wondered what was wrong.

Waiting for the child to come back, Sam headed into the kitchen. "Smells good in here."

"Spaghetti. Hope that's okay. Used up the last of our ration coupons for this month the last time I went to the store. Normally my housekeeper shops for me, but I knew exactly what I wanted, so I told her I'd stop at the market on the way home the other day. I had to get Italian sausage, beef, and pork for the sauce."

"I love spaghetti, but that doesn't smell like anything you'd buy from a general store."

Greg laughed. "It's not. My mother made her spaghetti sauce every weekend when I was a boy. Pretty much carried over the tradition myself. When I have time to make it, I simmer the sauce all day—usually on Saturdays. When holidays roll around, I sometimes have to be at the store, so I don't get to do it then. But my mother always makes sure we have enough in the ice box to whip out for emergencies like this."

"You cook your sauce all day?" Disbelief showed on her face.

"Certainly. Just like my grandmother taught my mom. She learned it from her family in the old country. Call it a family tradition."

"What's wrong with Missy's leg?"

The surprised look on Greg's face told her the change of subject caught him off guard.

"She broke it when she was two. Fell down the staircase at my parents' house. She'd climbed the steps when we weren't looking and it never healed right."

"Maybe they could operate and correct the problem." She sighed. "What am I thinking? Hospitals are too expensive for most people to go to. I understand if that's why you haven't taken her, but it's a shame—"

Greg's eyes clouded. "She's been through too much pain in her short life. I'll not put her through surgery with no promise it won't be a success."

"You can't carry her forever, Greg. What about when she begins school? Won't she start next year? Children can often be cruel. They might tease her."

"I don't want to talk about this, Samantha. Missy and I are doing just fine without you intruding."

He might as well have slapped her!

Shoulders straightened and chin raised, Sam glared at him. "I'm sorry to be an *intrusion*, Mr. Giovanni. Please make my excuses to Missy. I'm leaving."

She grabbed her purse and headed toward the kitchen door.

An arm reached around her and slammed it shut as soon as she opened it.

"Sam, I'm sorry." He placed his hands on her shoulders and turned her to face him. "Merciful Mary, I didn't mean that."

His eyes beseeched her. He looked miserable.

But she didn't stay where she wasn't wanted.

"I'm sorry, too, Mr. Giovanni, but this isn't going to work. I don't belong here. I shouldn't have said yes. Just tell Missy something came up and I had to leave."

She wanted to take away the pain she saw in his eyes. Wanted to stay. Wanted to go.

She closed her eyes. *I have no idea what I want.*

Greg felt like a heel. He'd been uncomfortable with her mentioning hospital costs and had taken his discomfort out on her. He could afford any treatment the doctors prescribed. Could buy the entire hospital if he wanted to.

But he didn't want to talk money with her. Didn't want her with him because his family was rich. Just once he wanted someone to want him...just for him.

Of course Samantha would ask about his daughter. She cared about people. It was one of the things that drew him to her.

He raised the palm of his hand to her cheek. Caressed it lightly. "Please, Sam. Stay."

Her eyes rose and met his, but she didn't move.

"Let me start over again."

When her hand reached up to cover his, something inside him snapped.

He wanted this moment. If he had nothing else ever again, he wanted this one moment in time with her.

Drawing her to him, he rubbed a hand along her spine as he looked down into those compelling eyes. He didn't have to drink any brandy to be drunk. Just looking into her eyes did that.

He cursed himself for being a thousand times a fool, but he was going to kiss her—and damn the consequences.

His hand moved to the back of her head, fingers lightly stroked the nape of her neck. When she moved to pull away, he anchored his fingers in her hair and lowered his mouth to hers.

He pulled her closer. Molded her body to his.

His tongue lightly traced her lips, urging them to open. They didn't. She wasn't going to make this easy on him.

He kissed her lips, her cheeks, her eyes. Moved his head and lightly swirled his tongue around the edge of her ear. Then returned to start over. When his hand cupped her bottom and urged her closer, he wasn't sure if the sigh was his or hers.

Not certain how they got there, he soon had her pressed against the icebox. He pinned her there, his body unyielding, his hands on either side of her.

"Kiss me, Sam." His eyes held hers.

When he lowered his mouth to hers again, her lips opened. He deepened the kiss, lost himself in the wonder of her.

"Daddy, where's Sam?"

Greg jumped back at the sound of his daughter's voice. Kept one arm on the icebox for balance. What had this woman done to him? Feelings he'd thought long dead coursed through him.

Breathing deeply, he faced Missy. She cradled her favorite doll to her chest.

"Oh, there you are, Sam. I didn't see you. Daddy was in the way."

Sam edged away from Greg.

"Your daddy was just...just..."

"Telling Sam about how Grandma makes spaghetti sauce every weekend." *What a ridiculous statement!*

"Yes, that's it. Doesn't it smell good in here?"

Sam pulled out a kitchen chair and sat in it. She looked shaken enough that she might actually have fallen if she hadn't done so. As her eyes met his over Missy's head, they revealed she'd wanted him as much as he'd wanted her. Still wanted her.

Thank God Missy had interrupted. Who knew what stupid thing he might have done if he'd kept kissing Sam? Why did she so affect him? He saw beautiful women every day. Women on the fast track to careers, fashion models in his high end stores throughout the United States. Not one of them had ever earned a second glance. Until Sam.

The woman who wore a green elf costume in one of his stores.

As soon as dinner ended, Sam told Missy, "I have to leave, sweetheart. Thank you for inviting me for dinner. Your daddy's a really good cook."

"Grandma taught him." Missy smiled as she hugged Sam goodbye.

Sam knelt and pulled the little girl to her. "She did a good job. The spaghetti was delicious and I haven't had chocolate cake for months. Not since they started rationing sugar."

"Yeah, Daddy does *pas-ghetti* really good." She turned to smile up at her father. "He does lasagna good, too. Want to have that tomorrow?"

Sam couldn't hide her shock. "I can't come back tomorrow, Missy."

"Why?"

"Well, because..."

"'Cause why?"

Sam turned to Greg to elicit his help.

He surprised her when he smiled—a cat who'd just cornered a mouse smile. "I do make good lasagna. Why don't you come over after church? We'll eat around two."

"Mr. Giovanni!" She shot him a glare, but he didn't rise to the bait. "I can't come here again and you know it."

He stood silent and thought a minute. "Well, all right. It will mean more work, but if you can't come here I guess Missy and I can bring the meal to your house around two. Might be two-thirty with travel time."

"Mr. Giovanni!"

"You said that already."

"And you aren't listening."

"Nope, I'm not. And I have no intention of doing so."

"Why not?"

"Missy wants to have lunch with you tomorrow."

"That's not reason enough and you know it."

"And so do I."

"You what?"

"Want to have lunch with you. So the only question is—your place or mine?" He wiggled his eyebrows like a lecherous old man.

How could he do this to her? He couldn't have forgotten *that* kiss so quickly. She couldn't see him again. If she did, she just might... What?

The answer was only too clear.

She just might fall in love with him.

"Oooooo, you have a kitty," Missy squealed when they walked into Sam's kitchen and a huge bundle of fur skittered away. "I want a kitty, but Daddy won't get me one." She made a face at her father. "Says I'm not old enough."

She got down on her knees. "C'mere, kitty, kitty."

"Her name is Tigger."

Missy smiled. "Like in Winnie the Pooh?"

"Yep, just like that."

"But Tigger's a boy."

"Not this Tigger. She's a girl. A very spoiled girl. When I try to work on my typewriter at night, she either drapes herself across my legs or insinuates herself over the keys."

"Oh. C'mere, Tigger." Missy turned to her father. "Daddy, what's sin-u-ate?"

Greg laughed. "It means the cat plops down on Sam's typewriter like you plop on my lap when I sit in my chair."

"Oh, okay."

Greg looked around the kitchen. "Your friend has a nice setup here. I see you're all set for us."

"You said you'd be here at two. I didn't want the lasagna to get cold." She turned away from him so she didn't have to see the taunting in his eyes.

She was a coward. She knew it. He knew it.

After lunch, Sam ordered Greg and Missy into the living room. "You cooked. The least I can do is clean up."

From the living room, Missy shouted, "Daddy, Daddy, look. A reindeer!"

Greg walked into the living room to see his daughter on her knees in front of the Christmas tree, a book in her hands.

His gaze shifted back to Sam. "How'd you get one of the books Montgomery Ward is giving away?"

"My cousin, Allison, lives in Chicago. Apparently she's been seeing some man whose family owns the general store. Allison said he's trying to make Christmas special for her daughter, Rebecca, so he took her to see Santa several times. That's how they got an extra copy. She mailed this one to me thinking I'd like it. How did you know where it came from?"

"I have to keep up with what all the stores are doing so I can stay competitive. Wards' handed those out five years now—although I've heard it was harder this year since there's such a paper shortage."

A smile lit Samantha's face as she watched Missy's obvious excitement. "I'm glad she sent it. Why don't you read it to her while I go clean the kitchen?"

Greg finally settled Missy with the book after reading it to her three times. Stretching, he strode to the Victrola to see what record was on it. *The Christmas Song* by Mel Torme. *I should have known she'd be playing Christmas music.* He wandered back into the kitchen. Sam was at the sink washing dishes. Walking up behind her, he pressed his body to hers, moved her hair aside and kissed her neck.

"Thanks for letting us use your kitchen, Miss Noelle. That was a wonderful meal."

"Searching for compliments, Mr. Giovanni?"

He turned her to face him. Wrapped her soapy hands around his neck. "No, actually, I'm searching for a kiss."

Her eyes closed. "Mr. Giovanni, please. We can't...we—"

His mouth closed over hers, silencing her words. He pressed closer, allowing her to feel his desire.

Breathing heavily, he backed away. "Are you going to tell me you don't feel the same thing I do? You're lying if you do."

Her eyes pleaded with him. "You know I do. But our lives are different. You're the manager of a fancy store. I'm the elf. Come Christmas, I won't be there anymore. You'll never see me again. You live in a beautiful house. I can't even afford the deposit on an apartment."

"Oh, I'll definitely see you after the holidays." He arched a brow, daring her to contradict him. "Let me help you with that deposit."

"I don't take handouts. I earn what I need. I don't have enough yet, but I'll get it. And I can't spend all my time with you. The elderly people I work with need me."

"I need you."

"Mr. Giovanni, please don't."

He backed away. "If you call me Mr. Giovanni one more time...I'll..." He ran a hand through his hair. "I kissed you, Sam. You kissed me back. You can call me Greg now." He sighed in frustration. "Okay, you need more time. I'll give you that time. Maybe."

Drawing her close again, he placed a chaste kiss on her lips, then whispered in her ear, "I want to take you out—just the two of us. We'll go out next Saturday. That gives you a week to come to terms with...us." Without waiting for her answer, he walked into her living room.

After drying her hands and placing the towel on the counter, Sam left the kitchen. Her heart slammed against her ribs at the sight that greeted her. Greg lay back in the recliner, his small daughter curled on his chest. With his arms loosely around her, both were sound asleep.

Sam knew her heart was at risk. This man and his tiny daughter were *sin-u-ating* their way into her life. *I'm even thinking like Missy now*!

Was she ready for this? Her life had been perfectly fine the way it was. She didn't need the complications of a high-profile man and his daughter.

Didn't need anyone else in her life right now. She had the senior citizens she helped. They needed her.

But who did she really have for herself? She had...no one!

Did she want anyone? Or was she happy as is? She'd thought so. She hadn't dated since her break up with Joseph several months back. He'd wanted different things than she did. Was focused on climbing his way to the top of his career. He wanted her at his side—to look nice. Be an asset in his business. Her life was more important than being an ornament on someone's arm. Her life was busy—full. Other than needing a place to live, her life was perfect—until now.

So why did she suddenly feel that if she let these people walk out of her life she would be making the biggest mistake of her life?

At six o'clock sharp Saturday night, Greg rang the doorbell to Samantha's house. He'd arranged for Missy to spend the weekend with his mother. Wanted to be alone with Sam. Had decided to tell her about his family.

He sucked in a breath when she opened the door. She was beautiful.

Long, brown hair had been swept up, with tendrils loosely framing the edge of her face. Her low cut, floor length black shift hugged her figure to perfection. When she moved aside to permit his entry, he saw the thigh-high slit along the side.

Mercy! He felt himself harden at the sight of her. Did they really have to go eat dinner? He wouldn't mind missing their reservation. What he really wanted to do was take that dress off her luscious body and explore every inch of her. Visions of her sprawled on the bed naked wrapped themselves around his mind. He might not even make it upstairs to the bedroom. From the impact to his already throbbing shaft, he'd be lucky if they made it as far as the stairs. Heat from the fireplace radiated through the room. Yes, making love in front of the fireplace would be quite nice. Not that he needed the heat. His blood was already aflame.

She smiled and he lost all sense of intelligence. Couldn't think of a thing to say.

"Greg? Is everything all right?"

Oh yeah, more than all right! "You look beautiful."

She blushed. "Thank you. I don't have many formal clothes, so I hoped this would be appropriate for wherever you planned to go. You said to dress up."

Appropriate? Hell, he'd be the envy of every man they saw.

"It's more than appropriate. On you it's stunning."

She reached for her wrap and he took it from her. Frowned. "You'll freeze to death in this flimsy thing. It's cold outside, lady."

Embarrassment crept up her cheeks. "I bought the fancy dress, but never got around to buying an appropriate coat. I go out so seldom, I could never justify the expense."

He slipped off his suit coat and wrapped it around her.

"Greg! You'll be cold."

"Leave it on, Sam," he ordered as she started to shrug it off her shoulders. "I'll only be cold a few minutes. I'll remedy this on the way to the restaurant."

Samantha looked like she didn't know if she wanted to kiss him or knock him to the ground.

"You can't do this."

His idea of remedying the situation had been to park the car, run in to the fanciest couturier in the city and buy the most elegant coat he imagined she'd ever seen in her entire life! He'd placed it around her shoulders as they got out of the car to enter the restaurant.

"But I already did. It's yours, Sam." The shocked look on her face delighted him. As did her expression as her fingers lightly caressed the elegant material.

"Greg, I can't afford this. It likely cost more than I make in several months."

"It's a gift, Sam." *More like a year on her salary would be closer to the actual cost.* "If you like it, keep it. If you don't, wear it tonight, then give it away to someone."

"Give it away! I'll do no such thing. You have to take it back."

"Can't. All sales are final."

She looked defeated and hopeful at the same time.

"So you'll just have to keep it. Call it a gift from Missy."

She harrumphed. "Missy would choose a doll or a game—not the most elegant coat I've ever seen. What were you thinking? This must have cost a fortune."

"So you like it?"

She exhaled frustration, a sheen of tears in her eyes. "What's not to like? It's beautiful, and you know it."

He couldn't keep a smile from spreading across his face. "Good, then that's settled. Now let's go inside the restaurant before we both freeze."

Samantha had never been to Guiseppe's, the newest Italian restaurant in the heart of the city. It wasn't the type of place her circle of friends frequented. Whenever the menu didn't list prices, it was waaaaaay out of their league. If they wanted Italian, they'd order from the corner pizzeria—not go to one of the most expensive restaurants in the city.

What had gotten into Greg tonight? Sure, profits at the high priced store were probably good with all the holiday shoppers that swarmed there over the past few weeks. Still, Greg had a daughter to look after. He couldn't be spending what had to be a large chunk of his manager's salary on one evening with her.

Granted, his fancy house was in an upscale neighborhood, but she imagined he was hugely in debt for that. Everyone was nowadays. Why was he throwing his money away on her?

Did he think he could buy her affection? He couldn't—and she had every intention of letting him know that.

Avoiding Greg for the next week, Sam made a point to visit Missy at the house during the early afternoon hours. She didn't want him there—was still too embarrassed about the coat—but she wanted to spend time with Missy.

This afternoon they were at the skating pond. Sam helped Missy put her rented skates on while the young girl kept shaking her head.

"I can't, Sam. Daddy's never taken me skating. My leg's not strong enough."

"It can be if you exercise it more, sweetheart. Just look at the progress we made walking around the block yesterday. You didn't think you'd be able to do that, either, and look how far we got. We made it all the way to the playground."

Missy's eyes widened and she nodded. "That was fun, Sam. Mrs. Watson never took me there before. I loved the see-saw! You made me go soooooooo high!"

Sam riffled Missy's hair before she helped her to stand on the skates. "You're going to be a little wobbly at first, but just hold on to me. I'll help you out onto the ice and then we'll take a spin around the pond."

As Sam helped ease Missy onto the ice, Missy called out, "Look at me, Mrs. Watson. I'm skating!"

Sam turned to watch the elderly housekeeper sitting on a bench at the edge of the pond. It was cold outside, but Sam didn't think the tears in the old woman's eyes were from the cold.

Missy was wobbly and her feet kept slipping out from under her, but Sam kept a firm grip on her. Each time they passed the bench where the housekeeper sat, Missy shouted, "Look at me, Mrs. Watson!"

After about an hour, Sam finally led Missy to the side of the pond and sat her beside Mrs. Watson to help remove her skates.

"Did you see me, Mrs. Watson? Didn't I skate good? I can't wait to tell Daddy."

The elderly woman's eyes locked with Sam's. "I'm not sure that's a good idea. I think we shouldn't say anything about today. Just like we didn't mention everything you did with Miss Samantha the rest of this week."

"But I want Daddy to come skating with me and Sam tomorrow. I bet Daddy can skate reeeeeeeeeally good. Did you see that lady in the middle of the pond who kept doing circles? I'll bet Daddy can do that!!!"

When Sam drove up to Missy's house to drop them both off, Mrs. Watson drew in a deep breath. "Mercy me. Mr. Giovanni's already home. We're in for it now."

As soon as Samantha pulled the car into the driveway, Greg walked outside. "Where have you been?

I've been calling for over an hour. I thought something horrible happened to Missy when I couldn't get an answer."

Missy rushed up the driveway and into her father's arms. "Daddy, Daddy, guess what? Sam took me ice skating!"

Mrs. Watson groaned aloud, and Sam didn't move away from the car. Her feet were rooted to the ground.

Greg looked into Missy's upturned eyes. "Ice skating?"

"Yes, Daddy. Down at the pond. Sam rented me skates, 'cause I don't have my own. Mrs. Watson said she's too old to ice skate, so she just sat on a bench and watched us. You should have seen me, Daddy. I went round and round the pond with Sam." She giggled as she turned to look at the housekeeper. "I yelled 'hi' to Mrs. Watson every time we went past her. Didn't I, Mrs. Watson?"

Samantha could tell the elderly lady wanted to drop through the ground. Her face was flushed, and Sam knew it had nothing to do with the cold.

Greg set Missy back on the ground. His eyes filled with anger, he calmly told his housekeeper, "Take Missy inside so she can get warm. We will discuss this later."

As Mrs. Watson took Missy's small hand in hers, Samantha stepped forward. "No, you'll discuss nothing with Mrs. Watson. If you want to fight, do it with me. Right here, right now."

He waited until his daughter and housekeeper had gone inside, then turned to Sam. "Do you want to tell me what you thought you were doing with my daughter?" The only telltale sign of his anger was a vein in his neck twitching. Sam knew the warning sign well. It's what her father did when he'd wanted to throttle her, but held himself in check.

"I know exactly what I was doing, *Mr. Giovanni*. Ice skating with Missy. She had a wonderful time playing outside and exercised her leg in the process."

"Exercised her leg?" His hand fisted at his side. Though he didn't raise his voice, his anger was palpable. "Did I not tell you there was nothing that could be done for it?"

"Yes, you did, but I don't believe that. You're looking at her as a father who doesn't want to see his child in pain. I'm looking at her as an outsider who believes it will get better if she's made to use it. Why, just this week alone—"

Greg's eyebrows rose. "This week? This isn't the first day you've forced my daughter to use her leg?"

Standing straighter, Sam raised her chin. "I forced Missy to do nothing. I've merely suggested activities she could do to have fun while strengthening her leg."

Greg's eyes narrowed. "Outsider is right. What right do you have to come here—when you knew perfectly well I wouldn't be here—and force my daughter to do something I didn't want?"

"I came when you weren't here because I didn't want to see you. I knew you wouldn't let Missy do anything if you were here. And you embarrassed me the other night when we had dinner and went dancing."

His voice as cold as a polar ice cap, he said, "I don't remember stepping on your toes."

"I'm not talking about your dancing—and you know it." By now Sam's temper was probably as hot as his. "I'm talking about you buying me that coat. What were you thinking? Do you really think me so shallow I would want you to spend your hard-earned money on me in such a frivolous fashion?" Frustrated, she paced up and down the driveway. "I don't understand you. I've heard you're backing the War Bond drive. That you offered to match the amount every employee has payroll deducted. How can you afford that? How can you afford to waste money like you did on that coat? I know how difficult it is for everyone with the war going on. Most people barely have enough money to make ends meet. Yet you—"

"I don't need to explain myself to you, Miss Noelle. You overstepped your bounds—our friendship. I don't want you around Missy again. I don't want to ever see you again. You're fired. Don't bother coming back to the store to get your final wages. My secretary will mail a bank check to you." With that, he spun on his heel and headed inside his house.

Sam watched him, heartbroken. She didn't care about the job—although she'd miss seeing Joe. More importantly, she'd miss seeing Greg.

She'd avoided him this week. Purposely had gone out of her way not to see him at work. She'd sensed when he'd been around, but she'd made a point of ignoring him.

She'd done it again. Lost someone that mattered to her. Only this time it was her own fault. He wasn't leaving her to further his career. He was leaving her because she'd pushed him away. And interfered with his life.

Deep in her heart she believed Missy would get better if she used her leg. But Greg was right. It wasn't her place to make that happen. She'd just wanted to do something wonderful for them both at this special time of the year—and helping Missy to walk without pain seemed the perfect Christmas gift to give them.

Wiping the tears from her cheek with the back of her fingers, she opened the door to her old car and got inside. Starting the engine, she eased away from the driveway to head home to an empty house.

Greg stood at the window and watched her drive away. He wanted to yell at her and comfort her at the same time. She'd looked so hurt when she got in her car and swiped away her tears.

Damn it all, why had she hurt his daughter? He'd thought she was perfect for him. Believed he was actually falling in love with her. No, there was no doubt about it—he was in love with her. And she seemed to really care for Missy. Why would she do something so foolish—so cruel?

It didn't matter. He'd ordered her out of Missy's life. Out of his life. He'd missed being with her this week while she'd avoided him. She'd been outraged when he bought her that silly coat. To her the cost had been astronomical. To him it was nothing. It had been a means to an end. He'd wanted to find out once and for all if she only wanted his money.

She'd put him in his place quickly enough. Told him she'd allow no one to waste their hard-earned money on her. That he needed to save it for Missy.

Missy. Yes, he needed to think about his daughter. Needed to forget about the woman who'd caused her so much pain.

When he walked into his living room, he was surprised to see Missy on the floor, her Lincoln Logs sprawled all around her. She didn't seem to be in pain—certainly wasn't crying. She chatted away to Mrs. Watson like nothing out of the ordinary had just happened.

She looked up when he walked into the room. "Come help me, Daddy. Mrs. Watson and I are playing with my Lincoln Logs. But she's not doing much. She keeps crying." She put her small hand on the housekeeper's arm and patted it.

"I asked if she has an owie, Daddy, but she keeps shaking her head no. But she won't stop crying. Can you make her stop, Daddy? You always make me stop crying when I have an owie."

This was his opening. "Do you have an owie now, Missy?"

She furrowed her brows as she raised her head to look at him. "No, Daddy. That's silly. I'm not crying. Mrs. Watson is crying."

"Your leg doesn't hurt from standing on it so long while you were ice skating?"

"No, Daddy. Sam held me the whole time we went around the pond. She's such a good skater. She held me there just like she held me when I climbed the slide at the park yesterday. It was really cold when I sat to slide down it. You should have been there, Daddy. I wasn't scared at all. Sam reached up to hold my hand—and she held it all the way down! It was so much fun, Daddy." She held out a Lincoln Log. "See, that's what I'm making now. A playground like we were at yesterday."

"You went to the park?" He turned his head and saw Mrs. Watson's embarrassed face.

"Yes, Daddy. We had a good time. Mrs. Watson only sat on the park bench and watched, but Sam played with me the whole time. And she bounced me on the see-saw, Daddy. Want to go do that now? I'll show you where the park is." She paused, and frowned. "Oh, I don't know where it is. But Sam does. She can take us."

Looking around the living room, she stopped again. "Where's Sam, Daddy? I want to show her what I'm building with my Lincoln Logs."

"Sam went home." He turned to his housekeeper, kept his voice low. "Mrs. Watson, if I may see you in the kitchen."

"Call Sam, Daddy. See if she'll come back and have supper with us. I love her, Daddy. Can you marry her?"

Marry her? He'd ordered her out of his life. Forever.

He bade Mrs. Watson good-night and closed the door behind her. He'd been angry enough to fire her, just like he had Sam. But common sense had prevailed before he'd made the same mistake twice.

Hell, what was he going to do now? Once he'd finally gotten his housekeeper to quit crying, she'd told him everything Sam had done with Missy throughout the week. He watched his daughter walk into the kitchen holding her favorite doll. She should be tired. Should be crying from the pain. She seemed to be neither. And she wasn't dragging her leg.

Could Samantha be right? That all it would take to help Missy walk correctly was to do exercises with her? But make them fun, like Sam had done?

He felt a fool. This woman had come into his life—wormed her way into his heart—and saw instantly what he'd been too blind to see. That Missy really could walk. The break may have healed incorrectly, but it didn't have to be debilitating. In wanting to coddle her—protect her from more hurt like she'd experienced when her mother walked away—he'd not done the best thing for his daughter. And in truth, Missy hadn't been hurt by Amanda leaving. She'd never known her mother. He was the one that carried the hurt—the anger.

And now he'd lost the best thing that had happened in his life since Missy was born. Lost her? No, it hadn't been that simple. He'd accused her of mistreating his daughter. Ordered her out of his life.

Now he just had to figure out how to get her back. *Please, God, let her forgive me.*

"Giovanni, tell me the rumor I just heard isn't true," Joe said as he stormed unannounced into Greg's office.

Greg wasn't going to back down. Joe and Sam had become fast friends, but he didn't have to explain himself to a man dressed in a Santa costume.

"Actually it is. I fired Miss Noelle."

"Of all the moronic things to do. First you insult her by buying her some extravagant coat, then you yell at her for helping your daughter, and to top that off, you fire the best elf this store has." He raised his hand to stop Greg's protest. "Don't try defending yourself to me. I saw Sam yesterday. Took a pound cake over to her that my daughter made." He glowered at Greg. "Do you know what you've done to that young woman? She cared for you. Cared for your daughter and you slapped her down as if she was no better than yesterday's trash."

He turned and walked to the door. Stopped with his hand on the doorknob. "If I thought you could find someone to replace me between now and the holidays, I'd quit right now. But I won't leave the children in the lurch. Our world is in enough turmoil with most of our men overseas fighting. I won't allow them to come here expecting to see Santa and be disappointed. But you're a disappointment, Giovanni. What you did to Sam was unspeakable."

Turning, he stormed out the door and slammed it behind him.

Two days later Sam heard a knock at her door. She opened it to find Greg and Missy on her doorstep. Greg held a casserole dish in one hand and her coat in the other.

"You left this in my car the other night." He held the coat out to her.

"I told you I wouldn't accept such a gift."

"You looked beautiful in it."

She glared at him. "You made me wear it! I told you I—"

"Couldn't accept a gift from me."

"Don't you dare twist my words. I didn't say I wouldn't accept a gift from you. I just won't accept something so expensive. Money is too dear these days. You need it for Missy."

Hearing her name, Missy looked up. "Isn't the coat pretty, Sam? Daddy said it's a gift from me and him to you." She furrowed her brows. "Don't you like it?"

Knowing she was cornered now, Samantha glared at Greg. "That's pretty low, Giovanni."

A smile lit his eyes. "Whatever works."

He crossed to the living room and sat in the recliner. "I really like this chair. I'll have to get one for myself." He turned to face Sam. "Now, while I'm resting and Missy's playing with your cat, go get ready. Missy wants to go to the movies. Disney's *The Three Caballeros* is playing at a theatre downtown—a few blocks from The Battery."

"And there's a cartoon with Goofy in it, too, Daddy," Missy piped up. "Don't forget that. Something about swimming. That's silly, isn't it, Daddy? People can't go swimming in the middle of December."

"No, sweetheart, they can't. But it will be fun watching it, won't it?"

Missy giggled and turned back to play with Tigger.

"You can't barge in my house and expect me to go out for the afternoon."

He looked unconcerned. "You have other plans?"

"No, I don't, but if you'll recall, you told me you never wanted to see me again."

"I haven't forgotten the spiteful things I said. It's all I've thought about. I've regretted every word.

"Hurry, Sam, or we're going to be late for the movie," Missy said. "Daddy told me it starts at 3:10. He said we had just enough time to get you to go with us, then hurry to the movie theatre." She smiled up at Sam. "He said he'd buy us popcorn, too!"

"Yeah, Sam, hurry or we're going to be late." A mischievous twinkle lit his eyes.

"I'm not going anywhere with you, *Mr. Giovanni.* You made your feelings quite clear the other day. I don't have to be beat over the head with a stick to get the message."

Greg glanced at Missy to make sure she wasn't paying attention. "Sam, please, I was wrong. Mrs. Watson told me everything you did with Missy last week. I realize now you were only trying to help. To—"

"You changed your mind about me because your housekeeper told you what a fool you'd made of yourself? How nice. I would have preferred you trusted me." She headed toward the kitchen. "I suggest you hurry, or you're going to miss part of the cartoon."

"Sam, I..."

"Goodbye, Greg. I have nothing further to say to you. Please leave."

Taking Missy's hand and leading her to the door above her protestations—"Why isn't Sam coming with us, Daddy?"—Greg opened the front door, then slammed it closed.

He knelt on one knee to look Missy in the eyes. "Sam's busy today, sweetheart. You and Daddy will have to go to the movies alone. Stay here just a minute. I have to tell Sam something."

He strode to the kitchen, walked up beside her and pulled her into his arms. Ignoring her struggles, he threaded his fingers through her hair and drew her close. His mouth claimed hers as a warrior going into battle. He had no intention of granting her quarter.

Pulling away, he breathed heavily. "Don't tell me you didn't feel as much as I did in that kiss. I was wrong the other day. I'm sorry. I've brooded for two days about how to get you back. Now you can think on that. I'm not giving up. If you don't want to make it easy for me, fine. But I will win you back."

He crossed to the front door, stopped and returned to the kitchen. "And I want you back to work tomorrow, Miss Noelle. Santa needs you there. The kids need you. Don't let them down." He returned to Missy, held her hand and walked out the door.

Greg looked at the clock again. For the fourth time in the last ten minutes. Three-fifteen. Samantha was late. She'd never been late. Too conscientious an employee not to arrive on time. So where was she?

She might still be angry with him, but she wouldn't let the children down. He'd counted on her sense of dedication when he ordered her back to work.

He jabbed his hands into his back pockets. *This is ridiculous. I have a shopping center to run. Yet here I stand looking at a clock. Worrying about a woman I've only known since the week before Thanksgiving.*

A woman he'd fallen madly in love with.

He'd lectured himself a million times over. She was too young for him. Too full of life. Too busy with other commitments to include him in her life. Too angry with him to give him a second chance.

None of that mattered. He wanted her. Needed her.

In the weeks since he'd met her, she'd turned his world upside down.

"Mr. Giovanni, there's a call for you," his secretary announced from the outer office.

"Not now, Mary. Take a message. I'm in the middle of something." *In the middle of waiting for a young girl just like some pimply teenage boy.*

She rose from her desk and came to stand in his doorway. "It's St. Martin's Hospital, sir. The emergency room."

Greg grabbed for the phone. Could barely breathe as he barked out, "Giovanni."

Please, God, don't let it be Missy!

"Sir, this is the emergency room at St. Martin's hospital. We have a young woman here who's been in an automobile accident. We can't find any contact information in her purse except your name and number. I'm sorry to bother you, but—"

"I'm on my way. Don't let her leave."

"She can't, sir."

Greg grabbed his stomach—his lunch threatening to return. "Oh, my God, is she dead?"

"No, sir, but I need to find a contact number for her."

"Then I'm on my way. I'm her contact."

He didn't have to ask who it was. His gut told him.

Sam!

His name and number had probably been in her purse from when he'd given her directions to his home the first time Missy invited her for dinner.

The day his life had been turned topsy-turvy. The day he'd fallen in love with Sam. As he ran out the office door, he called to his secretary. "Sam's been injured. Tell Santa. She's in the hospital. And call Mrs. Watson. I don't know when I'll be home. I may need her to stay over with Missy. Tell her if she can't, I need my mother to pick her up."

He revved his car engine, put it in gear and squealed out of his reserved parking space.

Please, God, let her be all right! I didn't mean what I said the other day. She was right and I was wrong.

She wouldn't listen to me. Please let her live so I can tell her how sorry I am.

Please let her live so I can—a sob escaped his lips—*tell her I love her.*

Reaching the hospital, there was no parking space at the emergency room other than the ten minute drop off. He didn't care. Let them give him a ticket. Let them give him a dozen citations. He had to see Sam. Had to know she was alive.

He ran inside. Stopped briefly at the Triage desk. "Samantha Noelle, please."

"Are you—?"

Years of executive training kicked in. They weren't going to keep him out. Weren't going to not let him see her. "Family? Yes, I am. Where is she?" He shot the triage nurse a look that said he wanted an answer now.

"Room seven." She motioned toward the door and he rushed inside.

Going down the long corridor, Greg saw the numbers over each room. When he reached seven, he pushed the door open and saw her lying on the narrow bed. Her face was pale, almost as white as the sheet covering her. The top of her head was wrapped in gauze, her right cheek had a deep scratch on it, and her arm was in a cast. Under the sheet she wore a hideous hospital gown, and on the chair beside the bed lay a green elf costume.

She'd been coming back to work after all.

He grabbed the doorjamb. Had to draw his breath to keep from passing out. She was asleep, but she was alive.

A nurse came up behind him. "You're here for Miss Noelle?"

"Yes, is she all right?"

"We don't know yet. The doctor is still running tests. She hasn't regained consciousness yet."

"She's unconscious? She's not asleep?"

"No, sir, she's not asleep. I'm sorry."

Greg thudded down onto the chair.

"I'll tell the doctor you're here. Maybe he can answer some of your questions."

She started to head back into the hallway.

"Wait. Do you know what happened?"

"All I know is what the attendants told us. Whoever hit her car said he was heading to an office Christmas party. Unfortunately, it appeared he'd already had a head start on his drinking."

"Was he injured?"

"No, sir. Being drunk probably saved him. The men who brought Miss Noelle in said both vehicles were beyond repair."

Greg nodded.

Why was life always so unfair? He'd thought his heart had been torn out the day Amanda walked out on him. That pain didn't hold a candle to what he felt now.

Samantha had brought him back to life. Had loved him. Loved his daughter.

And he'd thrown it in her face.

Not because he didn't want her. Because he wanted her too much. Was afraid of loving anyone that much.

Missy adored her. Children and animals instinctively recognized the good in people. Only adults were idiots. At least he was. He'd almost thrown away the best thing to ever happen in his life—other than having Missy.

He'd never do that again. If she woke up—*when* she woke up—he'd ask her to forgive him. Ask her to take him back. Ask her to marry him.

He moved his chair closer to the bed so he could hold her hand.

"Sam, wake up, sweetheart. It's Greg." He felt like a fool. Could she hear him? He'd heard somewhere that people in a coma could hear people talking to them. He didn't know if that was really true, but he wasn't taking any chances.

"Come on, now. You have to wake up so we can go home to Missy. She's waiting for you. Needs you to help her with her therapy. Wants you to take her ice skating again. I've decided to let her have that surgery the doctor's been talking about. The one you yelled at me the other day about her having. You were right, you know. Yeah, you heard that correctly. I'm admitting I was wrong. Don't do that lightly. You told me how stubborn men were. Guess you're right about that, too. You were right about a lot of things. But I need you to wake up now."

"Sir?"

A man—probably the doctor—stood in the doorway.

Greg stood and offered his hand. "Giovanni. Greg Giovanni. You're her doctor?"

"For the time being, yes."

"What does that mean?"

"Once she's stabilized, we'll have an ambulance transfer her to our county hospital."

"Why the hell would you move her?"

"I'm afraid the young lady has no visible means to pay us. We've gotten her past the first trauma."

Greg's eyes narrowed. Voice low, he took a step toward the physician. "You're telling me you're going to move my fiancée because you think she has no money?"

"We could find no proof of it on her, sir. It's not something I want to do, but the hospital can't absorb costs like this. I'm afraid we—"

With an effort not to lose his temper, Greg stepped back toward the bed. Picked up Samantha's hand and cradled it in both of his. He looked at the doctor, then dismissed him as not being worthy of his attention.

"I suggest you do everything you can to save this young woman if you don't want yourself and this hospital sued for every cent you and it have. Her bill will be paid. If you require payment now, give me an amount and I'll write a bank check."

"Sir, you don't understand. The cost could be enormous."

Greg didn't bother to hide his look of disdain. "Hospital bills are always outrageous. No one should be charged what such facilities bill people. That's neither here nor there."

He reached into his back pocket, pulled out his bank checks. "You want money? How much?"

"But, sir—"

"Let's don't waste time on trivialities. I own the Embassy Shopping Center. Have numerous other holdings. I have enough money to buy and sell this hospital ten times over if I wanted to." He stopped, looked at Samantha. Rubbed his fingertips back and forth over his forehead to ease his headache. "I don't want to do that, don't want to threaten you, but I'll do whatever it takes to ensure she's not moved."

Looking uncomfortable, the doctor said, "Let me have someone from Admissions come see you."

"Yes." Greg flicked his eyelashes at him in dismissal and turned away. "Do that."

So angry his entire body shook, Greg sat once again. He couldn't let Samantha feel how upset he was. She had to concentrate her energy on getting well. Couldn't know he wanted to wring everyone's necks right now. Probably just like she'd felt about him when they'd argued. He'd been as stubborn and unyielding as the hospital was being now. And their argument had been over something much more important than mere money. It had been over his daughter.

How foolish he'd been. Had been foolish for years. If he'd done what the doctors said years ago—what Samantha had done with her this week—Missy would probably be walking fine now. Instead, he'd coddled her. Hadn't wanted to put her through more pain. When in fact, he'd done just that. If he'd let her have the surgery and pushed her to walk, she might not still have the side effects of the painful break. Only time would see if that was true or not, but he had to take that chance for Missy. Had to quit thinking of himself.

It was time to put the past behind him. Amanda was gone. He had a future to look forward to now—if he hadn't blown it with Sam.

No, he wouldn't think like that. He wouldn't let her walk away from him. He'd make things right no matter what he had to do.

If only there was something he could do. Instead, he felt hopeless. Useless. He couldn't do anything but sit beside her and hold Sam's hand. He wanted to hold all of her. Hold her and tell her he loved her. But the hospital would frown on...

Well, damn! He could care less what the hospital thought. After all, wasn't he going to pay her bill? If they kept giving him grief, maybe he'd buy the hospital after all.

He heard a sound at the door. Turned and saw Joe standing there. Still in his Santa costume, the man's eyes looked wide with shock.

"Your assistant told me about the accident. I got here as quickly as I could."

Greg nodded. "I'm glad you're here. Help me move her."

Joe came closer to the bed.

"Can you lift Sam up while I move the pillows against the headboard? Those metal rungs would dig into my back."

As soon as Joe had Sam in his arms, Greg slid onto the bed.

Joe took great pains not to move her IV, carefully lifted Sam onto Greg's lap. Greg cradled her head against his chest.

Gently stroking her arm, her back, he kept talking to her.

Joe sat in the hard plastic chair, ran his hand through his already disheveled hair. "What happened?"

"I don't know much. Apparently some drunk got behind the wheel of a car. His vehicle crashed into Sam's."

Tears filled the elderly man's eyes. Greg imagined he willed them not to fall.

"She has to get well, Giovanni. She means a great deal to me."

Greg nodded. "I understand. She loves you, too, Joe."

"I called her cousin in Chicago. Didn't get to talk directly to her since she doesn't have a phone of her own, but I left a message at some general store. The man who answered said he'd be sure to tell her. Claimed he was a close friend."

When nurses or orderlies came and told him he couldn't sit on the bed, Greg's icy stare sent them on their way.

The Admissions clerk came in while he was holding Sam. "Hold the clipboard for me so I can sign your paperwork."

"You don't wish to read it over, sir?"

"No. The only thing that matters is Sam."

Joe furrowed his brow. "How can a store manager afford that?"

"I'm not just Nickel's manager, Joe. I own the entire shopping center. My family owns upscale shopping centers across the country."

Joe's eyes widened. "You're *that* Giovanni? The one with *connections* in Chicago?"

When Greg only nodded, Joe laughed. "Sam is going to be so upset with you when she wakes up. She was angry about you buying her that coat. She's one stubborn woman. Been determined to pay her own way about everything—then goes and falls in love with a millionaire."

"If she'd known, she wouldn't have gone out with me."

Joe corrected, "If she'd known, you wouldn't know if she loved you for yourself or for your money."

Greg briefly lowered his eyes, his only concession at agreement.

"I'll get back to the store now. Let everyone know Sam is going to be fine." Though he said it as a statement, Greg knew it held a question.

"She'll be fine, Joe. I'll make sure of it."

"Good, I'll call her cousin again. Don't want her worrying needlessly. I have to go home to feed my dogs after work—I have four Goldens that will be starving—but I'll come back after that to see how she's doing." With a nod and a final backward glance, Joe left the room.

Greg sat for hours, stroking her, alternated speaking in a soothing voice, a pleading voice.

"Come on, Sam. You have to wake up. We never got to go see a movie together. We can either take Missy back to see *The Three Caballeros*—she loved it you know—or you and I can go someplace by ourselves. I've heard *Meet Me in St. Louis* is an excellent movie. And knowing you, you'll cry when Judy Garland sings *Have Yourself a Merry Little Christmas*. Some of the men at the store said their wives couldn't stop crying when she sang to Margaret O'Brien."

Finally he could take it no more. Afraid he was at the breaking point, he shifted Sam in his arms.

"Samantha, this has gone on long enough. I insist you wake up. As your boss, I'm making that an order."

She moved.

Dear God, she moved!

"Sam? Sam, can you hear me?"

"Mmmmm."

"Sam!"

He tried to shift so he could move out of bed to call the nurse. His arms were numb from holding her so long. "Nurse! Room seven. Miss Noelle's awake!"

Sam's eyelids fluttered open. Seemed to take a moment to focus on him.

"Stop yelling, Giovanni. Weren't you the one that told me you could catch more flies with honey when we first met?"

He wanted to cry. Wanted to shout with happiness. She was going to be all right!

"Yes, I did. When you kicked the silly locker. If I recall correctly, you didn't pay much attention to me."

"Oh yes, I did. I wanted to kick you in your a... backside when you walked away."

He laughed. "I'll just bet you did."

"Wanted to do that the other night, too. You're one stubborn man."

"I've been told that by other people."

She reached up to touch the gauze bandages. "My head hurts."

Greg rubbed his hand lightly up and down her back. He pressed his lips together, trying to hold back tears. Men didn't cry. He had to be strong for Sam.

"Actually, my whole body hurts."

"I know, love, but you're going to be all right now. I promise."

"Did I hear Joe?"

Greg nodded. "He came to see you. He's worried about you. He went to work, but said he'll be back later tonight."

"I-I heard people talking." She furrowed her brow as if trying to think. "Someone said you're rich."

So she had been able to hear them. Greg bit his lip, nodded again. "I am."

"That's why you bought me the coat? Because you're rich?"

"I bought it because I'm stupid. I needed to know if you were with me because you like me or because you wanted my money. That's all most people want. I've built a wall around myself to keep people like that out."

"I don't like walls. They're meant to be knocked down—especially when they're around your heart."

Greg looked up as the doctor walked in.

"Young man, if you'll kindly get out of that bed, I'd like to run some tests on the young lady."

"My fiancée."

"I never said I'd marry you." Sam tried to focus on him as he slid out of bed and leaned her back against the cushions.

"No, you didn't. But you will."

"Why would I do something like that? You're too stubborn."

"You'll do it because you love me."

"I never said—"

"And because I love you."

Her eyes met his and her lower lip quivered. Tears spilled down her cheeks unchecked.

"It's not nice to take advantage of someone when they're laid up in bed."

"Maybe not. But I'll do whatever it takes—for the rest of my life—to convince you I love you."

"But—"

"You gave me the courage to risk my heart, Sam. Marry me. Make me the happiest man on earth."

"Young man, I need to—"

"Not now!" Greg glared at the doctor. "I need an answer from her. She says I'm stubborn, but she won't agree to marry me. Don't you understand? She has to be my wife. I can't live without her. Can't spend another moment without her in my life."

The doctor smiled.

Greg wanted to kick him. "What?"

"I believe the young lady is trying to get your attention. If you'll quit talking a minute, she might be able to say something."

Surprised, Greg shifted his eyes to Samantha. "Sweetheart, what's wrong? Are you in pain? Do you need the doctor to give you some medicine?"

"You said you loved me."

"Of course I did."

"Did you mean it?"

"Of course I meant it."

"And you really want to marry me?"

Realization started to sink in. Greg stared at her in amazement.

Despite his location and the many people milling around them, he dropped down on one knee. He didn't care what anyone thought—except Sam.

"Yes, Miss Noelle. I really want you to marry me. I can't think of a better Christmas present than you saying yes. You're the best present I've ever had in my life." He rose and ran a hand lightly over the bandages on her head. "The location isn't quite what I would have selected to propose to you, but you're everything I could ever want. All I want."

He leaned over and brushed his lips gently over hers.

"I love you, Greg." Tears ran down her cheeks.

"And I love you, Sam. I have from the minute you walked into my office—even though I did everything I could to fight it."

He turned to look at the doctor. "Well, what are you waiting for? Do whatever you have to so I can take her home for Christmas."

"I intend to, young man. Seeing you two together, this young woman is going to have her hands full with you as a husband. I hope you appreciate her. After surviving what she went through today—she's not just your Christmas present, she's your Christmas miracle."

Be sure to visit Leanne's website
http://www.leanneburroughs.com

The Power of Love

by Kemberlee Shortland

Limerick City, Ireland

The best feeling in the world had to be lying in a lover's arms, exhausted after a night of lovemaking, totally and absolutely sated. Elaine snuggled closer to Ethan, weaving her legs with his and grinning at how his leg hairs tickled her.

The warm, masculine scent of his damp body permeated her senses. He smelled delicious. So much so, she'd practically gobbled him up over the last several hours. Perhaps she would again, she thought, trailing her fingertips across the ridges of his broad chest, circling his nipples.

His strong hand grasped hers and brought it to lips framed with dark stubble, kissing the backs of her fingers. "Please, love. I can barely move."

Elaine glanced down the solid length of him to the twitch beneath the sheet just covering his hips. "Could have fooled me."

Ethan leaned over, propped up on an elbow and looked down at her. "Isn't it enough you kept me up all night," winking at the double meaning, "but you want to make me late for work, as well?"

"You weren't complaining an hour ago."

He bent to kiss her. His lips echoed the passion they'd shared through the night. When he leaned away, his deep voice was soft, his blue-eyed gaze intense. "And I never will, Lany. I love you and will always be here for you."

Tears threatened. "Will you?"

Nodding, he said, "Aye. Always."

"And you truly want this baby?" she asked, rubbing her belly. When he nodded, his grin answering more than his voice could, she added, "Oh, Ethan! You make me so happy." She slid her arms around his shoulders and he came to her instantly, burying his face in the curve of her neck, kissing her there.

All too soon, he pulled away. "I still need to go to work. Now let me go or we'll be raising our child on the Dole." He winked again before placing a quick peck on her lips then rose from the bed.

Elaine laughed lightly. "As if you'd accept unemployment money."

The sheet fell away as he left the bed. Elaine leaned up on her elbow and watched his firm arse flex as he strode out of the room. Something inside her swelled with admiration. Yes, no matter how exhausted she was, she could eat him up over and over again.

A moment later she heard him in the shower. He was actually singing! He must really be happy, she thought. She considered joining him, but he was right. He had to get to work, as did she, or they'd both be raising their baby on the Dole.

As she rose and threw on a robe, she laughed at her feelings of dread last night. She'd been so afraid to tell Ethan she was pregnant. They'd only been married a few short months and were trying to plan their future and keep to an agenda. That included birth control—for a while at least. But nothing was one hundred percent effective, as her pregnancy proved. She was so happy Ethan welcomed the baby much sooner than they'd planned.

In the kitchen, Elaine put the coffee on then turned her gaze out the kitchen window to their back garden. She tried to imagine a swing set, sand box and Wendy house rather than the clothesline, spotty lawn and tool shed. She wrapped her arms around her waist, wondering how they were going to give their child the life he or she deserved.

A moment later, strong arms encircled her, pulling her against a broad chest. Ethan kissed the curve of her neck and she melted against him.

"You okay?" He turned her to face him.

His dark hair was damp and shaggy, hanging just above his shoulders. Dark brows and lashes framed his crystal blue eyes. His gaze was both concerned and sexy. She wanted to rip his shirt from his shoulders and...

Instead, she just nodded. "Aye. I'm trying to imagine a swing set in the garden instead of the clothes line."

Ethan chuckled. "Everything is going to be grand. We've a perfect life. Nothing's going to change that." He kissed her on the forehead before releasing her to pour a cup of coffee.

Even as she watched the man she loved more than anything move about the kitchen, she couldn't quell the feeling of dread beginning to eat at her again.

Six months later

He'd practically killed himself getting to the hospital. When Ethan got the call saying Elaine had collapsed at work, he panicked and dropped everything to get to her side. He still hadn't been allowed to see her, as she was still undergoing tests, so he waited in the private room he made sure their health insurance covered.

A moment later his pacing was interrupted when the door pushed open and Elaine was wheeled in on a gurney. As assistants helped her into bed and the nurse made her comfortable, his heart pumped hard in his chest. Elaine looked pale and groggy. He wondered if she even knew he was in the room.

Then he was alone with his wife. She lay so still. His chest tightened, fear pumping the blood though his body at a fierce rate.

"Are you going to stand there all day?" Her voice

was thready.

Ethan stepped to her bedside and kissed her clammy brow, stroking her once lustrous golden hair that now fell in limp strands around her shoulders. He gazed into her tired green eyes and his heart squeezed again.

"How are you feeling, love?"

Elaine grasped his hand as he stepped back, encouraging him to sit beside her on the bed. He did so and kept her hand in his, leaning in to kiss her forehead.

"I've been better."

"What happened, Lany? They said you collapsed at work."

She shook her head lightly. "I-I don't know. I don't remember much. I was helping a customer, talking about babies, the next I knew I woke up here."

"Have you spoken with the doctor? What did he say?"

When she shook her head once more, he rose with the intention of going to find the doctor to get the test results. Then the door opened and an authoritative balding man with glasses perched on the end of his nose strode into the room. Dressed in black trousers and a white lab coat, a stethoscope around his neck and a clipboard in his hands, he had to be the doctor. He moved to the foot of the bed, going over the papers on his clipboard. It seemed he stood there for hours before he finally looked up.

"Are you the husband?"

The husband? "Oh, aye," said Ethan, not even trying to disguise his annoyance. "What's wrong with my wife?"

The doctor turned to Elaine. "I'm Doctor Gibbons. How are you feeling?" Before she had a chance to reply, he bent his face to the clipboard once more, flipping the pages one after the other. He finally looked up again and sighed heavily. He certainly wasn't making Ethan feel any better. And by the way Elaine squeezed his hand, she wasn't doing well either.

"Doctor..." Ethan finally started, tired of not only the delay, but also the doctor's bedside manner.

The doctor put his hand up to silence him. "Please, have a seat."

Ethan reseated himself on the bed, never once releasing Elaine's hand. The doctor stepped around the bed so they could see him easier and Ethan realized the man's demeanor stemmed more from agitation than rudeness.

"By the look on your face, doctor, you might as well just come right out and give us the test results." Ethan really didn't think he wanted to know, but if they were going to help Elaine get better, they had to know what they were facing.

"Yes, doctor. Please, what's wrong with me?"

Doctor Gibbons again sighed heavily. "There is never an easy way to tell patients when their test results are unfavorable. But you need to know you do have options."

"I've only fainted. I'm tired, but surely there isn't anything seriously wrong with me. Tell me what the tests say so we can discuss the options you mention."

"The test results show a weakness in your heart, Mrs. O'Donovan."

"A weakness?" Ethan and Elaine asked together.

"I've been healthy my whole life. Why is this weakness only now showing symptoms?"

"As your baby grows, it's pushing on your heart. With the weakness, the heart can't function properly. Other things can also affect the heart's function, such as diet, exercise and stress. Even bending over can force the baby against the heart, totally preventing functionality."

"But I wasn't really bending over. It's kind of hard these days." She rubbed her belly.

"Nonetheless, this is what we believe happened today. When the heart doesn't function properly, the oxygen supply to the body is diminished. When that happens, a person can faint." The doctor flipped through the test results again. "Is this the only time you've fainted? Have you felt weak or more tired than usual?"

Elaine glanced at Ethan. He knew by the look on her face she had. How could he have missed her distress?

Elaine shook her head. "No. I'm tired all the time and not sleeping well these days since it's hard to get comfortable. And with work and everything that's been going on at home, well... But I did go see my doctor. He said I was probably just down on my vitamins and to get some rest. I've been trying, but..."

Ethan sat up straighter, glancing at the doctor. "So, what does this mean? Elaine just needs more rest, right? Get those vitamins?" He turned to Elaine. "I'll call Mary and tell her you've worked your last day, love. You should have quit weeks ago."

"I'm afraid it's a bit more complicated than that," the doctor continued. "Mrs. O'Donovan, I fear your heart has irreparable damage."

"What are you talking about? She only fainted. You said so yourself. The baby pushed on her heart and she fainted." Ethan felt the air in the room become suffocating.

Elaine squeezed his hand again. He met her gaze and took all of her in—her pale face, tired eyes, the blinking and beeping monitors surrounding her.

"I'm sorry, Mrs. O'Donovan, but there's no easy way to say this. Your heart is too weak to survive the birth of your child."

Ethan's own heart stopped beating then.

He spun his gaze to Elaine when her fingers slipped from his hand. If it were at all possible, her face had paled even more. Her mouth opened and closed, but nothing came out.

Ethan looked up at the doctor again, rapidly blinking through the fog that threatened to engulf him. "Your tests must be wrong. You're wrong." Turning back to Elaine, he said, "We'll get another doctor, love. We'll have the tests redone." Then back to the doctor, not bothering to hide the anxiety in his voice, he said, "Get out. Just get out! You're wrong. Just—"

"Mr. O'Donovan—"

"Get out!"

Doctor Gibbons stepped away from the bed. As he turned away, Elaine spoke. Her voice was desperate but barely audible. "No, wait. You said there were options."

"Lany, he's wrong. We'll have the tests redone. You're just tired. We'll get them redone. Everything will be fine. You'll see." Try as he might, he couldn't keep the quiver from his voice or his eyes from welling. He had to stay strong for Lany though, so he took a deep breath and willed his emotions away.

Elaine struggled to sit up. Ethan took her by the elbow and put an arm around her shoulder and held her until she was comfortable. The doctor had stopped at the door, waiting.

She looked up at her husband, unable to believe her life had taken such a turn. It was amazing she could have awoken this morning thinking their lives couldn't get any better. She loved Ethan with every fiber of her being. Their baby was a symbol of that love. There was no way she was going to lose their baby.

She turned her gaze back to the doctor, blinking her tears away. "Tell me about the options."

Doctor Gibbons stepped back to the bed and motioned for Ethan to reseat himself. "This is a very serious situation. Even the options aren't a guarantee."

"You just told me I'm not going to survive the birth of our baby. I think any option, even if it's not one hundred percent, is better than no option, don't you?"

Gibbons held up his palm. "You're right. I'm sorry." He took a deep breath, laid out the test results on the bedside table then began. When he finished, Elaine wondered just what options he was referring to. In fact, the options he'd outlined seemed nonexistent.

"Those are my options?" she asked, incredulous. "Have a caesarean now or carry to term and end up having a caesarean anyway, and possibly injuring my child if its oxygen is cut off for too long before you can perform the section? Neither of which I'll survive? Where are *my* options?"

"Well...if you waited, you'd have more time together," Gibbons told her, glancing in Ethan's direction. "And we are talking about the health of your child. There's nothing we can do to change your outcome..."

"Her outcome?" Ethan gasped.

"Please, Mr. O'Donovan, I mean no disrespect. This is a delicate situation. We must think of the health of your child."

"And you're telling me I'll be bedridden until I die?

"Lane..." Ethan pleaded.

"What am I supposed to say, Ethan? I woke up this morning excited to be seeing our child soon, being able to hold him or her in my arms, to make you a father. And in the space of a few hours, our future has been destroyed. This morning I was living, really living, and tonight I'm dying...really...dying," she spluttered through sudden tears. She'd been stunned by the news, confused and now angry.

She faced the doctor again. "Tell, me. Will I ever see the outside of this hospital? Can I go home?"

Doctor Gibbons stared at her for a moment. "If you leave the hospital and have another episode, there's no guarantee the baby won't suffer adverse reactions."

"So, you're telling us the only option is *when* Elaine is going to...is going to die," stuttered Ethan, choking back his emotions.

Elaine's chest squeezed hearing his words. She felt the anguish in his voice. It was one thing to hear the doctor telling her she was dying, but something else entirely to hear the man she loved say the words. She felt slapped in the face. Not by Ethan. Never by Ethan.

Unsurprisingly, Gibbons didn't respond. What could he say? They all knew exactly what was going to happen. She had to face the truth. She was going to die. There was nothing she or anyone else could do about it.

Of all her non-options, there was only one thing she could do.

"Get out," she said to the doctor, turning her gaze to Ethan.

Gibbons gathered the papers from the bedside table and stepped away from the bed. If he were waiting for her to call him back again, it would be a mighty long wait.

Once alone, she lifted her palm to his cheek. "It'll be all right, Ethan."

"How can you say that, Lany?" Ethan's voice was filled with emotion. She knew he was trying to stay strong for her, but he still couldn't keep his chin from quivering.

She pulled him to her by the hand. He fell into her embrace and buried his face in her hair. Careful not to pull the IV tube from her hand, she wrapped her arms around him and held him. He wasn't crying, but she knew he would the instant he left her. When they were together, he always put on a brave face for her.

She wondered how he would survive raising their child on his own. Would he fall in love again? Would another woman be the one *her* child called 'mum'?

Swallowing hard, she couldn't worry about that now. She only had a couple weeks left before their baby was due...before she would die. There was a lot to do—a lot of things to say.

Christmas Eve

She'd been in labor for several hours now, but still her water hadn't broken. If Elaine hadn't felt weak in the last few days, she certainly did now. Her body felt wrung out and heavier than normal. This baby was sure to be a boy by the way he'd been kicking. Might even grow up to become a world-class rugby player.

The closer her due date got, the more she understood everything Doctor Gibbons had told her about her condition. Every day that passed, her body grew more fragile. Her bones felt brittle, her energy was non-existent and her skin had paled until it was translucent. She could no longer deny what was happening. The only thing that seemed alive and vibrant was her baby who tried its hardest to make an entrance into the world.

Elaine shook herself from those thoughts and remembered back to last Christmas Eve.

Today was their first anniversary, and their last. The irony wasn't lost on her. If she'd had the energy she would have laughed. She did smile though. Their wedding day had been the happiest day of her life. Finding out she was pregnant had come a close second.

Even with everything they were going through, Ethan hadn't forgotten. They both knew her days were dwindling to hours so he hadn't wandered far. He'd stepped out while she'd been taken for tests. When she'd returned, she'd been amazed at what Ethan had done. He'd decorated her hospital room just as he had their bedroom on their wedding night.

They'd been living together for a few months and Elaine had feared their wedding wouldn't change anything. They'd leave home in the morning and come home in the evening just as they did every other day. The only change would be the paper filed with the registrar and a new ring on her finger. They swore their love to each other daily, so what else could have changed to make the day more special?

Ethan.

He changed everything. He always changed everything. He made her life...beautiful. And he did it every day, regardless of how he felt. The night before their wedding, when she'd stayed with her family because it was bad luck to see the bride the night before the wedding, he'd decorated their bedroom to make up for the honeymoon they couldn't afford to take.

He'd strung tiny white lights across the ceiling, lit vanilla and coconut scented candles around the room, sprinkled flower petals on the bed, and had exotic music playing softly. Champagne and strawberries with chocolate dipping sauce waited on the bedside table.

Because it was Christmas Eve, he'd also set up a tree in the corner of the room. It was fully decorated with colored blinking lights. When she stepped into the room after taking her shower, he was laying beneath the tree propped on an elbow—nude except for a big red velvet bow around his hips. A tail end of the bow just barely covered his...

Elaine smiled at the memory as she looked around her hospital room. She knew how hard it must have been for Ethan to do this for her again...the decorations, lights and tree. But, typical Ethan, he sought to make her last hours happy ones.

Another contraction gripped her. They were coming closer together now. She hoped she lived long enough to see their child's face. A tear rolled down her cheek, praying she'd survive at least that long.

"Hey," Ethan said softly as he stepped into the room. "What's all this?" He stroked the tear away with the back of his finger.

She couldn't tell him what was really in her heart—regret and sorrow. As he tried to make her last hours happy for her, she too wanted their last hours to be happy ones for him.

She cast her gaze around the room then back to Ethan. "All this."

Ethan leaned down and kissed her lips. "Happy anniversary, love." His smile was forced, she could tell, but his tone was pure love.

"So, where's my bow?" She winked.

Ethan grinned, knowing what she meant. "And give the nurses a thrill?"

"Give me a thrill," she corrected. He sat beside her on the bed and took her hand in his. "You gave me a wonderful day to remember, Ethan."

She saw his eyes glaze over, but he stayed composed.

"Everything pales beside you, Lany. You were the most beautiful bride any groom could want."

"And you've always been a charmer."

Ethan's expression sobered. "There's nothing charming about me, love. I did some serious scheming to get you to notice me."

"It never took scheming, Ethan. I was yours from the moment I saw you." She pulled him down to kiss him. She wished she had the energy to kiss him the way he deserved.

Another contraction took the breath from her.

Ethan jerked back. "Are you all right?"

When she had her breath back, she nodded. "The contractions are coming closer together. It won't be long now until you're holding our baby."

"Until *we* are holding our baby," he corrected.

She squeezed her eyes shut for a moment then looked back to him. "Ethan," she started. "I-I don't think I have the energy for this. I can barely breathe as it is."

He shook his head. "Don't talk like that, Lany. Everything will be fine. You'll see."

Ethan's denial broke Elaine's heart. In another few hours the truth would be born with their child.

"Promise me something, Ethan."

"Anything, love. Just name it."

Elaine swallowed hard. "If it looks like...if the baby..."

"Just say it, Lany."

"If it looks like I'm not going to...survive long enough...I want the doctor to do the scan. I want to know if it's a boy or girl. I want to know its name before..."

"Elaine, please. It will be all right."

"Ethan, stop. You know what's happening. You have to stop denying it. I'm dying, and in all probability, it's going to happen before this child is born. Today. I'm just asking you to honor my last wish."

Ethan leapt from the bed to pace the floor to the

window across the room. This was hard for him, she knew, but it was hard for her too.

Before she could speak again, he turned back to her. "Okay, Lany. Okay."

Later that afternoon, her labor came in earnest. Ethan was beside her, holding her hand and wiping her brow. He couldn't help but be angry at the position he was in—seeing his child delivered and saying goodbye to the woman he loved more than anything else in his life.

The doctor was positioned to deliver the baby and the room bustled with activity preparing for the birth. Machines beeped, monitoring both Elaine's heartbeat and that of their child.

"All right, Elaine, I see the crown. Not long now," said Doctor Gibbons.

Elaine turned her gaze up to Ethan. She looked exhausted. They both knew her time was short, but she clung to life. He hoped she lived much longer than just to get through the birth. He wanted her around for the rest of his life. He couldn't imagine ever loving anyone the way he loved her.

His heart squeezed and his breath caught in his chest, blocking out the reality that they might only have a few short minutes left. He pushed back the tears that threatened and reminded Elaine to breathe.

"Give us a push, Elaine. It won't be long now. A little more," Gibbons encouraged. Elaine took as deep a breath as she could and pushed.

The monitor started beeping rapidly. Elaine turned her gaze to Ethan. "Eth-an," she gasped weakly. "I can't do it. I'm not...going...to make...it."

The oxygen in the room was suddenly sucked out and he couldn't breathe. Tears welled in his eyes. "You've got to hang in there, Lany. The baby is almost here. There's no time for a scan. Just hold on, love. Hold on."

Ethan spun toward the doctor. "You have to hurry, doctor. She has to see the baby before..." He couldn't finish his sentence. He couldn't believe this was happening. No amount of time could prepare anyone for this moment.

"The shoulders are through. One more push and we'll see your son or daughter, Elaine. Come on, now. One more big push."

Ethan stroked Elaine's brow, drying her perspiration and brushing the stray hairs from her eyes. "Come, love. The baby will be here with one more push."

Elaine blinked several times as if to clear her vision. "Ethan." Her voice was thready. He leaned in closer to hear her. "I...I love you. Always...remember..."

"Sweetheart, take deep breaths. Our baby is almost here. Please, Lany, breathe," he pleaded. It was all happening too soon, too fast.

"N-no, Eth...an. List...en to me. I love...you. I can't..." She blinked rapidly. "I can't...see." Her arms flailed weakly, reaching out to him.

The machine beeped wildly now. Ethan grasped her hands in his, kissing her fingers. "Lany!" he cried. "Elaine, hold on. Doctor, you have to hurry."

Doctor Gibbons worked quickly. "Ah, here we are. We're just snipping the cord." He stood quickly, then with the baby in his arms, stepped around the bed. Ethan's mouth fell open at the tiny bundle the doctor thrust into his arms.

"It's a boy," announced the doctor.

"Lany, it's a boy," cried Ethan, but Elaine's head lulled to the side. The monitor stopped beeping and was replaced by the flatline sound. "Elaine," his voice barely a whisper. "I love you."

Emergency doctors and nurses had managed to get Elaine's heart started, but she hadn't regained consciousness. Ethan now sat beside her hospital bed, their newborn son in his arms and the decorations he'd put up sparkling and winking. He cooed to his son and told him about the lights. All the while he prayed Elaine would wake up long enough to see their son.

He still hadn't chosen a name. He and Elaine talked about names but had never agreed on one. Now it was up to him and he wanted it to be something perfect—something she would have loved, too.

Until she woke up, he would sit here and wait so they could make the decision together.

Elaine wasn't sure how she'd gotten here. The last she knew, she'd been lying in the delivery room giving birth, monitors beeping wildly around her. She'd felt as though she was suffocating and her body had ached with incredible pain.

Then there was blissful silence.

When she'd finally become aware of her surroundings, everything had changed. Her body no longer ached and she breathed easier than she had in months.

She saw Ethan sitting in her hospital room beside her bed, his decorations lighting the room. The room was quiet except for the even beeping of the machine her body was connected to and Ethan's quiet weeping.

She moved to stand beside him. He held her hand in both of his, kissing her fingers and whispering something she couldn't hear through his tears. She reached out to touch his shoulder, but her hand passed right through him. His body jolted at the same time and his head shot up, looking around. Did her effort get through to him?

She saw the haggard look on his face. It broke her heart. He needed sleep, needed this to be over. It should have been. He knew her wishes about not wanting to be kept alive on monitors and other devices. Looking around, the only machine in the room seemed to be the heart monitor that continued to beep evenly, even if the numbers on the monitor showed her blood pressure was critically low.

Why was her body still alive if she wasn't part of it any longer and machines weren't keeping her so?

If she were able to weep, she would have. She ached

for Ethan and wanted closure for him. She saw how much the continued ordeal wore on him.

She didn't see their child and wondered if she had delivered it safely. She wanted to seek out the nursery, but Ethan shifted, drawing her attention to him again. He rose and closed the door, then returned to her bedside where he lay down beside her, wrapping his arm around her and lying his cheek against her breast. It was only then that he let his tears fall freely. His body spasmed with his wracking sobs.

Elaine spun around where she stood. She couldn't watch this. Ethan's pain melted into her body and she felt it inside her across the room.

If she were dead, why didn't she see a light to go to? If she were alive, why couldn't she open her eyes? Would she end up just surviving in the hospital for the rest of her life, living this way and never giving Ethan the freedom he deserved? Worse, her spirit surviving in Limbo and having to watch it all?

Grief welled inside her and she tried to cry, but the only sound was her tortured wail of frustration.

It was then she felt a hand on her shoulder. The voice was deep and almost familiar. When she turned, she had a hard time believing whom she saw.

The man standing beside her had a thick beard and silky looking hair. His voice was gentle, spiritual.

"You love this man," he said.

"Yes. More than you know."

The man's eyes sparkled like the lights Ethan had hung around the room, but more intense—no less than she expected from such a man.

"A Christmas wish, Elaine?" he offered.

Her eyes snapped open in surprise. "A wish?" The man nodded. She turned her gaze back to Ethan. What she wanted was for this all to be a cruel mistake. She wanted to wake up and put her arms around her husband, get up from her bed, collect their child from the nursery and leave the hospital and not return until she'd lived a rich and full life. That's what she wanted.

But wishes weren't for keeping. They were for giving away. And what she wanted was to give Ethan the life he deserved. She wanted his pain to end. She wanted him to take their child home and give it the life she couldn't. She knew Ethan would tell their child everything about her and share his love of her, but she wanted his pain to end. And that meant finding the light. So perhaps her wish would be for both of them.

"I want the light. I don't see it. If it would only shine, I could walk into it and Ethan could get on with the rest of his life, find someone else to love and raise our child in a family."

Elaine squeezed her eyes shut, trying to make the tears come so she could relieve some of the ache inside her. She didn't even know if she'd given birth to a boy or girl. If she had another wish...

"All things in time," he said.

Elaine gazed up at him. Could he read her mind? Her answer was in the twinkle in his eyes.

He turned to face the bed. Ethan's sobbing hadn't lessened. His grief was so great she still felt it within her. She couldn't bear it anymore. It was too painful. She would suffer childbirth time and again if this pain inside her would just end. They'd cried together in the last few weeks, but nothing like this, and it was tearing her apart.

The man beside her stepped up to the bed. He pulled a broad hand from beneath his floor-length white-trimmed burgundy cloak and placed it against her breast where her body lay on the bed. It sank through her, much as her spirit hand had done when she tried to touch Ethan. How could she feel it, yet be watching it at the same time?

A moment later he stepped away and looked at her.

"It is not your time, child." Then he was gone.

His lungs and throat burned, but Ethan couldn't stop the tears. How long would this go on? He didn't think he could take much more. The doctors told them

Elaine wouldn't survive the birth of their child, yet they'd brought her back. They'd acted before he could protest. He knew Elaine didn't want to survive like this.

He pulled himself closer to his wife. The beeping of the heart monitor told him her heart still beat, but he could barely hear it as he pressed his ear to her chest—wanting, no needing, to feel the life within her. Her frail body was almost nonexistent under the blankets. He couldn't let her go. Not yet.

When he felt a hand on his arm, he thought it was a nurse coming in to tell him to get off his wife's bed, but when he looked up, prepared to tell the nurse to leave him alone, there was no one there. But the hand remained on his arm. His gaze followed the hand and up Elaine's body. He nearly leapt off the bed when her eyes opened and focused on him.

"Elaine?" he gasped. "Oh, Lany."

Elaine reached up and palmed his cheek. Her hand was warm.

Warm!

And her cheeks were turning pink. The circles under her eyes disappeared before his eyes.

What was happening?

"Lany?"

She smiled weakly. "It's not my time." She glanced to the side of the bed and whispered, "Thank you." Ethan didn't see anyone, but he didn't care. His wife was awake. He didn't know how long he had, but he had to tell her everything he'd been thinking while lying beside her on the narrow bed.

"Elaine, I have so much to say," he said, stroking his thumb across her lower lip. She liked it when he did that. But when she reached up and pulled his hand away he wasn't sure what to think.

"Please, listen to me, Ethan. I'm going to be all right."

Ethan's heart pounded. What was she talking about?

Just then the door swung open and a nurse came in to check on Elaine's status. When she saw Elaine was awake, she spun around and left the room. A moment later she returned with Doctor Gibbons in tow.

Christmas Eve – one year later

The best feeling in the world had to be lying in a lover's arms, exhausted after a night of lovemaking, totally and absolutely sated. Ethan snuggled closer to Elaine, weaving his legs with hers and grinning at how the feel of her body so thoroughly ignited his own.

The warm feminine scent of her damp body permeated his senses. She smelled sweet and exotic. So much so, he'd practically gobbled her up over the last several hours. Perhaps he would again, he thought as he trailed his fingertips between her breasts then encircled a nipple with his thumb.

She raked her nails gently down his chest, across his belly and lower. He grasped her hand with his and kissed the backs of her fingers. "Please, love. I can barely move."

Elaine glanced down to the twitch beneath the sheet just covering his hips. "Could have fooled me."

Ethan leaned up on an elbow and looked down at her. It was hard to believe a year had passed since he'd been lying beside Elaine in the hospital waiting for her to take her last breath. And now, she was taking his breath away.

He still didn't understand it, but Elaine had been right about it not being her time yet. Doctor Gibbons couldn't explain her turn around either, and all the other specialists he consulted were sure the test results had been an error in the hospital's equipment. She was as healthy as the next person. Her checkups during the year proved it and her doctors had given her the all clear. She could even have more children, if that's what they wanted. And they did.

Whatever had happened, there was no doubt Elaine suffered from something that nearly took her away from him forever. Every day since bringing her home, he made a point to show her how much he loved her.

"Do you know how much I love you, Lany?"

She gazed up at him. "I have an idea, but if you get a little closer you can show me just how much." She wiggled her eyebrows at him. "Again."

"Be right back." He kissed her on the forehead and rose to check on their son.

When he returned, Elaine wasn't in bed. While he'd been in the other room, she'd turned off the overhead light, lit the candles and turned on the Christmas tree lights. She lay on her belly beneath the tree, nude with a bright red sash tied around her hips—the folds of the bow resting on the curve of her bottom.

God, how he loved her!

Ethan strode across the room and knelt before her, lifting her to her knees. He ran his fingers through her hair, stroking her cheeks with his thumbs. Sensations raced through her veins and enflamed her skin. His gaze bore into her, pooling passion in her belly.

"Elaine," he sighed, running his hands over her shoulders and down to her hips. He grasped her and pulled her against him. Her arms went around his shoulders automatically. She leaned in to kiss him, but he leaned away from her.

"Tell me what happened that night," he said.

"Which night?" But Elaine knew by the look in his eyes what he wanted to know, so she told him. Over the last year, she'd let him believe the reason she wanted to name their son Nicholas was because he'd been born at Christmas time. Now she hoped he understood the real reason. Saint Nicholas had given her every wish she'd thought of that night. He'd ended Ethan's pain and given baby Nicholas the family life he deserved. He'd given her back her life to make it all happen.

When she was done, Ethan pulled her to him, folding his arms around her and burying his face in the curve of her neck. The feeling of his hot breath on her flesh went right through her. She trembled at his touch.

"I love you, Ethan," she whispered into his ear, kissing him behind it and running her tongue along the lobe.

He leaned away and gazed down at her. She saw the glassy look in his eyes. His emotions were on the surface. "And I'm going to show you how much I love you, Lany. Every day for the rest of our lives."

Hours later, when they'd exhausted each other and hovered on the brink of sleep tangled in each other's embrace, something broke the silence of the room. Elaine turned to Ethan to see if he'd heard it—a distinctive jingle, soft clattering on the rooftop and jolly laughter.

A grin matching Ethan's broke across her face. They threw the blankets aside and raced downstairs to see what Santa left them, laughing like children all the way.

Be sure to check out Kemberlee's website
http://www.kemberlee.com

Sempre

by Aleka Nakis

"Alone. All I've accomplished, but I'm still here alone on Christmas Eve."

Damn! How could a woman immerse herself into her family and friends for years, only to find herself standing at the top of the Empire State Building watching the sunset on such a special day alone?

Amanda Law turned and walked to her right, absorbing a lonely view of Central Park. The cluster of trees in the center of the concrete jungle painted a picture of her personal life. Others surrounded her, she provided them an escape from their hectic lives, but rarely were her gardens tended to.

A tear streaked her cheek and she swiftly swatted it away.

Years ago, she'd watched the sunset here with the man who'd wrapped a tight fist around her heart. She'd smiled and leaned her head on his shoulder, feeling that this was the most beautiful place on earth. Then like an idiot, she'd told him it could never work out between them.

Idiota!

She shook her head and reprimanded herself. "No regrets, Amanda. If you'd made a different decision, you wouldn't have the light of your world." Jason wouldn't have been born and she'd have never had the joy of being his mother. No, she wouldn't trade him for the world.

Her lips curved into a smile as the image of her son, now a teenager, floated into her head. God she missed him. She hated the holidays he spent with his father and not with her.

A sigh escaped her lips, and she walked around the observation deck to face south. Staring at the emptiness where those incredible twin buildings once towered, she ran a long slender finger along the glass outlining where their image should have been.

There is so much misfortune in this world. Lives cut short, never meeting their potential. I'm blessed. I have Jason, my health and a dream career. What more could I ask for?

The orange and pink hues banding across the sky encased the observation deck and warmth flooded through the glass adding to Amanda's comforting thoughts.

Fishing in her coat pocket for change, she walked through the exit onto the outdoor promenade. Choosing a binocular stand, Amanda strode to it, slid in the coins, and lost herself in the spectacular beauty of the city.

Suddenly her skin prickled and a familiar awareness sank into her pores. She jerked back and swung her head searching the promenade. A German family touring, a Japanese couple cuddling, three beautiful Indian women enjoying the sunset, but she didn't see the Italian who used to make her skin tingle in the same manner almost twenty years ago.

Amanda couldn't ignore the sensation in her belly, but she tentatively returned to the binoculars. Raising her shoulders, she softly rolled her neck and tried hard to disregard what she believed was her subconscious playing with her.

A persistent heat permeated her coat and settled on her back. Amanda pulled away from the view and adamantly shook her head. No way was this mere imagination. He was near. His gaze was the source of heat she felt.

The sensation grew stronger. Squaring her body behind the metal stand, Amanda attempted to calm herself.

"*Ciao bella,*" a deep accented voice said behind her. The smooth velvety sound swirled into her mind, and the clean, woodsy scent of him threw her olfactory system into overload.

Marco Tamburi.

Inhaling deeply, her eyelids dropped. Did she dare to believe he was here? Her feet wouldn't help her turn to look at him. Rather she stood as still as the tall cement light poles decorating the streets below. She continued to stare out over the city, illuminated a little more each moment.

A large arm encircled her waist bringing a strong hand to splay under her breasts. Instinctively her body fell back and came to rest against him. He felt broader, fuller, more solid. Warm breaths caressed her ear.

"*Ogni tanto mi chiedo cosa mai stiamo aspttanto.*" He paused, and still standing behind her, ran his fingertips down the side of her cheek. "I saw you looking for me. You knew I was here. How do you always know when I am around?"

"I sense you," she whispered and watched her words escape into the coolness of the air.

"*Si Bella.* That is one more thing I love about you."

She closed her eyes again and attempted to steady her heaving chest. Did he say love or loved, present or past tense?

Taking her upper lip into her mouth, she scraped her teeth over it. Could she turn and look at him?

She'd walked away from Marco Tamburi on a cold winter day to preserve her identity. When she'd been with him, she'd felt part of him, him part of her. They weren't two individuals, they were one. The intimacy had terrified her then. Today she craved it. But she couldn't turn to look into eyes that would see into her soul.

"So, do you ever wonder what in the world we are waiting for?" He translated his previous statement and shifted to fit her completely against him.

She moaned softly at the intimate contact and covered his hand with her fingers, remembering the feel of his broad palm, the long fingers with the large knuckles and smooth nails. Her hand slipped into his coat curling over the edge of his shirtsleeve, and she couldn't deny he was truly with her. She could no longer refuse her desire to be with him.

"Marco, we're not waiting for anything. We're living our lives one day, one nightfall, at a time."

"This is the nicest sunset this week," he said, intertwining their fingers and pushing against her middle. "I didn't expect you to come on Christmas Eve, but I knew you'd be here one afternoon."

She stiffened in his arms. "You've been here before?"

"Yes. Three sunsets without you, and finally on the fourth, you're with me." He tightened his hold on her and placed a soft kiss deep into her thick brown hair before resting his jaw against the side of her head.

She relaxed again and they stood silently, watching the sun dip beneath the horizon into its nightly shelter. The final edge of the orange ball disappeared as he exhaled against her ear.

"What I've heard must be true. You're not with Robert anymore. Or else why would he let you come alone?" His voice carried an undertone of hope.

Forcing herself to breathe, she spoke slowly. "Robert and Jason are skiing in Colorado. I'm doing research for my next book."

"I know about 'Holidays in the City.' I found out you would be in New York on your blog. It is interesting you are using your maiden name and not writing as Amanda Jones. However, Law does have a better ring to your readers and identifies with your 'Rules of Travel' column. Still, I do not understand why you are alone. I would want to spend the holidays with my wife and would never leave her alone. Not for a separate vacation, not for work."

"No, you wouldn't. Robert and I divorced seven years ago. Jason spends alternate holidays with him."

The turn of the conversation brought her back into the realities of the day. She untangled her fingers from his, and twisted in his hold to look at him.

His brown eyes still looked like melted chocolate. His hairline had receded slightly, and he wore his hair at a longer length than most executives did. His jaw was more pronounced and set firmer than she remembered. He was the most handsome and the most beautiful man she'd ever seen.

Raising her hand to lay her palm on his clean-shaven cheek, she said, "Hello Marco."

He visually traced her face and then smiled revealing the sexy edges around his eyes that time had sketched. Reaching under her long hair, Marco grasped her nape and leaned forward sealing his lips on hers.

This wasn't the man-boy she cried over leaving; he was a man undeniably sure of himself and what he wanted. With firm, but tender lips, he captured hers and didn't allow her any possibility to pull away until his tongue had caressed every corner of her mouth.

"Hello my sweet Amanda," he said running the back of his fingers over her cheek. "We have much to discuss *cara mia*. Will you come to dinner with me?"

It wasn't truly a question; it was an explanation of what he had planned for them. Her heart pounded against her chest and her stomach did tumbles. He wasn't going to let her walk away this time.

"Of course, Marco. We have much to reminisce about and I would enjoy doing it over a good glass of wine." Despite the intimate greeting they'd shared, Amanda tried hard to sound casual and distant. She took a step back. "Will your wife be joining us?"

"No," he answered curtly. "Amanda, I guarantee Gabriella would have no issue with us being together. I will explain it to you soon. But, I need to know if *you* feel comfortable—or is there someone in your life who will object?"

A tight chuckle rose from her throat. "Do you care if there is?"

His face remained serious. "Not in the least. But I care for you to be relaxed."

"Then no, nobody would object. I don't feel at all uncomfortable, and I am hungry." Smiling, she placed her hand in his, and he put them both in his pocket as he headed toward to the elevator.

Retreating into her private thoughts, she tried to understand what was happening. He'd said Gabriella would have no issue. It had to mean they weren't together anymore since Marco wasn't the cheating type. No, he took his vows seriously.

Ten minutes later, they exited onto Thirty-Fourth Street, and Marco walked towards an impressive carriage teamed with a white horse.

"*Buonasera Signore Tamburi*," said the driver.

"*Buonasera Gio*. Are we set?"

"*Si, certamente*," Gio answered. With a slight bow at the waist, he offered Amanda his hand and assisted her aboard the elegant buggy.

Settling on the seat beside her, Marco tucked a blanket around her legs. "There. Are you warm and comfortable?"

"Very." She didn't need a blanket. His touch burned through her clothing and heated her in the crisp night air. "I thought carriages weren't allowed in this part of the city?"

"Gio is. Now come close and keep me warm *cara mia*." He pulled her against him as the carriage made its way in the city's holiday traffic.

Snuggled close, they rode in silence north along the festive avenue and into the park. Holiday lights twinkled on the trees lining the paved path, and the steely sky held the promise of a White Christmas.

The clickety-clack of the horse's hooves matched the racing beat of Amanda's heart. Shifting in her seat, she stole a glimpse of his handsome profile.

There was an inherent strength in his face. A smooth long forehead led to his Greco-Roman nose, which sat proud above his generous mouth and cleft adorned chin. His features were more pronounced, stronger and more determined than she remembered, making him more attractive to her than she could have ever imagined.

But, tension was present on his dark brow. Marco was uncharacteristically quiet, perhaps deep in thought. *Was I wrong to have assumed that he, too, is unattached just because he kissed me? No, maybe, but Marco wouldn't if—*

His glance met hers, and she quickly looked away. It hurt too much to hide her feelings from him.

Riding in silence, they passed the skating rink they'd spent many afternoons on. The carriage circled the lake where they'd rowed the small boat with such vigor, only to find themselves in the water laughing hysterically as they attempted to turn it right side up.

Stopping by the fort on the western part of the park, Gio turned to look at Marco. Marco nodded and stood. "Come *bella*. Let us walk a bit."

Taking his hand, she stood and stepped off the wooden platform. Walking along the lit path in the still darkness of the park intensified her desire to fill her world with him. He'd proposed in this spot. And this was where she'd told him it wouldn't work. So why were they here?

Amanda turned and raised her eyes to find him watching her. He stopped and pulled her against him. Placing a finger on her chin, Marco tilted her face up, and slowly kissed her temples, searing a path across her forehead, then down her nose, before finding her lips.

Marco's lips burned with anticipation as he sought entrance to her warm mouth. When she opened to welcome him, he delved deep with the hunger of a starved man. He wanted to taste her sweetness, to feel her softness under his hands, and to let her scent surround him.

Marco ran his lips along the length of her neck, nipping at tender skin at the top of her blouse leaving his mark there. Feeling like a teenager who couldn't control his hormones, his hands sought the curve of her breast under her coat, and his breath hitched when his fingers felt her taught nipple over the silk of her blouse.

She didn't protest. Amanda's fingers sprawled into his hair. Her eyes closed and her head fell back exposing more skin, and presenting the most enticing picture he'd ever seen. She arched closer, causing him to close his own eyes and pray for some physical control.

"You have such power over me *Bella*. You always have. A white witch stoking the slightest ember deep inside me to a full flame with unnatural ease." He groaned and then rearranged her clothes to their original condition.

Pulling her coat around her, he whispered against the satiny feel of her flowing mane. "But, no matter how much I want to take you in this very place and show you what you threw... No, I won't just yet. I have been a very patient man, and I believe you owe me an explanation, Amanda. Tonight is the night we settle the past."

He looked at her dark eyes and her soft parted lips quivering from his abrupt withdrawal. He wanted to say the past didn't matter. She was with him now. But he didn't. Instead, he asked what only she could answer.

"Why did you do it, Amanda? Why did you choose Robert?"

His question shot though her, sending a numbing cold up and down her spine. Suddenly she was twenty-one again, unsure of herself and overwhelmed by her love for Marco Tamburi. Her heart splayed in the corner of the street, exposed to everyone who crossed, and in danger of being trampled on and splattered through the city.

She'd been with him less than an hour and had ridiculously offered herself to him. In the middle of a public park! Yes, it may have been remote and dark, but she was such a fool to open her body and soul to a man, leaving it vulnerable to shame and ridicule.

In college, Amanda had fought the urge to relinquish her being and complete control to him for two years. What she'd felt for him had debilitating power. Nevertheless, she couldn't develop the thought, Marco's presence negated the doubts and fears she'd once used as a guide.

"I am waiting for your answer," he informed her and started walking again. "We have thrown away too much time and I count every minute that passes as a waste. After the way you just responded to me, I know your feelings are still there. Talk, Amanda."

She licked her dry lips and inhaled deeply. Closing her eyes, and trusting Marco with her next step, she found the courage to address the incidents that had determined the path she'd taken two decades ago.

"It was the Saturday after we left our fort. You'd been angry and called me irrational and immature. I called you at the house in the Hamptons. I needed to speak with you, to hear your voice and see you."

His gaze fixed on the carriage as they walked toward it. His strong jaw almost masked the small tick of the muscle beside his dark brow, but she knew him too well and didn't miss it.

Amanda continued, "My parents were having dinner with Robert's parents and insisted I contribute to the family by agreeing to marry him. Dad was running for office and he needed the support of voters behind Judge Jones."

Clearly shocked, Marco stopped and stared at her. "You left me to further your father's political career?" Then his nostrils flared and eyes narrowed. "You? The one with the high morals and the uncompromising ideals of doing what was right, regardless of the consequences to your career. I can detail the look you gave me when I told you we must do what is necessary to get ahead in business. Disgust and idealism all on one palette. Your face."

Oh how right he'd been. You did do what was needed to get ahead, to protect those you loved, and to shield yourself from being hurt.

"I called the house and your mother answered. You know, the woman your father's family never accepted because she wasn't born into aristocracy like your father?" Amanda's old fears gave her the strength to explain her thoughts.

"What does that have to do with us? I told you, I would never allow that where you were concerned. I chose you above everything and you walked away from me." He tightened his hold on her hand as he helped her back into the carriage.

"Your mother said you were out with Gabriella, and that you'd be out all day." Amanda rattled off the words in a quick whisper and diverted her gaze to the carriage floor. Biting her lower lip she added, "I was jealous."

"But you had nothing to be jealous of. I remember that day. I had driven Gabriella to take her SATs. That is why I went home that weekend. That, and the fact you refused to speak to me." He ran his fingers in his hair, a habit Amanda had found so sexy in college. "Gabriella was the little sister I never had. There was nothing romantic between us." He sounded annoyed that she'd not accepted his explanation.

"Obviously there was more than you admitted. You ended up marrying her!" she retorted with a sharp, hurt voice. "You spent your weekends with her, not with me. We were together only at school. Our relationship was hidden like a dirty secret in the depths of the dorms."

Disconcerted, he shifted in his seat, appearing flustered with her words. Amanda watched the park's bare trees wave goodbye as they exited into the lights of the city. She wanted to forget the pain of feeling alone and hollow. Embracing the distraction the busy streets of New York offered, she focused on the festive holiday storefronts and the clickety-clack of the horse's hooves, wondering why she'd never told him before.

Marco wouldn't let the past rest. "You were the one who did not want *me* away from school. I stayed in the dorms every time you left. I didn't leave. You are the one who went home without *me*. Not once did you invite *me* to your house, and when I finally convinced you to let *me* take you home, you said your parents would not appreciate *me* coming in. You turned me away on your front step."

Every word he said was true. She sighed with reluctance. "They didn't like it when I spoke of Italy. I was learning Italian and discussed you too much around them."

"They never met me!"

"No," she agreed. "But they knew you came from a wealthy and influential family, and you planned to return to Italy to take over your family's enterprises when you finished your studies."

"What was wrong—?"

"If I was emotionally attached to you, I'd go with you. Their little girl would live across the ocean, submersed in a culture they didn't understand. I didn't want to leave my family and simultaneously risk rejection by yours. The pressure and stress would have torn us apart. It would have made me bitter...as unhappy as it made your mother."

"You are not a little girl, nor are you my mother. Amanda Law is one of the smartest and most stubborn women I know."

"You're not hearing me. I was frightened and weak. I was terrified to choose you because I loved you too much."

There! She'd told him in two minutes what she hadn't been able to say in countless hours years ago. She'd been terrified of what she'd felt for him, scared she would have lost herself to him, and frightened of turning into a lonely woman surrounded by people. Much, she realized, like the woman she was today.

"You never told me you felt that way." His voice was softer now and a bit uncertain. "We could have changed our plans if I had known."

"Why? Would you have stayed in the States with me?"

"Yes," he answered quickly. "I would have done anything to make you happy."

Her chin rose in a determined stance. She wasn't willing to hear the words she once craved. "Be real, Marco. That wasn't what you wanted."

"What I wanted was you," he snapped. "Instead of trusting me, you came back from a long weekend at home engaged to Robert Jones. You refused to speak to me, and I camped outside your door for a whole night before my pride got the better of me."

Not knowing what to say, she stared at the floor of the carriage, which had come to a stop. From the corner of her eye, she saw him running his hand through his hair in frustration. However, it wasn't fair. He hadn't come after her, he'd walked away and later married Gabriella.

"We are at the hotel. Please, let us talk inside." He offered her his arm.

They were in the elevator when she spoke again. "I never mentioned the hotel on my blog. How did you know I'd be staying here?"

"The same way I knew you would be at the Empire State Building at sunset. That is your favorite time of day to look at the city." He squeezed her hand. "My suite is here as well. I remembered you wanted to spend New Year's Eve in Times Square. I guessed you would pick this place because it is near. Your room must overlook the Square."

"Yes." The elevator stopped and the doors opened.

He guided her toward his suite. "You see, I paid attention, too, and remember the desires you related to me. I know your dreams, your desires, and your goals."

She wouldn't look at him. Conflicting emotions dueled in her mind and she couldn't think straight. One moment she wanted to throw herself into his arms and yell, *We can be together now. I love you.* The next moment she questioned why he'd not fought harder for her and why he'd married Gabriella.

With lowered eyes, she watched him fit the card into the key slot. Opening the door, he continued speaking. "You wanted to travel the world and get paid for it. Today you are the most loved travel writer in America. The Amanda I knew loved the Big Apple and wanted to experience all the special moments it offered, including the notorious New Year's Eve celebration. Have you done that yet?"

"No, this is my chance." She entered the room. "You're correct about the reason I picked this hotel. It's close enough to avoid the security hassle, and if I couldn't make it physically on the street, I could watch from my room."

She walked toward the full-length window and gestured towards the magnificent view of Times Square. The colorful lights, the people on the pavement, the intricate advertising, all buzzing with life and transmitting energy found nowhere else on earth.

He glided her coat off her shoulders and threw it on an overstuffed chair. Excitement ran over her skin as he lifted her hair and brought his lips to the curve of her neck. She leaned her head back against his chest and closed her eyes.

Suddenly an image of Marco with Gabriella flashed in her mind and she pulled away from him.

"Stop, Marco. This is wrong."

Turning, she gathered all her strength to walk away from the man she'd loved since the first moment she'd seen him, and strode behind a desk erecting a physical barrier between them. She sat in the chair, facing him, and scooted her knees under the heavy wooden structure, negating the weak feeling in her legs.

Marco leaned over the desk and slammed his fist. "Why is this wrong?"

"You married Gabriella."

His eyes grew wide and he shook his head. He dropped into a chair in front of the desk and placed his elbows on the hard surface. Fingers massaging his scalp, and his gaze set on the dark mahogany, he spoke.

"I am sorry. I have been aggravated with you not telling me the truth, yet I am guilty of the same."

Amanda watched the veins at his temples bulge. His face was a slight shade of red and his Adam's apple was very pronounced.

"I did marry Gabriella. Years after you'd married Robert, and Jason was born. What you don't want to understand is that I never had romantic feelings for her."

Frustrated with his words, she pushed away from the desk, jumped up from the chair and strode to the window. She crossed her arms in front of her chest. How could he continue to claim he had no romantic feelings for his wife?

"Gabriella became sick. She had no family, and she was living off the remainder of her inheritance. A rare form of Leukemia attacked her body and she needed the best medical help in the world to fight it. The truth was she would get more attention as a Tamburi than as a Callone."

He crossed the room and stood behind her. Amanda welcomed his heat and comfort as he wrapped his arms around her, gently peeling her white fingers away from her upper arms.

"As I have always told you, I loved Gabriella like the sister I never had. I would do anything to help her. We married, but it was a marriage of necessity. She needed the support and money to get the best care possible. Unfortunately, the best was not enough. The disease claimed her, *grazie a Dio*, in her sleep...seven years ago."

Amanda shuddered, and Marco turned her in his embrace. Looking into bleary eyes, his thumb caressed her tear stricken cheeks.

"I'm sorry," she whispered.

"Thank you." He contemplated telling her Gabriella wouldn't initially accept his proposal. She'd said he should have gone after Amanda and told her how much he loved and wanted her. Gabriella had been a believer of true love and had claimed it would always prevail.

"The only woman I have ever loved romantically is you."

Amanda, unable to stifle the sobbing sounds deep in her throat, nestled as close as physically possible. She'd never fallen apart like this before. Not even after losing her parents.

"Oh, *bella*, my Amanda. Finally, you show me true emotion that exposes your beautiful heart. Do not hide from me anymore. Promise me that."

Amanda nodded into his shoulder, determined to gain a millimeter of composure.

"One more request," he said. "Make one of my dreams come true."

"Tell me how, *caro*."

Knowing she cared, didn't make it any easier for Marco to ask. What if she refused? Studying her face, he leaned toward her and feathered her lips with his own. Then taking a deep breath, he brought her hand to his lips and planted a kiss in the center of her palm.

"Christmas is tomorrow," he began. "I have always wanted to share Christmas morning with you. Please stay. Just think about our wants and desires this time around. Give us this holiday week, time for you and me, *cara mia*."

"Okay," she whispered.

Marco raised a triumphant hand before cupping her heart shaped face and sealing his mouth over hers. His heart pounded against his ribcage and his eyes couldn't stop devouring the most beautiful woman in the world.

No closed eye kisses for him. He needed to see her completely.

"I am going to take full advantage of every moment with you," he told Amanda. She'd agreed to share Christmas with him. Now all he needed to do was convince her to stay with him forever.

She leaned into him, tilting her face toward his, smiling and radiant. Marco threw back his head and laughed. Finally, she would be his. He then encircled her waist and crushed her body against him, lifting her off her feet as he turned them around like the lovers they were, meeting after a long time apart.

"*Ti amo, Amanda. Ti amo*." He brought his lips to her soft mouth, drinking in her essence. He didn't want the moment to ever end. He showered kisses around her lips, along her jaw, and down her long neck, feasting on the taste of her skin.

Rejoicing in the feel of her fingers digging into the flesh on his back, he lifted her effortlessly and carried her into the bedroom with a few long strides. Cradling her close, he smiled at his Christmas present.

"After years of playing this scenario in my mind, I am about to burst with the anticipation. You are mine, Amanda, *sempre*—forever. You are never leaving again."

"I want to stay. I need to be yours." She kissed the side of his neck. "I need you to be mine."

Placing her feet on the floor, Marco sat on the edge of the bed in front of her. Savoring every second, he painstakingly unbuttoned each tiny pearl on her blouse and then pushed it off her shoulders.

Running trembling fingers over the smooth lace trimmed material covering her peaked nipples, Marco brought his lips to it. The barrier teased his tongue and he removed it to taste her alone.

"Sweet, beautiful, intoxicating woman."

His hands and mouth explored the soft curves of her chest, her waist, and her hips. Marco reached behind her and unzipped her skirt. It fell to the floor, exposing a matching silk pair of panties and cream silken stockings held up by a lace garter.

His eyes moved over her as if in a trance. His hands followed and couldn't resist the temptation to lower the beautiful garment to her heels and lift her feet out of it. He didn't breathe as he felt the soft moist curls outlining the slick line of heat ready for him.

Heaven, she was his heaven.

"*Bella*," he sighed and buried his face between her breasts. Amanda responded, arching towards him and running her fingers over every inch of his body she could reach. When her fingers pulled at his belt, he stood and undressed, letting his clothes drop beside her skirt.

Her hot mouth burned his chest and as she scraped her teeth over his nipple, his control disappeared.

Instantly he laid Amanda on her back, covered her body with his, sinking into her with primitive possessiveness. A guttural sound escaped his throat as he moved within her warmth. He was home.

Amanda moaned aloud with pure pleasure as the passion and love they shared completed her. Captured by the heat of his intense dark gaze, she abandoned herself to the whirl of sensation he instilled.

"I love you, Marco." The words left her lips, and she fell into an abyss of ecstasy with Marco exploding deep within her.

They were sprawled on the bed as they looked out of the large window, their bodies naked and still moist from their lovemaking. The sun started to illuminate the pale sky and reflect the snow drifting in the air.

Amanda intertwined her legs into his and snuggled closer. Running her fingers in the dark curly hair on his chest, she raised her mouth to his and kissed the lips that had kept her from a minute's sleep. She couldn't get enough of him. She wanted him forever.

"Merry Christmas," she said.

"It certainly is, *cara*. And you are the best present I have ever received." He caressed her shoulder, then kissed the tip of her nose. "A present I want to keep forever."

"Forever is a very long time, Marco."

He turned his body toward her, and touched her cheek. "Not long enough when it comes to being with you. I want to spend the rest of my days with you, and to fill our home with love, love we have denied ourselves until now."

"I do love you, Marco," she said, giddy with joy from her admission.

"*Perfetto*! We will live our days to the fullest, grow old together, and pray our children and grandchildren find what we share."

She jerked up in alarm. Gathering the covers against her, Amanda pulled away. "Marco, we're not twenty years old anymore. I will be forty soon and my son is graduating high school this year. I can't have a child now."

"Why?" He sat up beside her, and in typical Italian fashion, began to speak with his hands. "Women much older than you have children. We are healthy, and we have so much to offer a child."

Turning her back to him, she slid her feet over the side of the bed and stood. "I can't think, Marco. This is too much. Can we talk after I shower?"

"We can talk whenever you want. But do not forget, I'll not let you take my present back." He stood behind her and kissed her shoulder. "We are going to grow old together. No more walking away with my heart, *cara*."

"No, but I do need to think." Walking towards the en-suite bath, she turned and smiled. "And eat. It seems I forgot to eat dinner last night."

"You think? I will call for breakfast." A smile teased his lips as he walked toward her again. Placing large warm hands in the small of her back, he pulled her close for a kiss. "I will ask for your things to be packed and brought here."

"No need. My things were never unpacked. My luggage is at the foot of my bed. The first thing I did after I checked in was go to watch the sunset and have a meeting with fate."

"I am happy you did." A look of relief spread across his face.

"Me, too." She blew him a kiss from the doorway. "Me, too."

Contacting the front desk, Marco instructed them of the room change and requested they bring Amanda's belongings up promptly. Stressing the need to direct all calls to his suite, he said, "It is Christmas and she is impatient to speak to her son. Please be sure to put Jason Jones through immediately. Regardless of the time."

The hotel staff delivered her luggage and released her room. Amanda had just finished pulling on her sweater when there was a second knock at the door. Room service. She popped her head into the bathroom. "Breakfast has arrived."

"*Si bella*, I will be right out."

Room service set the tray of fragrant coffee, cheeses and fresh baked bread on the table.

Taking care to give a good Christmas-worthy tip, Amanda opened the door for the young woman to leave. "Thank you and Merry Christmas."

"Merry Christmas." The girl turned and collided with a snow-covered young man.

"Excuse me," he said. "I didn't see you."

"Jason!" Amanda pulled her 'popsicle' son through the door and into her embrace. "What a wonderful surprise."

"Merry Christmas." Bringing his frozen lips to her cheek, Jason handed her a gift from the airport shop in Denver. "I couldn't be mistaken for Dad's new wife's boyfriend one more time. I had to get away from Kitty! She's nuts and a bimbo."

"Jason!" Amanda tried to sound serious, but couldn't stop her laughter. "Oh well, she's your Dad's problem, not ours. But be respectful to your father anyway."

"Whatever," Jason said shrugging his shoulders and throwing his wet jacket onto a chair. "Who cares? I'm here to spend Christmas with the best mom in the world."

She smiled and accepted another snow-frosted kiss. Taking his cold fingers between her hands, she guided him to the couch. "I'm happy you're here. Whatever your reasons. I have so much—"

Marco's voice sounded from the bedroom. "Coffee here, *bella*? I am famished, and not just for... Oh, sorry." He was now in the sitting room. "I did not realize...Jason?"

"What the hell is this?" Jason stood and glared at the man with a white towel wrapped around his waist standing in his mother's hotel suite.

Amanda placed a hand on her son's shoulder and nodded to Marco. "Yes, this is my son, Jason."

"Yeah, but who is he?" Jason's gaze burned into Amanda. "And, what is he doing in your room?"

Marco stepped forward and extended his hand to the shocked teenager. "I am Marco Tambu—"

"Tamburi," Jason interrupted. "I recognize you."

Amanda stared at Marco and raised her arms in question. How did Jason know him?

"Good," she said to her son. "Why don't we sit and talk while Marco gets dressed. I have a lot to tell you."

Jason moved like a robot under her direction. He sat on the couch, but continued to glare at Marco. After shooting a quick glance at Amanda, Marco nodded and walked back into the bedroom, leaving Jason and her alone.

Gingerly sitting on the edge of the couch, Amanda wondered how to explain Marco to her son without sounding as if she regretted the life she'd led. Her heart ached with the love she had for Jason, love she couldn't imagine absent from her life.

Holding his hand, she took a deep breath and began. "I've known Marco for a very long time. We lived in the same dorm during college."

"I know, Mom. I remember you telling me he was a good *friend* and all. I also remember you crying over his picture for a whole week after that."

A dim recollection of sitting at the kitchen table and talking to her first-grader entered her mind. She nodded and connected the pieces to the puzzle. "I didn't remember that, Jason. I'm surprised you did. You were so young."

"I remember. You were reading one of those Italian gossip rags you love. He was on the front page with a pretty bride, and you started crying when you saw it. You called him a liar and threw the paper in the trash. When I came into your room to ask why you were crying, you said it was because you'd known the truth all along and there was no second chance."

Amanda felt the blood drain from her face. Jason remembered bits and pieces of the day, but how did she put it all together for him now? "You don't have all the details."

"Obviously," Jason hissed, rising from the couch. "You've shacked up in this joint with a married man and are acting like a cheap—"

"Do not dare to speak to your mother like that!" Marco boomed entering the room.

"You can't tell me what to do," Jason challenged. "You're not my father."

"No, I am not. But I am sure he would agree with me on that demand." Marco's voice clearly displayed his effort at control. "However, no one talks to your mother like that. Not even you, Jason."

Jason's mouth dropped and he turned a bewildered gaze to his mother. Gone was the tough-guy act and in its place stood a confused boy unable to speak.

Amanda rose, stepped forward and took him in her arms. Stroking Jason's wet blond hair, she kissed the side of his head. Her gaze met Marco's and asked for his patience so she could explain to her son. He nodded and went to sit on a chair opposite the couch.

"Honey, I don't blame you for being surprised," Amanda began gently. "Please hear me out from the beginning."

Jason looked at her with blue eyes that begged for her forgiveness and pleaded for her to continue. She obliged her son's silent request.

"Marco and I met in college. We shared more than a typical boyfriend-girlfriend attraction and became very close. For my own personal reasons, I turned down his marriage proposal. We went our separate ways, but our love didn't fade. When I saw the wedding picture you remember, I cried because I thought I'd never again have the opportunity to tell him how much I loved him."

Holding her son's hand, Amanda paused to let him absorb what she'd said. She looked at the boy she cherished and prayed to find the right words for him.

Jason's eyes held tears in them. His lip trembled. "But you were married to Dad then. Why did you care about *him*? You had us."

"Yes, I had you, the best thing of my life. I would never change that for anything. Your dad and I wanted and loved you so much, that we tried to make our failing marriage work as long as possible. Then one day, we admitted to each other we could love you just as much if we weren't married and making each other miserable."

"The divorce?"

"Yes."

"Is he divorced, too?"

"Actually, Gabriella died a few years ago. Marco is widowed." Amanda swallowed the knot in her throat and contemplated her next words.

"Jason, a piece of my heart has always been with Marco and I love him. I want to be with him." She paused again, hoping her son would accept her decision.

"I would never do anything to jeopardize our relationship—yours and mine—and my wanting to be with Marco doesn't mean I don't love you. Please know that, sweetheart. I love you more than life itself. But in a few months you're coming to New York to start college, and you'll begin making your own way in the world. I'll always be there for you. I just don't want to be there alone."

Jason's eyes fixed on her face. He didn't speak, only nodded as she finished. Amanda felt Marco's hand caress her shoulder. She hadn't realized he'd come to stand behind her. She looked up at him, silently communicating she was done.

Marco cleared his throat. "We have something in common, Jason. We both love this woman and want her to be happy. We are both a bit quick to jump to her defense, even when she is more than capable and does not need our protection."

The two men's gazes met and held above Amanda's head. She felt their love surround her and she smiled as she took each of their hands in hers. "This is the best Christmas ever. The two men I love most are with me. I want you to get to know each other, and once you do, I know you'll like each other."

"Mom, I'm sorry I spoke to you that way. I was wrong...rude. Oh, Mom, I'm sorry." Jason stammered, then hugged her. Turning to Marco, he offered his hand. "And Marco, I don't like sharing, but if it makes Mom happy, welcome to the family."

Marco bypassed Jason's extended hand and gave the young man a quick hug. "*Grazie*."

"Thank you, both of you. Now let's have breakfast and get ready for Rockefeller Center. Honey, place your bag in that bedroom." A joyous Amanda pointed to the second bedroom in the suite.

The sun was low on the horizon as Jason witnessed his mother marry Marco on the last day of the year. The priest pronounced them husband and wife, congratulated them, and walked inside the eighty-sixth floor observatory for Jason to sign the marriage certificate.

Marco pulled her into his arms and gave Amanda the first passionate kiss as his wife. "Finally, *mia moglie*, my wife."

"Yes, my husband." Loving the sound, she repeated it. "Husband, how on earth did you manage to get a priest here on New Year's Eve?"

Marco laughed and placed an escaped tendril of hair behind her ear. "I told you, it helps to have influence, and for officials to owe you. I called in some favors."

"I'm glad you did." She leaned up on her toes and kissed Marco. "*Ti amero per sempre* is engraved in our rings. *Ti amero* means I love you. But what is *sempre*?"

"It is what I have been saying from the first time I met you. Forever, Amanda, I love you forever."

Be sure to visit Aleka's website
http://www.alekanakis.com

Christmas Masquerade

by Michele Ann Young

December 24, 1813

"Bloody Christmas." *Thwack.* The axe split the log with a satisfying ring. Gerrard picked the firewood out of the snow and tossed it on the growing pile beneath the lantern. At least his retreat from the joys of the season would provide his gamekeeper with enough wood for the rest of the winter. A gust of wind knifed through his shirt, turning the sweat on his chest to ice. He placed a new log on the block and hefted the axe.

"Excuse me, sir." A musical voice fought for attention above the wind's keening.

He peered into the darkness beyond the range of his lantern. Surely none of his servants had ventured forth to plague him with their pleas to return home? "Who is there?"

His jaw dropped as a raven-haired goddess stepped into the light. A pale gown molded against enticing curves. Her oval face bathed in gold, she floated closer, her cloak billowing as if she'd ridden to earth on the back of the wind.

Had he killed himself with the axe and been transported to heavenly delights or was this Hell's torment?

She raised her voice. “There has been a carriage accident on the road.”

The words clawed at an ancient scar, savaging his mind with images of funerals and solemn faces. He forced himself into the present with a steadying breath. Obviously this vision, with cheeks rosy from cold, was neither heaven-sent, nor a hell-born demon, but simply some marriage-bent female who’d tracked him to his bolt-hole. Hers wouldn’t be the first carriage to break down outside the Earl of Dart’s gate. Bile of disappointment soured his gut.

The forgotten axe slipped in his grip. He caught the shaft as the head hit the ground. Sparks shot from the flagstone inches from his boot. “Damnation.” He slammed the blade into the block and glared at the intruder. “An accident?”

A pair of wide, blue eyes assessed him from beneath arched black brows. “The carriage turned over at the crossroads. The post-boy must have hit his head. I could not rouse him.”

Nudging his hat back, he ran an insolent glance from her crown of tangled curls to her feet. Against his will, his gaze dallied on the outline of a pair of slender legs that took forever to reach her ankles. Ignoring the surge of heat in his blood, he mustered the control to meet her gaze with a blank expression. “No post-chaise would go out on a night like tonight.”

She stepped closer, gloved hands clasped, her brow furrowed. “You don’t understand. The boy is not moving.”

What type of fool did she take him for? He fisted his hands on his hips. “Where is your family, your maid, your traveling companions?” Those waiting to spring the parson's mousetrap.

Deeper color than the blush of cold flooded her cheeks. She lifted her chin. “There are no others, sir. How can you stand there asking questions when a life is in danger?” Snowflakes glinted like diamonds in her ebony hair. Rubbing her arms, she straightened her shoulders. "If you will not help, I must find someone who will."

The words tightened an iron band around his chest. An urge to promise to shield her from whatever had her running through the snow on Bodmin Moor tore at his throat. Worse, he wanted to believe she told the truth. Blast her to hell.

He picked up his greatcoat from the pile of logs where he'd thrown it aside to work. "Very well. I will check on this boy of yours. I trust he is still breathing?"

She flinched and twisted her fingers. "I am not sure. We must hurry." She turned to lead the way.

"Wait here." He damned his chivalrous instincts as he strode to the door of the cottage and shoved it open. "Warm yourself by the fire and do not touch a thing." At her startled glance, he shrugged. "Your presence will only slow me down."

Shadows swirled in eyes the color of a tropical ocean and deep enough to drown a man, if he cared to dive in.

He glowered. "You are wasting precious time, miss, if this lad of yours really needs help."

She recoiled at his harshness. He half expected her to admit the whole thing was a lie, a trap, then she took a deep breath and stepped past him over the threshold. The scent of snow and summer roses wafted up from her hair. He inhaled deeply and cursed himself for a fool. It had been years since he'd experienced such instant lust. Clearly he'd been too long without a woman. But the kind of woman he allowed himself no longer held any interest.

Hunched against the wind, he headed for a place in the road he knew all too well.

Clarissa jumped as the door crashed closed. She stared at the rough wooden planks. Could she have found a more sullen rescuer? She really ought to show him the way. She ran to the door, pulled it open. The man was gone. Oh Lord, let the post-boy be all right, else she would never forgive herself for insisting they continue their journey after dark.

A star very like the one she'd seen through the carriage window glibly promising her arrival home, twinkled slyly between hurrying clouds. A blast of wind rattled the windows. Snowflakes stung her cheeks and the heavenly body flicked out. She closed the door.

So much for wishing on stars.

The warmth and the smell of stew laced with herbs offered comfort. With a sigh, she stripped off her sodden gloves and crossed to the hearth. Holding out her skirts to the cheery blaze, she glanced around the one-room cottage. Furnished with a rough-hewn table, two chairs, a pine chest and a narrow cot covered in furs, it spoke of a Spartan existence. For some reason, it suited the stark beauty of the man who lived here.

The sight of him wielding his axe like some dark avenging angel had stopped her dead. A strange tingle had run through her body, not fear so much as an unsettling tension. The impression of leashed animal strength and suppressed anger had shaken her confidence, while his hard-angled face, as wild and stormy as the night, made her words come out in a breathless rush. In the split second his gaze caught hers, he suddenly looked younger and...lost. When she stepped closer he'd turned as surly as a wolf caught in a snare.

Strings of rabbit furs hung on one wall and a rifle held pride of place on the chimneybreast. He must be a gamekeeper, one explanation for his isolation. On the other hand, he might be a poacher, or a criminal hiding from justice. Either reason would account for his unfriendly reception. Thank God, she'd arranged for most of her luggage to follow in her traveling carriage and had tucked her jewels inside her valise's hidden compartment.

A sensible woman would leave before he returned. And go where? The nearest inn might be miles down the road. All her life she'd heard tales of people lost on the moors at night, led astray by boggards or faeries, only to be found the next day yards from their dwelling.

Besides, she couldn't leave before she knew the post-boy hadn't sustained some terrible injury.

The lid on a blackened pot over the fire rattled and a most delicious smell wafted up. She lifted the lid. At the sight of the meat and vegetables bubbling in rich gravy, her mouth watered, her stomach reminding her she'd not eaten for hours. *He* had said to touch nothing. It would be unconscionable to steal his dinner. She replaced the lid. As soon as she knew the post-boy was safe, she'd make her way to the nearest inn, order a hearty dinner and hire another carriage. With luck, she might make it home in time for Christmas dinner.

With nothing to do but wait, she perched on the edge of the chair nearest the fire. Surely, he'd return with the boy soon. She leaned back and let warmth of the fire seep into her bones.

The door banged back against the wall. Clarissa jerked upright, staring as snow swirled around the huge figure on the doorstep. He forced the door shut.

The bottom dropped out of her stomach. He was alone. On legs that shook, she pushed to her feet. "Where is he?"

He glared from beneath lowered brows. "Took to his heels, I presume. After dumping you on me."

The sharp edge in the deep voice flayed her nerves. "He cannot have gone. I left him unconscious. I thought he might be..." Her voice cracked and she swallowed.

"Dead? Well, apparently the corpse managed to ride off with the horses. Left the carriage with a broken axle." He dumped her valise on the floor. "I assume this is yours?"

She collapsed on the chair. "Why on earth did he not try to find me?"

The man shrugged out of his greatcoat, hung it behind the door and strode to the fire. He stretched his large hands to the blaze. The room suddenly seemed a great deal smaller. She edged back in her seat.

Cold air emanated from him in waves. He shot her a hard glance. "That is your story?"

"Story?"

"Your relatives can show up in the morning and make their demands, but it will not do you a scrap of good."

"Demands?" The man was touched in his attic. Living in the wilds had disturbed his mind. She rose and picked up her cloak. "Direct me to the nearest posting-house, please."

The man's eyebrows formed a dark straight line. "Are you mad? It is blowing a blizzard and already drifting. I scarcely made it back."

"Nonsense. It is a flurry." It had to be.

He crossed his arms over his expanse of chest. "See for yourself."

She ran to the window, rubbed at the frost on the pane. Snowflakes as big as moths whirled past. She swung around. "But I cannot stay here. It is Christmas Eve."

"Christmas." His lip curled. "A pagan feast adopted by early Christians to appease the masses. And you will not make it fifty feet outside dressed like that."

His gaze ran down her length with such intensity, it grazed the skin of her chest, her stomach, her legs. Her breath shortened. A delicious thrill tightened her breasts. She tried not to gaze like some besotted schoolgirl at his sensual mouth and the dimple in his strong square chin. A small knowing smile curved his lips and she wanted to taste them. Was he doing it on purpose? She narrowed her eyes. "My cloak is warmer than it looks and my shoes are perfectly serviceable." She lifted her skirts a fraction.

His gaze dropped to her hem and his smile broadened as he no doubt stared at her ankles.

She dropped her hem. "Unmannerly beast," she muttered.

He raised a brow. "You invited me to look."

"At my boots." Dash it, he was right about her attire. She'd left in such a hurry she hadn't thought to change into a gown more suited for the country. “Do you have a gig, or a horse I might borrow?”

“No. And if I did, I would not send any creature out on such a night.” He turned toward the fire. “I suppose you will want dinner?” He lifted the lid and once more the rich aroma filled the room.

She backed away, careful to keep the table between them. This powerful stranger had her at his mercy and she ought to be wary, even if she wasn’t fearful. The hunting rifle above the mantel caught her eye. Why hadn't she thought of securing it before he returned? “Thank you, but I would far sooner find an inn.”

He opened the cupboard and bent down. “You are stuck here, young lady. You might as well make the best of it.” He glanced over his shoulder. “Perhaps you might like to tell me who you are and just why you landed on my doorstep?”

The suspicion in his voice resonated through her body. If she told him the truth, it might well be her undoing. “My name is Clary...Albany.” Her mother’s maiden name was less well known than the Trevethon belonging to her wealthy father. “I-I'm a lady's maid.”

“Really?” He rose, and in two strides crossed to a cupboard set in the wall beside the outside door. He disappeared inside what appeared to be a neat little pantry.

Clarissa dashed to the fireplace and hopped up on the hearth. On tiptoes, she managed to get one hand on the rifle’s stock.

“Steady, lass,” a deep voice murmured in her ear. “The fire will catch your skirts if you stand too close.” Strong fingers caught her around the waist, held her against a hard length of strong, bay-scented male. Hard thighs brushed against her buttocks, sending prickles racing across her back. Bone-melting weakness invaded her limbs. She gasped and turned within the circle of his hands.

He gazed at her, a flicker of something hot flared in his eyes. Anger? Or something far more disturbing? It disappeared so fast, she wasn't sure.

She quelled a shiver. Lord, but the man was tall and broad. The top of her head barely reached the underside of his chin, a strange sensation when she could look most men in the eye. The fact that he was also strikingly good to look upon when he smiled didn't help slow her heartbeat one little bit. Energy crackled between them. Unless she moved soon, she'd burst into flames and melt in a puddle at his feet. She ducked out of reach. "I was admiring your rifle."

"An expert on guns, are you?"

Strangely breathless, she pressed a hand to her throat. "Not me. My brother."

"I see." He returned to the table now sporting a cottage loaf. He carved two thick slices, his muscles rippling beneath his fine linen shirt. Her mouth dried as she watched his strong hands control the blade. He brought the pot to the table and ladled stew into two bowls.

"Fetch the butter from the larder, please?" he asked. He tilted his head, indicating where she'd find it.

"Yes, of course." Anything to avoid the pleasure of watching him, though she suspected he'd only asked because he didn't want to leave her alone with the rifle.

Inside the shelf-lined pantry, she found the butter in a covered clay dish set in a saucer of snow. She set it next to the bread. Her stomach growled. Face hot, she clutched at her waist.

He eased himself into a chair and gestured for her to sit. "When did you last eat?"

"At midday, when we stopped to change horses." She'd barely had time for a mouthful of tea and a biscuit before they were off again.

"Well, then, set to." He lowered his gaze to his food and spooned up the stew as if she no longer existed.

What a strange man. As seductive as a rake one moment, sullen the next. Fortunately, he ate delicately for one of the poorer classes, no slurping or wiping his mouth on his sleeve, or indeed any other unpleasant habits—and his voice sounded far too educated for a gamekeeper. For some reason, she couldn't dredge up a smidgeon of fear, but she really ought to know more about this man before she gave him her trust.

She gingerly tasted the gravy in her dish. "Mmmm. Delicious. For a man without a wife, you are remarkably well fed." She slanted him an enquiring glance.

Eyes narrowed, he stared back. "I manage." He poured ale into his mug and water into hers.

"Thank you." At least he wasn't plying her with strong drink. Which meant he probably wasn't interested in having his wicked way with her. Despite a tiny flash of disappointment, her shoulders loosened and she attacked the stew with relish.

They ate in silence like old friends. She finished every morsel.

"I like a woman with an appetite." Rising, he strolled to the window.

Butterflies took wing in her stomach, her pulse faltered. Did he intend a double meaning? And if not, why had such a thing occurred to her? Never had a man so inflamed her femininity. She ought to be ashamed of her responses. Instead, excitement buzzed in her veins.

He glanced out the window with a grimace of disgust. "If this keeps up, the drifts will be too deep for anyone to cross the moors for days."

"Surely not? Perhaps I should return to the carriage, in case the postilion returns. At the very least, I should leave a note as to where he can find me."

He spun to face her, a faint curl to his lip. "You expect me to believe he does not know?"

Perplexed, she wrinkled her brow. "How would he?"

His dark eyes searched her face as if he would read her mind. If he did, he'd be very surprised to find her thoughts focused on the width of his shoulders. Heat flushed her face.

"Perhaps because this is the only dwelling for miles?" He glowered. "With the cottage but a few yards off the road, whoever comes looking will find us."

Why would that make him angry? "I must accept your judgment, sir, but please leave a candle burning in the window. Only a chance sighting of your lantern led me here."

He opened his mouth as if to speak, then nodded abruptly. Silently, he did as she'd asked before stacking up the dirty plates and utensils.

"Let me wash the dishes. It is the least I can do." She'd often helped Millie in the kitchen before Father made his fortune, and surely a servant would expect to offer help.

Eyes widening, he cast her one of his devastating smiles. "Thank you. While you do that, I will make tea."

She managed to halt her exclamation of surprise at the welcome word of tea. A wry smile pulled at her lips. No doubt it would be a bitter brew of twice used leaves.

As they worked at their self-appointed tasks, awareness simmered in her veins. His cologne overpowered the smell of the soapy water. When he passed, his warmth heated her skin. Cold chills slithered down her back when he moved away. Did he feel her presence, too? Somehow she knew he did, just as she knew unspoken questions grew between them like a hedge.

The urge to tell him the truth tightened the muscles in her throat until drawing breath became an effort. She knew nothing about him. If she revealed too much, might he pretend an attraction to better his lot in life, like her suitors in London? The acknowledgement of the risk brought her trembling back from the brink.

Dishes dried and stowed in the cupboard, she returned to her place at the table. "Are you lonely living here?"

He handed her a cup, and slouched in his chair, stretching out his long legs. The firelight cast his profile into stern planes and hid his eyes in shadow. “I prefer my own company.”

“I'm sorry to impose on your solitude.”

A begrudging smile tugged the corner of his mouth. “I might change my mind, if my company turned out as young and pretty as you.” He flicked her a wicked glance.

Heat scalded her cheeks. Did he think she’d fished for compliments? “There is no need for flattery, sir. I am fully aware of the extent of my charms.” Her fortune.

He lazily surveyed her from head to toe, the way he had outside. She wanted to wriggle like a happy puppy being petted.

“You are right,” he said. “Your features are too strong to be called pretty, your eyes too frank to beguile. I apologize.”

She gritted her teeth. Did he have to be so brutally blunt?

Again he shot her that piercing stare as if to uncover her secrets. “I also apologize for not introducing myself. I am Gerrard Blackstone.” He paused as if awaiting her reaction.

“Mr. Blackstone, while our meeting was unexpected, I am pleased to make your acquaintance.”

He rested one booted foot on his knee and leaned back, a picture of ease. A smile played about his lips as if he'd decided to be amused instead of resentful. “How about a game of cards to wile away the time until bed?”

Bed. The word rolled off his tongue, delicious and terrifying all at once. Her woman’s core jolted. Flutters pulsed in her abdomen as an image of his hard body pressed against hers danced in her mind. Enough! If she continued like this, she wouldn't dare close her eyes. She hauled in a deep breath. A game of cards might be the very thing to keep her awake and clear her mind of its wayward thoughts. “If you wish.”

“What shall we wager?”

He wanted to gamble? If he'd recognized her, it would be a novel way for a man to relieve her of her fortune, one that didn't require a long-term commitment. She tried not to let her bitterness show. "What stakes did you have in mind?"

A reckless light entered his gaze. "There is no point in a wager without significant risk." He gestured to the bed. "How about my fur quilt for a kiss."

A kiss? The thought of his finely drawn mouth touching her lips sent her heart beating wildly. Her head spun as if she'd drunk too much champagne.

Great heavens. She didn't need protection from him, she needed locking up and the key thrown away. None of her suitors, not the money-hungry ones in London, or those she'd danced with at the local assemblies in Wadebridge, had so inflamed her senses. How could she defend herself against his charm when her unruly body played tricks with her emotions? She darted a glance at the mantel. "I'll play for your rifle," she said, adding swiftly at his surprised expression, "it would make a fine gift for my brother."

His eyelids lowered, hiding his thoughts. The pause dragged on. Her heart thundered. Had she pushed him too far? Did he suspect her motives?

"Very well. The rifle for a kiss."

Her stomach took a long slow roll. Idiot. He would never get a chance to kiss her. She would win. "I play Whist. And I must warn you I am very adept."

A typically arrogant male, he grunted his disbelief, already moving to a drawer in the cupboard. He pulled out a well-thumbed deck of cards and slapped them on the table. "Deal."

Gerrard watched her skilful shuffling with a mild sense of shock. The captain sharps he'd favored in his misspent youth would have been hard put to fault her technique. Must be that brother of hers. He couldn't resist staring at her face, surrounded by unruly curls and so obviously determined. Pretty didn't do her justice. It was far too milk-and-water a word. Goddess suited her strong features and statuesque body. Diana, the huntress, perhaps. And was he the hunted? Surprisingly, the idea didn't rankle—rather it stirred his blood.

Had he lost control of his mind as well as his body? Dressed in the first stare of fashion, she was no lady's maid, but he still hadn't discovered the truth of who she was and why she was here, and he couldn't afford to relax his guard.

In the morning, he needed to act quickly to be rid of her or find himself legshackled against his will. In the meantime, a kiss would teach her a lesson about wandering the countryside preying on lonely bachelors. "Is your family expecting your arrival tonight?"

She nibbled her lush bottom lip and he wondered how her mouth would feel on his skin, on his ear, his... He crushed the thought beneath a metaphorical boot and maintained an expression of polite enquiry.

"We have not spent a Christmas apart since I was a child."

The pain of regret stabbed him like a knife blade to the heart. He stiffened against the crushing emotion. He thought he'd squelched the anguish years ago. He laid down an ace of diamonds.

Moisture glistened in her eyes and she blinked it away, making a good attempt at a rueful smile. "But no, my arrival is unexpected." She played a two of spades. "Oh, no." She stared at the window.

"Now what is wrong?" Damn. He sounded as surly as a bear.

"All the gifts for my family were in the boot of the post-chaise. They will be ruined." She looked utterly distraught.

Gifts? The world ran mad at Christmas. "Do not fret, I will go for them at first light." He snapped his mouth shut in disbelief at what he'd said.

"You will?"

Unusual warmth blossomed in his chest at the delight in her eyes. He wanted to bask in the first smile of genuine pleasure he'd seen from her. Bloody fool. You can't wipe out your closest relatives and expect a reward. This was indeed Hell's torment.

"Your play." His voice sounded rough.

She laid her last card. A trump. "My trick."

The chit played well, better than he'd expected. But not good enough. He filled his tankard from the jug and waved it at her glass. "Would you like some?"

She pushed her hair off her face with a frown. "Do not think I will let you addle my brain with drink so you can win."

Her spirited reply forced a rusty laugh from his throat. "I play better in my cups."

"Highly unlikely." She tapped the table with a fingertip. "Your deal, sir."

Good God, she was bold. He couldn't think of another woman who didn't simper and bat their eyelashes when his gaze fell on them. Not one of them would have insisted he check on the missing post-boy, either. They'd be too busy complaining about their discomfort. Curse her unwanted allure. Perhaps getting to the bottom of her lies would cool his ardor.

"Why would a mistress, even a generous one, allow a servant to go home at such a busy time of year?"

Once more, a beautiful wash of pink tinged her cheeks and graceful neck. His body tightened, his blood ran hot. Lust. It couldn't be anything else. He certainly didn't need a permanent fixture in his life.

"Ummm," she murmured, her gaze fixed on her cards.

Here came the lie, the dissembling little witch. He kept his expression bland awaiting her next invention.

When she looked him straight in the face, her eyes darkened. "I could no longer stay." The pain in her sapphire gaze said she spoke the truth.

The knife twisted in his chest. "Why?"

Once more, she looked down and for a moment he thought she would refuse to speak. She played a ten of spades, leading high this time. "I made a mistake. I had to leave."

More secrets. God, he wanted to plumb them all. He put down a Knave. She topped it with a Queen. The king and Ace remained buried in the deck, then.

He played a low diamond. "Do not tell me you kissed the butler behind the pantry door?" Although he'd intended it as a joke, the thought of catching her in the dark, up against a wall, quickened his breath. Ribbons of fire streamed through his veins, awakening a part of him he'd sooner leave dormant.

He never lusted after women, not like this. Hell, now he was thoroughly aroused while she sat staring at her cards with cool aplomb. Was it her ploy to distract him during this deciding hand of their game with visions of heated encounters, hot kisses and slick bodies? The scent of roses wafted across the table. The echo of her soft derriere against his groin tightened his balls. It took all his willpower to drown a picture of her lush lips parting to his questing tongue and her full bosom crushed against his chest or cupped in his palm. He swallowed a groan of frustration.

She put down her next card with a little snap. "Worse than that."

What the hell could have happened? And why did she look so sad? An unwanted urge to protect tensed his muscles. He unclenched his jaw. "What?"

The hand holding her cards trembled. "I prefer not to discuss it."

Someone, some man, had hurt her badly, or she was a consummate actress bent on gaining his sympathy. Dammit, her problems weren't his concern.

He counted up the tricks. They were neck and neck, but he never lost at cards.

He swigged from his tankard to ease the fever in his brain, well not his brain exactly. He shuffled and dealt the cards with lightning speed, ignoring how her eyes widened.

The play went back and forth, each taking a trick in turn. Only the wind whistling in the eaves and the rattle of shutters disturbed the sound of their shallow breathing.

Beads of moisture sheened her upper lip. A log crashed into the grate. She jumped. Oh, she was nervous all right. Perhaps she guessed she'd met her match. Or maybe he'd come too close to the truth about her cross-country flight.

He got up and poked the fire. Flames gamboled among the ashes, taunting the inferno in his blood. He returned to the table and softened his voice. "Would it help to talk about what happened?"

"No. Maybe." She closed her eyes, dark lashes fanning on her cheekbone for a moment. "I lost my temper."

Relief flooded through him as visions of the worst things that could happen to a woman fled. "Is that all? I lose mine several times a day."

"I created a dreadful scene. He was a nobleman. I should have said nothing."

The visions returned with a vengeance. He wanted to slam his fist through the table or into this unknown man's chin. "You were right to speak up."

Clarissa shook her head at his snarl. She stared into his burning gaze. A man who lived in the wilderness, away from society's pressures, couldn't possibly understand the terrible consequences of her *faux pas*. She would never live it down. Her father would be so disappointed, not for himself, but for her. "I disgraced myself. Now I must tell my family."

"Are there many to tell?"

The hesitant glance and the faintest hint of longing in his voice took her by surprise. "Besides Papa, I have four brothers and three sisters. My mother died a year ago. As the oldest, I am supposed to set a good example. What about you? Does your family live nearby?"

In an instant, his gaze shuttered, closing her out.

Clearly, the revelations were to be all on one side. The silence dragged, heavy and awkward, as he stared at his cards. He slowly lifted his gaze to meet hers as if he'd come to some kind of momentous decision. He shook his head. "I have no family. I prefer it that way." The words came out low and tight as if slivers of glass lined his throat.

"Everyone has family unless..." She closed her mouth, horrified by his harsh expression.

"They died," he finished. His mouth turned down in a bitter line.

She jerked back in her seat, her mind whirling in shock. "All of them?"

He squeezed his eyes shut for a second. "My parents, my older brother and sister were killed on Christmas Eve in a carriage accident. Right where your chaise went off the road."

A shiver slid through her stomach at the bleakness in his eyes. "I am so sorry," she whispered.

Regret obvious in his expression, his gaze held hers for a long drawn out moment. Clarissa swallowed, longing to speak, too overcome by the sadness in his coal-black eyes to utter a word.

"It was all a very long time ago," he murmured. Seeming to shake off his sorrow the way a dog shakes off water, he smiled his beautiful smile. "I have never talked about it with anyone before." He placed his cards face down on the table. "Your trick."

"I beg your pardon?"

"You win." He shrugged. "You have the Ace of spades and three trumps above six. I have nothing but low cards. I cannot beat you."

Her hand exactly. Her jaw dropped. "How could you possibly know?"

"I did not cheat, if that is what you mean." He laughed. "I simply regained my wits." He held up a hand to still her questions. "No matter. I have very much enjoyed this evening, but it is time to bring it to a close" He rose and bowed in a most gentlemanly way before going to the hearth and taking down the rifle. "Here is your prize." He set it on the table before her.

The metal glowed dully with firelight. She sensed she had insulted his honor.

He pulled open the drawer in the cupboard and returned with ball and powder. "A weapon is of no use without these. I assume you know how to load it?"

"I do." She peered up at him with a tentative smile. "The peril of younger brothers."

Gerrard heard the pride in her voice when she spoke of her family and knew they would embrace her, no matter what she'd done. He wished for a chance to seek forgiveness. For him it was far too late.

"Bed for me," he said. A cold lonely bed. He'd never thought of it that way before. He had his estates, his life's work, and a distant cousin who would make a fine earl one day. He didn't want the responsibility that went with a wife and family. At least, until today, he hadn't thought he did. No other woman had him thinking about children and firesides and warmth.

He buried his regret. He didn't deserve a family.

Startled out of his reverie by her rigidity, he realized her gaze remained fixed on the cot in the corner. "My bed is in the loft," he said.

"Oh," she breathed.

"I assume you have all you need," he nodded at her valise. "There is water in the kettle for washing."

She nodded, her lovely eyes huge and wary.

Was there anything he could do to assure her of her safety besides the rifle? "Do not worry that I will disturb you. It has been a long hard day, and once asleep it would take the crack of doom to wake me. I hope my snores do not interrupt your rest."

The smile of relief lighting her beautiful countenance warmed the ice protecting his soul. His chest ached.

He forced steadiness into his voice. "Good night, Miss Albany." He climbed the ladder and dropped the trapdoor with a resounding bang. Another sleepless

Christmas Eve and this time he mustn't allow the nightmares to invade his rest. Definitely the torment of the damned.

Clarissa tried not to look up as she scrabbled for her nightdress, tried not to imagine the powerful male above stripping to his skin. He certainly hadn't taken a nightshirt with him. Stupid. Male servants slept in their shirts for the most part. Any good housekeeper knew that. Still, he'd peel the tight buckskins off those beautifully muscled thighs and well-formed calves.

As if to prod her imagination, a boot thudded on the ceiling above her head. Then the second. She swallowed. This man labored for a living, not like the prancing popinjays she'd met and rebuffed in London. Well, they'd paid her in kind and now her reputation was in tatters. The sting of humiliation squeezed at her heart.

What would it have been like to kiss him, had she lost the game? His body had been hard against her back when she crashed into him like some awkward green girl, his hold firm, strong, yet incredibly gentle. A little flutter, full of wicked pleasure pulsed deep inside. Her body ignited. She'd felt a stir of feminine excitement before, but never with such undeniable force.

Prickles skittered down her spine. What on earth was wrong with her? Was it knowing this might be her last chance to attract a man making her feel so wanton? She ought to be ashamed of herself. In haste, she undid the ribbon at her neck, unhooked the fastenings and let the gown fall to her feet. After a quick wash, she unlaced her stays, pulled her nightrail over her head and leaped into bed. His bed.

She turned on her side. Inhaled the scent of bay and an earthy scent she couldn't name that teased her senses. Essence of Gerrard? She rolled on her back and stared at the flame-shadowed ceiling. Somewhere up there he slept. She strained to hear his promised snores, or footsteps on the ladder. Dash it, she'd forgotten to load the rifle.

She slid out of bed, shivering at the wind's chilly

fingers reaching through every nook and cranny. She loaded the gun beside the candle in the window. The click of the lock seemed to echo around the room. She held her breath. Had he heard? Would her lack of trust cause him more pain than she already sensed in those deep dark eyes?

On the table sat the remains of their game, her discarded hand face up, his face down. Imagine. He'd held nothing but low cards and not one of the high trumps had been played. Her teeth gripped her lip painfully. Why look? She'd won.

Fingers trembling, she flipped his cards.

Ace of hearts, King of hearts, Knave of hearts. She stared, numb, disbelieving. He'd won. Fair and square.

Blood pounded in her temples. She daggered a glance at the ceiling, imagined tearing him limb from limb. The shadows in those fathomless eyes had been the fear he might have to kiss her, not pain.

He owed her a kiss.

She picked up the rifle. Silent, she mounted the ladder. At the top, she flung back the trapdoor and ran up the last few steps to land on her knees beside a blanket laid out on straw.

A candle on an overhead beam wavered. "What the devil," he yelled, starting up, his hair tousled, his face sculpted granite.

She pointed the rifle between his eyes. "You won."

His mouth gaped. "What?" He came up on his knees, staring at her weapon. "Are you mad?"

She let her gaze wander his length. As she suspected, he wore nothing but his shirt. She glimpsed dark curling hair at the open neck and her mouth dried. "Why did you not wish to kiss me?" She hated the shake in her voice.

Enough heat to scorch her face flared in his eyes. He sat back on his heels and stretched out a hand. "Give me that gun before someone gets hurt. Have you no sense of propriety? No wonder you had to flee London."

So that's what he thought of her. "I refuse to leave without an explanation."

He blew out a sigh. "I will explain, but not with a rifle pointed at my head."

"Well, I hardly need it for protection." Nor did she really want to shoot the man. She uncocked the weapon and slid it across the rough planked floor. Her body trembled with anticipation, definitely not fear, as she scrambled to his makeshift bed. She plunked down beside him crossed legged and glared. "Well?"

"You want a kiss?" He sounded almost angry. He cupped her face in both hands. His wonderful mouth descended on hers, hard at first, but instantly softening to warm, soft, teasing. A shiver ran all the way to her toes. She moaned and parted her lips. His tongue traced the inside of her lower lip, slid into her mouth, swept her palate, entwined with her tongue and withdrew.

He groaned and pulled away. "Damn. I knew you would be too powerful to resist"

She flung her arms around his neck. "I don't care." Having decided not to sell herself on the marriage mart, she had to know what it would be like to be kissed properly, or better yet, to be thoroughly loved by a man who knew nothing about her wealth or position, even if she never saw him again. She nuzzled his neck, found his ear, bit the lobe. He tasted like smoke and fresh air and musky male.

He pushed her away, held her at arm's length, searching her face with smoldering eyes.

She drowned in his question, saw the promise, the heat, the desire. Her heart thundered, her pulse tripped and galloped until the room spun away leaving his face in the center of her vision.

"Young lady, you are taking a risk. Only one thing will quench this fire." His voice sounded rough.

She swallowed. "I know." At least, she thought she did.

His mouth descended, consumed, heated, demanding. She melted against him, her limbs liquid, her heart full to bursting, her body humming with pleasure and want.

Cradling her against his chest, he lowered her to the blanket. One heavy thigh moved across hers, a pleasurable weight, but not close enough. She arched against it, building a sweet ache between her thighs.

His hand skimmed her jaw, slid down her throat, came to rest on her breast. Her nipple tightened beneath his gentle touch. Unutterable desire streaked to her core. She cried out. He caught the sound in his mouth.

She ran her hands over shoulders made of steel and covered in satin, dipped into the shirt open at his beautiful throat, raked through the curls on his chest, finding his flat nipple, running her sensitive palm over the tight little nub.

In-drawn breath hissed through his teeth. Need shot to her core, ratcheting her tension.

"Witch," he muttered, tickling her lips. "Take this off." He tugged at her nightrail.

She pulled it over her head. "Devil. Take off your shirt." He complied instantly and lay alongside her, his palm cupping the place between her thighs. She shuddered in delight, raised her hips to grant access, seeking to satisfy primal hunger. He pressed hard, circled his hand.

Her whole being centered on that one place, on the need he evoked with cunning flicks of his nimble fingers. Moisture slicked her throbbing swollen female flesh as a finger slid inside.

"Do you like that?" he asked.

"Yes!"

"You want more." Not a question. His voice sounded rough, yet triumphant.

She parted her thighs, instinct overriding thought.

He eased between her legs, the rigid length of something hot and hard against her entrance pushing, stretching, tormenting her with the promise of heaven on earth. A little hiss of pleasure grazed her cheek and a small secret smile curved her lips. She pleased him.

"Ready, sweetling?"

Whatever it was, she wanted it before she expired with need. "Hurry," she whispered and closed her eyes, focusing on the source of her pleasure.

"Look at me. I want to see your beautiful eyes, Clary."

She gazed into his tortured face as he thrust his hips forward. A pinch of pain, a squeak she couldn't hold back, and then utter stillness. Agony twisted his features, his jaw set hard. "I do not believe it," he growled.

"A Christmas gift for you," she murmured.

"Perhaps I like Christmas better than I thought," he managed on a hard fought exhalation. "Are you all right? Do you want me to stop?"

She wriggled, felt the abrasion deep inside and tightened her muscles in response to the stab of desire. "I am fine," she said with a feeling of power at his soft groan.

"Thank God," he breathed. He pushed slowly inside her, then withdrew.

She moaned her disappointment.

"Slowly, love," he said moving forward, deepening his thrust, tilting his hips until she couldn't bear the spasms of pleasure without crying out. "The last thing I want is to win this race."

Once more, he eased back, only this time she was ready for his onslaught.

She drifted, melted, bit his shoulder to urge him on until he thrust harder, faster. She sucked his bottom lip until his tongue plundered her mouth and his hands played with her breasts. Her body vibrated like an overstretched bow. She moaned her need.

"My God, I hope you are ready," he gasped. "I cannot hold back."

He pounded into her, flesh slapping hot wet flesh. Blackness loomed agonizingly close. She drew back, afraid.

"No," he groaned. "Come with me. You must fly with me."

She entrusted herself to him, tipped over, fell, then flew apart into a thousand heated pieces, falling like burning embers to land softly like hot ash on an emerald lawn in sunlight.

"Oh," she breathed and felt him shudder, saw his muscles strain, his neck cord. He shouted, deep and feral, yet his voice held a joy that shimmered through her body and warmed her heart.

He collapsed, rolling to one side, pulling her close to his sweat-slicked body, his heart thundering against her ribs. "Definitely a goddess," he murmured against her temple. "I think I am in love."

"I know I am," she managed to whisper before drifting away on a heated ocean of bliss.

Sunlight streamed through a small gable-end window. Something stirred at her back. Gerrard. The stranger who said he loved her.

She rolled over and gazed into his eyes.

"Good morning," he said, smiling with a gentleness she'd never thought to see in such a harsh and surly man. He smoothed her hair back from her face. "How are you feeling?"

"Wonderful," she said and stroked his jaw, feeling the prickles of rough stubble that shadowed his cheek against her palm, inhaling the scent of man and lovemaking. "Happy Christmas."

He rolled on his back, taking her with him, nestling her head against his shoulder. "Christmas," he breathed, wonder in his tone. "I never wanted to hear those words again."

"The loss of your family hurt you deeply."

"I was six. I wanted them home for the holiday. I wished on a star, threw pennies down the well and when my tutor said they would never come because of the parties in London, I pretended an illness. The tutor sent for them." He planted a kiss on her temple and blew out a breath. "I tricked them. The next day my whole family was gone because of me."

She frowned "If you wrote to them the day before, they could not possibly have received the letter before they left. It takes three days to get here in good weather. I know that for a fact."

He raised himself up on his elbow and stared down at her, his eyes full of storms. "My mind knows it, but not my heart." His voice cracked. "Why was I not with them?"

She pulled his head down so she could brush her lips against his. "Do you not think they are happy knowing you are here to continue their hopes for the future of their family?"

"I will never have another family. I do not deserve one"

Her heart clenched at the bleakness in his face. She shook her head. "Would you want a child of yours to be alone all his life?"

His expression lightened. "No. I would not want that." He laid a warm palm against her cheek. "I love your sense of belonging, the way you see these family things so clearly. And I adore your honesty. Coming up here to pay your debt of a kiss instead of saying nothing."

A tickle of guilt stirred in her chest, her heart thumped against her ribs. "I have not been entirely truthful. My name is Clarissa Trevethon. Father is a baronet and very rich."

He propped himself up on one elbow. "Trevethon? You jest."

She shook her head. "No. Does the fact I have a large dowry trouble you?"

He raised a knee, rested one strong forearm on it. Mischief lurked in the depths of his eyes. "Would it bother you to know this is not my house? I own it, but do not live here. My name is Gerrard Algernon Blackstone, fifth earl of Dart."

"The Earl of Dart?" She punched his shoulder. "Why did you let me think you were a gamekeeper or some sort of poacher?"

"I thought you were another matchmaking miss out to catch herself a rich husband." He shrugged. "Why your pretence?"

"I went to London to find a titled husband."

He lifted his head and looked down at her, eyebrows lifted. "Aha. I was right."

"Not really. I found I did not like the London sycophants who chased me for my fortune. And the rest treated me like some sort of pariah." She swallowed. "I heard my most ardent suitor mocking my father for trading his plebeian daughter for a place in society. My father would never do such a thing." She bit her lip. "I slapped his face. Everyone blamed me for the scandal and I ran home like a coward."

He enfolded her in protective arms. "He did not deserve you. But that does not explain why you told me a false name."

The gesture filled her with comforting warmth. She nuzzled into his shoulder. "I thought you might also find my wealth a temptation. Father will be so upset. I ruined my chance of finding a husband and I always wanted a tribe of children."

"With blue eyes," he murmured. "Marry me, Clarissa? Help me be a family again."

Her heart pattered against her ribs. He'd said he loved her, but she hadn't dared expect a proposal. "Yes," she whispered as a church bell peeled somewhere in the distance.

"Happy Christmas, my darling," he murmured into her hair. "And if it pleases you, I will drive you home to your family in my carriage after breakfast and you can deliver your presents. Do you think they will approve?"

"They are sure to," she said, giddy with her most beautiful Christmas morning ever.

He kissed her, thoroughly, emptying her mind and filling her body with passion. "Do we have to wait until after we are married?" he asked politely.

She rolled him on his back and straddled his hips. "Oh, no," she said, her heart filled with melting and sweet desire tingling and burning where hot flesh met.

"Then let this be my gift to you." He lifted her hips and slid her down his hard length. "And you will receive it for Christmas every year for the rest of your life, if you will allow, my lady."

Desire built to need. "Oh, believe me, I will," she said on a groan of pleasure.

Be sure to check out Michele's website
http://www.micheleannyoung.com

Ballou's Christmas Wish

by Keelia Greer

"Behave, Ballou. Stay inside until we reach the pet food aisle." Melody Barton stroked the silky head of her West Highland white terrier then pulled the sides of the leather tote bag higher before entering the Big Tex grocery store. She needed a Christmas miracle. Her heart longed for the right man. Would this year be the one where her Christmas wish came true?

The automatic doors swished open, blasting her with heated air. The sound of Bing Crosby's *White Christmas*, the excited chatter of children and bright decorations sparkled in all directions--the perfect distraction for one curious little doggie.

Melody tugged a cart from the row and placed the bag containing her eight month old puppy, Ballou, on the seat reserved for children. Leaning forward she reached inside for a quick pat on his head. "Good boy," she whispered.

She wove through the crowd making quick work of arriving at the dog product aisle. Wouldn't you know Ballou's favorite—Woofies—were on the top shelf. She pushed aside a few off-brand cans of food to make a toehold on the shelf. *What demented person puts an eight-pound bag of dog cookies so high you have to climb to reach them?*

Placing her foot on the shelf, she grasped the metal above her head. Her thigh high skirt inched higher. Terrific. She could see the headlines—"*Woman Falls, Exposing and Busting Her Ass.*" Of course, she had to wear the shortest item of clothing she owned today. Melody suppressed a groan and prayed no one would choose this moment to come around the corner.

"Here, let me help you." A man's Welsh accent slid over her like warm honey drizzled over a biscuit. His voice reminded her of the days she'd spent in Wales as a foreign exchange student.

Damn and double damn. A pair of strong hands encircled her waist and eased her from her perch.

"Thank you." Hard muscle flexed beneath her palms causing her tummy to flip with delight.

He released her and smiled, then reached for the large bag of Woofies and plopped it into the basket right behind Ballou. Warm chocolate brown eyes, golden brown hair that brushed his collar, and an athletic body all made for a tempting package. He made making a Christmas wish worthwhile. Oh, would she like to have *him* for Christmas! One tiny quick prayer sent to Saint Nicholas.

What's wrong with me? I don't think about men like this. Melody tried not to melt into a mushy pile at his feet.

"I see you brought your friend." He raised a brow and the beginnings of a smile tipped his mouth.

As Melody moved to pull the edges of the leather bag higher, she edged closer and whispered, "The store manager isn't fond of dogs, so I have to hide Ballou."

He held out his hand. "Jorin Griffin. I've recently relocated from Snowdon, Wales."

"Melody Barton. Welcome to Texas. You're in for quite a shock if you're expecting a white Christmas in Houston." The sound of plastic ripping and an excited yip pulled her attention back to the shopping cart.

"Ballou! How could you?" Her Westie, nose deep in Woofies crunched away. Melody heard the rumble of laughter behind her. She gently lifted the eight-month old dog and shoved the bag aside.

"It's nice to see a dog that likes my product so much."

Melody gasped. His product? Wait a minute. This was *the* Jorin Griffin?

She had seen him and his pup, Bonnie, on the Woofies commercials. Mercy, the man looked even better in person. She turned to see the store manager, Mr. Whipple, rushing toward her. "Oh no. I'm in trouble now."

"I told you not to bring that animal into my store!" The manager shook his finger at her, then pushed his sliding spectacles back onto his beak-like nose.

Jorin moved to Melody's side holding out a ten-dollar bill. "Here, sir. The dog hasn't caused any serious trouble, just overeager for a few treats."

Mr. Whipple stuck his pointy nose in the air and took the money. "Get that beast out of my store." He turned and the small crowd that had gathered around parted for him.

"My little dog is not a beast, you old geezer," Melody muttered under her breath to the man's retreating form. Ballou's low growl elicited snickers from the dispersing group.

"Shhh." She made her way to the cashier, with Jorin close behind her. "Hi Dee Ann. Could you tape this for me? Ballou couldn't wait."

"Sure, Melody." The cashier quickly secured the treats.

Mr. Whipple stomped up, shoved the ten-dollar bill at the cashier and glared at Melody.

She ignored the store manager, turned to the handsome man beside her and reached into her purse to reimburse her knight-in-shining-armor. "Mr. Griffin, there's a pet-friendly coffee shop close to here. Would you care to join me after I pay for Ballou's treats?"

He closed her hand on the money. "Keep your money, my lovely. I would love to join you at the coffee house."

Jorin paid for his purchases and took the bag of Woofies from her cart. He followed her into the crisp December evening.

She tugged the edges of the tote close over Ballou to shelter him from the wind. Melody couldn't help but notice quite a few women stared in admiration at her companion. A little shiver of excitement shimmied through her.

She pushed a button on the key ring to open the door of her Xterra.

Jorin placed the dog cookies on the floorboard. "I'm looking forward to our visit, my lovely."

Melody secured an excited Ballou in his harness, then drove the three blocks and pulled into the parking lot of Coffee, Pastries and Pets. She eased into a slot by the front door. *Of all people for me to meet in the grocery with my butt in the air—the owner of Woofies.*

Jorin waited for her on the sidewalk, then escorted her inside.

"Hi, Cassie. Is it okay to let Ballou into the play area?"

"Go ahead, Melody. It's fine."

Melody didn't miss the teen eyeing the handsome Welshman. She released the leash and Ballou ran into the canine quarters.

"Mr. Griffin, I'm buying. You rescued me twice. Once from the Woofies bag. The second time from the dog-hating store manager."

They placed their orders and Jorin carried the tray to a corner table next to the pet corral.

"Before we go any further, please call me Jorin."

"Okay. Call me Melody." She sipped her mocha latte. "Are you always a knight-in-shining armor?"

"Truth be told, I haven't found anyone interesting enough to rescue until now."

She raised her latte and touched his arm. "I'm honored, Jorin." *I can't believe this. I'm flirting with a man I don't even know.*

"I'd like to stay in touch, Melody. Please feel free to call me anytime you need a knight-in-shining armor." He pulled a business card from his pocket and handed it to her.

"I'd love to." She placed his card in the zipper pocket of her tote.

Melody discovered she and Jorin had much in common. Celtic folk music, Italian cuisine and Westies. When she learned he admired the same qualities in people, her estimation of his character rose. Honesty and trust.

He glanced at his watch. "Melody, I've had a great time with you and Ballou, but I have an early conference in the morning."

She rose and picked up Ballou, who lunged for Jorin. "I've never seen him do that to anyone before. I think he likes you."

"Hey, fella." He bent and scratched the pup's ears. "I'll carry him to your vehicle."

Melody followed her knight. Her knight? *I've only just met the man.* But her heart warmed at the thought. She unlocked the doors and placed her purse on the driver's seat.

Jorin handed her Ballou. She secured the yawning dog. Her fingers scrambled inside the leather bag for a moment. She retrieved her business card holder, opened it and handed him her information.

"Thank you. I was about to ask you for your number." He read the inscription and smiled. "Can PR Designs take on another client? I've got a new project you might be interested in."

"I arrive at the office around seven in the morning. We can discuss it after your conference." She turned and rested her hand on his well-toned forearm. "Thank you again for saving me today." Liquid heat as hot as a Texas summer raced through her at the innocent touch.

"My pleasure. We shall talk on the morrow."

She removed her hand and walked to the driver's side of the SUV.

All the way home, Jorin Griffin occupied her thoughts.

Melody hefted a sleeping Ballou to his bed in her room. In a few more months, she wouldn't be able to carry him. She went back out for the Woofies and the tote bag.

She placed the treats onto the kitchen counter and a wonderful idea formed. Depending on the outcome of tomorrow's business discussion, she would invite Jorin to dinner. After all, he needed to experience good Texas hospitality and a home cooked meal. The man was here from another country for heaven's sake, away from family and possibly alone for the holiday. No one needed to be alone on Christmas.

She wasn't fooling herself, she wanted to see Jorin again.

What she couldn't explain was the electrical surge of heat when she'd touched him earlier. It had never happened before. Did it mean something? Too tired to think anymore, she readied for bed.

Ballou stretched on his pillow. *Mom Melody and Mr. Jorin are perfect for each other. He smelled of Woofies and a lady canine. The best scents to my way of thinking. A few well-placed sniffs and I know the personality of a human. The lad's a keeper and I want to meet his dog friend, too. I hope it's the beautiful Bonnie from the Woofies commercials.*

The next day Melody dressed in her best teal suit. She zipped the form fitting skirt, then slid a matching silk tank over her head. She studied her reflection one last time before removing the matching jacket from the hanger and laying it across the bed. Running a brush through her hair, thoughts of seeing him again filled her with excitement. She wanted to look her best in case Jorin wanted a face-to-face meeting.

Melody sighed as she twisted her hair into a chignon. Poking the decorative pins in, she admitted she wanted to see Jorin in more than a business capacity. How had the man captivated her in such a short time?

Ballou ran to the doorway, stopped and barked.

"I know you need your good morning cookie." Melody turned, scooped up the coat and made her way to the kitchen.

"Woof!"

Draping her jacket on the kitchen chair, she moved to the counter and grabbed the Woofies bag. She tugged on the tape until there was enough room for her fingers to wiggle in and snag a cookie.

"Here, boy." She stroked his silky fur. "I'm talking to Jorin today and plan on inviting him to dinner."

Ballou wagged his tail and crunched.

"So, you think this is a good idea?" Melody reached for the wiggly dog to give him his goodbye hug. "It's time for you to settle down. I have to go to work. Be a good boy."

As the owner of a graphics company, PR Designs, Melody loved being her own boss and having the creative freedom to bring her visions to life. Her first order of business—a strong, steaming mug of coffee.

A few minutes after seven, her private line rang.

"Good morning, Melody. Would you meet me for lunch? I'll bring the campaign documents I mentioned for you to review."

"Great! We can meet at Panera Bread a block from my office. You won't have trouble finding it. They have great food and a warm atmosphere. Is noon good for you?"

At twelve sharp, Melody stood in line and waved to Jorin when she spied his handsome face. She placed her order and took her number from the employee. When he stepped beside her the spicy scent of him made everything else recede into the background.

Grateful for a small reprieve, she walked to the beverage counter, sugared her iced tea, then found them a booth in the corner. She placed the laminated card in the metal holder.

Joining her, Jorin pointed to his drink. "This is my first time to try sweet tea, as you call it."

Melody laughed. "I think it's an acquired taste."

He took a tentative sip. "It's good."

The orders arrived and Melody took a bite of her turkey on asiago cheese bread. She swallowed and wiped the corners of her mouth. "What is the project you wanted to tell me about?"

"My company needs a graphics and marketing firm with vision. I've already been to your website and contacted some of the businesses you've worked with. All stated they were happy with the work you've done for them. Would you consider taking Woofies, Inc. as a client?" He pulled a packet from his briefcase and handed it to her.

"I'd be delighted, Jorin. PR Designs would be thrilled to work with you and Woofies, Inc."

The remainder of their lunch passed with friendly chatter.

That evening Melody decided she felt comfortable enough with Jorin to invite him to dinner.

She slipped off her shoes and went to feed Ballou before taking a hot shower. Melody wanted to be relaxed and refreshed when she phoned the sexy Welshman this evening. She'd hated to see their wonderful lunch this afternoon end.

Melody punched in the number and closed her eyes as his smooth, sexy voice washed over her.

"I was hoping you would call, my lovely."

"If you don't have any plans for tomorrow, would you like to come over for dinner at my house?"

Deep soft laughter floated through the line. "I'd love to. May I bring my Westie, Bonnie? I'm sure she would love to meet Ballou."

"We'd love to meet Bonnie, Jorin. Around six then?" Warmth flowed through her. Yes, she'd made the right decision in calling.

She gave Ballou a good boy cookie for not barking at the animals on the television and went to heat up her microwave dinner. Strange, but Ballou never barked at Bonnie on the Woofies commercial—just stared at her. Possibly a case of puppy-love.

Chili simmered on the stove, filling the kitchen with a rich, spicy aroma. Melody wanted everything about tonight to be perfect.

She showered and changed into a dark plum sweater dress and black high-heel boots. With a spritz of her favorite fragrance and a Victorian-style clip to hold her hair back, she was finished.

The chime from the doorbell echoed and Melody took a deep breath before opening the door.

"Hi, come on in." She stepped aside to let Jorin and Bonnie inside. "Oh, she's a puppy, too. Please, sit down. Dinner will be ready in just a minute."

Ballou pranced into the room and paused in front of Jorin.

"Hi, Ballou. This is Bonnie." He bent and placed her nose-to-nose with Ballou.

Tails wagged with excited yips.

Jorin released Bonnie and followed Melody into the kitchen.

She ladled the chili into deep bowls and placed them on the table. "Please, sit down. I'll get our drinks." Melody returned with two ice-cold beers and handed him a longneck bottle. "You can't eat Texas chili without the beer."

The pounding of little paws stopped Melody from sitting in her chair. Ballou ran and slid on the kitchen floor executing a perfect spin.

"Ballou, you have a guest. Behave." She rose from the chair and called Bonnie. "Here girl, this water bowl is for you." Melody placed the container next to Ballou's dish.

Melody sat and picked up her beer. Jorin raised his in salute.

"To a most gracious lady. Thank you for welcoming us."

"To a man with enough manners to help a lady in distress." The bottles clinked.

"Cheers to that, my lovely."

Jorin was everything she'd dreamed of. She wondered if he could possibly be the answer to her Christmas wish. Should she take a chance if the opportunity for more than friendship presented itself? *How can I be thinking like this, we just met?*

She refocused and tasted the chili, relieved to find the recipe turned out perfect. "I looked over the information you gave me this afternoon. The project sounds fun and exciting. I'm looking forward to being a part of it."

An easy smile touched the corners of his mouth. "I hoped my presentation would catch your interest." Jorin took his dish to the sink and rinsed out his bowl. "You're a wonderful cook, Melody. Thank you."

"Here let me do that for you..."

Boom. Boom. Boom.

She looked at him and placed the dishes in the sink. Who was pounding on her front door? She crossed the room and opened the heavy oak panel, but left the chain lock attached. "May I help you?" She asked the blonde-haired woman.

A cultured, sultry voice carried across the room. "Jorin, are you in there?"

Melody thought she heard Jorin mutter something behind her like 'bloody witch.' She looked at him and found a frown marred his handsome face.

She opened the door, but barred the rude woman's entrance. The chili she'd eaten churned and lay heavy in her stomach. "Who are you?"

Ballou trotted up beside her and released a menacing growl.

Jorin moved behind Melody and placed his hand on her shoulder. "Glenys, what in the bloody hell are you doing here in Texas? I told you to stay away from me."

A long claw-like fingernail poked through the doorway. "We are supposed to be making plans for our baby and our wedding."

The bottom fell out of Melody's stomach. Baby? Wedding? Clearly Jorin neglected to mention a few major details.

"Glenys, don't spout nonsense. What are you blethering about?"

Jorin's hand trembled on her shoulder while the other fisted at his side. Melody wanted to cry as the excitement of the promise of a budding relationship withered inside her. She'd finally found a man she felt comfortable with and wanted to see again, only to have another woman lay claim to him.

"Make no mistake—we will be married, Jorin. By the way, I just found out I'm pregnant. I'm staying at Silver Falls Hotel and Resort." Glenys glared at Melody before she turned and left.

Ballou barked at the retreating figure.

Jorin pushed the door closed. "I'm so sorry, Melody. I've known and worked with Glenys for years. Her husband died and left her deep in debt. I offered her a position last year to help her get back on her feet. She's always been a bit conceited. Then a few months ago, I suspected Glenys of embezzling funds from my company and began legal action against her. This is also the first I've heard of the possibility of her being pregnant." He turned to the coat stand and grabbed his leather jacket. "I'd better go."

"Is the baby yours?" Dread squeezed her.

"No." Obviously changing his mind about leaving, he tossed the leather jacket onto the sofa. Moving to the ottoman, he sat and ran his fingers through his hair. "Glenys used to be my executive assistant. Last month she drugged my drink on a flight back to Wales. From all appearances, we had sex, but damn, I don't remember anything. My marketing director, Charles, was there as well, but he refused to comment on the situation saying he didn't see anything clearly because of faulty contact lenses. I also suspect him of embezzling funds. So much for honesty and trust."

"So, there's a chance she's lying." Melody wanted desperately to believe him, but her ex-husband had an affair with her best friend, Cindie and got her pregnant. Then the demented woman had stalked her for months. Not quite the same scenario, but close enough she didn't want to get involved.

Pain clutched her heart. "I'm sorry, Jorin. Under the circumstances, I think we need to refrain from seeing each other until we learn the truth." Melody wanted to scream at the injustice of the situation, but God help the woman chasing Jorin if she were lying. Melody could dish out some Texas whoop-ass when the situation called for it.

A whimper at her feet caught her attention. Ballou and Bonnie were nuzzling each other. Damn it all to hell, she hated this.

Melody dropped to her knees and hugged both dogs. "Oh babies, I'm so sorry." She kissed the top of Ballou's head, then Bonnie's.

Jorin released a frustrated sigh. "I understand your decision, Melody. But I don't like it." He jammed his arms into the jacket. "I know myself. I don't believe anything happened."

"I know, but I need time to sort this out. I'll call you." She picked up Bonnie and handed her to Jorin.

With a bruised heart, Melody let him and his sweet dog out.

Ballou whined and ran down the hallway into the bedroom. He plopped on his pillow, laid his head on his front paws. *I can't lose Bonnie. She's my Christmas wish. I must find a way to bring Melody and Jorin back together. But how? Maybe if I don't eat much and cry, Melody will ask him to bring Bonnie over.*

Melody leaned against the doorframe. "Ballou, I know you're upset. I am, too. But until Jorin gets everything straightened out, I simply can't see him. I can't go through a situation like that again. It would hurt too much."

Ballou released a forlorn howl and turned on his pillow, giving Melody his back.

One week later

Melody paced and twirled the ends of her hair. On the third ring, he answered. "Jorin, this is Melody. Can you bring Bonnie over? Ballou is barely eating and all he does is cry."

"Of course. We'll leave straight away."

"Thank you."

Melody missed the sound of Jorin's voice. Tears burned and threatened to fall as she hung up the receiver. Truth be told, she hadn't been eating much either.

In the master bathroom, she checked her appearance. Ewww. Dang, she didn't want to scare him away. A few quick strokes of the hairbrush, a twist of her unruly curls and a dark green clip helped immensely. A few minutes later, the doorbell rang and her heart beat faster.

I shouldn't get my hopes up.

She peeked out the curtain to be sure it was Jorin, then opened the door.

Bonnie barked and wiggled in his arms. He placed the spirited puppy on the floor in front of a happy Ballou.

"Come in."

"I've missed you, my lovely."

Her heart leapt at his words. She heard the hurt and longing in his voice. She shut the door and Jorin followed her to the kitchen. "Want some coffee? I need at least half a pot to function." Especially since sleep had eluded her the past week.

"Yes, I could use a cup."

As she poured the dark brew into large mugs and handed him one, she noticed Jorin looked strained and tired. "Are there any new developments in our situation?"

Jorin's lips quirked into a half smile. *Oh no, had he heard her slip and say 'our'?*

"Yes. Just before you called, my attorney phoned. Glenys did have an accomplice in the Wales office. I was right about my former marketing director, Charles MacInnes. We had a bloody row before I left Wales and Charles confessed when my solicitor appeared. The pair is in custody and legal proceedings for the embezzling have begun. No pregnancy. No wedding. All lies."

Melody rose and stood in front of the man who'd come to mean so much to her in such a short time. She cupped his face in her hands. "Stay with me. Don't leave."

He tugged her onto his lap and brought his lips to hers. She moaned and savored the taste of him. Melody wrapped her arms around his neck and wiggled her hips.

"Do you think our wee doggies need a longer visit?" he murmured against her neck.

"Yes, oh yes." Melody reveled in the feel of his hands sliding up and down her back in a slow hypnotic rhythm.

"Do you want me Melody?" Jorin brushed a loose strand of hair from her eyes.

"More than you know." She kissed a trail down the side of his neck while her hand moved to the waistband of his jeans and stroked his hard length.

Jorin shifted Melody into his arms and carried her down the hallway. "Which is your room?"

"The door at the end of the hallway," she said between kisses and nips.

Jorin kicked the door closed and laid her on the bed. "Are you sure you want this? I won't be able to stop if I touch you again."

Melody brushed her lips against his and reached to unbutton his denims in answer to his question.

A groan escaped and he quickly discarded his clothes. "Let me undress you, my lovely." He licked and nibbled as he removed each item of clothing.

Melody arched into his touch, never having felt so hot and needy in all her life. When he slid his hand between her legs, she gasped.

"I need you now, Jorin." She wrapped her legs around his waist.

"Don't rush this, my love," he whispered as he placed kisses along the curve of her neck. "It's too soon. You are not ready yet, but will be soon." He smiled and lowered his lips to her mouth.

When neither could bear the sweet torture any longer, he eased inside and moved. The feel of his flesh against hers, the increase of his thrusts brought her closer to release.

She reached her moment of pure bliss, a heartbeat after Jorin. Her heart whispered he was the answer to her heart's plea.

"That was incredible." Melody sighed as she trailed her fingertips along his jaw.

He ran his thumb along the edge of her lips. "After we work on the new Woofies campaign, I'd like us to take a trip to Wales. I want you to meet my family."

"That would be wonderful, Jorin. Ballou, too?"

"Yes, my lovely, Ballou can come, too. Bonnie would never forgive me if he didn't. She refused to eat and cried the whole time, just as Ballou. I do believe our pups have fallen in love." He kissed her neck and lifted himself onto his elbow. "The master is following the lead of his Westie. I know we've only seen each other a short time, but Melody Barton, I've fallen in love with you."

"I love you too, Jorin. I kept trying to tell myself the same thing—we've only known each other a short while. It's too soon. It couldn't be real. But my heart knew the truth."

He leaned over, kissed the top of her head. "I have to leave right now. My VP in Wales will be contacting me for a video conference. Then I have a board meeting with our Texas stockholders. It will be late by the time I'm finished or I'd suggest we meet later on."

In no time, he was dressed. "I'll call you tomorrow morning and we can talk of housing arrangements. Make no mistake, Melody, I want you to be my wife."

Melody bounced on the mattress to her feet and threw her arms around his neck. "Yes, yes, yes!"

Ballou and Bonnie ran into the room barking and wagging their tails.

Melody grabbed her robe from the chair beside the bed and put it on.

"Come on, Bonnie. You can see Ballou tomorrow. And the day after, and the day after that. Forever!" Jorin scooped the puppy into his arms.

Melody followed Jorin with Ballou at her heels. At the front door, he kissed her once more before he left. She never thought falling in love could happen so fast. She locked the door and headed for the shower.

The next morning Melody let Ballou outside to the backyard to play while she ran a few errands.

An hour later, she pulled into the driveway then headed for the back gate. Her eyes scanned the yard. Where was Ballou? Panic welled inside her.

She unlatched the lock on the gate and ran into the backyard. "Ballou! Ballou!"

A pale pink paper fluttered on the backdoor. Tears blurred Melody's vision as she read the note. *If you want your dog back, give Jorin up. Glenys*

Melody fisted the linen stationery as worry and anger warred within her. Hands shaking, she pulled her cell phone out of her purse and called Jorin.

"Jorin, that woman dognapped Ballou!" She couldn't stop the sob that escaped.

"Can you drive or do you need me to come and pick you up?"

Melody sniffed. "I'm too upset to drive."

"I'll be right there. Don't worry, my lovely, we'll get Ballou back."

Melody grabbed a tissue from her purse and blew her nose. *My poor baby is with that hateful woman.* She stuffed the hostage note into her small handbag and tossed it into the leather tote bag.

At the last minute, Melody walked back to her truck. Opening the door she leaned over and added Ballou's extra leash. She locked the truck door as Jorin drove up.

He opened the car door to reveal Bonnie in the passenger seat. Melody picked her up, handed her to Jorin, and sat down.

"Hi girl." She placed her bag on the floorboard and snapped herself in, then held her arms out for Bonnie.

The pup sat quietly in Melody's lap and kissed her hand.

"Where are we going?"

Jorin eased into the traffic. "I'm taking you to the hotel. The solicitor called and said Glenys is also staying there, but I haven't learned which room. We'll speak to the manager about the situation."

Melody stroked Bonnie's ears and tried to rein in her fear. Her body shook at the frightening images in her mind.

"Will Glenys hurt Ballou?" She buried her face in Bonnie's clean fur, willing herself to stay calm.

"No, my lovely, I don't think so. Although she seems quite unbalanced right now, it would be messy and Glenys does not like anything untidy."

Jorin parked and they rushed through the lobby, then took the elevator to his floor.

She followed Jorin down the corridor, but stopped when she heard a bark. "Jorin! I hear Ballou." She pointed to the room opposite his. "He's in there!"

He opened his door, tucking Bonnie safely inside his room. He placed a finger to his lips, grabbed Melody's hand and rapped on the door.

"Who is it?" Glenys called in a challenging voice.

"Jorin. I've left Melody, open up." He eased Melody behind him.

Glenys quickly opened the door. The hem of her designer dress hung in tatters. Her high heels were smudged, and a huge snag ran the length of both stockings.

At that moment Ballou jumped and head-butted the back of Glenys' knees, knocking her to the floor.

Glenys screamed. "Get that hateful beast away from me!"

Ballou stopped. He looked up at Jorin and Melody, then back to Glenys. He trotted over to the woman, raised his leg and peed on her skirt. Head held high, Ballou marched out of the room and ran to Melody, who cradled him in her arms.

"Filthy animal," Glenys shouted.

"Ballou! Oh baby, are you okay?"

Ignoring the woman still sprawled on the floor, Jorin escorted Melody back to his room. He smiled and closed the door. "Ballou, leaving your mark on Glenys was pure genius. Well done." He reached over and scratched behind the dog's ears.

Jorin pulled out his cell phone. "Jorin Griffin here. Someone needs to attend to the woman in the room across the hall from me."

He led Melody and Ballou to his bedroom, while he made another call. "Griffin here. Glenys is in the room across from mine and dognapped my fiancée's Westie. I trust you to take care of this matter."

He turned to Melody. "I think we need to order in and discuss our Christmas wedding."

"Jorin, that's three days away!" Melody sat on the sofa and hugged Ballou close. "We couldn't possibly—"

"We can have a small intimate ceremony here and another one in Wales. That way our family and friends from both sides of the pond can attend. Later we can have a big celebration and invite everyone. Your friends—Kimberly, Kelly, Meagan, Billie and Melinda—have already contacted the people who need to know. I've secured us a lovely spot for the ceremony and reception." He crossed the short distance that separated them.

Melody lowered Ballou to the floor. "How can I say no when you've thought of everything, my knight. Thank you." She stood and claimed his lips in a searing kiss. "My hero." Melody took his hand and pulled him to the bed. "We're celebrating early." She stepped back, closed the door and began to show Jorin how much she loved him.

Ballou woofed and licked Bonnie's nose. *When Jorin and Melody repeat their vows, I will say mine to you, Bonnie. You are my Christmas wish and Jorin is Melody's.*

Woof!

Be sure to visit Keelia's website
http://keeliagreer.tripod.com/

The Christmas Curse

by Rachel Michaels

Jenna Malone gasped as a wave of icy water splashed her face. "Dammit!" she sputtered at the departing bus, wiping ineffectually at the dirty mess it had left in its wake. She must look a complete wreck. Black slush stained her camel colored peacoat and her lovely Manolo boots were ruined. Well, to be fair, those were already ruined, as she'd broken the heel off the right one not more than twenty minutes ago.

Why had she even left the house today? After all, it was Christmas. Okay, December 24th, but close enough. She should have stayed in her warm, cozy bed and read romance novels all day. Since Michael had dumped her earlier today, reading a spicy romance would definitely be the most exciting thing taking place in her bed any time soon.

Ah well. Michael was a jerk anyway. Jenna couldn't believe he'd had the nerve to dump her over e-mail. And after she'd given him the best six months of her life! Well, it hadn't really been the best six months, but it hadn't been the worst either. Still, she should have seen the break-up coming.

After all, it was Christmas.

She gave up trying to clean herself off and with the cold air stinging her still damp cheeks, hitched her large mahogany leather satchel into a more comfortable position. Criminy, it was frigid out! 'Tis the season...

Yeah, right! Sighing, she limped off toward home, trying to cheer herself along the way. She had five blocks to walk, plenty of time to improve her mental state. She tried to concentrate on positive things. As soon as she got home, she'd take a nice warm bath, listen to some James Blunt and dig into that bar of chocolate she'd been saving for emergencies. Then she'd go to bed, alone, have a restful night, alone, and wake up, alone, on Christmas morning. Hmmmm. This cheering up stuff wasn't as easy as she'd hoped.

The cold seeped through her clothes, causing her to shiver. Chunks of her soaked hair had frozen and now whapped the side of her head as she trudged along. *Stupid bus.* More like 'stupid car.' If her Honda Civic hadn't broken down last week, she could have driven it and avoided the bus altogether. But it would stay in the shop until she could afford to pay for the repairs. So here she was.

Jenna sniffed loudly as her nose began to run. She tugged at her heavy bag again. Why wouldn't the stupid thing stay on her shoulder?

Her eyes watered. She tried to convince herself it was due to the cold, but it was really because she felt sorry for herself. *Okay, time for the cheering up thing again!* Should she have gone to visit her family? No. It wasn't like she'd have a great time with her family anyway. After all, it didn't matter where she was—something was bound to go wrong. Just like every other Christmas.

Jenna sighed.

Her steps slowed as she reached the sidewalk leading to the old white Victorian housing her third floor apartment. Almost home. She paused, psyching herself up to climb the thirty steps between her and complete relaxation.

For what she hoped was the last time, she hitched her bag higher on her shoulder, trying to find a more comfortable place for the strap. Looking up, a bright star caught her attention. Huge, it looked as though it hung right above the house. Mesmerized, she stared up at it. An idea popped into her head. *Should I...* Her head whipped from side to side as she shook her head vigorously, but the idea wouldn't go away. With a sigh, she surrendered to the inevitable. *I can't believe I've sunk so low. Okay, Jenna, get it over with.*

"Star light, star bright, first star I see—oh screw this. Star, if you're listening, how 'bout a little help here? Even though you seem like some special Christmas star, which makes me justifiably nervous, I'm desperate here. I could use some good luck for a change. So I wish...I wish I could have, just this once, a merry Christmas." She stopped, still staring at the star, almost afraid to look away, worried if she broke 'eye contact,' she'd somehow mess up her wish. For several moments, nothing moved in the frosty night.

Finally Jenna shrugged, causing her satchel to slide off her shoulder again. Aggravated, she didn't bother to move it this time. She trudged up the sidewalk toward the porch steps, grumbling to herself. "What did I expect? Was Santa Claus supposed to show up? How about the three wise men? Maybe the baby Jesus himself? Or—I know! How about an angel?" She reached for the railing by the porch, but her errant bag snagged against it. She tugged on it and grumbled, "Yeah, that's it. An angel is just going to appear—aaaaaaaack!" Her last thought as her feet slid out from under her was 'Christmas sucks.'

Jenna slowly opened her eyes and turned her head to see where she was. Wow, her head injury must be pretty bad. She was hallucinating that an angel leaned over her, softly calling her name.

"Jenna? Jenna, are you okay?" the angel called.

Jenna started to pull herself into an upright position and regretted it instantly as dizziness rushed over her. She immediately sank back down into the slush covering the icy cement sidewalk.

She reached up and gingerly touched the back of her throbbing head, noting without surprise the large lump forming where she'd whacked herself after her losing battle with the ice. Trying to focus on something other than her excruciating headache, she looked back up at her angel, er, neighbor. Although he might be handsome enough to be a heavenly being, she now recognized the figure crouched next to her as her new neighbor from the downstairs apartment. Jim. No, Jeff. No, John! That was it! John something. He'd moved in at the beginning of the month. She'd noticed he was cute, and they'd had a few sessions of small talk while collecting their mail. Since she'd been dating Michael, she hadn't paid too much attention.

But now Jenna gave him a thorough looking over. All right, he might not be an angel, but he looked pretty dreamy. His tousled brown hair needed a haircut, but there was something very endearing about the way a lock of it curled right above his right eyebrow. And his eyes, wow, his eyes were the most gorgeous green. She thought she remembered him having a killer smile, but he wasn't smiling now. Why was he frowning at her? Oh, right, because she was lying on the ground, not responding. He probably thought she was brain dead, and not only because of the fall.

"I'm okay, John," she finally said. "Just got the wind knocked out of me."

"That must have been quite a fall! I heard you scream and came out to see if you needed any help."

"Thanks, but I'm fine," she said ruefully. "I think my pride is bruised worse than anything else."

"You're sure you don't need me to call an ambulance or anything?"

Jenna groaned. "That would be ambulance number six," she whispered under her breath.

"What?"

"Nothing. I'm fine, really. If you could help me up."

"Of course."

Jenna expected him to offer her a hand, or maybe an arm for leverage. Instead, he scooped her up into his arms, rose easily and headed up the porch steps. He even managed to sling her traitorous bag over his shoulder.

Wow! Cute, strong, and chivalrous! This guy looked better every minute.

After fumbling a bit with the front door, John carried Jenna into the foyer of the house. He paused, still cradling her in his arms.

"Are you going to be okay? You know, on your own? You're welcome to come in for a drink and to warm up by my fireplace."

Was he flirting with her? The shiver that ran through her had nothing to do with the bits of snow still stuck to her. Then she remembered what day it was—Christmas Eve. Not the best time for her to be starting something like this. Actually, it was the absolute worst time. She really ought to get out of range of the poor guy before the romantic-sounding fireplace set his apartment on fire.

"Thanks, that's nice of you, but I'll get out of your hair now." He gently set her down, keeping an arm wrapped around her for support. Did he seem reluctant to let her go? *Stay focused, Jenna. He's a nice guy. He doesn't need to get dragged into your troubles.* Planning a semi-graceful exit—or at least an exit more graceful than her entrance—she said, "It's Christmas Eve, and I'm sure you've got more important things to do than—owwwww!" The second she'd put her weight on her left foot, lightning bolts of pain shot through her ankle. Clinging to his arm, she began hopping around like a wounded duck, squawking all the while. "Ow, ow, ow, ow!"

"Okay, that's it." Without waiting for her approval, he scooped her up again. "I'm taking you into my apartment for a while. There's no way you can make it up all the steps to your apartment on that ankle."

As they headed toward his apartment, Jenna remembered the last ground floor tenant. He'd been 86 years old with three cats. She hoped John had redecorated, or at least gotten rid of the smell. She expected something sparse, dark and masculine. Instead, John opened the door to a winter wonderland. It was festive. It was bright. It was hell.

Jenna scanned the room, hoping it wasn't as bad as it looked. A lit fireplace dominated the cozy living room. The flames crackled merrily, casting a rosy light over the rest of the room. The fireplace was fine. She had no beef with it. Well, other than the stockings hung by it—with care, she was sure. It was the rest of the room that was the problem. The place was wall to wall Christmas! From the big Christmas tree in the corner, twinkling with little colored lights and decorated to the max, to the crocheted snowflakes hanging in the windows, to the dozens of Santas and snowmen seemingly scattered on every flat surface. There was even one of those miniature ceramic towns set up on a corner table. Granted the room had a certain warmth and charm to it, and all the decorations were interesting or amusing, rather than tacky or commercial, but there was just so much Christmas!

"Could you carry me up to my place after all?" she asked John, trying to keep the pleading out of her voice.

"I'm not sure I could handle all the stairs, to be honest. Besides, you might have a concussion. I think you need someone to keep an eye on you for a while. If you're still feeling okay later, we'll see what we can do about getting you up those stairs. Sound good?"

He seemed so reasonable, and so darn cute, Jenna felt like a Scrooge pursuing the issue. Surely she could handle all these decorations for an hour or so. Her fall had been a real doozy. Maybe something that big and painful meant Christmas was through messing with her for the year.

Yeah, right.

John lowered her onto his plush red sofa, careful not to jar her injured ankle. "Let's get you a little more comfortable. Can I take your coat?"

Jenna managed to undo the peacoat's buttons, but had somehow gotten it tangled under her.

"Here, let me help." John leaned around her to tug at the stuck coat. Their eyes met as he moved in. *God, he was so cute.* He was close enough that she could smell his breath...the exact peppermint of a candy cane. Of course. She sighed and pulled back a little, breaking eye contact. He eased the fabric out from under her and tossed it over a nearby chair.

He knelt beside the couch. "Let's get these boots off." The right one slid off easily, ruined heel and all. The left one proved more difficult, due to the swelling.

"Ow, ow, ow, ow."

"I'm sorry. I don't mean to hurt you. Let me take a look."

"Are you a doctor or something?"

"No, sorry, I'm an accountant." He stripped off both her ruined nylons and wrapped his hands around her injured ankle. "But I was an Eagle Scout, so I think I can help." He smiled as he gently squeezed and prodded the tender flesh above her foot. "I don't think it's broken. Probably just twisted." Cradling her foot with one hand, he dragged the coffee table closer to the sofa. Snagging a pillow off the foot of the couch, he set it on the table and eased Jenna's foot onto it. "I think I've got an ace bandage around her somewhere. I'll go find it. You keep your foot elevated. I'll grab an icepack for your head, too." John stood and headed out of the room.

Even through her pain, Jenna couldn't help noticing the way his faded Levi's hugged his butt. She sighed, then grimaced as the slight movement jogged her ankle. Great—a possible concussion and a sprained ankle. Not to mention that she'd met this great, cute, nice guy and then found out he obsessed with the very thing she hated most. This had to rank as one of the worst Christmases yet.

"I'm cursed!" she muttered.

"You're what?" John asked, as he returned to the living room with his first aid supplies.

"Nothing."

"I thought I heard something about a curse." John handed Jenna a bag of frozen peas. "Put this on the back of your head." She complied, wincing from the cold. "I brought you a towel for your hair, too. And I'm heating up some milk for hot chocolate. I thought you could probably use something warm to drink."

Could this guy be any nicer? Then she noticed the towel he'd handed her was red and green with a little snowman on it. She had to get out of here.

Jenna gently rubbed her damp hair as John knelt and wrapped the bandage around her ankle. Although he was very gentle, it still hurt. To distract herself, she tried to focus on something else. Her eyes landed on a miniature glass Christmas tree with little removable glass 'lightbulbs.' Her grandmother had owned a similar tree. Jenna still remembered her trip to the hospital to remove the little bulb she'd gotten stuck up her nose. Granted, she'd only been three at the time, but that had been the first time the curse had shown up.

"There. That should do it." John abruptly sat back on his haunches and looked up at her. Startled, she tried to refocus on him, but it was too late.

"I see you noticed my little tree. It was my Gram's."

"Yeah, my grandmother had one, too. Well, she used to."

"Oh? What happened to it? Did she give it to you?"

"Um, no. Actually it had to be put down." Before John could ask what she meant, she hurried on, "I'm not really into Christmas." *Geez, was that the understatement of the year, or what?*

"That's too bad," John replied as he stood up. "I'm sure you can tell I am pretty 'into' it. I think the milk is hot enough now. I'll go mix up the hot chocolate. Would you like a shot of peppermint schnapps in it? Or is alcohol bad for potential concussions? We didn't really get into those types of things in the Scouts."

"I'm pretty sure I don't have a concussion, so schnapps would be great. Thanks."

John headed into the tiny galley kitchen where she heard him banging about, getting their drinks. *I wonder if he has a girlfriend. If so, she's a lucky girl.* Although, come to think of it, the apartment didn't really give off a super masculine vibe, especially with the Christmas stuff everywhere. And schnapps wasn't too manly either. Perhaps there was a lucky *boy* in the picture. Not that it mattered. No way would she get involved with this Christmas freak. Even if he did have the cutest dimples...

"Here you go," John reentered the living room, balancing a tray with two steaming mugs and a plate of cookies. Jenna could smell the sharp molasses from across the room. Yum. Gingersnaps.

Handing her a mug, John rested the tray on the coffee table next to Jenna's propped up foot, and sank onto the sofa beside her. "Cookie?" He offered her the plate. She snagged a cookie and held it up to inspect it.

"What, just circles? No gingerbread men?"

Jenna couldn't believe she'd spoken out loud. How rude! Fortunately, John didn't seem to be offended. He laughed. "I usually make gingerbread men with my two nieces, but since we couldn't be together this year, I decided plain old circles were good enough for me."

"Nieces, huh? Do you have a big family?" Jenna bit into the tangy gingersnap.

"Not very big. There's only my parents and my two brothers. They're each married. One has two daughters—the gingerbread girls—and the other had a son in August."

Jenna couldn't resist the opening he'd given her. "So you're the only single one, huh?"

"Yep. Still single. Not even a girlfriend on the horizon. How about you?"

"No girlfriend on the horizon for me either." Jenna was so hung up on John's confirmation of heterosexuality that it took her a second to realize what she'd just said. "No boyfriend, I mean. Well, there was one, but we broke up today."

"Oh. I'm sorry."

"Thanks. Don't worry. He was kind of a loser anyway. He actually dumped me over e-mail. Tacky, right?"

"Well I'm glad you're keeping your sense of humor." He chuckled. "It doesn't sound like you've had a very good day."

"Let's not talk about my day. Let's talk more about you." If John knew every miserable thing that had befallen her today, he'd probably shove her out of his apartment and lock the door after her. Not that she'd blame him. She really should leave. But it was so cozy sitting here in front of the fire with him, the schnapps and hot chocolate warming her insides. She'd leave after she had a few more cookies.

"Ok, what do you want to know?"

What it would be like to kiss you. Dang, where had *that* come from? How much schnapps was in this drink anyway? Flustered, Jenna searched for a more suitable topic, desperately trying to ignore the idea that in a room so full of Christmas, there had to be mistletoe hanging somewhere.

"Um, tell me more about the little glass tree. You said your grandmother gave it to you?"

"Mmhmm. She gave me most of my decorations, actually. She really got into Christmas. We always spent the holidays with her, out at the old farm. Some of my best times with her were helping her bake Christmas cookies or helping her hang the snowflakes. There was this one time, when I was about seven, when I got to go with her to pick out the Christmas tree. Now, this isn't like getting a tree here in the city. This is farm country. So when we wanted a tree, we'd just go cut one down. Like Paul Bunyan, she told me. And I even got to carry a little axe with me."

Jenna tensed, waiting to hear about some terrible accident involving this axe.

John continued, "We walked along, dragging a big sled behind us, for what seemed like hours, but was probably only fifteen minutes, until we found the perfect tree. It had to be a little round, you see, and not too tall. Grams called it a squat tree. So we found the perfect tree, and I start swinging my axe, putting all my weight into it and barely making a dent in the thing. I've got branches hitting me in the face, sap all over my mittens, and my arms are killing me. But I can't let Grams down. Well, after a few minutes of this, I'm huffing and puffing and about ready to pass out when Grams pulls out a chainsaw from under the tarp on the sled and just goes to town on the tree. We had it down in minutes. She was sixty-eight at the time, and she took that tree down like it was nothing! And the best part? When we got back to the house, she tucked the chainsaw back under the tarp and told everyone what a great job I'd done cutting down the Christmas tree!"

Jenna gave a half laugh, half sigh. Thank God, no amputations had occurred anywhere in the story. If it had been one of her childhood memories...

She pushed away the thought and refocused on John. "Your Grams sounds wonderful."

"She really was. She passed away five years ago. I miss her a lot, especially this time of year. The holiday season really reminds me of her. I think that's why I like to put up all her old decorations. It makes me feel closer to her."

God, he was sweet! She wanted to cuddle up right next to him on the sofa and have his arms wrap around her, pulling her close...

"...favorite Christmas memory?"

"Excuse me?" Jenna blushed.

"I said, 'What's your favorite Christmas memory?'"

"Oh, I don't have one. These cookies are great. I think I'll have another one. Do you use dark or light molasses in them?" Jenna snatched up another cookie and stuffed it in her mouth, chewing dramatically.

John straightened up and set his mug down on the coffee table. He turned and looked at her, a frown on his handsome face.

"Okay, Jenna, what's going on?"

She tried shooting him her most compelling 'what? who? me?' look, but the frown remained. She washed down her mouthful of gingersnap with the rest of her spiked chocolate, needing the liquid courage. It was time to spill.

Looking into the fire, she muttered, "I'm cursed."

"That's what I thought you said earlier. What on earth do you mean?"

Still avoiding his eyes, she continued. "It means I'm cursed. Not a fun, interesting kind of curse, mind you, from an evil witch or an angry gypsy. Just your run-of-the-mill, average, the-universe-is-out-to-get-you kind of curse. Oh, and it's Christmas related."

Jenna waited for John to laugh. She knew she sounded crazy, which was why she didn't like to mention the curse to anyone outside the family. He didn't laugh. She risked a quick look at his face. Not a hint of a smile. Or a frown, actually. John just sat there quietly, looking at her. She didn't know how to react to no reaction, so she waited for him to break the silence.

Finally, he said, "So what exactly does this curse entail? I mean, I can see you don't have warts or a tail or anything."

"Well, the curse varies a lot. That's part of the problem. It's always something new. When I was younger, it was a lot of physical things. You know, a broken arm from tripping over my new dollhouse. Third degree burns from taking the Christmas cookies out of the oven. Eight stitches in my hand from a broken ornament. The emergency room staff knew us all by name by the time I was six, and if ambulances gave frequent flyer miles, I'd have earned quite the trip." She shrugged and released a sigh.

"But it wasn't only injuries. In third grade, at the church Christmas pageant, while I sang 'Silent Night,' MaryBeth Danvers pulled up my dress so the whole congregation could see my underpants. At the seventh grade holiday dance, my 'best friend' Emily Spires told Jimmy Donovan, the biggest bully in school, I liked him and he followed me around for the next two months. Then when I was a sophomore, my boyfriend broke up with me on December 23rd at Makeout Point because I wouldn't let him get to second base with me. And then, on our way home, his car got stuck in the snow and we had to sit there for two hours before someone found us and helped push us out of the snow bank."

She checked to see if he was laughing yet. He wasn't.

"The list goes on and on. It's a tragic saga of breakups, injuries, and embarrassments, some fairly minor, and others pretty serious. So I've become allergic to Christmas. I try to pretend it isn't even happening, thinking if I simply ignore it, the curse will leave me alone. But we can see how well that's going." She gestured to her swollen ankle. "I know it sounds crazy. Believe me, I do. But it's true."

They sat in silence for a few minutes, the crackling of the fire the only sound.

"What are you thinking?" she finally asked him.

"That this place must scare the hell out of you. It probably looks like Macy's Christmas Department came in here and threw up all over the place."

She laughed in disbelief. He didn't think she was crazy?

"No, no, it actually looks lovely in here. Everything is very cozy and homey. And now that I know about your Grams, everything is even more beautiful—special. But I admit when you first carried me in here, I was a bit...surprised. Overwhelmed. Okay, freaked out."

"I noticed, but I wasn't sure what was going on with you. I thought you might have decided you didn't want to be alone with me or something."

"Oh no, no, I really wanted to be alone with you." Jenna blushed again. "Okay, that kinda came out wrong."

"Oh, I don't know." He draped his arm around her shoulders and pulled her up next to him. "It sounds pretty right to me."

His green eyes held hers as he slowly leaned toward her. As he drew even closer, she closed her eyes, lost in the sensation of being so close to him. Her stomach fluttered in excitement as she waited for the imminent kiss. She completely forgot where she was, not to mention what day it was, until his lips were just a breath away from hers. *Dammit, it's Christmas Eve!*

Her eyes snapped open and she jerked back from him. "John, I don't think this is such a good idea."

"Why not? I thought things were going quite well."

"They were. They are. But weren't you listening to what I said? I'm cursed!"

"What does that have to do with us?"

She gestured around the room. "Gee, I don't know. Aren't all these decorations giving you a hint? It's Christmas Eve! Who knows what could go wrong! A fire, a power outage, a leaky pipe...the list is endless!"

"Hmmm. I see. Well then, I guess we only have one option."

Jenna nodded sadly. It was probably for the best, but she couldn't help feeling disappointed their relationship had to be over before it really even started. She started to lower her injured leg to stand up.

"We have to lift the curse."

Jenna flopped right back on the couch.

"What?"

"I said we have to lift the curse."

"That's sweet, John, but don't you think I've tried?"

"Maybe you haven't tried hard enough."

"I swear, I have! Just tonight, I wished on a star. It was so big and bright, I decided it had to be a Christmas star, so I thought what the hell, I'll take a chance—and I made a wish. And look what happened! I ended up with a banged up head and a swollen ankle! I honestly don't think the curse is breakable."

"I don't know, Jenna. I'm sure the fall wasn't much fun, but you have to admit something good did come out of it. After all, it got you into my arms, not to mention my apartment." He waggled his eyebrows at her.

Jenna smiled, but opened her mouth to start protesting again.

He put his hand to her lips, shushing her. "I'm serious. I've had the biggest crush on you since I moved into this place, but you wouldn't give me the time of day. You were friendly, but I felt like you never actually saw me. You always seemed so busy, rushing in and out. I'd almost given up on you. And then tonight I heard you scream and I got to be your knight in shining armor."

"Angel," Jenna mumbled. Fortunately, John didn't seem to hear her and continued on.

"Ergo, I'm not convinced this curse is all bad. But I know how seriously you take it, so I'm willing to give breaking it a shot. And I know exactly how to do it." He got up from the couch and walked over to the coat closet by the front door. He pulled down several boxes from the top shelf and rummaged through them. After a minute, he plucked something from a small red box.

"Aha!" he said, triumphantly holding his find aloft. "Mistletoe!"

I knew it! I knew he'd have mistletoe!

Part of Jenna still wanted to get out of this apartment, worried she'd cause disaster for this sweet, sweet man. But the rest of her had decided to stay exactly where she was, because the combination of this sexy, sexy man and a sprig of mistletoe was too good to miss.

John came back to the sofa and sat down.

"I think this is traditionally done by standing under it, but due to your ankle issues, I think we can forgo tradition this once."

Jenna managed a quick smile, but she was nervous.

"What if it doesn't work? How will we know?" she babbled nervously. "If the kiss is really awful, that might be a sign the curse wasn't broken. I don't want the kiss to be bad. It won't be bad, right? I'm a pretty good kisser. And how could someone as gorgeous and nice as you be a bad kisser? It'll be okay, won't it?" She started chewing on the cuticle of her left pinkie. "Do you think we need to say something? You know, like magic words, or anything? And does it have to rhyme? Those types of things always seem to rhyme."

"Jenna..." John caught the hand she gnawed on and set it back in her lap. "It'll be all right."

Then, before she could start up again, he held the mistletoe over her head and gently cupped her chin with his other hand. Looking straight into her eyes, he said, "Merry Christmas, Jenna."

Then he leaned in and kissed her.

The kiss was perfect. His lips were soft and sweet as they gently touched hers. He kissed her again, this time more firmly, slanting his open mouth across hers, his tongue slowly licking its way inside her mouth. He tasted like peppermint, chocolate and molasses, and Jenna wanted to eat him up. She grabbed his head and leaned into the kiss, eager for more. She heard a soft thud, and after John wrapped both his arms around her, pulling her even closer, she realized he'd thrown away the mistletoe. *Eh, who needs it?* The kiss had enough magic on its own to break a hundred curses.

Out of the corner of her eye, Jenna thought she saw a flash of light through the living room window. She reluctantly broke off the kiss and sat back, pointing to the window.

"Did you see something?"

"I don't see anything but you." John smiled and tugged her back into his embrace, raining kisses down her cheek and onto her neck.

Jenna was convinced the light she'd seen had been a shooting star. *Thanks, star.*

Maybe the curse really was lifted. But even if it wasn't, she'd met an amazing man, and this had turned into her best Christmas ever. *I guess anything really can happen—even magic.*

After all, it was Christmas.

Be sure to check out Rachel's website
http://www.rachelmichaels.com

Maggie at Christmas

by Diane Davis White

Maggie Donaldson opened the door, apprehension pulsing in her blood. “Hi, you must be Professor Spencer.”

“I am.” Ethan Spencer, Professor of Psychology, moved out of the porch shadows extending one very large hand to be shaken. Maggie watched in fascination as her hand disappeared in his grip. Such huge hands! The electricity that sparked through her at his touch startled her.

“Nice to meet you, Mrs. Donaldson. I appreciate you offering the hospitality of your home. You can’t imagine how relieved I was when your cousin Nelda told me you’d take me in for a few days. I need to get a handle on the curriculum before the semester begins at the University and get settled in before Christmas break is over.”

“No problem at all,” she murmured. “It’s not your fault there are three conventions in town filling up the hotels.”

Maggie’s breath caught at the size of him. In a London Fog raincoat that emphasized the breadth of his shoulders, a woolen scarf round his thick neck, he was easily a foot taller than her five-foot-ten. His voice matched his size—deep baritone and well modulated. The glimmer of heat in his eyes and his slow smile said he felt it, too.

Maggie stared at Ethan Spencer. His brilliant blue eyes were alight with intelligence, his deliciously sculpted lips curved into a friendly smile. A current of tension arced between them, stronger than the buzz she'd experienced when their hands had touched. Were *still* touching, she realized, glancing down at the loose grip of his fingers on hers.

"Come on into the kitchen. I baked cookies and fresh bread. Coffee's almost done."

"Help yourself, please. I'll be right back." She nodded toward the cookie jar, then excused herself.

Hurrying up the curving staircase, she rushed into her bathroom. Closing the door, she leaned against it, waiting for her heart to stop pounding in her ears. Her nerves were raw from her intense reaction to Ethan Spencer.

Splashing cold water on her face, Maggie stared at herself in the bathroom mirror. Large, haunted eyes stared back.

Guilt speared her as her gaze moved to the mirrored reflection of Stan's picture on her bedside. How could she be so moved by another man when her husband had been dead less than two years? Still, she knew she'd have to let go of Stan eventually. Maybe the time had come. Thrusting away the guilt, she turned from her reflection.

Changing her muddy slacks for a pair of well-worn jeans and soft peach sweatshirt, Maggie stood before her Cheval mirror and studied herself. She saw a woman ill-suited to romance—a little on the plump side and wide-hipped. Still youthful breasts redeemed the defects somewhat. Nevertheless, it wasn't enough to make her sexy.

Not that she *wanted* to look sexy, she told herself firmly.

Ethan took his coffee and settled into the oversized leather recliner facing the fireplace. It wasn't often that furniture accommodated his nearly seven foot frame.

Returning, Maggie paused—clearly unsettled to find Ethan in the recliner. He watched the flutter of her hands that indicated uncertainty, then her eyes shifted to the picture on the mantle.

He smiled. "Hope you don't mind. You did say make yourself at home."

"Of course not...it's just that...oh, never mind."

"This was your husband's favorite chair, wasn't it?" He stood, picked up his cup.

"How did you know that?" Maggie sounded perplexed.

"The look on your face, the way your eyes went to that picture on the mantle." His voice gentled. "Psychology. It's what I do."

"Let me show you where you'll work. It's a very nice den. My husband used it for an office." The strain in her voice wasn't lost on Ethan. He followed wordlessly as she hurried across the room, noting the pleasant sway of her hips.

"I have some shopping to do. If you prepare a list, I'll pick up anything you need." She brushed her hair behind her ears and took a deep breath.

Ethan couldn't help his eyes straying to the material stretched over her ample breasts.

He stared at the woman who would be his hostess. Maggie fascinated him. *She has the most beautiful eyes I've ever seen...and skin like milk and honey. A man could go far and never see such a soft kissable mouth.*

He drew back from an erotic image of Maggie—dressed only in his pajama top—sprawled across his lap before a roaring fire. He schooled his features to show no trace of his lustful thoughts.

"Get a grip, professor," he muttered to himself.

"What?"

"Ah...nothing. Just thinking out loud," he answered quickly. "I can't think of a thing I need at the moment. Thanks, anyhow."

Established in the first floor office with its private

bath, Ethan was eager to get to work. He set up his laptop on the old desk and sorted through papers he'd dragged from his briefcase.

Unable to concentrate, his mind wandered back to Maggie. Warm, sweet, and lovely were words that came to mind. Sighing, he gave in to the inevitable—he was attracted.

After dinner, Ethan—armed with detailed directions and the keys to Maggie's van—went to pick up some papers and visit with the professor he would replace.

Cradling a cup of cocoa, Maggie settled by the fire to contemplate the day's events. She threw on an extra log and sighed longingly, feeling empty. She wanted someone to talk to. Not just *anyone*, but Ethan Spencer—she admitted with painful honesty.

She reminded herself sternly that she didn't know this man. Told herself she was only reacting to basic human need—a feminine desire to be wanted, to be cherished.

To be loved.

He could be any man. Any man at all. I am going through a phase.

After a fruitless effort to erase the image of Ethan's brilliant blue eyes and wide, smiling mouth, she recounted the few moments they'd spent together, analyzing her reactions—or trying to. It all came back to one thing. She was attracted. Helplessly attracted.

Exhausted, Maggie drifted toward sleep. She sank down and curled into a fetal position on the wide couch. Vaguely aware of the throw blanket gentle hands smoothed over her, she curled into its warmth. Smiled at the touch of a fingertip tracing the line of her lips. Comforted beyond anything she'd felt in a long time, she slept deeply.

Maggie bustled around in her cozy kitchen, making coffee, whipping up crêpe batter and scrambling eggs. Refused to think why she was going to so much trouble—denying the intrusive thought that she might be trying to impress *him* with her cooking. Delicious aromas rose from a meal designed to tempt the most discerning pallet. She set the breakfast nook for two, and started up the stairs to her room.

She met Ethan coming down.

"Grab a cup of coffee and help yourself to breakfast." Energy and heat filled the few inches that separated them as they paused on the steps. Goosebumps prickled along her flesh.

"I'll wait for you, if you don't mind. I'd rather not eat alone."

"I'll just be a minute, then." Maggie hurried to her room.

Staring at her image, she wondered at the change in her looks in the last twenty-four hours. Her eyes sparkled, her skin glowed, her lips looked fuller. Some inner drive was making these changes and Maggie had a good idea of the cause.

A vibrant, handsome man was drinking coffee and puttering in her kitchen. Maggie smiled. One last glance in the mirror and she hurried downstairs.

Finishing the last bite of food on his plate, Ethan poured more coffee for them both and settled back in his chair. Determined to know Maggie better, he smiled. "Do you work, Maggie?"

"Yes, I'm a roving reporter for the Middleville Daily, but not full time. I don't *have* to work, but it's part of my keep-Maggie-busy-and-useful plan."

"Sounds like you aren't sure what to do with your life."

"Are you psycho-analyzing me, Dr. Spencer?"

"Of course. I do it to everyone." He grinned at her over his coffee mug. "I can't help it. I'm a naturally curious guy."

"Have you ever had a practice? Or have you always been a professor?"

"Private practice has never been an option for me. I

love to teach and can't imagine myself doing anything else. I'd rather turn out well-trained doctors than be one myself."

Elbows on the table, he leaned forward. "What else do you do, Maggie Donaldson?"

"I teach children to read and read to them as well." She paused, then added, "At the Children's Protective Shelter."

"And?" Ethan prompted.

"I work with teen dropouts and the elderly." Terseness crept into her voice. "And I don't have any problems figuring out what to do with my life."

Ethan smiled. Maggie with angry sparks in her eyes was a lovely sight. He held his cup out for a refill and she obliged.

"I...I'm sorry. That was unforgivable. I don't know why I said that."

He reached across the table, squeezed her hand briefly. "The only unforgivable thing you have done is call me Dr. Spencer. It's Ethan, please."

Perceptibly flustered by his touch, she glanced at the clock. "Oh my gosh! I have to leave. The children are expecting me for our reading session."

"May I join you? I'm just a kid at heart you know."

"You drive, professor. It's the best way to learn your way around." Ethan deftly caught the keys she tossed.

"So tell me about this foster care center. You work there?"

"I applied to be a foster parent, but they turned me down. So I volunteer to read to the children."

"Why would they do that? Just one look at the warm, loving atmosphere of your home should tell them about Maggie Donaldson. I find that unbelievably stupid on their part."

Maggie's heart lifted. He thought her home 'warm and loving'. Who was she kidding? This man had changed her life irrevocably. She'd never be the same—with or without him. Most likely without, she thought unhappily.

She shifted in her seat, facing the windows. It had been so long since she'd had someone to lean on. Someone strong and kind.

She sighed.

"Want to talk about it?" His voice drew her back. "That sad, despairing sigh. It was fraught with meaning, as they say."

Grasping the excuse he'd given her, she admitted, "Four of the children are special to me. I'd love to adopt them, but it's not going to happen."

"Did the agency turn you down?

"Stan and I applied to adopt. They withdrew me from the eligible file after he died." She motioned to a building up ahead. "That's it. My home away from home."

He sat at the desk in back, not wanting to intrude on the reading group. Ten children sat cross-legged on a round mat while Maggie lowered herself carefully to the floor. Obviously, she wanted to be on eye level with her group.

Maggie read and the children settled to listen. So did Ethan—as mesmerized as the little boy who'd come to lay his head on Maggie's knee, staring up at her with adoration. He let himself drift to the soft, melodious rhythm of her voice.

"Well, I've had a captive audience before, but this is the first time anyone ever fell asleep while I read to them. It's a good thing I didn't ask you to give a book report, Dr. Spencer."

Ethan came awake with a start, mortified he'd fallen asleep. He grinned sheepishly and gave the first excuse that came into his mind. "I lied. *Treasure Island*'s actually my favorite. *Tom Sawyer* puts me to sleep."

A solemn-eyed little girl gazed at him. Two small boys edged closer, smiling shyly.

Maggie laughed lightly, brushing a gentle hand over each child's head. "I would like to introduce you to Dr.

Spencer. Dr. Spencer, this is Anna Marie, Toby and Tommy Baker."

A boy about ten came up next to Maggie, sullen and remote. Maggie touched his shoulder lightly. The boy twisted slightly to avoid her touch. "And this is their older brother, Matthew."

Maggie ignored Matt's rebuff, but Ethan saw the puzzled look in her eyes. He was torn between wanting to tousle Matt's curly dark hair or turn him over his knee for such rude behavior.

"They'll all be spending Christmas Eve at my house, so I'm sure you'll meet again." Maggie patted Toby's head as he leaned against her. Tommy, less willing to be coddled, hovered on her other side, but didn't touch her. He kept a wary eye on his older brother, as though looking for a sign. The younger ones clearly depended on Matt and it tore at Ethan's heart that a young boy should have to shoulder such responsibility.

Matt scowled, pulled his little sister back from the desk, jerked his head at his brothers and started toward the door, back stiff and eyes to the front.

"Matt, where are you going?" Maggie appeared distressed and a surge of protectiveness rippled through Ethan at the sight of her frightened eyes.

The ten-year-old stopped, but didn't turn around. "We're in a hurry. Gonna have lunch soon. Bye." He hurried his siblings along and disappeared around the corner, his mute anger hanging in the air long after he'd gone.

On the way home, Maggie sat deep in thought, trying to figure out Matt's rude, hurtful behavior. They'd developed a trusting relationship over the last several months and this was the first time he'd displayed such abrupt discourtesy to her—though he often did with other adults. She cast a sidelong glance at Ethan.

Maybe the professor has a clue. I wish I had the nerve to ask him.

Ethan cleared his throat and broached the subject on her mind. "You know, sometimes children who've been through great trauma—like losing their parents—have a tendency to be just plain angry with the world. They show it in different ways, of course, like withdrawing, trying too hard to please, or getting into trouble just for the attention. Then there are the ones like your little friend, Matt. Want to tell me what he's like when he's with you and hasn't got a rival?"

"Rival? What do you mean?"

"You tell me what he's normally like around you and I'll answer your question."

"When they arrived at the foster care center Matt wouldn't talk to anyone. He wouldn't let his brothers and sister talk to anyone. He kept them apart, refusing to eat, refusing to cooperate with the staff. Their case worker finally separated the other three children from Matt, thinking if they did, Matt would come around. He just grew more sullen and silent. It lasted three days."

Maggie sighed and shifted in her seat, gazing at Ethan's profile. "One Thursday, I came in to read to the children and he sat in the corner of the reading room, drawing. I'd been told about him, and I decided to ignore him and let him sit with us if he wanted to. I began to read and the children gathered close. You saw little Toby lying against my legs today? Well, he did that right off, and when Matt saw him, he became angry."

She drew a long breath and stretched her legs as far as she could in the confined space of the van. "He came and pulled his brother away, scolding him for being *forward*, for goodness sake. He didn't leave though, just pulled Toby down beside him and sat listening with the other children. After two chapters of *Oliver Twist*, he approached me and apologized for being rude. It was a beginning, and it took awhile to gain his complete trust, but we've been great friends ever since."

"What changed his mind? Why did he suddenly decide to like you, Maggie? What about you in particular gained his trust?" Ethan asked quietly.

"He said I looked like his mother, told me she used to read to them all the time and that Dickens was her favorite author." Maggie grinned. "He made it very clear, however, that his mother *only* resembled me in the face. He informed me—in a proud little boy way—that his mother had been very small—not big and tall like me."

She heaved a sigh. "He said her eyes were like mine, but my legs were too long."

"Well, there is certainly something to be said for long legs, despite one little boy's opinion. Mine got me through college. Basketball scholarship." Ethan slapped one solid thigh for emphasis, then swung the van into the driveway.

"I find it hard to believe there could ever be another pair of eyes like yours, though."

Maggie smiled at his words, then dropped her gaze, overcome with shyness. A condition that seemed to happen a lot with this man.

Ethan turned off the engine. He turned in his seat and looked at her for a long moment, then spoke in cautious tones. "Maggie, did it ever occur to you to try again? Maybe if foster care saw how well you manage your lifestyle and the real affection between you and the children, they'd reconsider."

"I *did* think of it, but decided not to attempt it. I guess that sounds defeatist to you, but you have to understand why I'm afraid. I couldn't get their hopes up and then not be able to have them."

"You're not a quitter, Maggie Donaldson. I know that instinctively. I say go for it. You don't have to tell the kids unless you get the go sign."

"Thank you, Ethan. I'll think about it." She reached for the door handle. He stopped her with a hand on her arm, and so she waited for him to come round and open her door, loving his courtly gesture—how special it made her feel.

After dinner, they sat by the fire in companionable silence. Finally, Ethan stretched and patted his flat belly. "That was a good dinner. Where did you learn to cook all those fancy sauces?"

"Cookbooks. I've always loved to cook. My figure shows I like my own cooking."

"Your figure is perfectly nice." His gaze roamed over her in a display of intimate speculation. "It goes without saying that a woman as tall as you wouldn't want to be too thin. You'd look all out of proportion. "

"Thank you...I think." Maggie fidgeted beneath his passionate appraisal.

He tossed a couch pillow onto the floor and stretched out in front of the hearth, taking up a great deal of room. Clearly attempting to lighten the moment, he complained, "What I need now is a masseuse. I feel like I'm going to burst from all that food and the wine has made me groggy."

"And just what would a masseuse do for you that would cure your stuffed belly and boozy head?" Maggie smiled wryly, looking at him as though he were a little boy who'd eaten too much candy.

"Ah, I was addicted to massage parlors when I was in college." Offering an irrepressible grin, he glanced at her shocked face with a mischievous glimmer in his eyes. "Not *that* kind. I mean a real Swedish masseuse parlor. There are such things, you know. You get a massage, nothing more. I found when I was stressed, it worked great."

He faced the flames and propped his hands behind his head. Him looking so comfortable and at ease made Maggie nervous. The scene had gone from casual to intimate too quickly. She took a swallow of her white wine and seeing the glass was almost empty, slugged down the rest, feeling it wind its way into her bloodstream, warming her and loosening the tension in her neck.

"Stressed is stressed and stuffed is stuffed. What you really need is to curb your excesses at the dinner table," she teased with a smile.

"With a feast like you prepared? You've got to be kidding. It's hard to talk to you when I can't see your expression. If I didn't know better, I'd think you were chastising me for being a pig."

Impulsively, Maggie tossed a couch pillow on the floor, stretching out close to him. "I deliberately had a very thick carpet put in here, just so I could lie in front of the fire."

The wine had loosened Maggie up, given her false courage. Though she normally didn't drink, she'd made an exception tonight, and the effects of one glass of wine for a person used to total abstinence was dramatic.

Ordinarily she never would have lain on the floor next to a near stranger. Yet she felt at ease with this tall, introspective and handsome man. Contented.

"You said you would answer my question and you never did." She casually reminded him of his earlier promise, needing him to explain his use of the term 'rival' when he'd spoken of Matt.

Maggie yearned deep in her soul for him to declare himself a rival for her affections—even those given to a small boy.

"Question? Which one? You ask so many." He grinned at her. "Do you refer to the one about rivalry?"

"I do *not* ask a lot of questions. I just wanted to pick your brain, professor. It seemed a curious thing to say."

"Curious? Not really, when you think about it. Matt lost his mother to death, his father to prison and he has three siblings under his care. He's trying desperately to be an adult—you can see it in his old-young eyes."

He sat up and reached for a log, tossing it on the dying flames. "You come into his life, remind him of his mother. You're comfortable, safe, caring, and available. Matt allows himself to lean on you a little, probably has some vague hope of making a more permanent arrangement with you as his guardian."

"I don't see how he could think that. I've never said—"

"You don't have to." He interrupted softly. "It's in your eyes, Maggie Donaldson. You do have the kindest, most compassionate eyes I've ever seen. Moreover, they *are* like Matt's mother's eyes. Remember?"

"Okay, I'll concede, just for the sake of argument, he may have entertained a hope of that nature, but what has it to do with you?" She sat up, pushed her pillow up to the couch and leaned back on it, feeling less vulnerable sitting up.

"He sees me as a threat to that hope." He moved to sit next to her. "I'm a man who could be your boyfriend, for all he knows. I'm a stranger, and he isn't good with strangers, as you mentioned. Thus, I'm a rival for your time, your attention, your affections."

"Well, in that case, it will be simple to clear it up. Do you really think that's what caused him to be so curt, to run off?"

"Let's just say young Matt is very intuitive when it comes to spotting a rival." He moved closer to her, dragging his pillow with him. "I find you a fascinating study, Maggie. Fascinating."

"Study? What am I, a specimen in your lab?" She scooted away from him. The room was growing very warm and she wished he hadn't put another log on the fire. Irritated and confused by her reactions to his nearness, she snapped, "I don't think I want to be a study."

"All people are a study, Maggie girl." He smiled slow and sexy, eyes going smoky. "But not *all* people are fascinating. I never study women. It's dangerous. *You're* dangerous."

"Me?' Maggie made a derisive sound. "I'm about as dangerous as a...a..." She waved her hands, unable to find a suitable description of what she wasn't. "Well, anyhow, I'm not a *fem fatale*, or anything like that. The only danger with me is if I fell on somebody, I'd crush them."

"Stop it!" Ethan rose to his knees and leaned over her, his eyes blazing anger. "If you say one more damned stupid thing like that about yourself...I'll turn you over my knee."

He pulled her gently to a kneeling position, then

looked at her for a long moment. Lowering his head, putting his mouth close to hers, Ethan murmured her name.

Maggie stiffened and pulled back, but as though he'd anticipated her reaction, he put his hand behind her head, holding her in place while he plundered her mouth.

"Don't," she whispered against his lips, trying to pull away. Her control slipped to zero as her temperature rose, her body responding to the hard length of him, melding into the assault of his kiss. Light-headed, Maggie experienced a throbbing sensation in her breasts that moved downward, spiralling to her lower belly and beyond.

Never, even in their most heightened moments of passion, had she ever felt this with Stan. The sensation of guilt that had plagued her from the moment she'd laid eyes on Ethan Spencer reared its ugly head. "Please let me go..."

Ignoring her plea, he trailed his open mouth down her neck. By the time he lifted his head and ran his tongue along her jaw line, Maggie ceased to struggle, her hips moving with his as he pressed against her. What had started as a simple kiss turned into a molten, devouring exercise in unbridled passion. He captured her mouth once more and she met his kiss in total surrender.

Ethan drew back, breathing hard, as though fighting for control. Finally, his voice ragged and husky, he whispered, "Good night, Maggie Donaldson. I should say I'm sorry, but I'm not."

He got up with graceful ease and went up the stairs, not looking back.

Maggie slumped back against the pillow, her eyes brimming with tears of hurt and anger, her throat aching with the effort not to sob. She waited until she heard his door close, then replaced all the pillows, picked up the empty glasses and plates and went to the kitchen to wash them before she allowed herself to go to bed.

This simple exercise in self-discipline helped her clear her head. By the time she was ready for bed, she'd decided to tell her houseguest he would have to find other quarters.

Maggie spent a sleepless night tossing and turning. Though she'd made her decision, she wasn't happy with it and tried to find a way to justify keeping him around. She couldn't. Knew she was playing with fire and likely to be badly burned if she continued on this foolish route.

Ethan Spencer was a good-looking, charming, intelligent and oh-so-sexy man and she was just a very tall, slightly plump, available woman. A handy flirtation, seduction, whatever. No matter what he said, no matter how sweet and charming he behaved toward her, she knew she shouldn't trust him. He wasn't the desperate type and there were just too many tall, slim and beautiful women out there for him to choose.

Ethan spent a sleepless night, debating his determination to stay unattached and avoid serious relationships versus his strong and compelling desire to love Maggie and give himself over to the feelings he had for her. Loneliness—his constant companion for years—would continue if he turned away from her now.

Through the long night he came to terms with his fears, realizing Maggie was far different from his ex-wife—different from any woman he'd ever met. She was kind, compassionate, caring and intelligent. Maggie Donaldson was a first class woman.

Sensual fire burned in her—just waiting for the right man. He knew without a doubt he could be that man. He also knew Maggie didn't trust him, didn't believe in her womanly allure, and he burned to show her how wrong she was. Knew that no matter what, he had to gain her trust. Just before sleep overcame him, he decided not to walk away from this chance to have Maggie. Have a good life, free from loneliness.

Ethan tried to concentrate on the football game, all the while conscious of Maggie puttering in the kitchen. Every now and again he heard her humming and the sound comforted him. He was long past fooling himself about his feelings for her. In just eight days he'd managed to meet and fall in love with the most contrary woman he'd ever come across. When he let himself think about it he was astounded right down to his toes.

He actually wanted to marry this woman and adopt four kids that were total strangers, just to see the love light in her eyes. It was insane, but then most things in life made little sense. Marrying Maggie wasn't the folly it had first seemed.

She'd been down with the flu for three days and Ethan had taken care of her, despite her protests. He found he liked pampering her, loved the looks of appreciation, her sweet smiles and simple words of gratitude. It made him think of what it would be like to care for her all the time—be there for her. Be *with* her. Be *one* with her.

Worried that the children would want to know what happened to her, Maggie asked him to contact them. He'd visited the shelter, explaining about Maggie's illness, assuring the children Christmas Eve was still on—provided Matt write Maggie an apology for being rude. The boy agreed and the other three had raced off to get paper and pens and they'd all written to her.

When they'd asked him to read in Maggie's stead, he hadn't the heart to refuse, and found he really enjoyed it. That he would be a regular volunteer from now on was a given.

He held up the funny little drawing Anna Marie had scrawled in crayon. The very tall stick figures of a man and woman were in the center of the page and on either side were tiny stick figures of children—three with pants and one with a skirt. Apparently a picture of the six of them—Ethan, Maggie, Anna and her brothers.

He'd not shown this one to Maggie yet. He wanted

to use it as part of his proposal, and he couldn't wait for her to get better so he could give her the ring he'd picked up that morning at the local jeweler's.

"Ethan, what have you got there? I thought you said Anna's picture got wet."

He whipped around at the sound of her voice with a sheepish grin, clearing his throat nervously. "Well, not exactly. I just wanted to hang onto it for a few days."

"Whatever for?" Maggie crossed the room, her hand out for the drawing. "Sometimes, Ethan Spencer, you make no sense at all."

"If you must know, I've been studying this, trying to get more insight into our quiet little friend." He waved the paper distractedly, then dropped it in her lap. "You can see the obvious things in the content. Anna needs—wants—parents."

"Yes, I know." She smiled at him, then her eyes drifted back to the page. As she looked at the very tall man and woman, the significance of the drawing hit her and a blush rose on her cheeks. She handed back the picture, not looking at Ethan.

Rearranging a few bulbs on the Christmas tree, she tried to ignore the longing and desire for what the picture depicted. Wishing that picture reflected the truth.

"Maggie." He breathed her name, his body warming hers as he moved close behind her, his large hands drawing her back to him, melting her insides. One hand moved to her hair, lifted the heavy mass away from her nape. Ethan's breath wafted on her flesh as he moved against her, his lips brushing her skin, causing shivers to run the length of her otherwise heated body.

"Please, don't deny me. We're not children, we both know what's between us. I've felt it from the very first...and you have as well."

"Ethan, stop please." She didn't sound convincing, even to her own ears, and the way her body pressed back against him of its own volition belied her request. Having no resistance to him, she relaxed as his hands came up over her breasts, sighing at the tremor of desire that overcame her.

Turning her around, Ethan plundered her mouth until her knees were weak. Pulling away slightly, his voice hoarse with passion, he whispered against her lips, "Want to go upstairs?"

All Maggie could do was nod.

"Tell me, Maggie my love, is your bed any bigger than the one in my room?" His voice was teasing as he led her toward the stairs. "I've been thinking of sleeping on the floor, just to be able to stretch my legs."

"Poor baby, I feel so sorry for you." Teasing him in return, she pushed open the door to her bedroom and stood aside so he could see the massive bed—special made for very tall people.

"Heaven. Pure Heaven." He crossed the room and lay back on the bed, stretching like a lazy panther, then he lifted his hand, crooked his finger and beckoned her to him. She moved toward the bed, her eyes glowing with desire as she went to him.

Ethan entered the room, his bare feet silent on the thick carpet. It seemed intimate—like he belonged here. His unbuttoned shirt hung loose from his jeans. It flustered her.

"Good morning, Maggie." He moved toward the kitchen. "Wondered where you ran off to."

"'Morning," Maggie murmured, suddenly shy. "I fixed breakfast. Didn't want to wake you, you looked so peaceful."

Ethan held out her chair then seated himself, pouring them each a cup of coffee. "Smells good," he murmured, filling his plate.

Ducking her head, she took a bite of her breakfast.

"You're awfully quiet," he commented.

Maggie looked up with a brief smile. "Sorry..."

They sat facing each other, breakfast growing cold as they looked at one another, each seeking something in the other's eyes, not sure of one another's feelings, yet lost in the wonder and magic of the night and their loving.

She gazed out the window. “It’s beginning to snow. The children will be so pleased about it. Matt told me last week they always had snow at Christmas when his mother was alive. He said it was as though she’d brought the snow and when she died took it with her.”

“Think they’ll like the presents we bought yesterday?” He changed the subject, hoping to lift her spirits.

“They need a mother.” Her eyes were deep pools of pain that tore at his heart.

“Well, we could fix that, couldn’t we?” Moving the chair next to her, he reached into the pocket of his shirt and brought out the little silver box. “I got this for you.”

Passing her the jeweler’s box, he leaned back, watching as she took it with trembling hands, head bent so a fall of hair hid her expression. She sat for a long moment, turning the object in her fingers, making no move to open the lid. He lifted the curtain of hair, tilting his head to see her face. “Well? Are you going to open it?”

“Ethan, what does this mean?” She looked up, eyes questioning—hoping—while at the same time despairing. “I can’t accept this.”

“How could you know? You haven’t opened it yet.” He pried the lid open. The sparkling diamond engagement ring and plain gold band winked in the dim light.

“I know it will fit.” Ethan hurried his speech, rushing his fences, suddenly afraid she’d say no. “I borrowed one of your rings while you were ill and took it to the jeweler. We could be married tomorrow. Just say the word.”

“I don’t know what to say. It’s so sweet of you to offer.” She looked down at the diamond and brushed her fingertips over the hard, cold surface, then looked at him once more. “You are truly a nice man to offer to help me this way.”

She slowly closed the lid and held the box out to him. "But I can't let you make such a sacrifice, not even for the children. And especially not for me."

"Sacrifice?" His voice quivered with indignation and anger. "What makes you think I would be dumb enough to sacrifice my life? *I love you*, Maggie. Want to spend my life with you. How the hell—"

"Don't curse." She snatched the box back and flipped the lid open, slowly lifting the diamond ring from its nest. "If you're sure you really want to..." Gazing at him, her brown eyes sparkled. He'd said he loved her.

"Never been more certain of anything in my life." Ethan took the ring and slid it on the third finger of her left hand. He quipped nervously, "Well, is this a yes or a maybe?"

"Hmm, let me think." She lifted her hand and examined the sparkling gem. "I guess if you've gone to this much expense, I'd better say yes."

He gathered her close and kissed her until they were both breathless, his mouth seeking hers hungrily. As his lips played over her throat, her eyes and back again to her mouth, he reveled in the taste of her, her sensual whimper as he touched her. She arched against him, breath coming quickly as he aroused her to a fever pitch.

The ringing phone startled them both. Ethan pulled away reluctantly, reaching for the phone on the counter behind him. His decisive movements and take charge manner said master of the house. Mouth turning grim, he listened to the voice on the other end. "When?"

His clipped tone held secrets. "We'll be in touch." Hanging up, he pulled her close.

"What is it? What's wrong?"

"That was the Children's Center. The Baker children's father died this morning. Matt has run away with his brothers and sister." She stiffened at his words and he held her tighter. "Mister Chambers thinks they're coming here. Have they been here before?"

"Yes, several times for special outings. Do you think

Matt can find his way?"

Maggie looked at the wind-driven snow outside the picture window. "How will they survive in this?"

"Don't worry, Maggie. Matt is a smart kid. Evidently he borrowed your phone number and address from the rolodex on Chambers' desk."

"Did you hear that? Someone just called my name. It sounded like a child."

"Yes, I did." Ethan turned toward the door. "You stay inside. I'll check it out."

"Not on your life, mister." Maggie was right behind him as he bolted through the door.

Peering through the heavy snowfall, he spied four small figures coming up the driveway. Anna Marie broke away from Matt and ran to him. Ethan picked her up and bundled her close. Reaching an arm out, he was gratified when Matt snuggled against him. Tommy and Toby raced ahead, straight into Maggie's open arms.

Ethan heard sobbing and looked down to see Matt wiping his eyes. He hugged the boy harder. "Let's get out of the cold, son."

Maggie removed their coats, seated them on the couch, then snuggled them in a throw blanket. Sharing hugs and kisses with each child, she glowed with happiness. Ethan thought he could spend his life watching this single moment and be content.

"I'm going to call Mr. Chambers." She reached for the phone.

"Maggie, my love, you'd better scramble some eggs for these hungry troupers. I'll call Chambers."

"Maggie, my love?" Matt looked askance at Ethan. "You got married?"

"Not quite. Just engaged." Ethan ruffled Matt's hair. Matt didn't pull away. "But we're making wedding plans. In fact, we were just talking about all of you."

"You were?" Toby piped up. "What'd ya say?"

"We said we'd love to have you come live with us." Ethan looked Matt straight in the eyes. "But it would be up to you, Matt. Your decision."

"I guess it'd be all right," Matt mumbled, blinking to hold back tears. Ethan did the same.

"Who are the presents for?" Anna Marie eyed the packages under the festive tree.

"Some are for you." Maggie brushed the child's hair back from her face. "But it's not Christmas yet."

"It's Christmas Eve," Tommy informed her in a solemn voice. "Our Mom used to let us open one gift on Christmas Eve."

"Sounds like a great tradition to me," Ethan agreed. "I say let's go for it. What about you kids?"

"Yeah!" Toby and Tommy scrambled to sit on the floor by the tree, while Matt stood apart, saying nothing.

Ethan knelt and sorted through the packages. "Hmm, here's one for Toby. Tommy, this one is for you."

His heart warmed at their excited faces as the children crowded round him. He rattled a gaily wrapped box with a big tag that said Anna Marie. "Let me see, I wonder who this one is for?"

"Me!" Anna Marie jumped up and down. "It's mine, 'cause that's my name." Ethan laughed as she pulled the present from his hands and eagerly tore at the paper.

Matt stood back, hands in his pockets, eyes on the angel tree topper. Ethan found a present with his name and stood to hand it to him. "Here you go, Matthew. Merry Christmas. Careful, it's heavy."

"Thank you, sir." With all the dignity of a ten-year-old, he sat next to his siblings and slowly opened the gift. The Nintendo player revealed, Matthew managed a smile, though Ethan could see the boy's heart wasn't in it.

"Matthew, why don't you and I fix breakfast and give Maggie a break?"

"Yes," Maggie chimed in, her hands full of crumpled wrapping paper. "I'll clean up the debris in here while you two do that."

"Okay," Matt said without enthusiasm. "But could you call me Matt? Only my mom ever called me

Matthew."

"Sure." Ethan tugged the boy close to his side and drew him toward the big, cheery kitchen.

Giving Matt the bread and nodding at the toaster, Ethan whipped the eggs and poured them in the skillet, waiting for the boy to open up. Sensing he'd have to go first, he said, "You know, my dad passed away when I wasn't much older than you. It's tough, losing your dad."

"I don't care if he's dead," Matt said, slathering butter on a slice of toast. "He didn't care about us anyhow."

"No?" Ethan urged—hoping Matt would unburden himself and get past the grief that had to be bottled up in his young heart.

"Our mom died, then he went to jail. He just left us to...to starve."

"Starve?" Ethan thought Matt was paraphrasing an adult. Someone had done their work well to make this child bitter at such a young age.

"Yeah. Granddad said so. We lived with him for a while after..."

"After your dad went to jail?"

"Yeah. Granddad died, too, you know," Matt finished in a quavering voice. "They all died and left us."

Ethan turned off the fire under the eggs and pulled the sobbing boy into his arms. He moved to the table and sat holding Matt, soothing him with words of comfort only someone who'd been there could know.

When the youngster finally pulled away and slipped off his lap, Ethan let go reluctantly.

"You and Maggie are gonna keep us?"

"If you want us to, yes," Ethan answered softly. "I think you could use a nice break or two after all you've been through, don't you?"

"Yeah, I guess so." Matt looked sheepish. "I didn't hate my dad and I didn't want him to die. I just said that."

"I know, son. And any time you want to talk about it,

I'll be right here to listen."

"Hey! We're starving in here," Maggie called from the living room, breaking the tension. "Get a move on, you two!"

"Hold your horses, we're almost done," Ethan yelled back, then grinned at Matt. "Guess we'd better hurry or they'll get into the Christmas fudge. Won't be any left for us."

When Matt grinned back, his young-old eyes sparkling, Ethan was content to leave the sad subject of dying behind for now. There would be plenty of time for them—years, in fact.

When they sat to eat, Matt took a chair next to him. Ethan's heart filled with love and gratitude, aware of the gifts this Christmas had brought him. Maggie and these four beautiful children. The look she gave him across the table told him she felt the same.

"Let's have a prayer, shall we?"

"I know a good prayer," Tommy offered with more boldness than he'd ever shown. Ethan noticed the quietest Baker sibling was missing a front tooth, giving him an endearing smile.

Tommy said Grace and they all dug in like they were starving. Maggie's laughter and the children's giggles filled the house like spring blossoms. Ethan was content.

Leaving them to their happy chatter, Ethan went to the phone and dialed the Children's Protective Shelter. When Mr. Chambers came on the line, he explained the children were safe, and requested they spend the night.

"I see no problem with that, Doctor Spencer. I'm relieved they're safe."

"Mr. Chambers, Mrs. Donaldson and I are getting married next week," Ethan said without preamble. "We're going to apply for adoption of the Baker siblings. Can you see your way clear to let them stay here until we get the paperwork done? Naturally, I'll move out until the wedding for propriety's sake."

"I'll see what I can do. Since tomorrow is Christmas,

I can't accomplish anything until Thursday, but I'll certainly come and do a cursory inspection of the home tomorrow—just to be legal, of course."

"You'd take time from your family on Christmas Day to do that?" Ethan was touched.

"Well, you'll have to promise to play Santa at the center next year, but yes, I'll do that." Mr. Chambers laughed heartily. "Didn't know favors came with strings around here, huh?"

Ethan hung up and turned to find Maggie standing close. He touched a tear coursing its way down her smooth cheek. "What's wrong, love?"

"Wrong? Oh, absolutely nothing is wrong." Maggie hugged him. "Everything is perfect! I always cry when I'm happy."

"Do you laugh when you're sad?" he teased.

"No. But sometimes I laugh when I'm mad, so watch out, Mister." She grinned and hugged him again. Ethan hugged her back for a long time.

"Let's spend a lazy day. We'll bake cookies, play games—"

"You baked cookies yesterday."

"Yes, but it's more fun with the kids. I've got a feeling we're going to be baking a lot of cookies around here the next few years."

"Yeah, we sure will, baby." He kissed the tip of her nose and turned her toward the living room. Sounds of joyful children filled the air. "Why don't you read us a story later?"

Ethan awoke to the sounds of off-key singing and opened his eyes. Maggie and the kids stood around him giving a terrible, but beautiful rendition of Jingle Bells. He grinned and sat up.

"You fall asleep every time I read a story." Maggie mocked being angry, but her smile soon gave her away.

"We'd better get our kids tucked in for the night. Christmas morning comes early when you have children."

Maggie's joy radiated like a golden beam—from her smile, from her eyes, from her laughter.

Ethan thought there was nothing so beautiful in the world as Maggie at Christmas.

Be sure to visit Diane's website
http://www.dianedaviswhite.com

Rachel's Light

by Victoria Houseman

Charleston, South Carolina, 1783

"Miss Levine. Your presence is requested in the library—immediately."

"Coming, sir." Rachel turned to the children. "Go in to Cook and have her give you some cookies while I speak with your father." No sense in them hearing their father's roar.

Since becoming governess to Mr. Samuel Stein's two young children, Eve and Joshua, she didn't seem to be able to do anything to please the man. If not for the bond she'd formed with the children, she would have left his employ long ago.

She reached the massive doors leading to the library and paused, her hands gripping the polished brass knobs. She'd endured six months of Samuel Stein's quick to flare temper and sullen, withdrawn moodiness.

Determination to look him directly in the eye and let him know how insufferable he'd been, pushed past nervousness. Uncivil behavior was unacceptable—even from her employer. The moment had arrived for her to tell him so, in no uncertain terms. If he demanded her resignation, then so be it. At least she'd leave with her self-respect intact.

Rachel pushed the doors open, shoulders squared, head high. He sat in his chair near the hearth, his head turned toward the fire. His shirt open at the neck, the ties hanging down framed a patch of skin covered in dark hair. Firelight outlined his profile, giving his strong bones an almost ominous look.

All her resolve faded and butterflies danced in the pit of her stomach. She prayed he couldn't hear their fluttering wings.

The most beautiful man she'd ever seen turned to face her. More times than she could count, she'd wondered how much fabric it had taken to make one shirt to house those broad shoulders.

His chestnut hair tied back in a queue, he looked rough and dangerous. Rachel thought she'd faint from the sight of him. A few strands broke free of their moorings and he swiped at them with impatient hands. What would it feel like to be that hand brushing back those thick locks that refused their owner's commands?

His stern voice snapped her out of her fantasies. Her cheeks flushed hot when she realized he'd been calling her name repeatedly while staring at her with eyes the color of violets. How could God have pieced together so much beauty with such a mean-spirited soul?

"What is this?" He waved the offending object in the air.

Her throat went dry and tight. "It's...it's a *latke*, sir." *So much for bravery.*

"I can see that, Miss Levine. What is a potato pancake doing in my study?"

"It is almost the holidays, sir." She twisted trembling hands in the folds of her skirt. "And...well... this being the first holiday without their mother..."

Something dark passed over his eyes at the mention of his late wife.

She continued, "I decided their lessons for this month should focus on the meaning of Chanukah."

He pushed out of his chair, using his cane for support. Stalking the room in a circle, he continued to prominently display the latke in the air like a spoil of war. All the while he made the circle smaller, getting closer to her with each step. His boots thumped loudly on the wooden floor as his cane thudded with every step. His footsteps made a distinct sound due to his limp.

"While you were away on your recent trip, the children and I took their lessons in here. They told me how much they loved their papa's library as it made them feel close to you—especially since you're away so much."

He paused and glared at her, his jaw tightly set. She knew immediately that had been the wrong thing to say, but it was too late to call it back. "Cook made a wonderful surprise of samples of traditional holiday foods." The pitch of her voice arced unnaturally high like a squeaky little mouse and she wanted to kick herself. "Ummm...well, sir," she nervously gestured toward the offending item, "that one must've gotten away."

"Miss Levine." He spoke the words too softly.

Forcing her eyes to his, it struck her why she babbled when she spoke to him, why she avoided looking into his eyes. Overwhelming emotions emanated from them and they hit her heart with dagger sharp precision.

He looked...haunted. Was it the loss of his wife that had wounded him so? The household staff talked of an unhappy, often volatile marriage—one without love.

She searched deeper and in that moment she knew Samuel Stein's eyes told of a wounded soul. Something so powerful it went beyond the death of a wife he didn't love.

She walked toward him with an outstretched hand—slow, halting steps. She could almost feel the muscles in his clenched jaw and she longed to wipe the tightness away, to run her upturned palm down his cheek and trace his cheekbone with a light touch. "Mr. Stein. I..." Without ceremony, he dropped the *latke* into her hand before she could complete her sentence. She stopped, frozen.

Cold, icy water thrown on her couldn't have been more shocking than the realization of what she'd been about to do. If he hadn't dropped the pancake into her hand, she would have touched him—caressed her employer's face.

"...and furthermore," he continued, "this is the library, not the kitchen nor the dining room. The children have quite an adequate study area on the third floor—plenty of windows and light. I made sure of it myself. This room is off limits without my express permission. Do I make myself clear, Miss Levine?"

"Yes, Mr. Stein." She tried to force her voice above a whisper, to no avail.

Samuel turned to stare again into the volatile depths of the fire before she could see the regret on his face. He'd been a total bastard of late—hell, since Katherine's death, but to take it out on this lovely young woman was beyond cruel.

"May I please be excused, sir?"

The meekness in her voice suited her station. She wore hand-me down clothes that were too short, too worn, and too dull, yet she wore them with a quiet dignity that said they suited her as well as if they were the most expensive frocks made. She never acted above her station. A station that placed her under his employ and outside his reach and he couldn't bear it. She had hair as black as a moonless night and rich, brown eyes that seemed too big for her sculpted face. Now, because of his brutality, tears threatened to spill from those eyes. He wanted to take his damn cane and whip his own hide.

He tried to gentle his voice before he spoke. "By all means, Miss Levine, you may leave. I shall see the children at supper."

It took a piece of the remnant of his bitter heart knowing he'd pained such a kind, gentle soul. The early evening chill stiffened his mangled leg and he cursed the damn war that had done this to him. All his life he'd been a failure—a poor excuse for a son, a rotten brother to his only sibling, Grace, and he hadn't even found redemption by being a good soldier. He came home from The Siege of Charleston battered and crippled.

He thudded into the closest chair near the fire, a tankard of strong whiskey in hand. The chair skidded across the wooden floor. He held tightly to his tankard, but almost toppled in the process. Not a drop spilled. Ah! He found his one talent in life—not spilling his whiskey.

"Miss Levine."

She turned at the door and looked at him.

"Thank you..." He cleared his throat and forced himself to speak louder, clearer, "Thank you for all you've done for my children." He had a great need to say more, but couldn't. The words stuck in his throat.

The flames from the fireplace bathed the room in shades of red and gold, framing Rachel beside the doors. She looked like an angel against the rage of fire. An angel he wanted as his salvation.

I am a bitter old man before my time. He brought the glass to his lips and threw back his head, allowing the strong whiskey to burn a fast trail down his throat.

"Would you care to join the children and me for our walk on the grounds before supper? The air is brisk..." She froze when he turned to stare at her.

The loveliness of her offer created an ache deep inside he fought to ignore.

"Not tonight. My leg and the cold air don't get along."

"Yes, sir. I understand. I'm...sorry. I didn't mean to be insensitive. I'm sorry." She hurried from the room.

The doors clicked shut before he could stop her. Closing his eyes, he leaned his head against the back of the wing chair.

He struck his fist to his forehead and groaned aloud at his own insensitivity. He'd hurt her—yet again.

The faces of Eve and Joshua flashed behind his closed lids. His beautiful children so full of life, so pure of heart. He saw himself laughing while he swung them, one then the other in his arms on the lawn. It had been a glorious spring day—the kind only Charleston could produce. Had it only been this past spring? Then their mother had died and the children stopped smiling. Or, maybe they stopped laughing because of his sudden change after his wife's death—from loving father to foul-tempered tyrant. He knew his actions were wrong, yet he couldn't change the way he felt. He was lonely.

His leg didn't hurt as much as he'd led Rachel to believe. For some inexplicable reason, the thought of spending time with his children frightened him. They couldn't believe their once beloved papa had turned into this awful man. He saw it in their sweet faces whenever he drew near.

He silently vowed to do better, to try harder. He knew this vow by memory, for he had made it thousands of times before.

Rachel leaned against the closed door, confusion settling over her. His moods had shifted so quickly. Angry, frightening, civil. And, then, almost...kind. She rubbed the tension between her brow. To think he had looked at her with anything other than the eye of an employer was utter foolishness. The wishful daydreams of a love-struck girl.

What did she know about love? Although nearly two and twenty, love had never entered her life. How could it? As newcomers to this land, she worked all the time, helping her family as they tried to make a life for themselves.

She pushed away from the door and headed upstairs to get the children ready for their playtime outside, determinedly shoving all silly romantic notions out of her head with each step she climbed.

A quiet murmur drifting through the partially open

nursery door caught his attention. Samuel paused to listen. Turning his ear to the opening, he recognized the beautiful sound as singing.

He peered through the slight opening. Tapers burned low. His heart followed the sound before his eyes adjusted.

There, in a corner of the room, Rachel rocked Eve while singing her a lullaby. The child stared, mesmerized by Rachel's lovely voice. Every time her tiny eyelids tried to flutter shut and drift into sleep, she'd suddenly push them open wide so as not to miss a moment of the song.

An inner door opened and Joshua stepped into the nursery. He tiptoed in the exaggerated way of children and Rachel fought not to laugh. Shifting Eve in her arms, she patted her leg and the little boy eagerly curled in her lap, too. Rachel continued rocking and singing and before long, both children fell fast asleep.

Samuel softly pushed open the door. Rachel laid her cheek on each child's head and then pressed her lips to their hair, holding them tighter to her breast with each movement. Never had their mother shown such tenderness and love for these children. He wanted to weep for the beauty of it.

For the first time, love and warmth filled this room. All because of Rachel. Light seemed to emanate from her, pulling him in its glow like a drowning man to a safe harbor. He stared, transfixed, while she continued to rock his two sleeping children in her arms—one bare, beautiful foot pushing off from the floor, keeping the movement of the chair soft and fluid.

The rocking stopped and his attention came to rest on her face. Rachel stared at him— eyes wide and deep and full of...what? He didn't dare hope she had feelings for him—not after how abominable he'd been to her.

A tentative smile curved her lips.

"Here, let me help you," he whispered.

Rachel coaxed Joshua into his father's arms while she held onto Eve. Shifting Eve to both arms, she rose from the chair.

They walked in silence to the children's beds where they laid them down. Samuel pulled warm quilts around his sleeping son, covering the boy to his shoulders. The night threatened frost and he didn't want Joshua to catch cold. He bent and kissed his son's cheek. It had been a spontaneous gesture, one he didn't do nearly enough. "I love you, son."

Going to his daughter's side, he repeated the affectionate acts. Eve stirred in her sleep, a soft sigh escaping her china doll mouth. He quietly cupped one round cheek and she turned her head snuggling into his hand, the softness of her skin caressing his palm. The gesture of love from his child shattered him. He wanted to hurry from the room and run out into the night. He wanted to howl his hurt and anguish at the moon until empty from all the pain he held inside.

"Your children love you so."

Turning, he found himself staring into deep brown eyes that spoke of healing and hope. Samuel reached out a hand and saw it trembled. Rachel's hair felt like fine silk as he sifted it through his fingers. Curls wrapped around his fingers like living, breathing vines. They drew him closer.

His other hand stroked her cheek. "You are so very beautiful."

Rachel froze, her heart thundering so hard it threatened to break loose from her chest. "Mr. Stein, sir–" Her arms worked enough to get her shawl tighter around her shoulders. In doing so, her hand brushed the front of his open shirt, her knuckles grazing his skin. It felt warm and slightly damp. His labored breathing and the feral look in his eyes frightened and enthralled her at the same time.

"Samuel. Call me Samuel. Not proper, I know, but when has being proper ever been a part of my life?" One arm went around her waist while his other hand continued to caress her face. Her slightly parted lips invited him nearer. Moving forward, he lifted her chin with the tip of a finger to see her face. He trailed his finger over her full lower lip and knew he had to taste her.

When he lowered his mouth to hers, she didn't move. She stood motionless as he gripped her waist, brought her against his chest. He touched her mouth with his—a whisper of lips. The kiss deepened, slowly, tenderly. The tip of his tongue traced her lips, asking them to part. She opened them on a sigh. Nothing had ever felt so wonderful as having this woman in his arms. She placed tentative hands on his waist.

"Yes, darling. Put your arms around me."

Rachel obeyed, wrapping her arms around his waist and moving her palms up his back. She couldn't seem to stop herself. Her hands glided over his broad, muscular shoulders and the warmth they exuded seeped into her. He held her tighter—one arm around her waist and one hand tangled in her hair, the palm cradling her head.

The kiss turned hard and seeking. He tasted of whiskey—warm and intoxicating.

Cold air hit her back and she realized he'd moved his hand. She wanted it around her again, holding her close to his chest. His hand came between their bodies and rested on the open spot in her nightrail between her breasts. Where had her shawl gone? The warmth of his palm against her bare skin bled deep into her body and she moaned into his mouth. Slowly that large, strong hand inched its way over until his fingers encircled her breast through the fabric of her gown.

"No..." Shoving against his chest as hard as she could, Rachel stumbled backwards. Retrieving her shawl from the floor, she wrapped it tightly around her shoulders. "No. This is wrong, Mr. Stein."

Reaching a hand to her, he stepped forward. "Rachel, please, I am so sorry. I didn't mean to..." His heart broke when he saw her flinch at his proffered hand.

"I'll have my things packed by morning. Only, let me say good-bye to the children before I leave." The children. The thought of leaving those precious babies tore her heart in two–one half belonging to each of them.

"Don't go. I swear it will never happen again."

She wanted it to happen again, wanted more. She never knew anything could feel so wonderful. But, he was her employer and would never be anything more. She had to maintain her dignity. She'd not allow him to compromise her–no matter how badly she wanted him, how much she loved him. Leaving would resolve the issue.

"It's for the best." The anguish and pleading in his eyes caused her to look away before she relented.

Curling his outstretched hand into a fist, he dropped it to his side.

"As you wish, Miss Levine. I'll have my carriage take you wherever you choose to go. If you need a letter of reference, I will be more than willing to write one."

Rachel only nodded. Speaking would have betrayed the tears she fought to hide. She watched the only man she would ever love leave the room. Flickering candlelight brought her attention around. The glow haloed each child while they slept. Their breaths came even and soft, their hands open on their pillows in the trusting way of sleeping babes.

Rachel sank to the floor and wept.

He would be nothing if Rachel left. The void created would render him an empty husk, and eventually he'd break apart and blow away with the wind. He'd find enough time later to berate himself for his foolish behavior in trying to seduce her.

All sense had left him when the heat from her skin had come through the thin fabric of her nightrail and soaked into his chest. He wanted to lay in that warmth forever.

As he paced in his room, he ignored the muscles cramping in his leg. He'd been on it too long today and the damp, chill weather caused it to ache more than normal. Nothing mattered at this moment other than finding a way to keep Rachel by his side.

Eve and Joshua's sweet faces passed through his mind. He squeezed his eyes shut so he couldn't imagine their sad faces when they learned of Rachel's leaving.

It came to Samuel in a sudden rush of lighted awareness. He knew what he had to do to keep his beloved Rachel with him.

"May we call you mama, please?" Rachel had barely arrived in the dining room to say good-bye to the children when they came running to her.

"What?" Baffled, she looked from one upturned face to the next. "Eve, Joshua, I have come to say—"

"That you have accepted my marriage proposal and can't wait to become their mother." Samuel swallowed a prayer that this would work.

Straightening her shoulders, Rachel avoided looking at him, at the children, at anything in the room except a woven flower on the rug while she tried to take in what she'd just heard.

The children wouldn't allow her the luxury of catching her breath. Tugging on her skirts, they demanded her attention.

"You will be our mama now and forever." Eve spread her tiny arms wide and spun in a circle.

"Children." Sounding harsher than she'd intended, Rachel winced at the stunned expressions on their faces as they suddenly halted. She forced a smile, and gave them each a quick hug and said, "I need to speak with your father a moment. Run along to the kitchen and see if Cook has any Chanukah treats."

Their joy back in place, they skipped out the door.

"Would you please explain yourself, sir?"

He didn't miss the emphasis on the word, *sir*. "The children will be devastated if you leave. They've had so much loss in their young lives and since you refuse to stay on as their governess, I've decided to marry you." It didn't come out like he meant and sounded so much better when he'd rehearsed it last night.

"Marry me? A servant?" Shock framed her features.

"I don't stand on formalities. You should know that by now, Rachel. I don't give a damn what anyone thinks of the decisions I make." Putting his hands behind his back, he stared at a spot somewhere over her head. "I was terribly out of line last night. I treated you with the utmost disrespect and the least I can do is make some kind of amends. Besides, my children love you so."

Foolish, foolish girl. For one moment, she thought he might actually say he'd fallen in love with her as she had with him.

"I see. The merchants in town lock up their daughters at the thought of you, so I, a servant, who has never owned a new dress in her life, will be just fine to be mother to your children and share your bed?" That last should have made her blush, but she was beyond blushing now. He didn't intend to make amends for his behavior of the previous evening, only to assuage his guilty conscience for handling her in a drunken state. She wanted to forget how it felt to be in his arms, how his lips felt upon hers, the things he'd awakened in her.

"No, Rachel, that isn't what I meant, not at all." He ran his hands through his hair. "Damn, this isn't going at all how I'd planned." Did he actually think this wonderful woman would fall into his arms and profess undying love after how he'd treated her all these months culminating in his assault on her? Yet he couldn't forget how she felt in his arms. Her soft, warm body crushed to his chest, her sweet mouth open for his kisses. No, he couldn't forget. Didn't want to.

"We need to think of the children. They are all that matter." He'd resorted to blackmailing her emotions—knew it and didn't care. Desperate men employed desperate means. He watched her shoulders relax, seem to slump, and he knew he'd won. "I won't touch you, Rachel, not ever. Not unless you want me."

Yes, I want you to touch me, she wanted to cry out, but only said, "Fine, then. We shall marry. If only for the children."

"Yes, if only for the children," he echoed.

She stood there for the longest time, not moving, not breathing. Just stood and stared into his violet eyes. Those haunted eyes. He looked away first, turned his back and went to stare out the window. He stood tall and straight, with large, beautiful hands clasped behind his back.

At that moment her heart shattered, for she realized she would be wed—tied forever—to a man who could never love her.

Samuel ran his fingers through his hair and looked around the room at the guests, at their forced smiles while making strained conversation. The simple wedding had been mere formality as there was no marriage settlement between himself and her family. His eyes came to rest on his bride. She stared at him, the look in her eyes unreadable. He'd bullied her into marrying him, used her love for his children as a weapon against her. The means seemed to justify the end at the time. Now, overwhelming guilt washed over him.

This should be the most glorious day of her life, instead the room felt like someone had died and the guests sat *Shiva* as opposed to attending a wedding supper.

Was she as unhappy as he felt? He couldn't take his eyes from her face, wondering what was going through her mind. They stood, staring at one another, neither making a move. Slowly, she made her way to her new husband

"Would you..." He swallowed and began again. "Would you care for something to eat?" That was the best he could think to say?

"I'm fine, Mr. Stein...Samuel." She corrected her mistake.

A look passed over her face, behind her eyes. He thought she'd tried to hide it, but he saw it. "I promised you I would never force you to do anything you are not comfortable doing." He hoped this would set her at ease, though he didn't know how long his growing need for her would be put off.

"No. I wasn't thinking about that. I mean..." She turned away. "Here, Samuel, we are married now. Let me prepare a plate for you."

She hurried to the table laid with the feast before he could comment.

After the last of the guests departed, Rachel had no idea what to do next. Normally, she'd be getting the children ready for bed, but that had been taken care of this evening.

The air suddenly grew thick and heavy as Samuel moved behind her. She had no idea what to do, what to say. She wished she'd never agreed to this marriage–nothing about it seemed right. As long as she kept reminding herself she married Samuel for the children, then maybe she could manage.

"Would you like to go upstairs now?"

"What?" Rachel spun around, startled by the words.

"It is getting late. It has been a long day and I am sure you must be exhausted." He stated his case matter-of-factly.

Samuel softened his tone before continuing. "I've arranged for your belongings to be moved to the room connected to mine." He held up his hand before she could interrupt. "You may lock the door from your side if you still have trouble believing I will never force myself upon you. I wanted to spare you any embarrassment about our...arrangement...and so I thought I could, at the very least, make it look as though we have a real marriage." A real marriage with Rachel–filled with love and respect. How he wished it were true.

Taking his bride by the elbow, he escorted her to the stairs. They reached the second floor and he guided her to their rooms.

Entering the bedroom, she saw a fire had been set and two glasses of wine had been placed on a table near the hearth. Samuel handed her a glass and took one for himself. She drank it quickly, too quickly, for she'd had very little to eat, and felt her legs begin to give way beneath her. Suddenly, she was lifted into the air by a pair of strong arms. Soft pillows greeted her head and she knew he'd laid her on the bed. He removed her shoes and pulled the coverlet around her.

The last thing she remembered, Samuel placed a soft kiss upon her brow and called her his 'sweet wife.' Surely, the latter must have been a dream.

March brought brisk winds to Charleston. Rachel normally loved this time of year best–when spring announced its arrival and the air smelled clean and crisp. This spring, she didn't have her usual enthusiasm.

It had been three months since her marriage. Three months of putting on happy faces for the people who continued to wish them *MazelTov*. Three months of retiring for the evening together, only to sleep in separate rooms. Three months of family and staff staring at her belly, wondering when she would be with child.

The pretense exhausted her and she didn't know how much more she could handle before she broke down. In private, they acted polite to the point of utter frustration. Short of screaming at him to stop being so civil, she didn't know what to do. She almost preferred when she'd been the governess and he the master and he'd yell at her for the tiniest infraction. At least then he showed some emotion.

Yet, at certain times he'd smile and she knew he meant it for her. Times when their hands reached for the same dish at a meal and their fingers touched. And she didn't think it her imagination when he let his fingers rest against hers just a moment longer than necessary.

"Mama! Mama!" The children came running into the room, calling for her in unison.

"Hello, my darlings." She bent and gathered them close. Her heart sang knowing they thought of her as their mother. "Shall we go outside and look at the beautiful trees in bloom?"

Eve and Joshua looked one to the other, their small faces solemn. They turned and looked at Rachel–eyes wide and serious.

"Dear hearts. Whatever is the matter?" She knelt, her hands rubbing their arms.

"Do married people never look happy?" Joshua's innocent question sent a sigh through Rachel. Children perceived a lot more than they received credit for, and she knew sooner or later they would notice the strain between her and their father.

Standing, she took each child by the hand and led them to the settee. They sat, folded their little hands in their laps and waited for her answer. She inhaled a deep breath, looked heavenward for strength, though knowing she'd have to handle this on her own.

"You see, my loves, oftentimes when a man and a woman get married–"

"It's my fault, really." They turned to find Samuel standing in the library doorway. "I was so excited to marry your new mama that I didn't wait until I had finished conducting some important business." He crossed the room and sat down on the settee, drawing each child onto his lap. "I've been much too busy with business and have ignored you two and my beautiful bride."

With that last, he turned a warm smile on her. The sun couldn't rival the light emanating from his beautiful face and especially those violet eyes. Did she dare hope? Maybe he really did have feelings for her.

"All that will change as of today. No more business for a while. I am at the bidding of my two wonderful children and my lovely wife."

The children squealed with delight. Samuel stood,

never taking his eyes from Rachel. Hoping she'd see the promise in them. Tentatively, he reached out a hand to help her stand. Just as tentatively, she put her hand in his. He closed his fingers around hers and something inside him unraveled. Something tight, ugly and black that he hadn't even realized he'd been carrying in his heart and soul for a very long time. A light filled him and he knew it belonged to Rachel. A light reaching from her soul into his—filling him with happiness and peace.

He'd been such a fool. Could he undo the damage he'd done by not being honest with her? By telling her what she really meant to him? Whatever it took, he meant to try.

"Come wife," he said, his voice soft and low. "Shall we take our children to play outside on this glorious March day?"

The sun shone brightly in a cloudless sky. A gentle breeze drifted through the trees, carrying the fresh clean scent of renewal. Samuel brought a hamper of food. Rachel sat on a quilt on the lawn arranging the repast.

Eve and Joshua played tag, their once silent voices raised in joyous sound, their faces glowing with renewed joy.

Rachel called them for lunch and they fell atop the quilt in a laughing, tired heap. After feasting on the wonderful meal, the children fell asleep—Joshua comfortable in Rachel's lap and Eve curled near Samuel, her head on his thigh.

"Thank you for this wonderful day." Rachel smiled.

The late afternoon wind picked up, sending curls into her eyes. She lifted a hand to clear her vision and her hand collided with that of her husband's larger one.

"Here, let me." He gently brushed the hair from her face and tucked it behind her ear. "I've been wanting to do that for the longest time."

Rachel turned her face into his hand and laid a kiss on his palm. Realizing what she'd done, she yanked away. "I'm sorry," she stammered. "I had no right to be so forward."

"You have every right, sweet Rachel. You are my wife." He rubbed the spot she'd kissed with his fingers, wanting to contain the feeling of her soft lips on his palm forever. Leaning toward her, he cupped the back of her neck, holding her steady. With their lips inches apart, he hesitated only a moment, breathing in her scent. Slowly, he touched his lips to hers, a chaste kiss, a gentle brushing of lips.

Leaning back, his hand now on her shoulder, she looked directly at him, her face flushed and her lips slightly parted as if in anticipation of more. How he wanted to give her so much more. Instead, he rubbed his hand down her arm until he caught her hand in his. He wanted to go slowly so as not to frighten her–the memory of that awful night in the nursery still fresh in his mind. Today was a promising start.

Dusk settled over Charleston, painting the sky in soft purples and grays. Samuel gazed into the blazing hearth, his bad leg outstretched on a footstool. It throbbed from the day's exertions, but seeing the smiles on his children's faces and hearing their laughter made the throbbing worth it. Watching the discomfort leave Rachel's eyes, seeing her begin to trust him, made everything worth it.

She'd taken the children upstairs for bed and promised to meet him in their rooms for a glass of sherry. He wanted to talk to her about the possibility of them having a real future together. Of being man and wife, of having a child of their own one day.

The thought of making love to her, of planting a child in her womb, filled him with a contentment he never dared dream. He would make it happen. Somehow, Rachel would love him as much as he loved her.

A soft knock on the door startled her. Before it opened, she knew her husband would walk through the doorway. She'd decided the time had come to truly be man and wife. She loved Samuel and tonight she would show him. This joining between husband and wife was meant to be wondrous–especially if it brought forth a child. Her hand went to her belly and she wondered if she would be blessed with a child this night.

He walked over to where she sat before her mirror and stood behind her, hands on her shoulders.

"Aren't you feeling well?" Strong hands kneaded her shoulders.

"What?"

He looked over her head to their reflections in the mirror and motioned with his chin to the hand on her belly.

She saw concern in his beautiful violet eyes. "Oh, I'm fine. You needn't have knocked. This is your room, after all."

"Our room," he corrected.

"Our room," she repeated, liking how it felt to say it.

He raised her from her seat and turned her to face him, drawing her close in his arms. His arms wound tightly around her and he rested his head atop hers. From the top of her head to the bottom of her toes she felt peace, belonging, safe. In some way, she'd gotten through to him, had convinced him he could give her his heart and she would care for it always.

Pulling back, he traced a finger under her eyes. "Darling. You're crying. Now what have I done to put tears in those lovely eyes? I wanted today to be only perfect."

Seeing the distress in his eyes, she quickly quelled it. "These are tears of happiness. Oh Samuel, I am so full of love for you. It's time you knew." Lifting his hand, she kissed the tip of his finger that held her tears.

It became too much. Samuel lifted his wife in his arms and carried her to the bed. He placed her gently in the middle and followed her down.

"I love you, beautiful Rachel." He placed his hands on either side of her face, kissed her eyes, her nose, her mouth. "I think I always have. I will never forgive myself for how I've treated—"

She reached and placed two fingers on his mouth to silence him. "It's in the past, my love. We have tonight, tomorrow, and forever to share our love." Her arms wound around his neck. "Love me, Samuel. Make me your wife in every sense."

And he did. He loved her throughout the night, tenderly, passionately, completely. Rachel's light completed him, made him whole. He decided then and there if all he did the rest of his life was show her how much he worshipped her, he would die fulfilled.

Afterward, he held her in his arms and quoted from Song of Songs, "'I am my Beloved and my Beloved is mine.'"

"Forever, my love," Rachel sighed, sated with lovemaking. "Forever."

Be sure to visit Victoria's website
http://www.victoriahouseman.com

The Greatest Gift of All

by Candace Gold

Brittany Sykes waltzed into her older sister Claudia's room. "How do I look?" She whirled around in her red dress, acting like a contestant auditioning for some debutante reality show.

"Beautiful."

"I detect a hint of prejudice."

"Not one bit," Claudia replied, crossing her heart.

"Why don't you come to the dance with us?"

Claudia had been waiting for Brittany to bring the dance up again. Neither her mother nor sister understood her desire to remain at home.

"I'm sure Matthew is just dying to have your sister tag along."

"Don't be silly. You don't have to hang with us. There'll be other singles there."

"Yeah, Mom's age. It's a Valentine's Day dance at the *church*, for goodness sake."

Had Mom not paid for your ticket in advance, you wouldn't be going, either. "Besides, I have a ton of things to do."

"Such as?"

"Laundry."

Brittany rolled her eyes. "Claudia, it's time to put Andrew behind you. You need to get a life again."

"I *am* living."

"Like a nun. When was the last time you actually went out on a date and had some fun?"

"Who's having fun?" their mother said, walking into the room.

"Certainly not Claudia, Mom."

A frown formed across their mother's brow. "Aren't you going to the dance tonight?"

Claudia shook her head. *Please don't start.*

"For heaven's sake, why not?"

"She has too much laundry."

A look of disbelief crossed their mother's face. "The laundry can wait. All work—"

"I know the saying."

"Then follow it and *go*."

Between them both, they verbally tortured Claudia into going. Attending a Valentine's Day dance at the church was just about the last thing on her to-do list—somewhere between gouging her eyes out and walking barefoot on hot coals.

She hadn't desired to go out since Andrew broke their engagement a month before the wedding and ran off to marry some woman he'd met at a cousin's club get-together. Although almost a year ago, it still hurt. She guessed she didn't go out because she feared getting hurt again. Granted, not all men would act like Andrew, but if you don't start anything, you won't end up getting hurt— plain and simple. Of course running into Andrew and his new bride at the Swap Mart a few months ago hadn't helped her forget, either.

Anyway, Brittany, the social butterfly, was forever going out and easily picked up the slack for her.

Reluctantly she put on her favorite black silk dress and swept her long hair up to achieve a look of some sophistication. As she looked in the mirror, time rolled backward to the last time she'd worn this same dress...

She saw herself brushing her honey-colored hair into the same knot. Andrew was taking her to a Christmas party at his supervisor's home.

"You look gorgeous!" He'd popped out of his chair

when he'd seen her on the steps.

As they'd walked towards his car, he'd stopped and taken her into his arms. She remembered seeing a look of pride in his eyes just before he'd covered her lips with his.

Subconsciously she touched her lips. She still felt that gentle pressure. It had been a magical night and ended with their engagement. She'd thought herself the luckiest girl in the world. Too bad those smiling lips turned out to be lying ones. She never wore the dress again—until tonight.

Claudia pushed all those hurtful memories aside. Surely there'd be no one at the dance worth worrying over. Most of the single men would probably be fifty or older with pot bellies and receding or no hairlines. Their store-bought teeth might chatter and their hands would surely be clammy. She nearly giggled at the conjured image. She'd probably find herself alone hugging some corner to avoid them.

As she applied the finishing touches to her makeup, her mother walked over. "You look beautiful, Claudia. You should wear makeup more often."

She rolled her eyes. "I'm *already* going, Mom."

Her mother pursed her lips and hugged her. "I only want you to be happy. That's all."

A loud horn blast interrupted the conversation. Brittany shouted up to her from the bottom of the stairs. "Are you ready, Claudia? Matthew's here."

They drove to the Holy Trinity Church on Smith Street, where the dance was already in full swing. The band could be heard from the door and actually sounded good, which surprised Claudia. She figured the church would hire some half-baked band from nowhere to keep the cost down. It often held dances and bazaars to raise money to help the homeless.

Walking into the crowded room gaily decorated with hundreds of hearts and cupids, Claudia already regretted coming. The band began to play a slow song and Matthew and Brittany proceeded to the dance floor, but stopped when they saw a man heading in Claudia's direction. Before Claudia could find a spot to sit, she felt a tap on her shoulder. She turned around slowly to face a guy wearing black-framed glasses with round shot-glass thick lenses. What little hair he had left on his head was thin, lifeless and combed to the side. Prince Charming, he wasn't. And she very much doubted he'd even make it to the frog category.

"Would you care to dance?" he asked.

Brittany nearly pushed the man into her sister, clearly making sure Claudia didn't hide in the corner. Claudia opened her mouth to protest, but Brittany quickly said, "She'd be delighted to."

As the stranger led Claudia onto the dance floor, she tried to console herself with the thought he was probably a very nice person. Not everyone could look like an Adonis. Besides, she only had to dance with him once—not forever.

The man *did* have clammy hands and when he placed one on her bare back, she cringed. And that was only the beginning. From that moment on, everything went downhill. He was a terrible dancer, constantly stepping all over her feet. Though he apologized profusely, her poor feet didn't feel any better.

"You live around here?" he asked.

"Yes," she said, careful not to tell him where.

"Me, too. My name is Howard Dolan."

She felt tempted to give him a fictitious name. "Claudia Sykes."

"Oof, sorry," he said, coming down hard on her left foot.

"Ugh...that's...okay," she managed to say through the lingering pain, praying for the dance to end.

"I think you're the prettiest girl here."

"Thank you." She tried to concentrate at keeping her feet out of harm's way.

"Maybe we can get together some time..."

At that exact moment the music mercifully stopped.

She took it as her cue to escape.

"I must run to the Ladies' Room." She fled as fast as her two wounded feet would take her.

Feeling like a coward, Claudia ducked into the bathroom. Realizing she couldn't remain in there until the end of the evening, she decided to sneak out and look for a nice, dark corner to hide in. Hopefully Howard had found someone else to stomp on while she hid.

She opened the door a crack to see if the coast was clear. Howard was nowhere in sight. Opening the door the rest of the way, she slowly walked out. She half expected him to dart over and grab her, but he didn't. She exhaled and began to breathe normally again as she spied the nearest corner behind a pole. Just as she reached the safety of her chosen haven, she felt a tap on her shoulder. Thinking Howard had found her after all, she whirled around and said defiantly, "Go away!"

Only, it wasn't Howard.

A tall, good-looking man wearing a tailored blue, pin-striped suit stood there with a surprised look on his face. Talk about feeling like a total moron, she wished she was anyplace, but there. All she heard was a tiny voice in the back of her head screaming, 'Idiot!' over and over again. Come to think of it, the voice wasn't tiny at all.

She put her hand to her forehead and groaned. "Oh, I'm so very sorry...I didn't mean...I never...I thought... but you're not..." She finally stopped and took a deep breath before pleading, "Can I start over?"

By now his shocked expression had been replaced by an amused look as she continued to feel and behave like a total fool. The only thing she'd accomplished was to open her mouth to switch feet. Time to flee. However, the tall, handsome stranger stopped her.

"Please don't run off just yet. My name is Adam Devine."

Yes, you certainly are, she thought, but said, "When I'm not totally embarrassing myself, I'm Claudia Sykes."

"Well, Ms. Sykes, I'd be delighted if you'd dance with me."

"All you have to do is ask." She smiled.

He returned the smile. "Would you care to dance?"

Claudia placed her hand in his and he led her to the dance floor. When they reached it she glided into his arms. They swayed to the music, and to her relief he danced exquisitely. Not once did he step on her feet. Truly enjoying dancing with him, she wished for the music to never end.

Something about this man intrigued her. Merely having his strong arms around her, sent shivers of delight throughout her body. She hadn't felt such feelings since Andrew, which made her truly regret her earlier actions. She feared he was merely being a gentleman and after the song ended he would leave in order to find a more stable woman.

The moment of truth came. The music stopped. Claudia steeled herself for his goodbye.

Instead of thanking her and walking away, he asked, "Would you like to continue dancing?"

Joy coursed through her entire body. For the first time that night she actually felt glad her family talked her into coming to the dance.

Then when everything seemed to be going right, her world nearly stopped spinning.

Howard appeared out of nowhere and tapped Adam on the shoulder, wanting to cut in. She shifted her gaze to him, pleading with her eyes for Adam not to step aside. Being a gentleman, she was afraid he'd let Howard have the rest of the dance. Once again that night, she found herself holding her breath.

Then she heard Adam say, "Sorry, guy, but Claudia's my date."

"But—"

"Listen, man, that's the way it is," he said, hammering the point home.

Howard stomped away fuming.

"Thank you," Claudia whispered into his ear as they

resumed dancing.

"By any chance was he the reason for your earlier outbreak?"

"Uh-huh."

"You're definitely forgiven. The man has awful taste in clothing."

Laughter overwhelmed her. Adam's chuckle quickly joined hers. Not only was he easy on the eyes, he had a wonderful sense of humor, as well. They danced until the band took a break.

Adam's eyes searched the room.

"There," he said, cocking his head in the direction of an empty table. "We can sit for a while and talk." He placed his hand on her lower back and urged her toward the table. "You stay here while I go get us some drinks."

He must have been gone barely five seconds when Howard materialized out of nowhere and sat down in the chair opposite her. This was beginning to get out of hand. She no longer cared to spare his feelings.

"Why are you back?"

"I like you."

"Howard, this may come as a shock, but I really don't want to be with you—now or later."

"But, you hardly know me. Once you get to know me, I know you'll change your mind."

"I hate to be blunt, but I won't. And when Adam comes back he's going to be angry that you're sitting in his seat."

"Are you going to give me your number or not?"

She shook her head. "Goodbye, Howard."

"You have no idea how sorry you're going to be!" he snapped, before he walked off.

"Did I see our obnoxious friend back again?" Adam asked, returning to the table a short while later.

"Unfortunately, yes. For some reason, he doesn't seem to understand the meaning of the word no."

"Hopefully he won't return." He handed her a glass of white wine.

"Thank you for braving the crowd and getting me

this. Suddenly, I'm quite parched."

"We make a great team, you and I."

"How so?"

"You guarded the seats."

Facing her as he sat, Adam gazed into her eyes with his beautiful, warm brown ones.

"Now Claudia Sykes, tell me everything there is to know about you."

"Where shall I begin?"

"Anywhere, as long as you leave nothing out."

"Okay. Can we narrow the field down just a tad?"

"All right. What do you do when you're not dancing the night away?"

"I'm a loan manager at First National Bank."

"That's good to know."

"Why? What do you do?"

"I'm a history professor at Carlyle."

"I got my associate degree in business there."

They talked about their jobs and Claudia told him a little about her family before he interrupted. "You know something?"

"What?"

"I'm glad I came tonight."

"Me, too," she replied.

"I almost didn't," he admitted.

She chuckled.

"What's so funny about that?"

"My mother and sister ganged up on me to get me to come."

"So maybe there is something to that saying 'there's a reason for everything.'"

"I'll drink to that," she said, clinking her glass against his.

A few minutes later, the band returned and began to play. As the music wafted through the room, Adam took her hand in his and led her back onto the dance floor. Claudia glided into his strong arms and laid her head on his shoulder. They swayed as one to the music.

She felt so at ease in the web of this man's arms—as

if she belonged there.

Brittany noticed them and gave her the victory sign. She seemed to be having a good time, as well.

When the last dance of the evening was announced, Adam said, "We've danced the night away."

"It feels as if we've only just begun to dance."

"It doesn't have to end here. I'd like to see you again. Perhaps for dinner?"

"I'd love to."

"How about next Saturday, say seven-thirty?"

"Fine."

"Then it's a date." Smiling, he took her hand in his.

After the dance ended, she wrote down her address and telephone number and gave them to him. He held the paper—and her hand—a bit longer than necessary.

By then Brittany and Matthew had walked over to them. After the introductions, Adam turned to her. "May I drive you home?"

Brittany seemed thrilled. From the look on her sister's face, Claudia had a feeling she and Matthew had no intention of going directly home.

Claudia's heart quickened at his question. Funny, how things often turned out. In one short evening her world had changed and seemed to be spinning in a new direction, promising a brighter future. Had she not come to the dance in the first place, none of this would have happened.

Adam turned toward her as he slowed the car for a stoplight. "Would you like to get some coffee?" At her nod, he stopped at the nearest diner.

She was hungry, but not for food. Instead she was eager to learn everything she could about this attractive man who had just entered her life.

"There's not much to tell," he answered as she posed question after question. "Since I had nobody left in Dayton to keep me there, I accepted the teaching position at Carlyle."

She must have had a questioning expression on her

face, for he added, "My parents are both dead."

"I'm sorry."

"Don't be. Things happen in life. We learn to deal with them."

"That's quite a philosophy."

"It works for me. My sister took it harder. Being older, she lived with them longer." A hint of a smile touched his lips.

"Where does she live?"

"On a ranch in Montana, of all places." He raised his cup, sipped the coffee.

"That must be exciting. Does she have a family?"

"It's not too romantic being married to a rancher. She helps run the place, taking care of the smaller animals, not to mention her kids."

"Her days must be long."

"But she loves it. Calls it God's country."

Claudia smiled, imagining the implications.

"And what about you?" he said, clearly changing the subject.

She found it easy to talk to him and surprised herself by telling him things she rarely talked about. Although she couldn't explain it, she had a feeling it was okay. That this man was going to be a permanent fixture in her life.

At her front door, after having told her a number of times how much he'd enjoyed the evening, Adam took her in his arms and kissed her. They parted, letting their eyes drink in the moment, before their lips came together once again, more passionately this time.

As Claudia watched him go, she knew she'd be counting the hours until she saw him again.

Their first official date turned out wonderful. He insisted on taking her for dinner at a small Italian restaurant. The food tasted scrumptious, the company divine. Afterwards, they parked on the bluff overlooking the ocean, while stars twinkled above in the canopy of endless black sky. She felt as carefree as a school girl. It was a picture-perfect evening, one that would remain forever in her memory. Had she fallen in love with this man? She hardly knew him—yet what she did know was enough. Had he asked her to drop everything and run away with him, she would have done so without giving it as much as a thought. Never one to advocate happy endings, she saw nothing but clear skies before her as months passed and they truly became a couple.

During one of their early talks, Adam mentioned he was in the Army Reserve. Although she hated being separated from him, once every month he had to go away for a weekend. However, when the United States became involved in Afghanistan and Iraq, things changed. A few of their acquaintances in the Reserve had been deployed there, but it didn't become personal until Adam told her about his orders to go to Iraq.

"But, what about your classes?"

"I've already spoken to the chancellor. They'll be divided up amongst the other professors until I return."

"But..."

"What?"

Tears filled her eyes and started to slip slowly down her cheeks.

"I don't want you to go."

"I don't want to go either, baby, especially now. But I have to."

She sobbed uncontrollably, unable to stop herself.

He drew her close, enfolded her in his arms. "Shh, don't cry. I'll be back before you know it."

They sat like that for a very long time. The thought he'd be flying out of her life in a few days hung over her like an axe waiting to fall. She feared he wouldn't come home. In the end, it would be just like Andrew. She would lose Adam, too. Nothing had changed after all.

Claudia's world fell apart when Adam left. Her heart splintered into a million tiny pieces—never to be repaired again. In her mind, she thought never to see him again. First Andrew and now, Adam. Was she only to fall in love with men who left her in the end?

Clearly sensing the black funk she'd fallen into, her mother sat down beside her one evening shortly after Adam shipped out.

"He's coming back, Claudia."

She shook her head.

"Nonsense! Of course he is."

"Nothing is certain, Mom. You know that better than most."

"But you can't put the cart before the horse. You, of all people, should think positively."

"Why?"

"Because you and Adam were meant to be. You said so yourself," she replied.

"That was before he shipped out."

"Destiny can't be altered."

Why couldn't she believe that? Unable to stop them, tears poured from her eyes. "I'm so scared, Mom." Feeling like a child again, she buried her head in her mother's ample bosom.

Her mother stroked her head the same way she had when she'd been small and afraid. Finally she whispered, "I hate to see you so sad. Everything always works out for the best. You've got to believe that, sweetheart."

Claudia didn't answer. Instead, she sobbed her heart out.

Adam wrote and called whenever he could. Listening to him on the phone and reading the words from his heart kept hers beating. She religiously read the newspaper every day, and watched the news on TV in an attempt to keep up with the country's peacekeeping efforts in Iraq. He couldn't really tell her much about what his unit was doing there, but she knew he had to be scared. Between suicide bombings, insurgents, kidnappings and beheadings, how could a non-career soldier not be frightened?

Then the worst happened. Adam's letters stopped. There'd been increased activity by insurgents in the area where his unit was stationed. After not hearing from him for over a week, she feared he was hurt—or God forbid, worse.

"Be logical, Claudia," her mother pleaded. "If they're under fire, how could any mail get in or out?"

She had a point. Getting supplies or reinforcements had to be their number one priority, but being aware of this didn't help her eat or sleep any better. In fact, nothing Brittany or her mother said soothed her. She finally contacted her congressman for help. She had to find out what had happened to Adam. The congressman's office gave her a sympathetic ear, but Claudia doubted anything else would come from the call.

Weeks turned into months and still no word. Claudia was nearly out of her mind with grief. What else could she imagine, but the worst?

Then the very thing she dreaded happened. Her congressman contacted her with news: Adam was missing in action. His unit, a supply platoon, had gone out on a mission to deliver food, water and fuel to soldiers stationed in a combat zone. They'd been ambushed by insurgents. More than half of the platoon was killed. Two went missing in action—her Adam one of them.

"There's always a chance the two men could be found alive," he'd said, but Claudia knew his words were merely ones of consolation and held no weight.

As she put the phone down, she felt as if every bit of air had been sucked from her body. All she wanted to do was crawl into a corner and die.

Claudia watched out the window as Brittany and her new boyfriend, Tom, drove away. They'd been going together for nearly a month. Her flighty, younger sister never let herself get attached to any guy for long. She used to think less of her for doing so. Now, she looked at it in a different light. Perhaps Brittany had the right idea, after all. If you didn't get attached to one guy, you couldn't experience much heartbreak when you broke up...or lost him.

The only thought never far from her mind was—where's Adam? Each time someone detonated a suicide bomb in that God-forsaken place, she wondered if he was in the midst of it. Not knowing whether he was dead or alive tore her apart.

"Claudia, I know you're hurting," her mother said, coming up behind her, "but you've got to keep believing Adam's all right."

"Mother, how can I? I haven't heard from him in over five months."

"God is watching over him."

"There is no God. If there were, there'd be no war."

"Claudia Sykes! You know better than that. Your father and I made certain you understood such things. God doesn't declare war on others. Man does."

"Why doesn't He stop them, then?" Claudia asked defiantly.

"Because the Lord gave man free will."

"What a mistake."

No matter how hard her mother tried to console her, the more she fought her. She simply couldn't look at the world through rose-tinted glasses.

As the months dragged on, it seemed so hopeless. Claudia threw herself into her work, trying to forget. It didn't help. Nothing would ever ease the terrible pain in her heart. She'd lost Adam. She tried not to think of him, but his smiling face came to mind every time she closed her eyes. Memories made her feel his mouth on hers or his hands gently caressing her body. Nothing seemed to dam her constant flow of tears.

Work was her refuge. It felt good whenever she helped a young couple secure a loan, allowing them to make their dreams come true. Sometimes, they'd come in with their children. Yet often she found herself envying their good fortune. They reminded her of the sweet times when she and Adam had talked about marriage and having a family.

He'd wanted at least three kids. She'd dreamed of having his children, but the dream quickly became impossible, for each passing day proved Adam wasn't ever coming back.

Claudia sat at her desk in the bank staring at the calendar. Tomorrow was Christmas Eve. Without Adam it would be a very blue Christmas. She'd prayed he'd be home for the holidays. They could've gone to the upcoming Christmas dance at the church. How Adam loved to dance. She smiled at memories of them dancing—of the night they'd met. He was such a good dancer.

Tears filled her eyes. She'd never dance with him again. What good were her tears? They weren't going to bring him back. She dabbed at her eyes and cleared her desk.

Claudia grabbed her purse and coat when the clock chimed six. She wanted to stop at the store on the way home to pick up a few things for her mother. She wrapped her scarf around her neck and pulled on her gloves as light snow flurries swirled around her. The street was lightly covered with new fallen snow. Just the way Christmas Eve should look. Head down, she headed towards her car parked at the back of the lot near the light. She looked up as she approached and noticed somebody by her car. Why would someone be standing by her car? A rapist? A mugger? Although her favorite time of year, many people were down on their luck and often chose the holidays to steal from other people. She was too far away to see who it might be.

Should she go closer, or run back to her office for help? Her feet kept moving of their own volition. She slowly approached the car...

Claudia rubbed her eyes, thinking they were playing

tricks on her. She blinked, but the man was no mirage or figment of her imagination. Her heart slammed against her ribs! She ran towards him laughing and crying at the same time. She wanted to fling her arms about his neck, but seeing his crutches nearly stopped her.

"Oh, Adam," she cried as she kissed his beautiful face, his eyes, and then his sweet mouth.

As their lips clung together, her heart beat wildly in her chest.

"Oh, my love, I imagined this moment over and over again as I lay in the hospital. Knowing I would come home to you got me through it," he murmured as he kissed her hair.

"Are you in pain? Do you want to sit? Oh Adam, how did you get here?"

He chuckled. "Slow down, baby. We have all the time in the world."

"I can't believe you're actually here." Gently she stroked the side of his face.

A car horn blared and Claudia looked up to see Brittany wave and drive off. A grin shone on her face from ear-to-ear. She'd brought Adam tonight.

"It's cold," she said, reaching up to caress his cheek. "Let me help you into the car." Fumbling with her keys, she turned and unlocked the door.

Holding on to the frame of the car, Adam handed Claudia the crutches as he lowered himself into the bucket seat. She reached inside and put the crutches in the back.

"I won't have to have them forever. They're only temporary. The doctors say I'll be able to walk without them soon."

"Adam, I wouldn't care if you did need them forever. I'm just so glad you've come home. Are you hungry?"

"Not for food." A teasing gleam filled his eyes.

Claudia drove to the closest motel and booked a room. She didn't care who might see them. She needed to be alone with Adam. There was so much to say and so much she wanted to do.

Entering the room, she put her purse down and crossed to the phone. “Mom, it’s Claudia. I just wanted to let you know I won’t be home for dinner. I didn’t want you to worry.”

Laughter filled her mother’s voice. “I didn’t expect you.”

Adam was stretched out on the bed watching her as she spoke to her mother. His eyes hadn’t left her since she ran to him in the bank’s parking lot. Now he opened his arms and she rushed into them, her heart racing so fast she could hardly breathe. His lips captured hers, practically devouring them before they continued down her body as if to reclaim what was his. Shivers of delight followed the path of his lips.

They became one quickly and then cuddled together in love’s aftermath while their hearts slowed to a more normal pace. Not letting go, he began to make love to her once more. This time they took their time and savored every kiss, every touch.

Then they talked. There was so much to say. Claudia clung to him, so afraid if she closed her eyes he’d disappear. Her fingers trailed lightly over his chest.

“Each day I didn’t hear from you made me think the worst.”

“I know. And I’m so sorry for making you worry. But I couldn’t contact you. After escaping the ambush, an Iraqi family hid me until they thought it safe to be turned over to the Americans.”

Claudia imagined the terror he must have experienced.

“Once in American hands, they flew me to Germany for medical treatment. My legs had been shattered, the rest of me badly wounded. One leg was fractured so badly the doctor feared they might have to amputate. He thought the other might be salvageable. Hearing his prognosis, my world seemed as shattered as my legs. I begged them not to notify you.”

“But, why, Adam? I love you—want you with all my

heart. I wouldn't love you any less had you lost your legs."

"In my heart I knew that, but I didn't want to become a burden. I saw what my father's stroke did to my mother."

"I'm not your mother—"

He placed a finger on her lips. "I know, but I was out of my head, strung out on meds."

"I don't care about any of that. You're here with me now and I don't intend to ever let you go again." She kissed him with all the passion she felt.

Adam shifted her slightly away, raised himself on both elbows. "Do me a favor, baby, and hand me my jacket."

She got off the bed and walked to the table where they'd laid it.

"I don't intend to ever leave you again, either," he said, as she handed it to him. He reached inside a pocket and took out a small box. He patted the bed beside him and Claudia sat. Love filled his eyes as he handed it to her. "I want you to be my wife."

Claudia's hands began to shake as she opened the blue velvet box to find a beautiful diamond ring. Her eyes widened and tears filled her eyes, but she quickly slipped it on her finger.

Not caring about who might be in the nearby rooms, she screamed, "Yes! Yes! Yes!"

"Merry Christmas, Claudia," he said before he took her in his arms and kissed her.

Be sure to visit Candace's website
http://www.candacegold.com

Victoriana

by Heather Hiestand

Even the local dollar store looked inviting at Christmas. As Robyne pushed through the door she noted the decorations, complete with evergreen branches over the door and a gay wreath on the wall behind the cash register, but Catherine added the eccentric charm no other store could capture. Standing behind the cash register, dressed in an old-fashioned costume complete with bustle and ornate velvet trim, the dear friend of Robyne's late grandmother smiled and blew her a kiss as she turned the corner into the toy section. Robyne understood why Catherine might be hiding in the past, but she was drowning in the issues of the present, shuttling severely disabled children to and from school.

She hoped to find presents for the kids she thought of as her own. Though she couldn't afford much, Catherine would give her a discount.

Robyne ran her hand down the shelves as she looked through the toy section. She discarded the idea of board games, metal toy trains and the like. Most of her kids had poor motor skills. A couple of dolls, dressed not unlike Catherine, caught her eye, but just as quickly she returned them to the shelves when she saw their poor quality.

After half an hour, getting frustrated, she shuffled through the kitchen aisle. She considered a display of teacups. Maybe the girls would like to play tea party? Taking a second look, she saw the cups were cracked and let out a sigh. Maybe the dollar store wasn't the place to look for Christmas gifts after all.

The bell above the door rang as another customer entered. The open door let the wind in, and a rush of evergreen-scented air wafted over Robyne. She closed her eyes, breathing in the energizing scent of Christmas.

When she looked again, she saw a Christmas cracker on the shelf below the teacups. *Perfect!* All you had to do with a cracker was pull the ends apart, and then you got a satisfying boom and the toys or other goodies tucked inside. *Please let there be more than one.*

The light didn't reach into the lower shelves very well. Robyne thought she felt the shiny paper of additional crackers as she reached down. Her hand only grasped one dusty object. She blew on it, and a spray of dust filled the air. When the dust settled, it revealed a surprisingly ornate multicolor design of red, yellow and blue.

She blew again. This time the central image on the cracker was revealed, a charming little world. Giving it an experimental shake, she was disappointed when nothing rattled inside. Maybe it wasn't any good, or had something boring like a paper hat in it?

Trying to think of other gift ideas, she tugged absently at the two ends of the item in her hands. Boom! A large explosion knocked Robyne backwards, and the world around her dimmed.

As Robyne regained consciousness, she felt a hard, curved surface behind her, like a pipe. Dusky light concealed much of her surroundings and a bitter wind stung her cheeks. Above her, she found an iron lamppost glowing dimly. With a bit of concentration things came into focus. She sat at the end of a street of sinister looking buildings. Fog swirled around her, bringing with it the acrid scent of coal. She sneezed and shivered. Where was she? How had she gotten outside?

As she hurriedly tugged her mittens out of her coat pockets and put them on, she remembered the loud noise she'd heard.

She reached into her pocket again. Shock rippled through her as she pulled out the cracker. Still intact despite the explosion, the colors shimmered in the fog, making the toy appear alive. The pattern on one end coalesced, and she saw it formed a lamppost, just like the one behind her. Shaken, she fumbled the cracker and dropped it. She crouched to retrieve it, shoving it into her pocket for safekeeping. When she looked up, a pair of legs encased in dark plaid trousers stood in front of her. Male legs.

"What the devil have we here?" A large hand encased in a leather glove reached down to help her stand. Though not tall, the man loomed over her. She noted sleepy eyes, a sharp nose and wide mouth, with a thick chestnut moustache completing his handsome face.

"Thanks," she gasped through chattering teeth.

"What's a lad like you doing out at dusk? You're much too clean to be a street urchin."

He had a low voice, one that relaxed her at some elemental level.

But...a lad? Robyne looked down at herself. Did he mistake her sex because she wore black corduroy pants?

"What are you doing out in the evening air?" she countered, reluctant to reveal too much to a stranger.

"Cheeky, aren't you." The man tilted his head. Now she could see the top hat he wore. He appeared to be wearing the male equivalent of Catherine's clothing, and smelled like cigar smoke.

"Why are you dressed like that?" she asked. "Are you on your way to a party?"

He chuckled. "There's little else for me to do in Victoriana."

"Victoriana?"

"Yes. You are visiting from elsewhere?"

"I guess," she said in a small voice. "I don't know

how I ended up here."

He nodded. "This, I have heard before."

Despite her mittens, she shivered uncontrollably. "It's awfully cold."

His tone became doleful. "It's always December now."

"What?"

"There are rules, you know. And our scientists broke them."

Feeling thoroughly confused, she began to wonder if she'd hit her head harder than she'd originally thought. "What rules?"

"As a visitor from elsewhere, you won't have heard of the Big Bang theory?"

"The one about how the universe was created?"

"No, the one that states it will take a big bang to get time started again. Some madman of science was experimenting three years ago and broke time. It's been December 17th ever since." His tone was so matter of fact, and the past hours had been so strange, she almost believed him.

"So it's always winter until time is fixed?"

"Yes. And the solution has to come from the outside. You see, the theory states there are many earths, many versions you might say, and we don't have the tools inside our version to fix our problem."

"I see. The outside?" Robyne said, thinking of the big bang that got her here. It hadn't made winter vanish, though.

Through the fog, she saw the man's teeth flash under his moustache as he smiled.

"Yes, the other places. As I said, this is Victoriana. Where do you come from?"

Robyne blinked. "Tacoma, Washington—umm, America?"

He nodded thoughtfully. "I'm afraid we haven't been introduced. I am Edward, Earl of Chester."

"It's nice to meet you," she said automatically. "I'm Robyne Arthur."

He took her hand in his. His light touch could hardly be felt through her thick Christmas mitten, but her hand tingled nonetheless.

"So you are a lass," he said as he straightened. "From outside."

"It appears so," she agreed.

"And you have nowhere to go, being a stranger?"

"No." She sniffed. "I'm afraid to leave this spot." She gestured. "The lamppost."

"I know where we are," the earl said, flashing his teeth again. "Why don't we get you out of this cold air, and I'll bring you back to this lamppost tomorrow."

Robyne thought. "How do I know I can trust you?"

"Have you a better option?"

She sighed. "Will my money be any good here? I'd prefer to go to a public place, like a hotel."

He shook his head. "I think not."

She bit her lip. His air of command was unnerving, and these foggy streets had her thinking of Sherlock Holmes and Jack the Ripper. She didn't think she should trust him, and yet, what choice did she have? At least he seemed to be kind.

"I guess I have to count on you then."

"I assure you, you don't want to be out on these streets at night. The wealthy and poor are mixed in among each other. A footpad or worse could accost you at any step. You are lucky I came upon you when I did."

"That remains to be seen," Robyne muttered, but took the arm he offered. She noted he was careful to stay on the street side as they walked along, his walking stick tapping the way.

She counted off seven streets before they arrived in front of a metal gate. They hadn't gone in a straight line, but she tried to remember their route. She didn't know what she might find when she returned to the lamppost where she woke, even so, it was her only tie to home.

Robyne hadn't seen the outside of the house in the gloom, but the inside was palatial, even fancier than what she imagined a five-star hotel would look like. A uniformed maid, who raised her eyebrows when she espied Robyne's manner of dress, brought in a tea tray. Robyne sat next to a blazing fire in a wood-paneled study.

She felt like she'd dropped onto a movie set. So far, she hadn't seen any sign of electricity. Sconces on the wall had flames behind them–gas, she supposed. This place was called Victoriana. Did that mean it was December 17th some time in the nineteenth century on this version of Earth? And how had she come to be in England? She was certainly a long way from Tacoma.

Considering, Robyne pulled the Christmas cracker from her pocket. Her sole intent that afternoon had been to find gifts for her kids. Now this toy was her only link to home. Who would drive her bus tomorrow if she didn't make it back? She ran her finger across the lamppost design on the wrapping, and now noticed the next set of intricate squiggles and swirls looked like a building, perhaps the one she was in now. Could the cracker be a map?

The double doors opened, and the earl strode in, magnificent in his long coat. She'd always loved the look of a man with a luxurious moustache. His polished boots gleamed in the candlelight thrown by the tall candelabra by the door. She sighed, wishing men as attractive and courteous as he existed in her world.

As he came closer, he smiled at her, then suddenly froze a few paces away.

"What, my, uh, Lord Chester?" Robyne stammered, not liking the expression of shock on his face.

"Where did you get that?" He pointed a shaking finger at her lap.

She looked down at the cracker. "It's what brought me here, I think. I was playing with it at a store, there was a loud bang, and then I woke here."

He reached out a hand to her, his eyes eagerly fixed on the toy. With a protective feeling, Robyne tucked the cracker into her pocket.

"I need that." His tone offered no room for argument.

"So do I," she said, attempting to stand. The plush chair proved difficult to get out of, and the earl held out a hand to steady her as she got to her feet. She shrank from his touch.

"I'm not going to hurt you." His voice softened immediately.

"You're making me nervous." She took a step away from him. Unfortunately, his solid form, the chair and the fire blocked her. She was trapped.

"I'm angry at myself for not recognizing a traveler might have the solution to our problem. Of course you might. How do travelers arrive here? It makes sense someone like you would carry our salvation." He trailed off.

"I hope what I'm carrying is my ticket home." Robyne pulled the cracker from her pocket, knowing there was no escape any other way. She would pull it apart again.

"Please!" He held out his hand. "I beseech you, do not do this!"

"Why not?" Robyne hated the quiver she heard in her voice. "I need to go home. I have a job—and my children."

"You have children?" His voice immediately calmed as he tilted his head.

"They aren't mine, exactly, but I work with them. They need me."

"The family can find another governess."

Robyne decided not to press the point. She held the edges of the cracker with her fingers.

She saw the shock in the earl's face; almost saw his brain at work behind his eyes.

"Miss Arthur, you must be tired from your labors with those children." His voice held an air of desperation.

Suspicious, she held the paper's edge, but didn't tug.

"Wouldn't you like to rest?" He waved his hand.

"Here, in these pleasant surroundings? No one will disturb you. You could regain your energy in comfort for a few days. Surely no one would deny you this. Your travel here, the ordeal you suffered. You should rest."

Robyne yawned despite herself. She was tired, but how could she trust him? Of course, she hadn't had a vacation in years. Of course his home was luxurious, and of course she could never expect to be in such beauty again. You'd have to be a billionaire to live like this. Or a king. If she didn't stay vigilant, someone might steal the cracker. Even Lord Chester might steal it, though she didn't want to believe he'd be capable of it, that he'd stoop to such lengths to obtain something belonging to another.

"I don't trust you," she said finally, belying her thoughts.

"I have given you no reason to question my integrity. My sister is here visiting, so you will be chaperoned. I assure you I am no seducer of innocents."

"I'm more worried about thievery than seduction," she snapped.

He chuckled. "Miss Arthur, I am a man of honor. You and your cracker are safe, far safer here than on the streets late at night. We will have a truce on the issue until morning."

"What of the others here? Will they steal it?"

He shook his head. "No one but me knows your secret. On my honor, it will be safe."

In the firelight, she could see his green eyes. Her father, who'd died in the line of duty in a warehouse fire, had the same eye color. For this inconsequential reason, she decided to trust the earl and tucked the cracker away.

"Be careful with it," he cautioned. "You hold life in your hands."

"My life," she said softly, but he'd turned away and she doubted he'd heard.

The next morning, Robyne woke to the sound of a

tea tray clattering, as a maid brought it to her bedside. What luxury, she thought, then remembered the reason for her excellent night's sleep on a fat feather bed—the too handsome, too controlling Lord Chester.

"Good morning, miss," said the maid cheerfully. "I 'ope you 'ad a good night's sleep."

"Yes, thank you," Robyne said carefully. She struggled to sit up. The maid swiftly moved to her side and plumped her pillows.

"Do you need anything else?" the maid enquired. "I've stirred the coal, so the fire should be nice and toasty soon."

Robyne asked the question most concerning her. "Is it true it's always winter here?"

"Why, miss, it's always December 17th 'ereabouts."

So he's honest, at least. Every day here, December 17th started over. "Is your master a good person?"

"Oh, 'e's the best, 'e is. Kind as the day is long, if not especially a gentle man. But you can't expect such as 'im to be. A good soul, though, cor blimey," she exclaimed.

Robyne opened her mouth to ask more, but the maid turned away as a knock sounded at the door.

It opened and a chubby, brunette teenage girl entered the room, dressed in a bustled black gown with ornate embroidery around the sleeves and hem. The maid curtseyed.

"Hello, Miss Arthur, my brother asked me to check on you."

"Thank you, Miss...?"

"Lenchen," the girl said. "Just Lenchen."

"All right," Robyne said. "I'm just getting up. I don't know what I should wear."

"I've clothing for you, miss," the maid said with a newly timid air.

"I shall see you in the dining hall in an hour, then?" Lenchen queried.

Robyne nodded and smiled. Unlike her strong-willed and authoritative brother, Lenchen seemed reserved. Robyne was never at her best with people so sure of themselves as the earl. How did they come by their assurance?

An hour later, Robyne went downstairs, moving slowly in the heavy dress and corset the maid had helped her into. The food on the sideboard didn't excite her. It all looked so heavy after her delicious tea and toast with marmalade upstairs. Lenchen had clearly tucked away a great deal of food, however, and was wiping her mouth as Robyne walked in.

With the heavy dress, and heavy food, not to mention the weather outside, Robyne started to wonder if she really needed a vacation after all. It was time to say her goodbyes and get back to her kids. Then she saw him.

The earl stood at the sideboard. Her heart gave a funny leap as she viewed his elegance in dark formal attire. Good grief, did she have a crush on the man? That was no good—she was going home. Soon, this would be nothing but a memory. Already, she knew she would regret saying goodbye.

"Ready?" he asked.

"Are we going to the lamppost?" Robyne was glad he kept his word, but sorry he was willing to let her go so easily. "Shouldn't I wear my own clothes?"

He smiled slightly. "You will draw less attention this way."

Robyne saw the truth in that, but patted the pocket that held the cracker anyway. Didn't they have pickpockets in Victorian England?

Another maid helped them bundle into outdoor garments. Lenchen, a footman and the maid came along behind them.

Robyne enjoyed the crisp air, even if the smell of coal hung heavy. At least there was some daylight to war against the cold. As they meandered through a market area she didn't remember from the night before, she saw an amazing cross-section of nineteenth century life. Stalls were available with all manner of goods–meats, pies, goats and cows for milk. Most shop people looked tired, as if they hadn't rested well. Her heart caught in her throat when she saw a little boy with a crutch, so like Tiny Tim in Dickens' tale. And there were girls selling matchsticks, too, their eyes huge in too thin faces. Robyne scrambled in her pockets, but of course she had no money to give them.

"I used to come here for flowers," Lenchen remarked. "Of course, there's none now, with the winter always upon us."

"I'm sorry," Robyne said. She felt bad, though wasn't sure why exactly, until she realized she felt guilty. But why should she? She couldn't know if the cracker really would restart time, and she needed it to get back home.

"Sad, isn't it?" the earl remarked, giving her a significant look.

Robyne pursed her lips, trying to remain strong against all these sorrowful children. "We don't seem to be heading toward the lamppost."

The earl took her arm, pulled it into the crook of his elbow. Her resolve melted at his touch. "I thought you might like to see the city a little."

"I suppose." She slowed her steps and leaned slightly into his warmth.

Their party promenaded down the main thoroughfare. Men in top hats like the earl's greeted them with slight bows as they walked down this more prosperous avenue. Robyne recognized the Gothic edifice of Westminster Abbey across the street as they entered a large building.

"Where are we?" she asked.

"This is St. George's Hospital."

"Why are we here?"

The earl regarded her seriously. "I wanted to introduce you to some of Victoriana's children."

"Are you trying to find me a job?" Robyne asked. The next words tumbled out of her lips. She was getting dangerously cozy with the earl, enjoying his touch too much. "Because I'm going home. As soon as we've finished sightseeing."

He smiled. "Perhaps."

He led them up a flight of steps, into a large ward. As he released her and put a hand to her back, pushing her deeper into the room, her breath stuck in her throat. Each bed held a child.

Children, suffering children. She, who knew the pain of disabled children so well, but also knew their resilience and capacity for uncomplicated joy, could see these children had no hope. No one to love them. At least her kids in Tacoma had mothers. These wards were empty, except for the children.

"Scurvy, Miss Arthur. Rickets. Pneumonia." The earl led her past bed after bed. "That orphaned lad fell on the ice and broke his leg. That motherless child fell on slippery steps and broke her back. Yet they live, I know not how."

Robyne tried to blink away her tears. "Why have you brought me here?" She stared down at one little blonde girl with skin so pale she could see the blue veins in her forehead that stood out in stark contrast.

"You must know," he said hoarsely. The earl turned to her and took her hands. "You must know," he repeated, "the cost of this ghastly winter."

He shook her hands for emphasis. "Miss Arthur, you have the power to help these poor children. Reach into your heart, madam, and show them mercy."

Robyne pulled away from him and walked down the ward. The earl left her alone as she clasped hands and kissed foreheads of the dear little souls. Within her heart she felt the same love for these children as she did for those she'd transported for the four years she'd been a driver. None of these children had the chances her kids did.

How could she consider merely saving herself with all these children in so much pain? She would survive somehow, perhaps as a governess as Lord Chester had suggested. But she now knew she couldn't go home and abandon these children, leave them to die. She vowed to help them. They were the neediest children she'd ever seen.

When she returned to the earl, she had the Christmas cracker extended in her mittened palm.

"Take it," she said, her voice trembling. "You were right. Your need is far greater than mine."

The earl's face grew solemn as he gazed at her. A long pause transpired before he spoke. "I thank you, Miss Arthur. You are a heroine."

Robyne blinked and took a deep breath.

His face softened and he smiled at her. "Let us go."

She glowed with pride at his words as she took the arm he held out to her. They left the hospital, with Lenchen and the servants trailing behind them. The earl moved with purpose as they entered a park. They walked down wide lanes edged with bare trees. When they reached a windswept clearing, the earl stopped.

"Here," he said, his voice holding a note of uncertainty for the first time. "Stand back, everyone, I'm not sure what will happen."

"It knocked me unconscious," Robyne reminded him.

"Exactly. Remove yourselves." Lenchen and the servants hastily retreated into the trees, but Robyne shook her head.

"I'll stay with you."

"Are you certain?" The earl searched her eyes.

She nodded firmly. "What if my presence is somehow part of the process?"

"Very good thinking." The earl took off his gloves, careful not to drop the cracker.

The colorful designs flared in the weak sunlight, now defining the marketplace, the hospital, and the park. The world in the center almost appeared three-dimensional to Robyne.

"I have an idea." His eyes searched hers as though probing her soul. "Would you pull it with me?"

"I'd be honored." Robyne removed her mittens and stood across from him. They each took one side of the cracker. The wrapping felt alive to her, buzzing slightly against her fingers. "It knows something important is about to happen."

He smiled. "As do we." He leaned forward, and almost before Robyne could react, he kissed her cheek. The sensation of lips against skin was even more electric than the cracker against her fingers. She looked at him in surprise.

"For luck," he said.

Robyne grinned at him. "That wouldn't bring us very much luck." Amazed at her daring, she touched her free hand to his cheek and pressed her lips to his. His lips were soft, smooth, and his moustache tickled her nose and above her lips. As she broke the kiss, she saw his joy and wished she could share happy moments with him always.

A twinkle still in his eye, he said, "Thank you, Robyne Arthur. I do not know quite what will happen, but I am humbled to be with you today."

Robyne smiled tremulously, feeling her crush blossom into something deeper, knowing this was the most important day of her life, whatever the consequences.

"Ready, then. On the count of three, it seems sporting," the earl said, then smiled at her.

She nodded, and as he counted, she grasped the cracker firmly despite its increasing warmth.

"Three!" Robyne pulled the cracker with all her strength.

BOOM!

She came to, blinking, and realized she lay flat on her back, staring into a blinding sun. A warm sun. Around her, she heard cries from passers-by at the sudden warmth. Where was the earl, she thought frantically, blinking her sun-blinded eyes until she saw his form through the spots, lying several feet away. She got up, feeling an ache in her bones, and crawled over to him.

The earl's eyes were closed, but as she shook his shoulder, he opened them.

"Did we do it?"

She nodded, tears sliding down her face. He reached out an arm, pulling her close. She dropped her head to his chest as he clasped her tightly.

Robyne woke from a deep sleep the next morning, when the maid bustled in with her tea tray.

"'ow's our 'eroine, then?" the maid asked, as she drew the heavy velvet curtains aside. "No need to stir the coal this morning, eh?"

"I guess not." Robyne pushed back the too warm covers.

The maid looked critically at the curtains. "We'll be replacing these with cotton soon, I expect."

"It's certainly warmer," Robyne said. The sip of hot tea still felt good against her parched throat, however. She'd spent the evening with Lenchen, learning local songs as a maid played the piano. The earl had disappeared after their hug in the park, had the footman escort them home through the cheering throng of Victorians. Robyne longed to celebrate the victory with the earl. He was her only anchor in this strange place and she didn't know what she'd do without him.

She passed the morning with Lenchen, reading the morning papers full of news of the season's change and glowing predictions for the future. Just when she was about to go out of her mind with impatience, the earl strode in. She noted the lack of a topcoat or gloves and was glad the warm, sunny weather held. He smiled at her, and she wanted to fling herself into his arms.

"Miss Arthur, may I see you in my study?"

"Of course." Robyne rose, heart thumping, and followed him into the room where he'd brought her that first night.

He directed her to an overstuffed red velvet sofa while he leaned against the carved mantelpiece.

She drank him in, as he gathered his thoughts before speaking. "Miss Arthur, I have a confession to make."

Robyne raised her eyebrows. "I'm listening."

"I told you of our men of science. A few months ago,

they developed a method of returning those like you home. I believe I have the power to return you as well."

She drew in a breath. "Why didn't you tell me before?"

"I think you know the answer to that." His eyes burned into hers and heat not from the newly activated sun, crept into her face, as she remembered her selfishness.

When he spoke again, his voice was slightly hoarse. "Are you ready to return?"

Robyne closed her eyes. She had no reason to stay, now that the children were safe from winter. She looked at the earl for a long moment, and saw nothing but reserve. She'd never forget him, but how could he be hers? He was an earl.

"Yes," she replied and couldn't understand why she wasn't happy about it.

The earl nodded and left the room. Robyne held back tears as a maid escorted her to a carriage. The earl climbed in after her, and she leaned into the seat. The horses moved them away from his house and she watched the landscape ease past. Silently, she said goodbye to each child at the hospital, to the market folk, to the maids, and Lenchen. But her heart wasn't quite ready to say goodbye to the earl.

He never spoke a word. Halfway through the journey though, he took her hand and tucked it into his arm. She tried not to clutch at his arm, but wished she could find a way to stay with him.

In well under an hour, far too soon, the carriage deposited them at a great building, which Robyne soon realized was a train station. A footman escorted her in, with the earl bringing up the rear. Inside the vast entry, she turned to him.

He held his hands out to her, his face solemn. "Miss Arthur, I can send you home on the train—or you could stay."

Her voice trembled with tentative joy. "I could?"

"Yes. I must tell you the truth. I am really Albert

Edward, the son of Queen Victoria. Someday, I will be king here."

Robyne's heart sank. She could stay, but without him.

"Miss Arthur." He clasped her hands in his, and all her hope was restored. "Robyne. Your selfless actions have taught me much. I am certain you are meant to be queen here. My darling, Robyne, please do me the honor of becoming my wife."

She exhaled with a laugh or a sob, she wasn't sure which. "Are you certain? How?"

"I have discussed my feelings with the Queen. She approved. Your heart, my dear," he nearly stuttered on the words. "You put me to shame with your goodness. How could I not love you?"

"You showed me the way," Robyne whispered. "You have such care for your people."

"You can go back to your home, if that is your wish. I wanted you to have the choice. But my love is true."

She saw it in his eyes. "I know."

He nodded solemnly. "Your answer?"

"It is yes, of course."

He shouted his approval and pulled her into his arms. With a joyful laugh, Robyne threw herself into his embrace as he twirled her around.

It might be springtime in Victoriana, but forever after, Robyne knew she would hold the magic of Christmas in her heart.

Be sure to visit Heather's website
http://www.coffeeonsundays.info/_sgt/m1_1.htm

Tempt Me Twice

by Anna Kathryn Lanier

Yorkshire, England, 1844

Meghan Shelton de Vries followed her daughter into the garden maze, lifting her skirts to keep the hems out of the light dusting of snow covering the ground. She knew the way through the twist and turns by heart, but she allowed six-year-old Marissa to take the lead.

"Papa would have loved this," Marissa said as she turned to the left.

Meghan's heart twisted. It was the sort of thing her gentle husband enjoyed. "Yes, he would have."

Eduard had been her best friend. Though they'd not shared passion in their marriage—and what good had passion done her anyway?—Meghan would be forever grateful for the kindness Eduard had shown her and the security he bestowed on both her and her daughter.

"You must remember what he told you, sweeting. As long as you hold him in your heart, he will always be with you."

Marissa nodded, then turned to the right and Meghan knew the girl had discovered the secret of the maze. Her thoughts on Eduard, she followed blindly and ran straight into a rock hard body, the breath knocked out of her.

"Oh!"

Two hands gripped her arms to steady her.

"Pardon me," a deep voice said.

Meghan sucked in frosty air. Her fingers turned to

ice. *Dear God, it couldn't be.* Only one week back in England and she ran, literally, into Peter Bourne, Duke of Prestwick. She wouldn't have imagined a man of his esteem traveling to Yorkshire to attend a wedding set two weeks before Christmas.

"Are you all right, madam?" Prestwick asked.

"Goodness, Meghan, it is a wonder he didn't knock you down," Lady Sarah, her cousin and the bride-to-be, said. She and a half dozen people were returning from the center of the maze.

The fingers on her arms increased pressure, but she refused to look at Prestwick. Instead, her gaze fell on the stickpin in the duke's cravat. Her eyes narrowed. *The bastard wears the gift I've given him as if a trophy.*

"Quite, Your Grace. You may release me now."

For a moment his fingers dug in, then dropped from her arms.

"Ah, you know the Duke of Prestwick?" Cousin Stephen, Earl of Winston asked. "I had not realized."

She raised her eyes to meet the duke's depthless, jet-black gaze, familiar eyes seen most recently on another. She turned to her cousin. "Did you not? His Grace was most kind during the short time I had a Season. He danced with me on several occasions and his small attention drew several other partners for my dance card." She smiled icily. "As you know, when a man of the duke's ranking pays attendance, no matter how minute, other men also find one of interest."

Winston darted a look to the duke. His eyes fell onto the stickpin and widened a fraction. He looked back at Meghan. She gave a warning shake of her head.

"It was my pleasure, madam, to have been of service to you," Prestwick said.

"I am sure it was, Your Grace."

Prestwick's eyes narrowed. Her doubled-edged words were clearly not lost on him. He knew she was not speaking of their dances.

Winston cleared his throat. "Mrs. de Vries, do you recall Mr. Brickman? When he learned you would be here for my sister's wedding, he hoped you would remember him from our visit."

Meghan turned to the younger man and beamed him a smile, glad to have her attention diverted from Prestwick.

"Of course I do, sir. How good it is to see you again. I trust the rest of your time spent on the Continent was pleasant?"

Brickman blushed. "Indeed it was, but not nearly as pleasant as spending time with you and your family. Do not tell me this is your daughter?"

Meghan's heart seized in her chest and panic welled in her throat. How she wished the man hadn't drawn attention to Marissa. She quickly swallowed her fear. *Please do not let Prestwick look at her too closely.*

They turned to Marissa, who talked with Lady Sarah.

"Yes. This is Marissa."

Introductions were exchanged among the party.

"You are as pretty as your mother," Prestwick said.

Marissa wiggled her fingers and Meghan realized she was squeezing the tiny hand. She released it.

"Thank you, Your Grace. Please excuse us, as we desire to find the center of the maze." Meghan tried to sidestep the man.

"May I walk with you a moment, Mrs. de Vries?" he asked.

Anxiety spurted through her and she noted Winston puff up like an angry rooster. *Oh. He has deduced it.*

"Prestwick, I did actually wish to show you my new billiard table," Winston interceded.

Meghan didn't know if she should be grateful or not. What would he say to the duke? Prestwick glanced from Winston to Meghan. She lifted her chin. He bowed. "Another time, perhaps."

"Certainly, Your Grace." Meghan curtseyed, then stepped around the group and followed Marissa to the center of the labyrinth.

Peter followed Winston into his study. A quick

glance confirmed there was no billiard table.

He had no doubt he was to be reprimanded. He'd seen the look on Winston's face when the man saw the stickpin Peter wore to remind him of his foolishness.

Reeling from his unexpected encounter with Meghan, his hands tingled from touching her through the layers of gloves and clothing. Her rose perfume, soft and tantalizing, still filled his nostrils. Had it been only seven years since he'd last seen her? It seemed a lifetime.

The door clicked shut. Winston crossed to the window, peered through the glass and clasped his hands behind his back. For several minutes he didn't speak.

"I will make this short and to the point, Prestwick. You are to stay far away from my cousin, Mrs. de Vries. You are not to address her in any way, nor should you ever be within ten feet of her. If I discover you have done either of those two things, I shall have you thrown off my property. Is there anything I have said you do not understand?"

No one ever threatened him in such a manner. He was a duke, Winston a mere earl. People didn't treat him as Winston just had and under normal circumstances he would have called the man on it. This, Peter knew, wasn't a normal circumstance.

"No, I understand perfectly, Winston."

The earl nodded. Puzzled, Peter stood in indecision. Had he been dismissed?

"She refused to give us a name," Winston said, surprising him. "I thought it was because she was ashamed, but I see now that was not the reason. She surmised if I knew who had debauched her I would have called him out. She did not want me hanged for killing a duke's heir."

She had told her family of the affair? Why do so, then not reveal his name?

Winston turned to face him. The light from the window framed the man. Peter couldn't see his face, but his rage was palpable.

"I would appreciate it, Prestwick, if you would remove the stickpin from your person and not wear it while in this house. Neither I nor Meghan needs to see your conquest trophy. Trust me, we are very aware of what you did to win the wager."

Peter's hand flew to the onyx and gold stickpin. "I do not wear it to remind me of a conquest, Winston. I wear it to remind me of my stupidity."

Winston's hands dropped to his sides and clenched into fists. "You will not wear it in this house, Prestwick. Meghan does not need to be reminded of her lack of judgment. She lives with it every day."

Peter removed the pin and clutched it in his fist. "She told me it was a gift from her mother to her father on their wedding day."

For a moment, Winston made no comment. "It was a family heirloom. It has been a wedding gift from wife to husband for six generations. Meghan was premature in giving it to you, was she not? I believe two days after receiving it you announced your betrothal to another."

The stone dug into his palm, but Peter didn't feel it. He recalled the expression on Meghan's face the night of the announcement, the utter look of devastation and betrayal. She fled the ballroom before he could reach her and had seen her only once since then. He moved his fisted hand over a table top and let the pin drop onto the polished surface.

"Then your family should have it back. It was never meant to be given to me."

"But it was given to you, Prestwick, and once given cannot be returned. Neither I nor Meghan wants it. Take it with you when you leave this room. Just do not wear it again in my presence." Winston turned his back and Peter knew he'd been dismissed. He picked up the stickpin and dropped it into his pocket.

Meghan was the love of his life and staying away from her was not a choice. He had to know if she was happy.

Charles Bates, Viscount Casterbridge and soon-to-be groom, stepped into the library. "I thought I saw you come in here."

Peter turned from pouring a drink. "I wished time alone."

Charles closed the door firmly behind him. "No doubt. Did Winston call you out?"

Peter stared at his boyhood friend. Did everyone know of his relationship with Meghan? He'd thought no one aware of the complete indiscretion seven years ago.

Charles crossed the room and poured a glass of whisky. His gaze lifted to meet Peter's.

"We were young and foolish, were we not, Peter? So arrogant and sure of ourselves. I look at Lady Sarah and burn red when I think of a man doing to her what we did to those gels—betting to see which one of us could get the first kiss, the first compromise."

Charles took a long drink before continuing. "No matter that our attention elevated them in the eyes of men looking for wives and some married better than any thought possible. In hindsight, I know we could have hurt them beyond measure. Unlike you, though, I never fell in love."

Peter sipped the burning liquid, when he wanted to gulp it in one swallow and refill the glass. How did Charles know? He shrugged. "It was merely a bet, Charles. One which I did win."

"Of course." Charles sat and crossed a leg over one knee. "Diane has been dead four years. I am aware your marriage was a sham, Peter. Diane lived with her lover longer than she ever lived with you. She did not love you, nor did you love her." He swirled the whisky.

"I can understand why you would not be anxious to remarry after that dismal affair. However, old chap, you are in need of an heir and your father is dead and cannot choose another unwanted bride for you. You have the luxury of finding a love match, or at the very least, marrying a woman you care for in some capacity. Yet you have not."

Peter refilled his drink and sat, aware of his friend's intense scrutiny. "It is not a great secret, Charles. I simply have no desire for a bride."

"We were only to compromise them with a kiss," Charles said, "to be witnessed by one of the other three. You had done so four weeks prior, winning the hundred pounds, Peter. Why did you continue to court her at balls and such?" Charles placed his crystal tumbler on a table. "I watched you dance with her. I saw the way you looked at her. Can you tell me truthfully, you did not love her then? Do not love her still?"

Peter stared at the liquid in his glass and shook his head, unable to answer. If she hated him for what he did, what good would voicing his love do? Besides, she was married.

"I did not know," Charles said, "if she would be here. Lady Sarah told me last month her cousin Meghan might attend our wedding, but I did not know she was here until I arrived."

"You could have warned me just the same. I could have prepared myself to look upon her again. Is her husband with her?" He didn't know how he would react to seeing them together again.

"She has no husband."

Peter's head snapped up. "Yes, she does. I saw them together in Brussels shortly before I married Diane."

Charles raised a brow. "You knew she was in Brussels? When did you learn?"

Peter stared at his friend. "I searched for her. I had some grand scheme I could convince her to forgive me and marry me, that I would defy my father's wishes. She was hard to track. She did not come here to Wingate Manor as I thought she would. By the time my man picked up her trail, she was in Belgium with her widowed aunt, the one who returned to her homeland after her husband's death. When I arrived to fetch her, Meghan was already married to de Vries." Peter downed his whiskey.

"And so you came back and married Diane."

Peter shrugged. "It mattered not who I married, as I could not wed the one I cared about. She was already married. What do you mean she is not now?"

"Sarah told me she is widowed. Her husband died eighteen months ago."

Peter nodded, too stunned to speak. Meghan was unmarried. Could he make amends?

Charles studied him in silence for a minute. "What are your plans now?"

Peter recalled the look in Meghan's eyes when he gripped her arms. "I do not know. I believe she hates me."

"I have heard hate is very akin to love, Peter." Charles stood. "If you still love her, you would be wise not to let her go without telling her how you feel. Was that not the root of your mistake seven years ago?"

Meghan slipped into the conservatory. It was a place not where many found comfort during the cold December. However, she'd always liked the room with its tall glass windows overlooking the garden, even in the winter.

She'd managed to dodge Prestwick for the past two days, but was she not ten times the fool? After discovering him at Wingate Manor she wanted to confront him, yet feared doing so. And why? Because she was scared he would laugh in her face at her foolish desire to know if he had cared for her, even a little bit, seven years ago when he'd seduced her.

She rubbed her aching temples. Had she truly deluded herself into believing she would be the next Duchess of Prestwick? Yes, she admitted, she had, but she understood the way of the *ton*. If he had but told her the truth, she would have understood. Instead, he allowed her to learn of his expected marriage in a ballroom full of people. That should tell her more than anything he'd not cared for her.

So why did she wish to confront him? What good would his apology, if he even lowered himself to dignify her with one, do now?

She wished she'd realized who Viscount Casterbridge was before she'd agreed to come to her cousin's wedding. Seven years ago, he'd not held the title. He'd merely been Mr. Bates. If she'd known his identity, she wouldn't have come, for she would have surmised Prestwick would attend the nuptial celebration of his best friend.

She released a sigh and leaned her head against the cool glass pane. How she wished the magic of Christmas her mother had always spoken of would find her now. All she'd ever wanted was to be loved and to love. Was that too much to hope for? She'd fallen madly in love with Prestwick, but he'd only sought her out to win a bet among his friends. A tear tracked down her cheek. He'd been so charming, seemed so sincere and she, a little country mouse in London for the first time, had taken his words to heart.

Seeing him again rekindled the feelings buried deep in her heart. She could easily fall prey to his *je ne sais quoi*, sensual smile and handsome looks again. He'd tempted her once. She could not afford to allow him to do so again.

She mentally shook herself, swiped the tear from her face and straightened. Magic or not, Meghan had more than her heart to protect now—she had her daughter to shield as well. She needed to stay far away from the Duke of Prestwick.

"I hope I am not disturbing you, Meghan."

Meghan jumped at the voice and whirled to face Prestwick. He stood in front of the closed door, blocking her exit.

"Your Grace." She gave a curtsey.

"*Your Grace*," he taunted. "I recall a time you called me Peter."

"Yes, well, that was an age ago, was it not?"

His dark, steady gaze held hers. "A lifetime ago, Meghan." He seemed to shake himself. "I owe you an apology for the way I treated you back then."

If he'd kicked her, she wouldn't have been more surprised. She realized the apology, so long in coming, made no difference. He'd not cared for her back then. It was merely his mature years forcing him to regret his past actions. Was she so pathetic that she would accept his hollow regret? She gave a humorless laugh.

"Oh, really, Your Grace, do not tell me you have dwelled on *that* all these years. I assure you, you did not take anything that wasn't offered."

"Winston believes differently."

She arched a brow. "You men are such odd creatures. You think you must protect the women of your family from the very things you encourage women of other families to do. Winston keeps a mistress and yet he would tell you I suffered greatly because you chose to dally with me for a short time." She stuffed her hands into the pockets of her dress when she noticed they trembled. "I assure you, Prestwick, my emotions are not so fragile as that. They never were."

"You were too young to know—"

"But you were old enough to know my mind?" she interrupted. "How condescending, Your Grace. I begin to see why you men think you must control us. We are too foolish to make up our minds."

She prayed he couldn't detect the wild beating of her heart.

He stared at her. "I never meant to imply you do not know your own mind, Meghan. I only wished to tell you I regret the way I treated you."

She blew out a breath. *In what way,* she wanted to ask. Instead she said, "And so you have done. I am meeting Lady Sarah for a game of cards, Your Grace. Please excuse me." She tried to step around him.

"I think not. You are keeping a secret from me, are you not?"

Panic gripped her. She drew in a shallow breath, clinching a hand to her abdomen. "N-no, Your Grace, I am not."

"No? Are you sure, Meghan? Did you think I would

not realize the truth?"

Shear black fright swept through her. How had he found out about Marissa? Did he plan to take her daughter from her? She would die first.

"I know not what you speak of. I have no secret from you, Your Grace."

He moved from the door with long, purposeful strides and stopped in front of her. "It has taken me a few days to work it out, but trust me, I have finally discovered the truth of the matter."

Meghan's lungs seized in her chest. "You cannot have her. Do you hear me? She is mine and you cannot have her. Have not you taken enough from me, *Peter*? Do you plan to also take my daughter? I would fight you to the ends of the earth first."

He stared, complete surprise on his face. "What are you talking about? Why would I take your daughter, Meghan?"

Too late she realized her mistake. Already she could see the wheels of his mind working. Tears burned her eyes. A deep moan rose in her breast. "Nooooo."

He gripped her painfully by the shoulders. "Dear God, Meghan, do not tell me she is mine."

She jutted her chin forward, determined to get control of her panic. "She is not. Eduard is her father. He was from the moment of her birth."

His fingers dug into her flesh. "From the moment of her birth, but not from the moment of conception?"

"She is mine and you cannot have her." She shook free of his grip and stepped away.

He dropped his hands to his sides. "Meghan, you carried my child when you left London and did not tell me?"

She stood her ground at his accusation. "When was I to tell you, *Your Grace*? Before or after I learned you were engaged to marry another and had been for three years before I met you? Before or after I discovered your seduction of me was only a means to win a wager?"

He raised a hand as if to caress her cheek.

"Do not touch me." She stepped back. "I did not know I carried a child until I was gone from London. More than a month after your engagement had been announced. Why would I inform you? You had made clear, most publicly, what you thought of me. What would knowing you had planted your seed in me have accomplished? Would you have broken your engagement to Lady Diane?" Why was she explaining to him? He was the one in the wrong. Meghan moved to step around him.

"Yes," he rasped.

She stopped in mid-stride. "What?"

He faced her, his eyes dark with emotion. He searched her face, as if seeking an answer, then shook his head. "Your husband did not mind you carried another man's child?"

What had he meant? Would he have married her if she'd told him? What foolish thoughts. If he had, it would have been out of a sense of duty, nothing more, to give his child a name. It would have had nothing to do with love, for he'd not loved her. She released a breath and answered his question.

"He did not mind. He knew it would be the only child he would have."

"Why?"

She owed him no explanation, yet she felt compelled to tell him. It was his fault—his action—that had led her to a passionless marriage.

"His attraction did not fall to women. He was in love with a man and could not bring himself to bed me."

"Meghan." He stepped toward her.

"Do *not* touch me," she repeated. "I meant what I said, *Your Grace*. You did not take from me anything I did not freely give. I gave because I wished to, because I cared for you. You took so you could win one hundred pounds, caring nothing of the consequences of your actions."

She moved to the door and felt for the brass knob. "I have lived with those consequences for seven years. I disgraced myself to my family. I married a man who could not love me as a wife should be loved. But I have gained from those consequences as well. I have a daughter, who is *mine*. I had a best friend, who did love me in his own way and who, in the end, left me very well off, so I need not worry of the future." She clenched her hand on the cool metal handle.

"You will only take Marissa from me if you raise a scandal and then the whole truth of the matter will come out. And I will fight you every step of the way, Duke Prestwick. Eduard de Vries is listed as her father on the church records in Brussels. And that is how the whole of England will know of my daughter's parentage. I will deny any accusation you make against her parentage."

She opened the door and stepped out of the conservatory.

Peter stood on the terrace that afternoon and watched Meghan stroll through the garden with her daughter—*his daughter*—and Lady Sarah. Pride and anger churned within him. Pride at knowing he'd fathered a daughter, one as lovely as her mother, sharing Meghan's honey-colored hair and soft, oval face. Marissa's eyes, he recalled from their one short meeting, were as dark as his, not Meghan's light gray. It was an enchanting combination, honey hair and dark eyes. She would draw the beaus when she had her coming out and he would have to weed out the cads.

He clamped his mouth tight. Yes, he would have to ensure a man such as himself did not attach to his daughter.

Anger surged through his body. Though not at Meghan. That moment of resentment toward her for keeping their child a secret from him had passed quickly. He knew Meghan wasn't to blame. He, Peter Bourne, Duke of Prestwick was the one responsible for the travesty of seven years prior. He should have had the strength, the belief in his love for Meghan to tell his father no before the announcement had been made, but he'd not realized how deeply he loved Meghan until he'd lost her.

Charles stepped beside him, a teacup in hand.

"Do you know how old Meghan's daughter is?" Peter asked.

Charles squinted his eyes at the trio walking through the dead rose arbor. "I had not thought on it. Four or five I suppose."

Peter clasped his hands behind his back. "She is six and will be seven on the seventeenth of March." He had learned the date of birth from Meghan's maid, though the girl was of the opinion Marissa was only five, turning six.

Charles sipped his tea, then spewed it across the marble terrace. "What?"

A muscle ticked in Peter's jaw. "Your betrothed came to me yesterday afternoon for conversation. She was of the opinion that her cousin, Mrs. de Vries, did I not remember her from the maze the other day and did I know she was recently widowed?" Lady Sarah tended to babble at times, Peter had noticed. Meghan never babbled. "Lady Sarah said she was of the very considerate opinion Mrs. de Vries was a tiny bit in love with me because she constantly looked at me when she thought no one watched and I, too, looked at her, so perhaps I was the tiniest bit in love with her as well."

Charles made a choking sound. Peter ignored him.

"I, being an idiot yet again, considered Lady Sarah's words and concluded she was without a doubt correct. Meghan had loved me seven years ago. She had told me so on several occasions. Had showed me on many more. I had not stopped loving her, so therefore, she must still love me."

Peter continued to watch the women and child as they traveled the garden path.

"I followed her into the conservatory this morning. My plan was to apologize, confess my stupidity years ago and ask if I might court her. She all but threw my apology into my face and made to leave. I told her I had discovered her secret and did she really think I would not?"

Charles set his teacup down and faced him. "What did she do?"

"She told me I could not have her daughter. I had taken enough from her already. Too late we both realized the other was not speaking of the same thing." He fisted his hands.

"She must not have been far along when she left town," Charles commented.

"She said she did not know until a month after she left that she carried a child. She did not, I suppose, feel comfortable in telling me the news then. Instead, she left the country and married a man who would give a name to her child."

"What are you going to do?"

"I do not know. I cannot take her child from her. As she says, to do so would cause a scandal and harm both Meghan and Marissa beyond repair. But I cannot let either of them out of my life. I was a fool seven years ago not to fight for her. I will not be a fool again."

The wedding ball was in full swing. Winston had gone all out to celebrate the marriage of his sister. The ballroom sparkled with hundreds of candles reflected in the mirrors lining the room. Fresh, hothouse flowers decorated the room couples danced in. Meghan had danced four times. Twice with Winston, once with Brickman and once with the groom, Casterbridge. Peter had danced only once, with the bride, Lady Sarah.

He stood on the edge of the dance floor, sipping wine, and watched Meghan slip through a door and down the hall toward the ladies' retiring room. A moment later a footman approached and handed him a piece of parchment.

Peter unfolded the note. *I am in the conservatory.* Though unsigned, he knew who had sent it. He stuffed the note in his pocket and reached to touch the stickpin hidden under his lapel. Winston be damned. He'd worn the pin everyday for seven years and didn't plan to stop doing so now at the demand of an outraged cousin. He moved the pin to the outside of his lapel.

She stood at the same spot as the other morning, her back to him. As he closed the door, she turned. She looked angelic in her ice blue velvet gown and her honey hair gathered atop her head like a halo. Aside from the dark green gown she wore to the wedding, it was the first time since he'd met her again she didn't wear mourning gray. Her eyes searched his face, stopping on the stickpin.

"Lady Sarah, Viscountess Casterbridge, told me you have worn the pin everyday, until a few days ago," she commented.

He unconsciously touched the gold and onyx pin. "I have worn it everyday, Meghan, since you gave it to me, even these past few days. But I was told by your cousin not to be seen with it while in his house. He said you needed no reminder of what had happened, for you remembered everything quite well."

She nodded slightly. "So you wore it so it could not be seen then?"

"Yes."

"As a reminder of what happened?"

He fingered the pin. This was the chance he'd hoped to have and she was laying the opportunity before him. He blew out a breath. He prayed she had a modicum of feeling left for him. He wished for nothing less than to have her as his wife.

"No, at least not in the way you think. It was, it is, the only thing I have of you, Meghan, save the sweet memories and those I cannot touch. This stickpin, this symbol of your affection for me, is the only thing I have to touch, to hold that is of you."

"An affection you laughed at, Peter."

His breath caught in his chest. He had so much to make up for, to be forgiven for.

"I never laughed at you, Meghan. I was a fool not to

fight for you back then. For not telling my father I would not marry Lady Diane." He stepped closer to her, wanting to smell the scent of her rose perfume he remembered so well. "I was not engaged to Diane for three years, as you seem to think. There had been talk of an arrangement between my father and hers. It was never formal, though it may have been implied. I did know of it, but did not take it seriously. I went to my father the day of the ball and told him I wished to marry you."

He heard her gasp.

"He said I could not marry anyone but Diane, because he had signed the marriage contract the week before. I demanded to know why I had not been informed of it. He laughed and said because it was not my concern." Peter gave a hollow laugh now, as he recalled his father's shocked expression that he should have informed the groom of the plans. "He said the engagement would be announced that night at the ball and the wedding would take place in six months time. I argued with him, but he pulled out the contracts and explained there was nothing that could be done to prevent the marriage. He said I had known of the arrangement and my infatuation with another was not going to change anything. I would soon forget you."

Meghan hugged herself, rubbing her hands up and down her arms, as if cold. She didn't comment. Why had she sent him the note?

"I looked for you, Meghan, after you left London. Your family was closed mouthed as to your whereabouts. It took me months to discover you were in Belgium. By the time I arrived, to defy my father's tampering, you were married to de Vries."

Meghan's eyes rounded in surprise. "I did not know."

"I saw the two of you on the street in Brussels. He was very tender with you. I did not interfere. You were married and I could not undo that. I returned to London and married Diane."

She remained quiet for several minutes. When she spoke it was a mere whisper. "I am sorry. I did not know. You never professed affection toward me. Never."

He closed his eyes against the pain of her words.

"I know. I was a fool. I did not realize how much I lost until you were gone." He found he still could not say what needed to be said.

She looked out the window into the dark night. "Lord Casterbridge said your marriage was not a happy one."

"Charles? When did he speak to you?"

"After the wedding breakfast he asked if we might walk in the gallery. He told me you did not love your wife, nor did she love you."

Peter gazed out the conservatory window as well. A pristine blanket of snow glittered— untouched, unsullied, as Meghan had been before he'd touched her.

"No, Diane loved another. She wished to marry me even less than I wished to marry her. She lived as my wife for less than six months. Then she went to live on one of my estates near her lover. She died in a carriage accident when I summoned her to London upon my father's death."

"I see. And so you had no children by her?"

He caught her gaze in the reflection of the glass. "No."

He had never consummated his marriage. Diane wouldn't allow it and as he didn't love her, he'd never force the issue, as had been his right.

"I cried with joy that the baby was a girl. I feared if I'd had a son, you would have discovered it and taken him away from me."

His heart seized. He had caused her so much grief, so much pain. "Meghan, I will never take your child from you. I would not dishonor you that way."

She moved to a plant and plucked off the dead and dying leaves. "Casterbridge said you would never marry again."

Charles had a big mouth. "There is only one woman

I would marry, Meghan, but I do not know if she loves me still or if she can forgive me for what I did to her."

Her hands stilled on the plant. He heard her breathe in deeply, slowly. She glanced over her shoulder at him, her eyes fixed on the stickpin.

"Do you want her forgiveness?"

"If she is able to give it, but I would understand if she could not."

"What do you want from her?"

Hope bloomed in his heart. "Her love. Her presence in my life. Her by my side forever."

She turned to face him. "And what would she get in return?"

"My undying love and devotion. I would every day, in every way, make her see that she is the only woman I have ever loved, that I am sorry for what I did to her seven years ago, that she is my everything."

A tear tracked down her cheek. Her lower lip trembled. "You never said such before."

"I was a fool, Meghan, in so many ways. To think I could seduce you and not be touched by your kindness and love. To think I could make love to you and leave you. To think I could be happy without you in my life." He closed the distance between them and wiped the tears from her face. "I love you, Meghan. I never want to be without you again. Please, marry me."

She tilted her head to look at him. "Tell me truthfully, are you saying these things because of Marissa?"

He shook his head. "I am pleased to hear I have a daughter, Meghan, but she is not the reason I want to marry you. If she did not exist, I would still be asking you to be my wife. I love you."

She chewed her lower lip, driving him insane with images of doing it for her.

"Tell me you forgive me. Tell me you love me still," he rasped.

She touched him then, for the first time in seven years. She cupped his face with her hands. Warm, smooth, loving.

"I have not forgiven you. Yet," she said. "But neither have I stopped loving you. Even after what you did, I never stopped loving you."

He lowered his head and touched his lips to hers. Softly. She arched against him, slipping her hands around his neck while his slid about her waist, pulling her close. He deepened the kiss, tasting her again. Sweeter than he remembered.

"Marry me," he said against her lips. He felt her smile.

"You are persistent."

"I will not let you leave this room until you have said yes."

She pulled away from him and searched his face. "Yes."

He crushed her to him, body and soul.

A new blanket of snow greeted Christmas Eve. Its fresh, unspoiled sparkle covered the ground in front of the chapel. Meghan smiled as she shook out the skirts of her new gown. Marissa bounced from one foot to the other, her excitement palpable.

"Mama, how much longer until I have a new Papa?"

"Just a few minutes more, sweeting. Winston is coming now," she said, spying her cousin as he moved through the nave of the church.

Marissa bit her lip. "Mama, do you think about Papa. I mean..." She shifted her eyes away.

Meghan knelt before her daughter and cupped her chin. "Your Papa loved you very much, Marissa, but it was his most favorite wish for us to be happy. Are you happy?"

Marissa nodded. "Are you?"

Joy splintered through her. "I am happy beyond words, Marissa."

"I think," Marissa whispered, "The Duke is happy, too, even if he did scowl the whole day long."

Meghan looked past Marissa to Peter standing at the

altar, scowling. Her grin broadened. She knew why he glowered. He'd wanted to marry the very night he'd asked her, but Winston had put him off for two long weeks. Each day had been torture for him—and her as well. But in just a few minutes Winston would escort her to the only man she'd ever loved and she would become the Duchess of Prestwick. More importantly, Peter would be her husband and the magic of her Christmas wish would come true, just as her mother always said it would.

Winston entered the narthex and Meghan kissed Marissa's cheek. "You will always love your Papa, Marissa, but it's okay to love someone else as well. He wanted our happiness above all else and the Duke will ensure that we find it. Go now, to Lady Sarah. It is time for me to marry Prestwick."

Meghan rose and watched Marissa skip down the aisle to sit beside her cousin. Her eyes met Peter's and she smiled. He smiled back and the magic arched through the air, touching her heart to his. Winston took her hand and placed it on his arm and she stepped toward the man who had tempted her twice and won.

Be sure to visit Anna Kathryn's website
http://annakathrynlanier.tripod.com/

Blue Christmas Cat

by DeborahAnne MacGillivray

Dara Seaforth hung the receiver in the phone cradle, then groaned. Amplifying her irritation, the television played Elvis singing *Blue Christmas* to advertise a re-release of the King's *If Every Day Was Like Christmas* album for the holiday season.

"Blue Christmas? Yeah, is it ever! This promises to be the worst Christmas Eve in my entire life, Dext—" She glanced down at her feet. *No cat.*

Depressed by the prospect, she sighed. It was hard adjusting to the empty space now Dexter had passed over the *Rainbow Bridge*. It'd been six weeks, yet she still missed the silly cat so. Her first Christmas in eighteen years without him. It didn't feel strange nattering aloud to a cat. Talking to thin air had her pondering if she'd lost her marbles.

She glared at her laptop on the kitchen table, her *Deadwood* screensaver reminding she needed to be writing not complaining to an 'invisible cat'. The January deadline loomed, and with time ticking away, she wasn't anywhere near typing *The End.*

"How can I write a hot sexy romance when life is so dreadfully dull?"

Her sister Leslie's call had been to wish her a Merry Christmas. She wouldn't be coming home for Christmas this year. Her younger sister was in love and spending the holiday with *Mr. Tall, Dark and Sexy* and his small daughter. Oh, Leslie hadn't admitted it, but the emotion was clear in her voice when she spoke about Keon Challenger.

"Bloody hell, with a name like that I'd fall for him, too," she muttered. Naturally, she was happy for Leslie, yet admitted in the same breath that she was envious. "I'm the last Seaforth sister not coupled with some sexy stud. Leslie's a year younger than I. Least she could've done was wait her turn. In olden days, the younger sister couldn't marry until the older one found a lad. Of course, it isn't as if I had any prospects. And like some blethering eegit, I can't stop talking to a cat who's not there. Am I pitiable or what?"

Dara glanced out the window at the swirling snow. A snowstorm dumped a meter of the white stuff over everything the night before, blocking her from reaching the airport to catch her flight to her grandfather's home in Colchester, England.

"Bloody airport is probably closed anyway," she grumbled.

Going home for the Hols had lost its appeal when Leslie broke the news a couple days ago that she wouldn't be there. Past dinners were a gauntlet of *are you seeing anyone special?, why didn't you bring a young man to dinner?*—or the guaranteed to make her teeth grind, *you're so pretty, I can't understand why you haven't landed a husband.* Her aunts, great aunts and grandfather, bless their souls, could make life a virtual hell with their old-fashioned way of still viewing anyone over twenty-five as an *Old Maid.* Without Leslie's presence, all that would be focused on her. Worse, when they heard Leslie was in love it'd be even more, *tsk...tsk...poor Dara.*

She caught herself starting to tell Dexter she'd love to see Great Aunt Janet's face if she wickedly replied the reason she was minus a husband was she couldn't find a tall, sexy, elegant man that gave her hot sex three times a day—and had a name like Keon Challenger. She sniggered.

The chuckle died as an image of a man with pale eyes, a light hazel that bordered on yellow, shimmered before her mind. *Welsh eyes.* Strange after all this time his image remained so clear in her mind. Over the years, at odd moments such as this, she'd wondered about Rhys St. John and gleefully tried to picture him as bald and potbellied. No such luck. She'd seen him several times over the past weeks since his return. If anything, he was as lean and hard as ever, age only sharpening his male beauty.

"As if I care, the bloody bastard." She tossed another brick of peat on the fire, ignoring the tightness around her heart. *But she did care. Always had. Always would.* "Oh, Dexter, up in Kitty Heaven, if you hear me, send me a friend. Please. I'm not picky. He doesn't have to look like you, he doesn't even have to be a *he*, just a feline friend to make this cottage less empty. Someone I can talk to and not feel a loon."

As she replaced the fireplace poker in the stand, a cat yowled. She paused, feeling twenty kinds of a fool for hearing it. "*The mind is a terrible thing to waste*—especially on a cat who doesn't exist anymore."

"Meeeeeeeeeeooooooooooooooooow!" The howl persisted, louder.

"Och, I give up. I *am* losing it. Next thing, Sci-Fi Channel will be investigating me—*see the woman who talks to a ghost cat.*"

Strong winds buffeted the house, rattling the windows. Shivering, she reached for her oversized jumper and slid her arms into the warm, fisherman's knit. The lights flickered, causing her to glance to the chandelier, fearful power would go out. After a few tense seconds, the electricity returned to steady.

"Meeeeeeeeeeooooooooooooooooow!"

Dara sighed. "Next time I'm facing a deadline, I'm going to Aruba where the temps are hot and sexy cabaña boys are hotter and will wait on me hand and foot. That way, if I lose my marbles there'd be someone to call the men in the white coats to come and take me away… haha."

Instead of visions of cabaña boys dancing through her head, the image of Rhys St. John roared back into her consciousness. "Where's a voodoo doll when I need one?"

She couldn't recall a time when she hadn't loved Rhys. The memory of when she first knew she loved him was clear. She'd been eleven-years-old, out riding bikes with her sisters, Leslie and Jenna. Rhys had zoomed past in his white MGB and swung into Castle MacNeill's long driveway. Top down, wavy black hair rippling in the wind, he was everything her pre-teen heart could want in a hero. From there, as she'd grown and changed, so had her love for Rhys, though she doubted he ever paid her more than fleeting attention. Nine years older, he was always too busy to notice the adoration she found hard to hide.

She'd spent a large portion of her life just watching Rhys St. John. Wishing. Knowing it could never be. Ruining her life, she was ashamed to admit. How could she ever commit to any man, knowing she'd never love him as she loved Rhys?

"Gor, how utterly pathetic is that?"

The sexy half-Welshman had finally come home and taken possession of Castle MacNeill, the medieval fortress down the road. She hated absentee owners, especially owners who weren't Scot…well, full Scot. Scotland's heritage should be treasured, protected. Rhys had inherited the castle from his grandfather nearly three years ago, but this was the first visit he'd deigned to pay since becoming owner. The arrogant man obviously had been too busy with his jetsetter life to return to the wee village where his father had been born. Keeping to himself, few had seen him since his arrival. Oddly enough, she'd spotted him frequently from a distance on horseback, riding in the woods. Other times zooming about in the midnight black Ferrari Testarossa.

"Och, silly man won't get very far in the 'rari tonight." She chuckled, thinking how the sleek black car wasn't built for the thigh-deep snowdrifts of the Highlands.

It seemed she couldn't set foot outside her cottage that Rhys wasn't about somewhere, lurking. Last week, when she'd peddled her bike to the village to pick up a few things, she saw him pull up at the end of the castle's long drive. He looked over at her, making contact with those pale, amber eyes, almost a gold seen only in those with ancient Welsh blood.

Curse his black head! She'd felt the power of the man's gaze so strongly, the force ripping into her soul, as if he could strip her mind of every thought. No secret would be safe from him. The strength of her reaction made her vulnerable, reminded she'd always loved this man too deeply, always would. While he was married he was safely out of reach, no possibility for her dreams to ever come true. Now he was divorced, it was harder to remind her Cinderella heart of the realities that Rhys would never want her. Fear, fear of pain, fear of opening herself to a heartache that wouldn't die, pushed her to run from him, to get as far away from him as possible.

Rhys was trouble with a capital T. Even so, she couldn't do anything but stand flatfooted and want him with every fiber of her being. Then the warlock eyes moved away, and with a flick of those long black lashes dismissed her as not worthy of his note. She'd blushed, ashamed of her reaction to this arrogant man. Hurt seared through her.

Rhys hadn't remembered her.

Why did that pain so much? That he'd forgotten her was a lance to her heart. He hadn't recalled the dance under the moonlight on Halloween fifteen years ago. Hadn't remembered the kiss. That magical kiss.

The pain was a familiar one. By eighteen her love had matured from that of hero worship to that of a woman's. She couldn't sleep or eat and found the old expression *living on love* had been rather accurate.

Despite that, Rhys and everyone else had thought it nothing more than puppy love. They refused to see she was nearly nineteen and no longer a child.

In her first blush of womanhood, she believed all things were possible. A future shimmered in her mind of Rhys continuing to live at the castle with his grandfather and over time come to see her there, waiting, and so much in love with him that it hurt to breathe.

At night, her heart spun castles in the air, so vivid, she was convinced they'd one day come true, that their love was fated. Instead, she'd watched him move away, marry. Thought she'd die from the agony of knowing her dreams were shattered forever. Rhys belonged to another. Not for one day had that pain lessened or gone away. Eventually, she'd learned to get on with her life. Even so, she still loved Rhys. Never stopped loving Rhys.

"Why did he have to come back, start the ache all over again?" She hated him all the more for carelessly dismissing from his memory something so special to her. A night when those dreams took on reality, if only for a moment.

"Meeeeeeeeeeooooooooooooooooow!"

Dara closed her eyes and counted to ten. "I'm *not* hearing a cat. It's bad enough I talk to a cat who's not here anymore. If he's answering, I'm in trouble. Next, I'll start talking to a head in a box like Al Swearengen. Geesh, that's what I get for opening and watching the *Deadwood* DVDs Leslie sent me for a Christmas present."

"Meeeeeeeeeeooooooooooooooooow!"

"Bugger. I refuse to converse with a Jacob Marley cat."

"Meeeeeeeeeeooooooooooooooooow!"

The last one sounded so insistent, so poignant, she gave up and believed. However unlikely, there had to be a cat outside in the snowstorm. Going to the door, she opened it a crack, braced herself against the gusting wind that nearly jerked the door out of her grip. She finally looked down to the stoop.

Sitting, nearly white from the snow, was a British Blue cat, the blue-grey so dark it was almost blackish. The poor, pudgy thing was hunched, shivering. “You pitiful darling. Would you like to come inside?”

She glanced toward Kitty Heaven and mouthed, “Thank you.” to Angel Dexter.

This kitty looked at her with amber eyes. Odd, for some reason they reminded her of Rhys St. John’s. Since the man wasn’t welcome in her mind, she tried to blink away the illusion, thinking it a trick of light. The peculiar impression lingered, stayed to the point where she half-expected to see the cat shake off the snow and suddenly morph into the sexy, conceited man.

“A werekitty!” Dara giggled. “Cat, I’ve spent too many weeks in this isolated cottage with no one to talk to but my characters now Dexter’s gone. Come on through—but no shapeshifting.” She wagged her finger at him. “Rhys St. John is the *last* person I want to see tonight. Life is simply too sucky to put up with his arrogance on Christmas Eve.”

As if he understood the instructions, he shook off the heavy snow and dashed inside and straight to the fireplace. Sitting next to the metal-mesh spark guard, he proceeded to tongue bathe his wet fur.

Figuring kitty would be hungry, she went to the kitchen cabinet and took out a tin of cat food left from Dexter. As she started to set the saucer on the bricks before the preening cat, she noticed he wasn’t solid British Blue after all. He had a little white ‘moustache’ rather like he’d been drinking milk. Strange, this cat was dark where Dexter had been white and white where Dexter had been dark grey. They could be the positive-negative of each other. Noticing he wore a collar, she looked at it, spotting a nameplate.

“Elvis the Cat.” Dara laughed. “Move over, Alice, I’m late for a very important date.”

“It’s getting late.”

Frustrated that night put in an appearance in early afternoon in Scotland this time of year, Rhys St. John glanced at his watch and muttered about 101 uses for a dead cat, thinking of the black humor paperback out a few years ago. At the time of its release nearly all cat owners were outraged by the premise.

"Given the circumstances of the moment, I could easily pen suggestions 102 and 103. Maybe even a 104. Damn creature. Why pick Christmas Eve to go walkabout—as Paul Hogan would say? My mood's crappy enough without having to chase down a cat that shouldn't be outside. That fat puss couldn't outrun a snail if his life depended upon it."

After following the tracks across Castle MacNeill's grounds, he stopped and glanced back. It was weird. The cat wasn't wandering about. He seemed intent on heading somewhere. Silly feline didn't know the terrain, so it was almost as if someone guided him. The heavy snow coming down had already half-filled in the path of his paw prints. Fearful they'd soon be covered entirely and he'd be unable to track Elvis, he broke into a jog.

In the distance he spotted a faint orange glow. As he paused to get his bearing, the corner of his mouth tugged up. He was nearing the cottage where Dara Seaforth stayed, a small hunting box on the edge of the Seaforth estate, which bordered Castle MacNeill. A romance writer, the villagers said. Somehow, it didn't surprise him Dara wrote romances. His mind cast back to fifteen years ago to a night under the autumn full moon and to a lass with stars in her eyes.

Too bad you couldn't hit the *Restore* option like on your computer and turn back your life to a time where it carried the sheen of hope. All futures were possible. If he had the choice to make all over again, he'd go back to that night, fix in his mind he had a couple years before he could claim Miz Dara Seaforth. He was a patient man. He would've waited. The instant she'd turned twenty-one, he would've married her so fast it'd make her pretty head spin. Instead, he'd allowed his mother and grandfather to push him into a loveless marriage just to save the family's fortune.

He swallowed regret. Had he chosen another path on that Halloween night, they'd have children by now and would be spending this Christmas Eve preparing to play St. Nick and watch their eager faces come alive.

"Well, I was stupid once. No more."

His mind conjured the image of Dara, her soft brown hair, long and about her shoulders.

The penetrating grey eyes are what he carried with him the most. Forever burned into his soul. Long into the night, those eyes haunted his dreams. Being a fool, it'd taken him several years to admit he was in love with Dara, never stopped loving her. Then it had been too late.

Since his return, he'd seen her here and there, watched her. Stalked her, if truth be told. He couldn't seem to stay away from her, though she was unaware of his new diversion. She'd grown into a sexy woman. One he wanted. One who could hold the key to the future—if she chose to give him a second chance.

For the past two weeks, he'd debated how to break the ice, scared spitless on messing this up. He'd almost made up his mind to approach her last Friday when he happened upon her at the end of his drive. She'd stopped her bike and just stood staring up at the castle. As he got up his nerve to speak, she'd looked at him with a strange mix of hunger and intense loathing. That'd thrown him.

Puzzling. Maybe not the initial reaction he'd hoped to see from her, but it gave him room to work. For the first time in years, he felt alive again, determined.

He'd returned to Dunnagal trying to find a new direction in life. Strange, the direction he now took in following the errant cat was straight to Dara's cottage.

"Maybe that cat isn't so stupid, after all." He smiled, blood of the predator rising within him. "Here, kitty, kitty, kitty. Ah, Fate moves in wonderful and mysterious ways."

Elvis finished his meal and stretched out as close as he could get to the screen guard, then proceeded to purr.

Dara wasn't sure where Elvis the Cat had come from, but she was glad for his presence.

"I don't have to spend Christmas Eve alone now, Elvis. Thank you."

He yawned a 'you're welcome' and then stared at the undecorated tree, a curious expression on his intelligent face. He almost seemed to ask the question of why? It was a bit unnerving, this cat being the negative to Dexter's positive. Only he didn't have Dexter's eyes. He had human eyes. Rhys St. John's eyes. It was spooky.

"Remember, you promised—no shapeshifting. I haven't bothered decorating, Elvis. It's just me. It didn't seem worth the effort."

The cat snapped his tail angrily. *That's no excuse*, was in the eerie eyes.

A rap on the door startled her. "*By the pricking of my thumbs...something wicked this way comes.* I don't know anyone with sense who would be out on a night light this."

She opened the door and her heart stopped. Looking so sexy he should be outlawed, Rhys St. John hunched his shoulders against the snow. Stupid man was in a lightweight coat not suitable for this wet snow. No cap on the black hair that was damp and mostly covered with white stuff.

She stiffened as if she received a blow to her chest, nearly reeling. *Oh, Rhys.* Why the bloody hell turn up on her doorstep tonight? On Christmas Eve when she was alone except for a cat named Elvis, when she was so low, she wanted to curl up and cry. She had no defenses against a man she'd loved for over fifteen years.

She drew upon her last ounce of pride and asked frostily, "May I help you?"

Rhys smiled, but it was a mask. So that was how she

planned to play it—as if they were strangers. Fine. He'd give her plenty of rope before he gave a good swift yank on it.

"I'm looking for a cat. A British Blue, yellow eyes with a white mustache, answers to the name of Elvis."

She tried to block his view into the room. "A cat? You're out on a night like this in search of a cat? Sorry, I'm afraid I can't help you."

"You were never a good liar when you were growing up, Dara." He arched a brow at her audacity.

"I don't know what you're talking about." She huffed and stiffened her spine.

Rhys glanced past her shoulder at the cat on the fireplace, and pointed. "That cat– Elvis. Or did you fail to notice him?"

"Oh, *him*."

"Oh, him?" He echoed softly. "Going to jail for *catnapping*?"

"Actually, I did forget about him. I was busy writing. I don't take notice of things sometimes."

A chuckle vibrated through him. "Good thing Elvis can open cabinets and use a can opener then, eh? He might've starved waiting for you to pay attention."

She had the grace to blush and shrug. "Well, cats are intelligent creatures."

"Dara, while I'd love to stand here and natter, I'm bloody wet and cold and you're letting all the heat out of the house." Not waiting for her to graciously step back and ask him in, he pushed past her, moving to the fire to warm up.

She turned, her mouth hanging open, though finally closed the door after another gust of wind blasted the side of the house. "I'm not sure I should let you in. How do I know you aren't a deranged killer?"

"Deranged? Not yet, lass." He unbuttoned his coat, but didn't stop there. He tugged off the pullover sweater, tossed it down by his coat and started to undo the buttons on the flannel shirt.

Dara backed up a step. "Maybe I should call Hamish

Macduff..."

Rhys laughed. "Oh aye, do that. By the time the snow stops and he pumps up the tire on his bicycle, it'll be New Years."

When the shirt came off, she was momentarily distracted by the expanse of his naked chest. He liked her wide-eyed expression. Only it changed to shock as he reached for his belt and began to unbuckle it.

"Rhys St. John, what are you doing?"

"Ah, you remember me now. You're a writer, Dara lass—of sexy romances—you figure it out. I just walked miles in the snow, am soaking wet from trying to catch that stupid cat before he fell into the burn and drowned or got lost and died in the storm. Now I'm doing what any intelligent man would do—getting out of the wet clothes before I take pneumonia."

"But...ah..."

"It's dark out. I'm not walking home in this storm, Dara. Once you get over drooling at my chest, you'll come to grips with you have Elvis and me as Christmas guests now. Get me a blanket to wrap up in, lass. Next stop is *what waits below*—and I'm so cold I can't recall if I bothered with underwear today. Or is it your wish to drool over more than just my braw chest?"

"Rhys St. John, you're a candidate for Bedlam!"

Rhys smiled as he noticed she kept the couch between them as if that was any sort of protection. Ah, thanks to Elvis, Christmas Eve suddenly was looking up. He made a mental note to get Elvis a truckload of *Armitage Good Girl Catnip Drops*, enough to last through the coming year. This silly beastie had played matchmaker! Here was the opening he wanted and he planned to press every advantage. He was staying today, tomorrow...and beyond.

"Determination is my middle name," he said under his breath.

"Damn you, Rhys, you've been back to Dunnagal for weeks and not even said hello. Now you think you can barge in here, strip to your skivvies without a by-your-leave—"

"I'm not stopping at my skivvies, lass. I warned you. I'm wet. I need to get dry and warmed up. So stop standing there ogling me and fetch a blanket and a dram of Whisky."

When he acted as if he was unzipping his pants, she let out with a squawk and rushed from the room. He laughed at her skittishness. Well, she'd just have to get over that. Sitting down on the footstool, he undid the Wellies and tugged them off, then the socks.

He leaned over and patted Elvis. "Thanks, lad. I appreciate it. You got me in and I'm not leaving."

He stood as she came back carrying a fluffy blanket and unfolding it. Winking at the cat, he started to unzip his fly. She gasped and held up the blanket like a screen to the middle of his chest.

"Ah, Dara lass, don't tell me you're modest."

She blinked, trying to keep her eyes off his chest and on his face. "Don't try to call me a prude, St. John. You come shoving your way in here, accusing me of stealing your cat and now play at being a candidate for Chippendales—"

"Playing at?" He leaned close to her, inhaling her soft perfume with a hint of tuberose and the woman underneath. His body went from frozen popsicle to a slow burn faster than he could count one, two, three. "Lass, hang onto that blanket because that's all that is separating us right now."

Her fist tightened on the soft covers, just as he intended. Dara was so focused on preserving his modesty that she was an easy target. His hands seized her waist and yanked her hard against him, his mouth closing over hers. This was no gentle wooing, this was picking up that kiss where it was left off fifteen years ago. This was him silently staking his claim.

A kiss with a promise of endless tomorrows.

Their lives had come full circle.

For the first time since that night fifteen years ago, he actually felt in control of his life again. Dara and he could be so happy, if only he could convince her of his love, of the future they could build. Her shock translated in her remaining stiff as he plundered that sweet mouth, took the heat from her and let it warm his body, his soul.

She leaned back, trying to break his hold on her. Though he didn't want to let her go.

She started to step back, then recalled her hold on the blanket. Trembling, she said, "Here," tossed it at him and fled.

"Oh, Dara lass, it's a night to believe in magic," he said to her retreating back.

"Way to go, St. John." Rhys' tone was chiding. "You're twelve kinds of a bloody fool."

Disgusted, he tossed another peat brick on the fire and closed the glass spark-guard.

Poor Dara was hiding in her room, door locked against the madman stalking back and forth in the hallway. A grimace etched his mouth when he conjured the image of her in there, crying. At one point, his impatience had driven him to pound on the door, even considered breaking it down. His last shard of common sense warned she wouldn't appreciate his caveman routine. It severely taxed him to wait. He was anxious to see Dara, kiss away the tears staining her cheeks, then explain why he'd been such an eegit.

Hold her through the night.

He lay on the comfortable sofa, staring into the flickering blue flames while he made up his mind how to put things right. By coming on too strongly he feared he'd botched everything.

The peat in the fireplace was warm, heady, the scent making him crave a cigarette. Last year he'd given up smoking because it caused Elvis to sneeze. Rarely did he miss the habit, but right now he really could use a nicotine buzz.

Over the past couple of weeks, he'd watched Dara puttering around the village. The small notions store on the village green had Dara's Romance novels prominently displayed in the front window—proud of the local lass now a bestselling author. He'd bought them all. Outside of fetching supplies or taking his stallion out for exercise, he'd been holed up reading her books—all thirteen of them. She had range, with the mix being half Historicals and half zany Contemporary Romances. After the first three, he got over the shock of seeing himself portrayed as the hero in each of them. Oh, there were variances in her characters, slightly taller, maybe just a bit prettier, but it was clear to him he'd been the seed for her inspiration.

Fifteen years ago she'd been eighteen years old, a breathtakingly beautiful eighteen. And she'd been in love with him. He had to have been blind not to see. Of course, at twenty-seven, he feigned ignorance of her adoring eyes when she came with her grandfather every Sunday when he played chess with his grandfather.

It'd been a good time in his life. *Salad Days*. He'd been preparing to follow his dream of being a historian. Then grandfather explained the realities of the family's financial situation—or lack of it. Suddenly, he had to put his whole life's work away and learn big business fast. St. John's Ltd. was a department store chain throughout Britain, Canada and US. Through his father's mismanagement, it was in near collapse. Now it fell to him to save it, even if it meant giving up on his passion for history.

Each time she was around, Dara's grey eyes had followed his every move, worshipped him. The pretty lass with the incisive mind intrigued him, challenged him, too much so, thus when she began turning up in his dreams he'd thought it best to keep his distance. Of another mind, Dara had taken to following him around. Oh, not blatantly. She just *happened* to be wherever he was. Had she been three years older, things might have been different. So he assumed the role of big brother, much to her disappointment.

Except that one night...

That Halloween night saw him restless, edgy. Bags already packed, in the morning he'd take a plane to New York, where he'd assume command as the new head of St. Johns Ltd. His task was to save the seventy-five stores that were in imminent danger of going under. Like a horse chaffing at the bit, he hadn't wanted to leave Scotland. Making matters worse, there was *something* holding him here, an indefinable pull.

The answer to that riddle remained illusive and just out of reach.

Seeking diversion from the itchy feeling clawing under his skin, he'd gone to the *cèilidh* to forget he no longer had choices in his life. He'd spotted Dara in the corner, watching the dancers. Oddly, he saw she kept turning down offers from the local lads to dance. She hadn't noticed him lurking in the shadows. In a pensive mood, he, too, hadn't felt like joining in with the merrymakers. When she excused herself and stepped outside, he followed.

Big mistake. There under the full moon, he saw she was no longer a kid, but was nineteen in three weeks, a woman.

A woman he wanted.

He'd approached her and asked if she'd like to dance. Her poleaxed expression was so enchanting. He'd taken her wrist and pulled her into his arms to slow dance to an old Gene Pitney tune, *Something's Gotten Hold of My Heart*. He guessed something had a hold of his heart, too, for halfway through the song, he stopped and stared down on the beautiful woman Dara had grown into. Unable to resist, he kissed her. Lightly at first. Then with the full passion rising within him. It was only with the last shred of sanity that he ended that kiss.

Ended with despair and regret, because he finally had the answer to that riddle. And it was too bloody late.

"Sometimes, I think the only thing right I did in my bloody whole life was kiss her that night," he confided to

Elvis, sitting on the couch beside him.

"Why do you say that?" She spoke from the shadows, tears choking her words.

He hadn't realized she'd been standing in the shadows, watching him. "Because it's the truth, the whole truth and nothing but the truth."

"Oh, Rhys..."

"I'm sorry, Dara. I didn't mean to scare you by coming on like a steamroller. It's just this is Christmas Eve and I am here with you—"

"Only because you followed the cat." She put a hand to her neck massaging it, obviously tense from emotions.

"Fate. Tonight's Christmas Eve, maybe the first one I've looked forward to in fifteen years. I think St. Nick granted me a wish—with a little prod from Elvis. Come sit." He noticed her hesitation. "I promise not to jump your bones. We can just talk."

Skittish, she came forward, but instead of sitting on the couch, she sat on the floor, crossing her legs. "Why did you come back to Dunnagal?"

"For you. Oh, I belong here, want to see the Castle is taken care of, find where I need to go with my life. I'd finally like to do what I always wanted, restore the family records, preserve the past. I can afford to follow that dream now. Only, it's you that pulled me here."

"I didn't think you recalled the kiss."

He smiled, "Oh, I recalled it...deep in the night...in my dreams." His hand reached out and touched her cheek. "I love you, Dara. Took a while to fully understand that. Then life was too bloody complicated. I feared you'd moved on. I've read your books you know."

"My books?" Her cheeks burned red. "You really read them?"

"All of them. I guess that's why I feel so close to you. I see of lot of your heart in the books, a lot of your dreams." When she looked down, his crooked finger lifted her chin forcing her to meet his gaze. "I see a lot of me in those books, too."

"Rhys...please don't play games. I couldn't take it. I'd die."

"No games, Dara. I want my life back. *My life*. Not what my grandfather decided was best, or what my mother shamed me into through guilt. I now have things back on track—but I need you. I lived too long in a cold, loveless marriage that I never wanted. I want magic, I want to know someone loves me, that I count."

"What happened? I heard you left the business, gave it up after the divorce."

"Gave up? Yes, I guess I did. There was a hostile takeover of the company I helped build, to take into the 21st Century. When the blood bath was over, I lost the company, but was very rich because my stock tripled nearly overnight. The new owners wanted a new CEO, so they offered me a golden parachute, which I took without looking back."

"I'd think they'd have wanted you to stay on, since you built the company, knew it better than anyone."

"The new owners figured I wouldn't work well with them and their vision for my company. You see, my ex-wife and her lover were heading the takeover consortium."

"Ohhhhhhhhh."

He grinned. "Yes, ohhhhhhhhh. I started to stay and make their life a living hell. Then I didn't see anything to hang onto, a reason to go on. When they offered the golden parachute, with a bonus to get hell and gone, I jumped at it. I was tired, had no personal life. The business took too much from me, I lived for it. St. Johns Ltd. is a cold mistress, love. I kept my stock so I can be a thorn in their sides come stock voting, only I wanted to go some place and find myself. *Me*. Not Rhys St. John, CEO of St. Johns. I went for a long walk, thinking. Stopped before this pub and looked in the window, reflecting like a mirror. I didn't know who I was, what I liked in life, where I wanted to be five years from now. That's how I ended up with Elvis. While I stood, trying to figure out who I really was, he waddled up. Thin, hungry, shaking from the cold. He seemed about as lost as I."

"Why Elvis?"

"Why else? Elvis the King...uh hun. The bloody beast went from grateful for shelter, food and a few pets, to running my life. Also, because the pub was playing *Blue Christmas* on the juke box when I found him." He reached out and petted the smug cat. "I've been wanting to approach you the last couple of weeks, but I was still finding myself. Your glaring at me like I crawled out from under a rock wasn't encouraging either, lass."

Dara leaned against the couch to be closer. "I thought you didn't remember me. My heart was breaking. How did you expect me to look?" She choked on a sob, trying to keep the tears in.

He cupped the side of her face, his thumb stroking her eyebrow. "If I died tonight, the last thought I'd have would be your eyes. I've found it's never too late, Dara Seaforth. Life, fate, people pushed us away from each other. Those nine years between us that seemed too wide to bridge fifteen years ago doesn't matter anymore. Strange isn't it? Oh, sweet lass, what better way to start Christmas Eve than with each other?"

The cat pushed between them and meowed. They both chuckled and petted him.

"And with Elvis." He took her hand and kissed the finger where he'd place a wedding ring. "Marry me on Valentine's Day in a big wedding at the castle. We can invite the whole village, all your family. Until then, come live with Elvis and me and be my love, my life. You can write sexy romances while I translate obscure Gaelic poetry. We can be so happy."

A smile finally cracked at the corner of her mouth. "Are you really naked under that blanket?"

"Unwrap me and find out. I'm your very own personal Christmas present."

After pouring an eggnog, Rhys tiptoed into the living room to add a couple bricks of peat to the fire. The only light in the room came from the twinkling Christmas tree. He paused to admire the decorations. They had made love, frantically, tenderly, crying, laughing. Then they'd gotten up, ate supper and decorated the tree. He smiled thinking of making love on the couch by its twinkling glow. He had a feeling he would be sore from head to toe tomorrow, but wow! Did that lass of his make love! He smiled at the grey puss sleeping before the fire, a smug expression of contentment upon his face.

"The wench is greedy, Elvis. But then, I think I can keep her satisfied." Elvis lifted his head and yawned a sleepy smile. "Proud of yourself are you? I didn't know cupids wore fur and had long tails."

"Meeeooooooow," he rumbled.

Rhys took a sip of the eggnog and then poured some out on the saucer. Elvis stretched and lazily dragged himself over to lap at the thick liquid. "So horribly bright of you to come here. Still, it's so odd how you knew to come straight to Dara's cottage...like someone guided you."

"*Hmm...thankyouverymuch....*"

Rhys froze upon hearing the male voice. He knew there wasn't anyone in the cottage but Dara, the cat and him. So who was speaking? The cat stopped drinking the nog and looked past Rhys to the tree, staring at something.

"Either you're suddenly a ventriloquist, Cat, or I'm barmy. Neither possibility is comforting." He shook a finger at Elvis. "Stop staring at the tree like that. I'm not going to look only to have you go *gotcha hahahaha, fooled the silly person again.*"

Dara, dressed in only socks and his flannel shirt, rushed out, put her arms around his waist from behind and squeezed. "You took all that wonderful male heat away. The bed's cold without you, Rhys."

He turned so he could pull her into his arms. "Warming up a bed with you is my idea of a way to spend Christmas Morn." He kissed her, feeling her renewing energy pouring through every fiber of his being, making him whole, making him alive again. Breaking the kiss, he turned to follow Dara back to bed, only to see the cat was staring at the tree again.

Unable to resist, he followed the line of the cat's vision to see what drew his attention.

He fought the instinct to reel from the shock. For in the shadows stood a man dressed in black leather. As Rhys stood, mouth slightly agape, the black-headed man winked as he made his finger and thumb into a gun. So startled, Rhys blinked once, but then the vision was gone.

"Rhys what is it?" Dara's concern was etched in her voice.

Rhys chuckled and hugged her. "Just a guardian angel that helped Elvis find his way here in the snowstorm."

"Rhys, I love you so. Always have, always will."

"Dara, my love, my heart, it took me a bit longer to reach that understanding, but it makes me recognize how precious that love is. I have loved you and always will love you."

As he kissed her, letting her feel all the joy within him, the DVD player came on in the living room behind them. The soft crooning of Elvis Presley filled the air, *"I'll have a blue, blue blue blue Christmas..."*

Be sure to check out DeborahAnne's website
http://www.deborahmacgillivray.com

Also Available from Highland Press

Highland Wishes
No Law Against Love
Blue Moon Magic
Blue Moon Enchantment
Rebel Heart
Christmas Wishes

Coming:

In Sunshine or In Shadow
Almost Taken
Pretend I'm Yours
Recipe for Love
The Crystal Heart
No Law Against Love 2
Second Time Around
Dance en L'Aire
Enraptured
The Amethyst Crown
Eyes of Love

Cover by DeborahAnne MacGillivray
2006

LaVergne, TN USA
22 July 2010
190478LV00002B/178/A